ALSO BY
DARCY COATES

THE
CARROW
HAUNT

DARCY COATES

Poisoned Pen
PRESS

Sourcebooks, Poisoned Pen Press, and the colophon are
registered trademarks of Sourcebooks.

Published by Poisoned Pen Press, an imprint of Sourcebooks
P.O. Box 4410, Naperville, Illinois 60567-4410
(630) 961-3900
sourcebooks.com

Originally self-published in 2018 by Black Owl Books.

Library of Congress Cataloging-in-Publication Data

Names: Coates, Darcy, author.
Title: Carrow haunt / Darcy Coates.
Description: Naperville, Illinois : Poisoned Pen Press, [2020] |
   "Originally self-published in 2018 by Black Owl Books."
Identifiers: LCCN 2019050869 | ISBN 9781728221724 (trade paperback)
Subjects: GSAFD: Ghost stories. | Horror fiction.
Classification: LCC PR9619.4.C628 C37 2020 | DDC 823/.92--dc23
LC record available at https://lccn.loc.gov/2019050869

Printed and bound in the United States of America.
VP 10

CHAPTER 1
ESTEEMED GUESTS

REMY WAITED, SHIVERING, ON the wide stone porch as the van crunched along the gravel driveway. The near-full moon washed light across the overgrown topiary garden and stone guesthouse as distant waves battered unseen cliffs.

Despite the chilly autumn air, she had a full tour booked. From her vantage point, she could see faces pressed against the van's windows, trying to glimpse the building, some grinning, others looking apprehensive. Remy tried to bite back a grin of anticipation.

The bus crawled to a halt, and Jones leaped from the driver's seat to wrench open the sliding passenger door. Remy held a lot of fondness for Jones; he was nearly eighty but still had a quick energy in his wiry frame. She paid him to shuttle her guests to and from their hotels or homes. He did the job with an unfailing smile and an eager, bobbing bow. But, though he'd worked with her for nearly two years, Jones had never accepted Remy's invitation to see inside Carrow House.

Eight visitors, a mix of young adults and older guests, descended from the van. Jones greeted them with a quick bow and waved them toward the porch. They clustered just short of the first step, glancing across the house, the gardens, the imposing stone gables, and the dark windows.

Remy adopted the familiar pose, one leg ahead of the other to highlight her costume's silhouette, her right hand on her hip and her left thrown toward the sky. She took a deep breath and projected her voice so that it boomed through the night. "Welcome, esteemed guests, to the infamous Carrow House. I sincerely pray no misfortune will befall you during your stay."

She knew she must look hilarious in her elaborate 1900s-inspired dress, but that was part of the fun. Guests weren't just paying to visit the state's most haunted house; they were paying for an *experience*. And Remy, lover of period dress and dusty books, was more than happy to oblige. The stiff black-silk uniform made her a passable impression of a Gothic Edwardian-era housekeeper, and perfectly matched her story's vibe.

The guests responded positively, some chuckling, others nodding. One middle-aged lady clapped twice. Remy lowered her hand and twisted, swinging both the black skirts and her long dark hair in what she hoped would be a dramatic way, then fixed her audience with an intense stare. "Tonight, you will hear tales of the macabre and the nightmarish. You will see firsthand the rooms where unimaginable horrors have transpired. And perhaps you may even be visited by a being from beyond the mortal realm." She held up a finger and raised her eyebrows. "Your driver is about to depart, and he will not return for nigh on three hours. If any of you fear your courage won't endure, this is your final chance to leave unscathed."

The small crowd glanced among themselves, but no one moved. They never did, but Remy let the silence stretch a few seconds, enjoying the rising tension. Then she relaxed her pose and dropped the theatrical act as she beckoned them forward. "All right, great! Come on up here, gang. I'm Remy, and I can't wait to show you this house."

After a few more chuckles, the tour group shuffled up the four worn stone steps. Remy moved back into the shadowed doorway to make room for them. She took a second to assess her group: two middle-aged women, probably sisters or close friends, had locked their arms together. The three young adults gave off a touristy vibe. One balding man squinted through round glasses and kept smoothing his jacket. A woman who looked equal parts embarrassed and thrilled to be there squeezed her lips together to repress a grin. And a tall, dark-haired man hovered near the back of the group, his face impassive but his eyes bright in the dim light.

Remy put her hands on her hips. Her short height meant she had to crane her neck to see everyone in the group, but she made sure to make eye contact. "Anyone here suffer from seizures? Heart conditions requiring medication? Is anyone likely to struggle climbing stairs or walking for an extended period?" They were all questions the guests had been asked when booking the tour, but Remy made sure everyone shook their heads before waving to Jones, who remained standing by the van.

Smiling, he gave her a quick nod then leaped into his seat, slammed the door, and hit the accelerator. The engine's roar and the crunch of gravel faded as he sped back to town. It was an hour's drive, but Jones seemed to prefer being on the road to waiting outside Carrow.

"All right." Remy grinned at her group. "I'm glad you could all join me tonight. It's going to be a real treat. I've been running this tour weekly for close to two years, and this house continues to surprise me. Some quick housekeeping before we begin. Don't leave the group. Some parts of this building aren't as structurally sound as they look, and I'd rather not have to fill out any insurance paperwork tonight. Don't touch anything, no matter how pretty and tempting it is. Most of the furniture in this building is antique, and the owners have been very generous to let us tour their house. Let's keep it clean for them, okay?"

She paused to wait for more nods then continued. "I'll point out bathrooms as we pass them. No photography is permitted inside—sorry, that's the owners' decree, not mine—but you're welcome to take pictures of the outside. You'll have a chance to do just that before you leave. Some guests have actually caught some supernatural phenomena in their pictures. If you find anything of the sort, I'd love you forever if you emailed them to me. That's about it. We ready to begin?" More nods answered, so Remy swept backward and beckoned her guests through the gaping doorway.

Although she'd been at Carrow for close to an hour before the tour started, Remy had purposefully turned off the lights in preparation for her visitors' arrival. She flicked the switch, lighting the foyer and bringing its treasures into sharp relief. The guests gasped and oohed appreciatively. Remy couldn't keep the grin off her face as she dipped into her theatrical voice a final time. "Welcome, dear ones, to the dreaded Carrow House!"

CHAPTER 2
HIS COLD EYES

REVEALING CARROW HOUSE TO her guests was one of Remy's favorite parts of the job. The building was the perfect blend of decadence and desolation. She gave the group a minute to appreciate the cobwebbed chandelier suspended high above them, the magnificent twin staircase cloistered in shadows at the back of the room, the slashed portraits hung on the walls, and the mahogany armchairs that still bore ax marks.

She beckoned them farther inside. "Carrow House was originally built by John Carrow and his wife, Maria, in 1901. John was a highly respected physician, though possibly not the greatest business mind the world has ever seen. He designed the building as a health retreat, believing the briny ocean air would cure a wide array of ailments. Health resorts had been hugely popular among society's elite for close to a decade, but unfortunately, interest in the fad had begun to wane by the time John opened the Cliffside Health Resort and Sanatorium's doors."

She led her guests to a series of black-and-white photographs on the wall near the door and gave them a moment to examine the pictures. They showed a building not too different from the modern Carrow House—a sprawling stone mansion dotted with dozens of lofty, dark windows. Clusters of patients sat in a neater and younger front yard, some swaddled in blankets, others in wicker wheelchairs, with nurses lingering nearby. "Those who were wealthy enough to afford the resort's exorbitant fees didn't enjoy the rules. John Carrow enforced a strict seven-thirty bedtime, insisted his patients bathe in the freezing ocean twice daily, and cut all forms of sugar, fat, and alcohol out of their diets. The institution struggled financially from its earliest days."

Remy kept shifting backward, gradually leading the tour toward a collection of blackened antique items arranged on a table in the foyer's corner. "In 1906, barely five years after the building's construction, a fire caught in one of the sitting rooms and spread through the building like…well, fire."

The pun was awful, but it always earned her a few laughs. Remy waited for the chuckles to subside before continuing. "The lower west wing and upper floors were severely damaged. While it was eventually ruled an accident, many suspected either John or his wife, Maria, of starting the fire in a bid to escape what had become their white elephant. If that was their plan, it certainly worked. They received a considerable sum from their insurance company and used it to remodel the building."

Remy indicated the photos showing wicker wheelchairs, tile bathtubs, and nurses in uniform then spread her hand toward the opulent foyer. "They converted the resort into a luxury hotel and renamed it Carrow Hotel. Salt baths were exchanged for silk sheets. Health tonics became cocktails. The medical staff were all fired and replaced with maids, butlers, and a troupe of entertainers. Over the course of three weeks, Carrow Hotel went from being an outdated bore to the trendiest place to visit, despite its remote location. It stayed that way for six peaceful years."

She raised her eyebrows ominously then turned toward the wingback chairs in front of a magnificent fireplace adorning the opposite side of the foyer. "John and Maria Carrow, in their eagerness to revitalize their hotel, hadn't thoroughly checked the backgrounds of their employees. If they had, they would have discovered their gardener, Edgar Porter, had been acquitted of murder just four years previously. He was accused of killing his wife but released due to a lack of evidence. I wonder if the jury would have come to a different conclusion if they'd known the victim was his *third* wife, and that the previous two had both gone missing within a year of marriage and never been seen again."

Murmurs ran through the group. One of the younger women clapped a hand over her mouth to muffle a nervous laugh.

Remy, loving the reactions her tale elicited, tilted her chin down so that shadows would play across her features. "During the evening of November 10, 1912, a fire broke out in the kitchen. Although it was extinguished quickly and caused minimal damage, John and Maria evacuated the building. When the staff returned the following morning, the doors had been locked, and a note nailed to the wood said Carrow Hotel would be closed while the building was restored. As you can imagine, rumors flew. Two fires in six years? Either the house was one of the unluckiest in the country, or foul play was in action.

"Carrow Hotel remained shut for nearly four months. When it reopened, John stood at the door alone. His wife had passed away, he claimed, bowing his head and placing a hand on his breast. The misery of seeing her hotel in flames a second time had eaten away at her heart and stricken her dead." Remy mimicked the motion, putting one hand on her chest and dipping her chin. Then she glanced up. "Guests blamed grief for the change in John's appearance."

"Ooh." One of the middle-aged ladies, understanding Remy's meaning, clutched her companion's arm closer.

"Based on what we now know, it seems that the gardener, Edgar Porter, set the fire. He hid in the house while guests and staff were evacuated, then murdered both John and Maria once they were alone. He'd been living with them for near to six years and had spent that time studying John's speech patterns, his mannerisms, and his laugh. People claim there was already a significant likeness in place, which was only enhanced when Edgar donned his old employer's clothes. A whole new set of staff were hired for the Carrow Hotel's reopening, and no one questioned that the man welcoming them inside was an inch taller and a sliver gaunter than their old host."

Remy turned back to the fireplace and lifted a hand toward a magnificent oil portrait above. A thin man with sunken cheeks, steel-gray hair, and sharp eyes glared down at them. "Edgar had this commissioned six months after taking charge of Carrow Hotel, perhaps to reinforce his ownership of the building."

"He looks twisted," the plump, bespectacled man said. He nudged his glasses up his nose and rocked on the balls of his feet. "Like his brain's full of sick thoughts."

"Perhaps it was. He's almost single-handedly responsible for Carrow House's reputation as the state's most haunted building." Remy let her gaze linger on the familiar image for another second. It had been skillfully rendered, and the gray eyes seemed to follow Remy no matter where she stood. A prickling sensation crawled across her skin. She turned her back to the image and flashed her visitors a grin. "Let's head upstairs, shall we?"

She led them across a dusty, worn rug and toward the staircase at the back of the room. The wood groaned as they began to climb, and Remy noticed both of the middle-aged friends were clutching the banister as though afraid the structure would collapse.

The bespectacled man jogged up the steps to get closer to her. "Does anyone still live here?"

"No, not for close to twenty years." The staircase turned, so Remy stopped on the landing to make sure the other guests heard her. "You'll find out why as I share more of its history. There were talks in the eighties about knocking the house down and building something less grim, but the land isn't valuable, and it's too far away from town to be much use. The most recent owners have embraced its reputation as a highly haunted location and were very kind to let me run these tours."

From their vantage point of partway up the stairs, they had an excellent view of the foyer. Remy indicated to the chairs, the age-worn rug, and the elaborately carved doors. "Most of this is the same furniture from Edgar's time. It spent a while in storage but was brought back out when the hotel closed for the final time. You'll also get to see some of the original beds and dressers in the guest rooms."

She continued up the stairs and raised her voice to make sure it would carry. "Carrow House has twenty-two guest rooms, plus downstairs recreational areas and lodgings for the staff in the attic. The house's owner—first John, then Edgar—always stayed in the room with the best view of the ocean. We'll visit that a bit later, but first we're going to Room 8." At the top of the stairs she turned left into the high-walled hallway that led deeper into the building. Even with the ceiling lights turned on, the passageway felt suffocatingly narrow and dark. Remy kept one eye on her guests as they followed her to a door bearing a little bronze Room 8 placard. Sometimes claustrophobic visitors struggled with the hallways, but that evening's group seemed to cope well enough.

Remy opened the door and stepped back to let her group enter. On the surface, Room 8 didn't look much different from its counterparts. Tall arched windows overlooked the ocean—though it was hard to see, except for tiny glitters of moonlight on the rolling waves—and decadent, ancient furniture filled the space. Remy entered the wallpapered room last and dusted her palms on the black-silk dress. "In 1913, eighteen months after Edgar replaced his employer, Albert Geiger went missing while staying in this room. The last official sighting was by a butler who helped the inebriated Geiger to his bed. Edgar told police he had seen Geiger riding out from the property early in the morning, though some people noted this story didn't make sense. First, Geiger had arrived at the hotel by coach, not horseback. Second, the wardrobe still held his clothes. Third, Geiger was notorious for sleeping in until after noon, especially on the mornings after binges. And finally, none of the staff—not even those who had been working on the grounds since four in the morning—could corroborate Edgar's story.

"But Edgar—or John, as the police knew him—was a well-respected gentleman, so his word was believed above others'. Geiger's disappearance remained a mystery for years. But nine days after he vanished, guests staying in Room 8 complained of a bad odor. They were promptly moved to a new room, and later that night, a maid included a very strange entry in her diary."

Remy reached into a hidden pocket in her skirts and extracted the black leather-bound book that contained her tour notes. She flipped to the first tab and began reading. "Couldn't sleep; went to the kitchen to get a drink. On the way, I saw Mr. Carrow dragging a sack from Room 8. He appeared surprised to see me. The sack smelled fouler than anything I had encountered before; when I asked what was in it, he replied that an animal had died in the room. Did a guest forget their pet? The sack was large, but he would not permit me to help him and sent me back to bed. It is very strange." Remy snapped the book shut. "The maid, Josephine, went missing shortly after starting her chores the following morning."

"Was that other guy in the bag?" the light-haired lady asked. "Geiger?"

"There was never a definite conclusion, but it seems more likely than any other possibility." Remy put the book back into her skirts then ducked between her guests to approach the wardrobe. Its heavy carved doors groaned as they opened, and she was greeted by the familiar musty smell. "As for how the body had been hidden in Room 8 for so long—well, every wardrobe in Carrow was constructed with a false back, possibly for storage purposes. The police later found traces of bodily fluid in this little cavity."

She pressed a hidden latch at the back of the wardrobe, and the wooden panel came out. The tour group clustered up behind her, some pressing their hands over their noses as though the toxic smell might linger. The cubbyhole was small, one foot deep and four feet high—just barely large enough for a grown man to be stuffed into. It was hard to see in the dim light, but patches of wood were discolored.

With her companions gathered so close, Remy could lower her voice and add a note of warning. "Some guests have claimed to hear knocking coming from this wardrobe, even before the murder was discovered. The stories are all the same: the guest will be in bed, minutes away from sleep, when they hear a soft *tap, tap, tap…* One woman said it sounded like someone asking to be let out."

The guests reacted by either leaning closer to the cavity or recoiling. A couple of the ladies chuckled nervously, and the spectacled man began bouncing on the balls of his feet again.

"He was caught, though?" The quieter of the middle-aged ladies spoke. The quiver in her voice suggested the tour had been her companion's idea. "If the police found blood…"

"They didn't find that until nearly eight years after Geiger's death." Remy carefully fitted the fake wall back into its slot, covering up the cavity. "During his career as Carrow's owner, Edgar murdered at least twenty-nine guests and staff and could be responsible for as many as sixty-three other disappearances."

The statement was met with a mix of gasps and whistles. That wasn't uncommon. Although Carrow House was notorious for its paranormal incidents, most people didn't know the extent of its bloody history. Only the tall, dark-haired man who hung at the back of the group seemed unsurprised.

"Carrow Hotel had two kinds of guests," Remy continued as she closed the wardrobe door. "Wealthy socialites who came to stay for the views and the entertainment, and travelers who were moving along the coastline. As the hotel grew older and less trendy, the proportion of the less-wealthy visitors increased.

"Traveling long distances—especially alone—was a risky endeavor back then, and it wasn't unheard of for people to disappear partway along their route. Even though a staggeringly high number of them vanished around when they were supposed to arrive at Carrow Hotel, not all the disappearances were reported to the police, and even fewer were investigated. Geiger's story is significant because he was the first well-known patron to go missing. But he was far from the last." Remy flashed the group a grim smile and nodded toward the door. "We'll go to Louise's room next."

CHAPTER 3
WASH THE STAINS FROM THESE WALLS

REMY LED HER SMALL group down the hallway toward the other side of the house. She kept her pace slow, ensuring they had time to appreciate the faded red-patterned wallpaper and the oil paintings hung between doors. A runner muffled their footsteps, but the boards still groaned as they were strained. "Most of these rooms would have seen death at one point or another. Edgar's favorite method of murder was to choose his victims when they checked in and assign them a room as far away from other guests as possible. He would then visit them in the middle of the night and either strangle them or, less frequently, slit their throats. While no accomplices were ever formally accused, many people think he had assistance from at least one or two loyal staff. He would have needed help to wash bloodied sheets and dispose of the corpses and their possessions." She stopped outside Room 19 and grinned as she opened the door. "In you go."

Just like before, Remy stood back while her guests filtered inside. The room was nearly identical to the previous, except for the mahogany bureau. A long, ugly crack ran down its glass. "Louise Small and her personal maid stayed here for two nights before vanishing. Another guest, who had become friendly with Louise, called the police. The officers searched her room and found a crack on the dresser's mirror. Edgar claimed Louise had cut her stay short and that one of the maids had tripped and fallen against the mirror while cleaning. The police accepted his excuse and closed the case."

"Just like that?" One of the touristy young adults scratched his long hair out of his face as his eyebrows pulled together. "They just took his word for it?"

"Remember, John Carrow was a respected member of society. And especially in small towns like the ones nearest Carrow House, there was a pervasive, subconscious assumption that the rich and influential couldn't be criminals. Vagrants stole and killed; the wealthy were above such base behaviors." Remy shrugged. "At the risk of stepping into politics, I sometimes wonder how much that attitude has changed. Even now, someone can spend years in jail for stealing from a convenience store, but bankers who siphon millions out of trust funds get a slap on the wrist for bad behavior."

The man with glasses leaned forward to examine the mirror. "But wouldn't the police look more closely as the number of missing-person reports increased? You said he was doing this for eight years, didn't you?"

"That's right. And especially toward the end of his career, some people in the community had grown suspicious. But evidence was hard to find, and there was always one or two staff members who could vouch for their employer's alibi. Edgar Porter was, from all reports, a highly intelligent man. He seemed to plan his crimes carefully." Remy indicated to the cracked mirror. "Louise's body was never found, but her story doesn't stop there. The bureau's mirror was removed and destroyed the day after the police investigation. Edgar had an entirely new mirror installed. Then, two nights later, while the room was unoccupied, it cracked again."

"No kidding," one of the young adults muttered.

"A maid reported it in the morning. Once again, the mirror was replaced. And five nights after *that*, a couple staying in the room woke half the hotel with their screams. They claimed they'd been disturbed by a woman's weeping, and while they were trying to figure out where the sound came from, they'd seen the glass crack in two."

Remy, careful not to touch the mirror, let her finger trace the length of the dark fracture. "After that, the bureau was put into storage, but the house's most recent owners returned it to this room. Several people, including two paranormal investigators who stayed here a few years back, have reported hearing the sound of crunching glass when the lights are turned off."

Remy let her words hang for a beat. Most of the group seemed excited by the story. Only the shyer of the middle-aged ladies looked nervous.

Remy licked her lips. "A couple of those accounts have come

from guests on these tours. This isn't something I offer to every group, but...would you like to try listening with the lights off?"

That prompted a flood of murmurs and nervous chuckles. Even the light-haired woman lost her earlier embarrassment as her eyes lit up.

Remy made sure to meet each guest's eyes and wait for a yes or a nod in return then crossed to the door. "I'll stay by the switch in case we want the light back quickly. Everyone keep as still and quiet as you can, and don't touch the mirror."

She pressed the button. The ceiling light went out. With the window's curtains drawn, they were submerged in perfect darkness.

Remy closed her eyes and let the room's ambient noise flow over her. She could hear faint breathing. One guest swallowed audibly. Someone shifted their weight, and the board below their feet creaked.

Out of the twenty-odd tours she'd offered this option to, only three had heard an audible phenomenon. Remy counted the seconds. She didn't want to leave her guests in the dark for too long when every beat increased the anxiety in her chest.

Thirty seconds.

A woman took a deep breath. Someone else shifted their weight again.

Forty-five.

"Did you hear that?" the sharply whispered question came from Remy's left. She turned in its direction.

They all held their breaths. Very faintly, almost imperceptibly, came a high, grinding noise reminiscent of glass crystals being scraped against each other. Remy's heart rate kicked up. Her fingers were pressed over the plastic light switch, but she hesitated to flip it. Her ears strained to catch more of the noise.

"Turn the light on. Please!"

Remy pressed the switch and blinked in the sudden, harsh illumination.

One of the middle-aged women had her arm around her companion, who was wide-eyed and shaking. "Did you hear that?" she cried, her eyes darting around the room. "Did you hear the glass?"

The spectacled man peered at Remy. "That wasn't a prank, was it?"

She held up both hands, palms out, to show she wasn't holding any glass. Her fingers were trembling, so she dropped them and folded them behind her dress.

"Might've been something else," one of the young adults said. He had his arms crossed, but his eyes were bright with excitement. "Like, this window looks out over the ocean, right? Could've been a big wave or something."

"That's possible," Remy agreed good-naturedly. She was glad her voice didn't waver. "This is an old house, too. Sometimes floorboards will settle in the cool night air."

The middle-aged woman shook her head. "I know what I heard. It wasn't waves, and it wasn't floorboards. Get me out of this damn room."

"Of course." Remy opened the door and held out a hand to

beckon her guest through. "Are you okay? The kitchen is warm and comfortable if you'd like to wait there for the rest of the tour."

The woman shot Remy a sharp look as she passed. "I want out of the room, not out of the tour. Just don't turn the lights out again, okay?"

Remy nodded. "That's a promise. All right. Everyone else doing okay?" She scanned the faces passing her. A few were dotted with perspiration, but her little group seemed happy otherwise. "Then we'll keep going. I wish I could say the tour gets better from here, but Carrow House doesn't make my job so easy."

CHAPTER 4
UNFORGIVABLE

REMY PULLED AN ANTIQUE pocket watch from the folds of her dress and checked it. The timepiece had belonged to her great-grandmother, and it fit in with the Edwardian-era aesthetic better than a wristwatch. The tour ran for three hours—the longest an average guest could tolerate before fatigue and sleepiness took the fun out of it—and there was never enough time to cover all of the house's mysteries. Remy recounted some of her favorite stories as she led her group through significant rooms.

Hobby researchers had taken photos showing a faint white blur in the servants' quarters, so she pulled the pictures out of her black book and passed them around. They spent some time in one room, examining torn wallpaper that had reportedly been caused by one of Edgar's victims, and she showed them the path the infamous Gray Lady's spirit looped through. At last, when only twenty minutes of the three hours remained, Remy led them back to the stairs. "We've looked at Edgar's deception, his victims, and his triumphs. Now I'm sure you want to hear about his downfall."

A chorus of agreements came, and Remy chuckled as she stopped on the landing that had the best view of the foyer. "Tiny hints of suspicion against Edgar had been accumulating for years. Each accusation carried no weight on its own, but they collected like drops of water in a cup, making it fuller and fuller until a nudge spilled it over. That nudge came from a maid called Sarah. On the second of March, 1921, she ran into a police station, hysterical and bleeding from a gash on her neck. She'd held her hands over the cut for the entire four-hour run from Carrow to the town, and gasped her story while the physician was called.

"She'd gone into Carrow's basement to fetch a bag of flour for the kitchen, she said, and found a corpse lying on the stone floor. Before she could fully comprehend what she was seeing, John stepped out of the shadows and cut her neck. She fled the house, barely escaping with her life.

"Her story made the cup of suspicion overflow in a major way. A riot began, and by the early evening, a mob of thirty civilians stormed Carrow Hotel. Some went to see the basement; others had brought axes, knives, and guns and looted the entryway." Remy pointed to the cuts in the high-backed chairs and the slashed paintings.

"Leading the mob was Annabelle Carrow, John Carrow's estranged sister. A rift in the family meant they had only talked through letters for the previous decade. Whether she'd intended to protect or accuse her brother is uncertain. All we know is that Edgar met her on the stairs and failed to recognize her. She screamed, 'Imposter, imposter! This man isn't John—he's an imposter.' At the same time, the men who had ventured into the basement came running out, yelling about a profane burial ground. And the mob, already overwrought, descended into a frenzy.

"Someone threw a rope over the chandelier. Edgar was bodily dragged to it, and before the police had a hope of interceding, he was hanged."

The guests all turned toward the dusty chandelier, and Remy could tell they were picturing the gray-haired man kicking at the end of a rope as a crowd cheered around him. She didn't let them linger on the picture for too long but beckoned them farther down the stairs. "The subsequent police investigation lasted for nearly four years. The bodies in the basement were retrieved, as many as possible were identified, and they were given respectful burials. The investigation wasn't finalized until 1925.

"The old furniture was put into storage, and the building renamed Carrow House. It remained closed for nine years until Mr. Preston, a well-off business owner, bought it to be a luxury seaside retreat for his family. He hired four separate construction companies to renovate the building, but each one canceled their contracts after crew members died. Mr. Preston passed away from a heart attack before he ever got the chance to stay in his house.

"Carrow House changed hands close to a dozen times over the following decades. There's a recurring theme of tragedy befalling anyone who lives in the building. The most recent is from twenty years ago, during one of the building's stints as a struggling hotel: a young child wanted to explore the house at night, became tangled in the attic's ropes, and was strangled. The hotel closed for the final time the next day, and except for brief research-related stays, no human has attempted to live in it since.

"The current owners bought Carrow House for virtually nothing a few years ago and restored as much of the original fixtures as they could. Unlike previous owners who tried to remodel it, they're happy to embrace Carrow's notorious history and celebrate it for what it is: the state's most haunted building."

Their shoes echoed over the dusty tiles as the small group crossed the entryway. There wasn't much time before Jones's van would rattle back up the driveway, but Remy had one more location to show her guests. She picked up the oil lamp she'd left on a small side table at the back of the room, lit it, and waited for the flame to stabilize before turning to the narrow door beside the kitchens.

"The basement doesn't have electricity," she explained. "The stairs are steep, so please move carefully and watch your step."

The nervous lady gripped her companion's arm tightly, and even the young adults looked uneasy. Remy went first, lamp held high to share its light, her spare hand brushing along the rusted metal handrail that stood between them and a steep drop to the flagstones below. Dozens of maids rushing up and down the steps each day had worn indents into the stone.

The cold, moist air tickled Remy's nose. The basement always sent uneasy prickles running up her spine like invisible spiders.

As the realm of maids and footmen, it had none of the luxurious proportions of the rest of the house. The stairs were steep, the ceiling low, and no attempt had been made to soften the stark stone walls.

"They used to store the wine and dry goods here." Remy reached the base of the stairs and moved back to make space for her companions. "Please don't go past the barrier. This is one of the less-safe parts of the house."

A cordon surrounded a ten-foot square at the base of the stairwell. Remy's guests clustered to the edge of the area, and she raised the light to help them see. "This is where they found the bodies."

The basement stretched onward for more than forty feet. A dozen of the huge, worn stones had been torn out of the floor and propped against the wall. Where they had once lain, dark holes tunneled four feet deep into the dirt.

"We're not allowed any closer," Remy said. Noise traveled too far in the basement, so she kept her voice soft. "The bodies were removed, but there are still tiny bone fragments in the dirt, and the house's owners don't want them disturbed."

One of the middle-aged ladies moaned and clutched at her companion.

"He buried all of his victims here?" the bespectacled man asked.

"Not all. That's why his total number of victims is unknown. Twenty-nine bodies were retrieved from the basement, and they're what he was posthumously convicted for, but it's likely that many more travelers and servants from that time met their end at his hands. Researchers have theories for how he disposed of them. He could have thrown them into the ocean, buried them somewhere away from the house, and—this is one of the less-savory theories— one historian believes a chef was Edgar's accomplice and some victims were turned into the next day's lunch."

The middle-aged lady moaned a little more loudly. Remy squeezed her lips together. *I probably shouldn't have told her about that part.*

"There's a horrible atmosphere down here," the blond woman whispered. "It feels...bad."

Remy rubbed at the goose bumps on her arms. She'd always mistrusted the basement, and not just because of the safety risks it posed. There was something unseen in the space that turned her stomach sour and made her heart feel heavy. A lone spider descended from the ceiling, spinning its web to hover in front of her face, legs twitching. "I know what you mean. Head back up the stairs when you're ready. The kitchen's at the opposite side of the foyer."

CHAPTER 5
THE PROPOSITION

THE KITCHEN'S SHINING TILES, clutter of bronze pots, and wide counters were a welcome relief after the basement. Remy could hear her guests release their breaths and see them flex their shoulders as she crossed to her oversized thermos and began pouring hot chocolate.

"Congratulations on making it through the night," she said as she passed out the steaming mugs. Even after two years of tours, she still felt a small measure of relief when they ended. "Jones will be here to pick you up in about five minutes. The doors behind you open onto the front yard. If you'd like to take some pictures from outside the house, now is a great time. And if you need a hug, come see me. I've been told I'm a world-class hugger."

Chatter filled the room. The spectacled man stood still just long enough to accept his cup before pulling a camera out of his pocket and speed-walking for the doors. The two middle-aged women and one of the tourists, who pulled out a pack of cigarettes, followed. Remy settled in to take questions from her remaining companions.

She had plenty of practice at coping with late nights, but the exercise and after-midnight hour were clearly weighing on her tour group. They leaned on the counter as they chatted, looking wrung out but happy. The blond woman who'd seemed embarrassed at the beginning of the tour couldn't stop giggling.

Empty mugs began to filter back to the kitchen, and the rest of the guests moved outside to wait for the van. Remy piled her mugs into the sink and checked her pocket watch. It would take an hour for her to clean and lock up once the guests were gone, and if she took the scenic route back to her town, she would arrive just as the bakery opened…

"Do you have a moment?"

Remy startled. The tall, dark-haired man lingered in the kitchen's shadowed corner. He shot her an apologetic smile. "Sorry, I didn't mean to alarm you."

It was the first time he'd spoken all night, and his voice was surprisingly deep and sharply enunciated. Remy laughed and pressed a hand to her jumping heart. "My fault, I'd thought everyone was outside. What's on your mind?"

"I enjoyed the tour." The man clasped his hands behind his back and crossed to a china cabinet. "You must know a lot about this house."

"I sure do." Remy kept her voice friendly, but something about her companion struck her as a little strange. He hadn't relaxed like guests normally did at the end of the tour but seemed to be growing tenser—almost anxious. His eyes flicked across the cabinet's contents, apparently without seeing them.

As Remy unscrewed the thermos lid, her mind strained to remember the man's identity. The booking forms ran together after a while, but she thought he was either Mark or Piers. Both men had given local addresses.

"You run the tours fairly often, don't you?" Mark-or-Piers was still focused on the cabinet, but he shot her a glance out of the corners of his eyes.

Remy tipped the thermos's excess milk down the sink. "Weekly during the warmer months. And as often as the weather will allow me during winter."

"And you enjoy it?"

"I wouldn't do it if I didn't."

He finally turned to face her. His eyes were bright and keen. "I have an offer I hope you'll consider. I'd like to hire you for a private, extended tour."

Remy blinked at him. *Private…extended… This isn't a come-on, is it?* "Uh, thank you, but I'm happy with my current job."

He reached for something in his jacket's pocket. "You haven't heard the proposition yet."

Remy swallowed and glanced toward the door. "The van's going to be here in a minute. Why don't we head outside?"

Mark-or-Piers pulled a business card out of his pocket and held it toward her. Remy mutely took the white rectangle but only glanced at it long enough to see her companion's name was, in fact, Mark. The card didn't list an occupation.

"I realize the house's owners would need to give permission," he said, "but if you pass my details on to them, I can handle the negotiations."

Remy frowned. "Wait, this is a real offer?"

He blinked twice, and his eyebrows pulled even closer together. "It's not a joke, if that's what you mean. I'm very interested in the supernatural and the phenomenon of this house in particular. I'd like to study it for a stretch of time. Two weeks, ideally."

It took Remy a second to readjust her assessment of the man standing before her. He was strikingly tall and thin in a way that made Remy think of a sleek cat. The stilted way he spoke suggested he was rusty at social interactions, but he didn't seem crazy, at least. "Two weeks is a lot of time to spend in this house."

"It is. But I think it would be the ideal length of time to become familiar with the building."

"Right." The faint crunch of the driveway's gravel told her Jones had arrived to collect his charges. "Well, I'll pass your details on to the owners so you can discuss it with them directly."

"I'd like you to be there, as well." He took a step nearer and licked his lips. "I believe I'd be hard-pressed to find someone who knows the building's history better than you, and so I want you to act as consultant. I wrote my offer on the back of the card."

Remy was starting to feel as though she'd fallen into a very strange, very confusing dream. She flipped the card over and found a dollar amount written in black ink. It was more than she would earn in three months at her day job. *I don't need the money. But even so…*

"I would also pay the owners rent, of course, and provide food and any other supplies we might need." Mark's eyes continued to rove across the kitchen's stone walls, wide counters, and long stovetop. "I can handle all of the preparation. All I require from you is your availability and willingness to contact the spirits here."

She turned the card back to its front to see his full name: Mark Sulligent. "Sulligent... Your name's familiar. Have we met before?"

"Maybe you know my father. He's a surgeon at Royal Henry Private."

"Right." Remy remembered seeing articles about him in the newspaper. She cleared her throat. "Mr. Sulligent, thank you for the offer. I can't accept, but I'll send you the contact details of some other local historians."

His restless eyes finally returned to her face. "But they won't know the house like you do. They won't *care* about the house. I saw the way you looked when you talked about it—you were *radiant*."

Remy felt color spreading over her face and across her ears. She was spared having to answer by the sharp toot of a car horn. Jones wanted to leave. "You'd better go. Sorry I can't help."

Mark appeared to be lost for words. He looked from Remy to the door and back, blinking rapidly. "You didn't even think about it. Is it the money? I can give you more."

Hot, frustrated anger rose to tangle with Remy's embarrassment. "Look, I don't want to be rude, but it's not the money. It's..." She floundered, hunting for some way to convey her feelings without offending. "I barely know you. I can't just spend two weeks with a complete stranger."

Motion drew her eyes down. Mark flexed his hands at his sides, coiling and uncoiling the long fingers almost reflexively. She looked back at his face and saw faint perspiration shining over his sharp bones. He was anxious.

Because of me? Why?

Mark's gaze didn't quite meet her eyes. His voice was quick, hushed, and tight. "I'm sorry; I've explained this all backward. It wouldn't just be us. I've already contacted a spirit medium as well as a paranormal researcher. And of course you would be welcome to bring any guests of your own choosing. I would ideally like a group of seven or eight persons who are open to the supernatural. But your knowledge of Carrow is invaluable. I doubt I could replace you."

Remy, still flustered and confused, looked back at his card. It didn't list Mark's job, only his address and phone number. Jones hit the car horn again and held the harsh, high-pitched note for several seconds.

"I'll think about it," Remy said at last.

Mark's tense expression broke into a cautious smile. "Ah—good. Good. Thank you. You have my number."

He gave her a quick nod then crossed to the exit and disappeared into the night. Remy followed him as far as the door but stopped while she was still inside the well-lit kitchen. Mark's lanky silhouette was barely visible as he jogged across the lawn to the van and leaped through the door. She listened to the faint murmur of voices as he apologized for making Jones wait, then the engine revved as the van turned back toward the town.

He wants me to stay here two weeks, researching Carrow? I'd love to spend more time in this building…but there's got to be a catch. Things like this don't happen outside of movies. Remy blew out a slow breath as the van's headlights disappeared from sight. *You'd probably save yourself a lot of angst if you just threw his card in the bin now.*

She looked down at the innocent rectangle of white paper in her gloved hand then flipped it over to reread the offer he'd written on the back. She hadn't seen him holding a pen; he must have prepared the card at home, before he came on the tour.

Just throw it out.

She rubbed the smooth paper for a second then snorted, slipped the card into her pocket, locked the door, and set about the long task of cleaning up.

CHAPTER 6
NEGOTIATION

REMY BLEW ON HER steaming cup of tea. She'd arrived at the little bakery café behind her house just as Michelle opened its doors. Remy felt drained after a night of no sleep, but practice had taught her the day would go better if she had something to eat before collapsing into bed.

Tucked into her favorite corner, she was the only patron in the little brick building at the early hour. Michelle dropped off a plate bearing a generous cheese croissant on her way to put salt and pepper on the outdoor tables, and Remy picked a corner off her breakfast. The business card felt as though it weighed a ton in her skirts' pocket.

Obviously, you need to say no. You shouldn't have even told him you'll think about it, because now it will be harder to reject him.

The croissant was chewy and fatty and should have helped sedate Remy, but her mind was jumping so badly, she wasn't sure she would get *any* sleep that day. She tore off another strip, but her chews slowed to a halt.

Why can't *I say yes?*

Mark *had* painted a tempting picture. Exploring the mansion and digging up its long-dormant secrets alongside a spirit medium, a researcher, and a handful of spiritually in-tune souls...

Despite voraciously researching Carrow and visiting the building nearly every week for two years, she knew she'd only scratched the surface of what it offered. Being responsible for the tours had meant being cautious, and as a result, her experiences were tame compared to what others claimed to have seen in the house. She'd never glimpsed the Gray Lady, never felt poltergeist activity, never heard the widow's wails in the early hours of the morning.

Remy scowled and shoved a large piece of the breakfast into her mouth. For a second, she allowed herself to imagine leading a new tour group through the building and saying, "Here's where I saw Lady Eleanor's ghost. She looked at me, then *whoosh*, she was gone."

It would be nice to be able to share some firsthand experiences. Right now, I'm only parroting other people's stories.

Remy exhaled and flopped back in her chair to stare at the ceiling. *I've got to stop being stupid. I can't say yes.*

And yet, that frustrating, niggling *why not?* refused to dissipate.

I don't even know the guy. He wants me to spend two weeks in a remote house with him. That's a crazy level of stranger danger right there.

There was nothing stopping her from doing a little research, though. Remy fetched her phone out of her skirts. She typed *Mark Sulligent* into the search bar and skimmed the results.

35

Mark didn't have much information about himself online, but she was faintly surprised by what she did find. Most of the results were small news articles applauding his charitable contributions to various causes. He'd bailed a no-kill animal shelter out when government fees had threatened to overwhelm it. He sponsored a college education for twelve underprivileged children. His money was responsible for many of the first-response efforts after a hurricane had left sixty people homeless the previous year.

He's rich, then. That shouldn't be surprising, considering he plans to fund this operation. He'd probably be insufferable to work for.

As soon as that thought passed through Remy's head, she realized how wrong it was. Mark had been almost painfully awkward when making his offer. He wasn't used to dealing with people face-to-face, Remy was sure. But he'd been scrupulously polite.

How did he make his money, then? His father's a private surgeon, but even that's not enough of an income to be a philanthropist on.

Remy returned to the Internet. It took nearly ten minutes of digging to find Mark's business name, which led directly to her answer. Mark designed web apps, developed them until they were profitable, then sold them to larger companies. He'd been doing it for close to eight years and had gone through nearly a dozen programs in that time. Remy whistled.

She put her phone on the table next to her empty plate. The sun was starting to reach over the tree line, and thin, long lines of its light speared through the café's windows and shimmered up the walls. Remy chewed on the inside of her lip.

The financial offer was generous, but she didn't need money.

Between her day job as a freelance graphic designer and the weekly ghost tours, she lived quite comfortably.

The other guests staying at Carrow could either be the best or the worst part of the deal. It was rare to meet people who were involved in the supernatural in her tiny town, but on the other hand, an out-of-control ego could make the fortnight unbearable. Without knowing who Mark had contacted, the assembly could go either way.

"Guh." She rested her head in her hands and used her thumbs to massage her sore eyes. *I'm actually considering this. And why not? I don't have any family waiting for me, and I can take time off work. If the offer is genuine...*

"To hell with it." She directed the words to the crumbs of her croissant. "When did I get so boring?"

A sharp laugh made her startle. Michelle swept past on her way to the kitchen, still fighting snickers. Remy could barely hear what she said to the chef.

"Get a load of this, Paulie. The ghost tour lady thinks she's *boring*."

Remy bit her lip so that her own laughter wouldn't overflow. It wasn't quite six in the morning. She was sitting in a tiny bakery café, wearing a black Edwardian-era dress and considering throwing herself into an escapade unlike anything she'd been a part of before. Michelle had every right to laugh at her.

Mark's business card waited on the table, seeming almost dangerously innocent in its simplicity. Before she could second-guess herself again, she dialed the number.

The phone had rung twice before Remy remembered the

time. Unlike her, Mark would have almost certainly gone to bed when he got home, and the call would ruin his night's sleep even more than the tour already had.

She was about to hang up when a groggy, slightly dazed voice answered. "Hello? Mark here."

"Oh. Hi. Mr. Sulligent." She'd thought using his surname would bring some sobriety to the situation, but it only made her feel more ridiculous. She cleared her throat. "It's Remy. Your, uh, tour guide from last night."

"You're going to do it?" All tiredness had melted from his voice. She could imagine his keen eyes glittering in the half-light of dawn.

"Yes. I mean, possibly. On a couple of conditions." Remy ran a hand over her face. She was starting to wish she'd slept before making the phone call. She knew she should put boundaries in place before committing herself, but her sluggish mind was struggling to think of what they should be.

"Yes. Absolutely. Go ahead."

"First—" She couldn't believe what she was about to say, and squeezed her eyes closed as though that would make it better. "First, I won't accept any payment."

"Oh." Confusion tainted his polite tone, but he recovered quickly. "I mean, if that's what you want…but I really feel that you should be compensated for your work."

"That's exactly why I can't accept payment. If I'm going to do this, it has to be as an equal partner, not an employee with job obligations." *Being trapped by a contract could be disastrous if the trip turns sour.* "This leads into my second condition. I, and by extension anyone else staying in the house, have to be free to leave at any time and for any reason."

"Yes, of course. I'm hardly going to keep you there against your will."

"Okay." Remy chewed her lip. "And, uh, I can bring some of my own companions?"

"I'm hoping you will. Ideally, we would have seven or eight people there total. As I mentioned, I've already hired a spirit medium, Marjorie McAllister."

"Oh, I know Marjorie." They'd met at a convention several years before. Although Remy hadn't had much of a chance to talk to her, she'd seemed like a pleasant woman.

"Good! Marjorie is coming with her assistant. I've also met a gentleman named Taj Sadana who will bring video cameras and other equipment."

Remy frowned. "I haven't heard of him before."

"He has a YouTube channel. Very enthusiastic. I don't think he's been in the business for long, so he's eager to record and observe as much as possible. So, including you and me, that makes five. Another two or three guests would be ideal. Does that sound all right to you?"

"Sure." Her tours normally topped out at eight, so Remy was comfortable with that number of companions. She chewed on her thumb for a second. The only problem would be coming up with her guests. She'd struggled to make friends since moving to the small town, and none of her family lived nearby. "You still need permission from the house's owners."

"You're right. I don't suppose you have their phone number?"

"Hang on." Remy reached into her skirt pocket and pulled out the black leather notebook where she kept their contact details. She recited the number to Mark then added, "That will contact Patricia Mahon. She acts as an intermediary for bookings, so it might take some back-and-forth to work out a deal."

"I don't mind. Thank you, Remy." Mark's smile was audible.

She shook her head. "All right, well, good luck. Give me a call when you have some concrete details."

"I'll do that. Phone me any time if you have questions or suggestions."

Remy hung up and tapped the phone on her front teeth. She wondered how Mark would react when he found out that Carrow House belonged to a very peculiar seventeen-year-old girl. April Mahon was technically too young to own property, but the house was hers in all but title. Her mother, Patricia, signed the contracts, but April had the final say about what would happen to her building.

Remy didn't doubt April would say yes. Like Remy, the teen was fascinated by Carrow House and would eagerly welcome a research team.

I'm really doing this, huh? Remy slid the phone into her pocket, left payment on the table, and turned to the café's doors. The sky was brightening, but all she could think about was her bed. *Two weeks in the state's most haunted house. This is either going to be a great decision or the worst experience of my life.*

CHAPTER 7
WELCOME TO CARROW HOUSE

I CAN'T BELIEVE THIS is actually happening.

Barely three weeks after her phone call with Mark, Remy slid out of her car to open Carrow's main shed. The space had once been a stable for the guests' horses then later been used to store the building's original furniture. Now, it would protect the research team's vehicles for the next two weeks. She drove into the vacant shed, easing her car into the back corner, then returned to the expanse of grass leading toward Carrow.

She'd grown used to how the house looked at night, and it was hard to adjust to the area's atmosphere during daytime. In the dark, it was easy to forget Carrow sat on what was essentially an island. Crashing ocean surrounded it on three sides, and its only access came from the massive stone bridge that crossed the strait dividing the house from the mainland.

Despite being separated from the true shore, Carrow had more than eight acres of land. A crop of pines grew along the cliff edges, twisted and weathered by countless storms, and Carrow's own front yard—though largely dead—would give them plenty of room to stretch their legs if the house's atmosphere became overwhelming.

Remy checked her watch. She'd arrived an hour early to open the house and pull some light into the neglected rooms. As she began moving toward the building, she was surprised by an engine's rumble. A small van appeared on the stone bridge and clattered its way onto the quasi-island. Remy watched as it pulled up at the front garden's gate.

I shouldn't be surprised, she thought as Mark Sulligent emerged from the driver's seat. He was dressed just as impeccably as he had been for her tour but had at least been sensible enough to wear jeans and boots.

He waved as she neared him. "I see we had the same idea to arrive early," he called. "I'm grateful. I was halfway here before I remembered I don't have a key."

Remy laughed as she reached him. "I was just going to let some air through the house before everyone got here. It's horrifically stuffy for a building that's constantly buffeted by wind."

"No cancellations?" Mark ran a hand through his dark hair as he stared up at the house.

"None that contacted me."

"Good. We should have a full party of eight, then."

They passed through the stone fence that bordered the house's front yard. Remy noticed Mark's dark eyes dance across the haphazard shrubs, stone figurines, and crumbling seats.

"John Carrow loved English aesthetics," she supplied. "So he decorated both the yard and the house to match, even though it didn't fit the climate."

"Talking about climates, they say we're likely to have some storms while we're here."

"Oh, I don't doubt it. As soon as winter hits and the current shifts, the area can be blanketed in rain for days on end. That's why winter tours are subject to the weather. Almost a third of the time, I have to cancel them because the roads are too dangerous." Remy shrugged. "We'll be fine inside the house, though. Once you light some fires, it's not as cold as it looks."

"I brought plenty of firewood." Mark ticked points off on his fingers as he followed Remy up the stairs to the front door. "Food. Clean mattresses and blankets. Spare toiletries, in case anyone forgets theirs. Candles in case the electricity goes. Bottled water in case the plumbing goes. A two-way radio for worst-case scenarios. And a medical kit. Plus I did a refresher first-aid course last week."

Remy stopped at the door to give Mark an amused, faintly impressed grin. "Ha. You're almost as paranoid as I am."

A hint of color flushed over his ears as he shrugged, not meeting her eyes. "The course might have been overkill. You already know my father's a surgeon. He's nagged me into attending them every year since I was eight."

"Well, better to be too prepared than the opposite." Mark was surprising her. He seemed so much more relaxed and jovial that morning compared to the awkwardness of his proposal. In fact, he was downright charming. *Maybe it was just nerves?*

43

She fit the key into the lock and enjoyed the screeching wail that greeted her every time she turned it. The doors shuddered on their hinges as they ground inward. Remy snorted to clear her nose as dust and stale air swirled around her, then she stepped back to let Mark inside. "We'll leave the doors open to circulate the air. See if you can budge some of the windows over there. I normally don't open them for the night tours, but they'll be worth it today."

Huge casement windows adorned both sides of the foyer. Remy worked on the right side while Mark tackled the left. The handles were stiff from decades of infrequent use, but she managed to shift one of hers open a crack. She turned just in time to see Mark straining against his, one hand on the handle and the other applying force directly to the frame.

"Try not to break it," she called.

The window groaned as it opened, and Mark, breathing heavily, stepped back.

"That should help." He rubbed his hands on his jeans as he joined her on the worn rug in the center of the room. "The wind's pretty sharp, so we might need to close them again before night."

Remy nodded as she surveyed the room. "Talking about night, we've only got a few hours of daylight left. It might be wise to start bringing in the supplies and choosing where we'll sleep—"

"Oh, bloody hell."

They both turned to the sharp voice that came from the front door. A teenager glowered at them as she drummed her fingers on the wooden frame. "I wanted to get here first. I swear I hit every red light in the country, and now you two are early, to boot."

"Hey, April," Remy called. As the teenager moved inside, Remy quickly made introductions. "You two haven't met yet, have you? April, this is Mark. Mark, April Mahon, Carrow's owner."

To Mark's credit, he greeted April with the same respect he showed Remy. "I'm glad you could come."

"I'm looking forward to this," April said as she shook Mark's hand. She'd dyed her hair since the last time Remy had seen her, adding a marine-blue streak to the long black waves.

Remy secretly found the teen fascinating. April's family was rich enough to own properties across the country. When their daughter had begged them to buy and restore the state's most haunted house so that she could "develop her psychic gifts," her parents had put up minimal objections.

April's fascination with spirits and ghosts was so all-consuming that she'd accepted Remy's ghost tours proposition without a second of hesitation. And on hearing that Mark intended to spend two weeks there, April had called Remy to simultaneously beg and demand she be included in the party. Remy was quietly pleased. If nothing else, April would keep them from being bored.

April blew a wisp of dark hair out of her face as she surveyed the room. "This place looks older every time I visit."

"Well, technically, I guess it is." Remy matched April's grin. "You said Lucille was coming, didn't you? Is she here?"

"Yep." April stepped to one side and gestured to the yard with a dramatic flourish. "The mud is in the process of consuming her shoes, so don't wait up."

Curious, both Mark and Remy moved forward to see the slim, immaculately dressed woman mincing her way up the path.

Remy had only met Lucille Price once, when April had wanted to come on a tour. The tall, glamorous-looking woman's role seemed to be something between a family friend, a nanny, and a modern-day chaperone. Any time April wanted to see or do something her parents deemed even mildly risky, Lucille was dispatched to accompany her.

"Good afternoon!" Remy raised a hand as Lucille neared them, earning herself a grimacing smile in response.

"Yes, I suppose it's wise to stay optimistic under such circumstances." Lucille's heels wobbled on the uneven stone steps, and for a second, Remy was afraid they would have a broken ankle on the first day. Lucille made it to the top of the porch safely, though, and exhaled as she smoothed her skirt. "Be honest, dear. You don't think this lark is likely to last a full two weeks, do you?"

Remy managed a laugh. "I guess we'll find out. Lucille, this is Mark Sulligent. Mark, Lucille Price."

"Oh! Charmed." Lucille's smile widened discernibly as she shook Mark's hand and added with a wink, "Call me Lu. All of my favorite people do."

Remy only had a second to note that she'd never been invited to use the pet name, then she caught sight of April standing behind her guardian. The teen gave such a prolonged, excessively melodramatic eye roll that Remy had to bite her tongue to keep the smile off her face.

"Well." Mark looked faintly uncomfortable as he nodded

toward the van. "I'd better start unpacking. Lovely to meet both of you."

Lucille exhaled heavily as she watched Mark jog down the stairs. "I didn't realize he was the host. Have April and I been assigned rooms yet? No? That's fine. We'll go and choose them now. I'd like one with an ocean view."

"That's good. You don't have much choice in this place," Remy said. "You're welcome to any of the guest rooms on the second floor."

"Very well. Come along, April."

April gave her guardian a deadpan glare as she leaned against the door. "Nope. I'm going to help unpack. This visit is only for two weeks. We need to start strategizing to make the most of our time."

Lucille looked ready to argue. Then she shrugged, patted her hair, and turned toward one of the double staircases. "Suit yourself, dear." As the blond started climbing, Remy heard her say, "Only two weeks. *Only!* The child's demented."

CHAPTER 8
CAUTIONARY

"WE'RE GOING TO HAVE séances, right, Remy?"

"Possibly?"

Remy and April waited at the back of the van. Mark stood inside the vehicle, gathering plastic crates full of supplies and passing them to Remy, who stacked them next to the garden's stone fence.

April seemed oblivious that there was work to do as she paced back and forth, rubbing her thumb over her lower lip. "Can we do that thing where someone goes into a trance and writes ghostly messages on a piece of paper? I saw them do that in a movie one time, and it looked super cool."

Remy laughed so hard that she almost dropped the carton of cereals Mark passed her. "That's psychography. And it's not as exciting as the movies make it look. But we might try it. I'm not a spirit medium, so I'll leave that side of things to Marjorie."

"Do you think she could teach me? I'm sure I have some crazy abilities. I just need the right environment and a good mentor to bring them out. A catalyst." April wheeled back to stare up at the building. The sun neared the horizon, creating dusky red streaks across the sky and silhouetting the house's shingle roof. "Yeah, Carrow's going to be my catalyst."

Remy carefully placed a carton by the fence but kept silent. The ability to communicate with spirits was a gift people had from birth. Most spirit mediums could recall seeing and speaking with ghosts as some of their earliest memories. If April's talents hadn't appeared by her seventeenth birthday, they were likely nonexistent.

That didn't mean that regular, nongifted individuals never saw ghosts, but the spirits had to manifest strongly. Remy likened it to eyesight: someone with great vision might be able to read every letter on an optometrist's chart, but someone with poor eyesight would only see the biggest letters, while the smaller ones disappeared into a blur. Most spirits were small letters. Only the strongest—poltergeists, ghosts that were able to physically manifest, and exceptionally powerful specters—could be equated to the chart's largest, clearest letters.

But unlike eyesight, twenty-twenty spiritual vision was very, very rare. And there were no glasses or contact lenses to improve it. Most people would go their whole lives without perceiving a single ghost. Some glimpsed one or two, often fleetingly. A true, strong spirit medium could see them all.

Remy's ability was slightly above mediocre, but only slightly.

She'd seen two ghosts in her life—the first when she was a child and the second as a teen—but neither had been clear or visible for long. She hoped she would have a chance to exercise her modest gift during the stay at Carrow.

She was contemplating the difficult task of explaining spiritual sight to April without shattering the girl's heart when a hand touched her shoulder.

Mark had jumped down from the van and approached without her hearing. "Are you all right? You look worried."

She blinked then grinned. "No, I'm fine. Just thinking about some stuff. Nothing serious."

"Good. I didn't want to lose my tour guide before the visit had even begun."

They both picked up a carton of food and began carrying them through the yard, up the stone stairs, and into the foyer. While Remy had been lost in thought, April had wandered off. It took her a moment of searching to spot the girl's red jacket and blue highlights near the copse of pine trees. Remy grimaced. She wasn't sure if she should let April wander around the hazardous island alone, but then, it *was* her property.

"The others should be arriving soon, as long as they're on time," Mark said. "Once introductions are over with, what should our first tasks be?"

They dropped their burdens in the center of the foyer and returned to the yard for another armful.

"Dinner, I'd say." Remy glanced behind them at the dipping sun. "Then setting up our rooms. If there's time, we might be able to discuss a plan for the next few days. But I don't think we'll get to the actual researching today—not unless we pull an all-nighter."

Mark handed her one of the lighter crates then hefted two jugs of water. "No, you're right. Better we're well rested."

"You're not disappointed?"

He laughed. "No, there's not much about today that could disappoint me. Except..." A hint of mischief brought light to his eyes. "If I'm being honest, I was rather hoping you'd come wearing that black dress from the tour."

"Ha!" *He's so lively compared to that night in the kitchen. I don't mind this change.* Remy jostled her companion then jogged up the stairs. "Not a chance. I only cosplay at night."

They stepped into the foyer. An ethereal figure stood in a band of dying light that flowed through the window. The sunset's glow sparkled off her glossy gold hair and gray dress, and her pose reminded Remy of the female saints that often adorned renaissance paintings. Then the woman turned, and Lucille's decidedly unsaintlike face glowered at them. "These rooms are disgusting."

Remy gave her a tight-lipped smile as she set down her carton. "Well, no one's lived here for a couple of decades. There's going to need to be a bit of cleaning before bed, I'm afraid."

Lucille stalked forward, her face contorted in repulsion. As she neared, Remy noticed a cobweb had become caught in the woman's bangs. It took all of her self-control not to stare.

"Dust everywhere." The words escaped Lucille as little staccato gasps. "Rat excrement in the hallway. Filthy windows. And blood on one of the walls! I can't believe you let our building devolve into such a wretched state. What are we paying you for?"

"Uh…" Remy blinked aggressively to collect her thoughts. "Wait… Hold up… You're *not* paying me. *I* rent from *you*. And what did you say about blood?"

"Sprayed across the wall!" Lucille threw out a hand to demonstrate. "Do you have any idea how unhygienic that is? Where's April? I've got to talk some sense into her."

Remy exchanged a look with Mark. "I check all of these rooms after my tours. I didn't see any kind of stain last time I was here."

"Perhaps…" Lucille massaged the bridge of her nose. "Perhaps April and I can stay in a hotel in town. She's only slightly unreasonable. Surely we can come to a compromise."

"Which room?" Remy pressed.

"Oh, I don't know. One of the bedrooms."

Remy was already jogging up the stairs. She could hear Mark's quick, sharp steps behind her.

"Does anyone else have access to the house?" he asked as they reached the landing.

"Not that I know of." Remy looked down both sides of the hallway and chose the right first. The doors were already open, so she checked inside each room before moving farther into the house. "I'd suspect vandalism, except it's nearly impossible to get into this place without a key. You saw how hard it was to open the windows."

They reached the end of the hallway without finding anything unusual, and started back up the opposite way. Remy was beginning to think Lucille was either mistaken or exaggerating—until she stepped into Room 9.

"Oh…no, that definitely wasn't here during my last tour."

Mark came to a halt at her side. Together, they stared at the dark-red marks blooming out of the wallpaper near the window.

"It does look a bit like blood, doesn't it?" Wonder tinted his voice. He stepped nearer to the marks, hand extended, but didn't touch them.

The stains weren't big—the largest was smaller than Remy's palm, and the rest could have come from fingertip taps—but close to a dozen of them spread across the wallpaper in a vaguely oval shape. Remy frowned as she scanned the pattern. "Tell me if I'm talking crazy, but I don't think those marks look like something was splashed on the paper."

He glanced at her. "What do you mean?"

"They look like a liquid is seeping *out of* the wall."

Mark blew out a breath and scratched a hand through his dark hair. "Yes…yes, I see that." He reached for the window handle. It squealed as the long-frozen pane moved, but he persisted until the opening was wide enough to poke his head through. His body contorted as he examined the external wall, but when he pulled back inside, he looked more confused than ever. "I can't see anything out there that could cause it."

Remy leaned close to the wallpaper. She touched the largest mark and grimaced as her finger came away slick with red liquid. "It's still wet."

"Well, damn." Mark's laugh was shaky. "The only person who's been up here since we arrived is Lucille. And I can't imagine she did this."

Room 9's door slammed open, making both Remy and Mark jump. April entered, followed closely by a dark-haired, stubbled man Remy didn't recognize.

"Lucille wasn't joking," April said, her eyes round. "This is bloody amazing. What do you think it is, Remy? A spirit's manifestation? Ectoplasm?"

Remy didn't answer. She rubbed her wet finger against her thumb, feeling the fluid's distinctly tacky consistency. She could smell a biting metallic undertone. It was hard not to think about blood, and the idea made her stomach flip unpleasantly.

"Well, what are you waiting for?" April flapped her arms. "Tear the wallpaper off! I want to see where it's coming from!"

Mark looked from her to the wall. "Oh…are you sure that's all right? Isn't this antique paper?"

"It's my bloody house—tear the bloody stuff down!"

Mark gave Remy a final, questioning look, as though seeking her approval. She shrugged to indicate it wasn't her choice to make, so he retrieved a Swiss army knife from his pocket. He flipped out one of the blades and used it to score the discolored patterned paper.

Remy retreated to stand beside April and the strange man, whose expression was almost as rapt as the teenager's.

He caught Remy looking at him, and thrust a long-fingered hand toward her. "Taj Sadana, ghost hunter."

"Hi. Remy. Tour guide." Remy, reluctant to extend the

liquid-tainted hand, offered him the opposite one. It was awkward, but they managed to shake. "I'm glad you came."

"That's a joke." He grinned good-naturedly as his hungry eyes returned to the wall. "*I'm* the grateful one here. A dozen of my peers are turning green from jealousy as we speak."

Mark was working at the wallpaper carefully but diligently. He pulled back a long strip, exposing a second, dingier layer of paper below.

Remy knew the pattern from photos. "That would be from the 1955 renovation."

"Keep going," April urged.

Remy silently agreed. The stains appeared to be bigger with the first layer gone.

He nodded, returned the knife to the paper, and scored deeper lines. A second strip of paper came down. The stains were larger. Remy recognized the gold-and-red paper. "That's the house's original layer. Try removing it, too. There should be plaster behind it."

For a moment, the room was silent except for the sound of ripping paper. Then Mark stepped back from the wall and continued backing up until he'd joined them in the doorway. Even April was speechless.

Gore, bright red, seeped out of the plaster as though from an open wound. The distinct spots that had been visible on the top wallpaper layer had merged into an egg-shaped patch that was almost as large as a person's torso.

April broke the quiet with a loud swear word. "You're all seeing this, right? I'm not imagining it?"

Grinning, Taj shook his head. "We need to document this. I'll get my camera."

"Yes." Remy's voice sounded hollow in her ears. She looked back at her hand, where the bright-red liquid marked two of her fingers, and nausea rose. "Get a camera. I need to wash this off."

Taj was already at the door. "Can someone help me carry my equipment?"

"I'll do that." April pointed at Mark. "Stay here and guard the…the…whatever that is. We'll be back in a moment."

Taj and April barreled out of the room at the same time, thumping into the hallway walls in their eagerness to collect the cameras.

Remy waited until their footsteps had faded, then she turned to Mark. "Will you be okay here alone?"

Despite looking a fraction paler than he had earlier that day, he gave her a bright smile. "Absolutely. Go wash your hand."

She nodded mutely and left the room. It seemed easier to breathe in the hallway, and Remy began collecting her thoughts as she jogged to the nearest bathroom. *This has to be of supernatural origin. Doesn't it?*

The small bathroom's off-white tiles glittered when Remy flicked on the light. She twisted the sink's tap and sighed as cold, clear water erased the red marks from her fingertips.

None of the accounts about Carrow talked about blood coming through the walls. What does that mean? Have we unintentionally angered the spirits? Is it a warning?

Her mind flashed back to the photos of bruises, cold burns,

and cuts that ghost hunters had earned while investigating Carrow. But in all of those cases, the researchers had spent prolonged periods—sometimes days—taunting the ghosts to provoke a response. There had been plenty of calmer research projects where nothing threatening, let alone violent, had been recorded. And Remy's own tours had run without a hitch for nearly two years. *Despite all of that, maybe it would be wise to cancel the visit…even if April throws a fit.*

She kept the tap running longer than was really necessary and scrubbed her fingertips until they were pink. She was drying her hands on her jeans when a muffled, furious "*No-o-o-o!*" echoed through the house. Remy slammed the tap off and raced back into the hallway, her focus recentered on Room 9.

CHAPTER 9
THE DINING ROOM

THERE WASN'T FAR TO run between the bathroom and Room 9, but anxiety had Remy breathless and her heart pounding by the time she caught herself on the doorframe. April and Taj had returned from collecting his equipment, and April, the source of the cry, had slumped against a wall.

"What's wrong?" Remy grabbed the teen's shoulders and pulled her around as she searched her face. "Are you hurt?"

"Only my morale," April spat and waved a hand toward the wall.

Mark stood near the stain, shoulders hunched and hands clasped behind himself apologetically. "I'm afraid this was a false alarm. Listen."

He knocked his elbow against the wall a foot away from the red marks. Remy frowned as a low clattering, gurgling noise rose from the house. The stain glistened as fresh liquid seeped out of the plaster.

"You mean—"

"From what I can tell, it's a burst pipe." He shrugged. "I made the mistake of leaning against the wall, and it started rattling."

Remy pressed a hand against her chest, where her heart was still fluttering. "Rust could account for the reddish color. And the metallic odor." She laughed as tension slipped from her shoulders. "Sorry, April."

"This is literally the worst thing that could possibly happen," the teen muttered.

Taj, his cheerful attitude unchanged, nudged her. "Stay positive. Maybe a ghost burst the pipe."

"Either way, you'll need to hire a plumber," Remy said. "If the pipe is going through the house's external wall, it's probably carrying water from the roof. This'll only get worse with rain."

April curled her lip to show Remy exactly what she thought of plumbers.

Chuckling, Taj nudged her again. "I'll get a camera set up, just in case. But I wouldn't complain if you guys helped carry the rest of this stuff back downstairs."

Remy noticed he was standing near an impressive stack of equipment: a camera and tripod, an EMF recorder, audio recorder, black light, and several odd-looking pieces of equipment she didn't recognize. He'd come prepared, at the very least. "Yeah, no problem. C'mon, then. It's getting late, and I'd like to be in bed before midnight if possible."

April shot a final, regretful look at the wall then joined Remy and Mark to take a share of the equipment. The others followed Remy single file down the hallway then the stairs.

Lucille's sniffles were audible as soon as Remy entered the foyer. She'd perched herself on the edge of one of the fireside seats, apparently trying to touch the dusty upholstery as little as possible, and directed a thousand-yard stare at the opposite wall. A familiar, portly figure sat opposite, hat held neatly on his lap, and he leaped to his feet as Remy appeared.

"There you are!" He pressed a handkerchief to the perspiration on his forehead. "What's happened? She's been wailing about blood, then those two ran past like the devil were on their heels, and I heard a cry—has someone been hurt?"

"No, no, nothing like that!" Remy placed the boxes on the ground and gave the man an apologetic smile. "Sorry, Piers, it's been a bit of a strange afternoon."

Following Mark's confirmation that he had a booking for the house, Remy had sent an email to her database of past tour guests, offering a spot in the extended stay. Although close to twenty had replied to say they wished they could come, only one had committed—Piers, the spectacled gentleman who had coincidentally been a part of Mark's tour.

Remy supposed she shouldn't be surprised by the low turnout. Two weeks was a long time for people to take away from their jobs and families, let alone spend in a haunted house. While discussing the plan's details, Piers had shared that he was recently retired and wanted to dedicate more of his time to exploring a subtle supernatural gift he believed he possessed. Gift aside, Remy was grateful to have him there. He'd struck her as pleasant and enthusiastic, two traits that would help defuse the irritability that inevitably crept over people stuck together for an extended time.

Remy quickly introduced him to Mark—even though they'd been on the tour together, they hadn't actually spoken—then to April and Taj. Piers let slip that he believed he was paranormally gifted, and April's eyes lit up as she latched on to him, demanding he tell her everything. Lucille, still sitting on the edge of the seat, sniffed and glowered at the pair.

Taj excused himself to retrieve the rest of the equipment from his car, leaving Remy and Mark together.

"Now we're just missing our spirit medium and her assistant." Remy checked her watch. "They're a bit late. Do you think we should start dinner while we wait for them?"

"Yes, definitely. I'm starving." He beckoned her toward the stack of cartons in the center of the room and began digging through them. "Where do you want to eat? The kitchen?"

"There's a dining room, but it'll be phenomenally dusty."

"Can't be worse than the rest of the house," he said cheerfully as he unpacked a stack of plates. "Lead the way."

The dining room was, as promised, phenomenally dusty. Remy and Mark spent a few minutes washing the table and serving counter and dusting the chairs to get it to an acceptable state, then Mark returned to the kitchen to prepare their food while Remy set the table.

She had to make several trips to carry the tableware and food into the dining room, and each journey took her past the foyer, where Lucille pointedly ignored everyone around her and April and Piers continued their excited discussion in hushed tones.

It would have been less work to eat huddled around the kitchen counter, but Remy was glad they weren't having dinner there. She wanted to make a good impression on their first night in Carrow, and the dining room was a surefire way to achieve that.

The vaulted ceiling that stretched high above their heads was fitted with skylights that would have allowed the day's natural glow through if there had been any left. A banquet table large enough to seat thirty filled the room. Serving tables stood at each end, and velvet drapes shuttered the tall, narrow windows overlooking the grounds.

The table was too large even for their group, so Remy clustered the food and drinks at one end. The sconce lights fitted to the walls provided poor lighting, so Mark went to find candles while Remy rallied their small group.

"Serve yourself," she said as she ushered April and Piers, who were still talking, through the doorway. "There's wine for anyone of legal age and soft drinks for April. We're still missing two of our party, so save some food for them."

Lucille's offended glower faded as she looked about the room. She exhaled a murmur as she took the seat beside April. "This place could be glorious if it were fixed up."

"That's exactly what the last eight owners thought," Remy said with a wink. She waited by the door until Taj, having run down the stairs, entered, followed by Mark. "It's an incredible house but not in a good location. Plus, its history doesn't do it any favors. It hasn't been profitable since Edgar Porter was hanged."

"Still, though." Lucille directed her attention toward her ward.

"I'm sure we could do *something* with it. Turn it into a luxury spa, perhaps. Or maybe a convention center."

April looked at Lucille as though she'd gone insane. "But it wouldn't be *spooky* if we did that."

"Dig in," Remy interjected loudly enough to interrupt the brewing argument. "Don't let it get cold."

For several long minutes, the room was silent except for the rhythmic clatter of cutlery as the pastas and cold meats were consumed. While April, Taj, and Piers all wolfed down their meals, Mark seemed distracted as he picked at his plate, and Lucille refused to eat anything except the salad and the wine. For her own part, Remy was lost in her thoughts. It felt surreal to be staying in Carrow rather than visiting for a handful of hours at a time. She only prayed they would find something to justify the hefty price Mark must have paid to bring them there.

Taj stopped chewing, and his eyes flicked toward the door leading to the foyer. "Did anyone else hear that?"

"No." Remy glanced behind them. "What was it?"

"Don't know. Like...voices or something."

April leaned forward in her seat, her eyes huge. "Are the spirits trying to speak to us?"

He grinned and shook his head. "Doubt they'd make it that easy. I can't hear it anymore. It was probably just the wind rattling a window; this house is noisy."

Even so, the entire group held still and listened. They could hear the wind tugging at the building, the dulled roar of crashing waves, and a groan as the wood above their heads flexed. Then a door slammed.

CHAPTER 10
GATHERING

"I KNEW IT!" APRIL leaped to her feet, but Lucille clutched at her arm to keep her at the table.

One by one the group stood, all turning toward the double doors leading to the foyer. Remy glanced toward Mark and saw he was already looking to her, apparently waiting for her lead. She licked her lips and took a step toward the doors.

The grand, carved doors burst inward, making Lucille shriek and Piers knock his chair over.

Remy exhaled and pressed a hand to her fluttering heart as she saw the tiny, wrinkled woman in the opening. "Marjorie!"

"I see you've started dinner." Marjorie trotted into the room, her narrowed blue eyes scanning the occupants with a quick sweep. "I suppose it was a bit rude not to call and tell you I'd be late. You must have worked yourselves into a frenzy if a closing door is enough to startle you."

Lucille sniffed. "You did a bit more than simply *close* it."

A tall, sallow man entered after Marjorie, carrying a suitcase in each hand. He inclined his head a fraction in greeting but remained silent as he placed the suitcases on the ground, took two plates, and began filling them with food.

Remy cleared her throat. "Everyone, I'd like you to meet Marjorie McAllister. She's a highly talented spirit medium who has worked on several significant haunted locations with great success."

"This is a lovely little gathering," Marjorie said as she stripped off her gloves. "Sorry we couldn't be here earlier. I sensed a strong psychic connection on the freeway, and we had to pull over to clear it. Young man killed in a car crash a few years back. Wasn't keen on moving on."

The sallow man, still silent, tightened his lips and turned his eyes toward the ceiling. Remy suspected he wasn't as pleased about the detour as his employer.

"This is Bernard," Marjorie continued as she wiggled into a free seat beside Piers. "He'll be assisting me during these next two weeks. Say hello, dear."

Bernard exhaled a barely audible response as he placed a plate in front of Marjorie, then chose a seat at the opposite side of the table, next to Lucille.

"Thank you for coming." Mark folded his hands on the table as he glanced about them. "That makes our party complete. Would now be a good time to make some plans?"

He turned toward Remy, and she nodded. Apparently—she

wasn't sure when or how—she seemed to have been elected the leader for that evening. She enjoyed playing the role during the tours, but it felt strangely foreign that night.

She cleared her throat and spread her hands. "Uh, welcome, everyone! I'm glad you could all make it. If no one minds, maybe we could go around the table and introduce ourselves and our purpose here? I'm Remy Allier, and I know a library's worth of mostly useless trivia about Carrow. My experience with ghosts is limited, but I've always been fascinated by them—and especially haunted locations like this house. I'll be acting as a guide and fact checker and helping out anywhere else I'm needed." She nodded to Mark, who sat at her right.

"Mark Sulligent." He raised a hand in a brief, awkward greeting. "If I had to sit in a box, it would probably be labeled *sponsor.* Like Remy, I'll help out wherever I'm needed."

Remy would have liked Mark to share more—she still didn't know his underlying reason for coming to Carrow—but he motioned to Piers before she could ask.

"Well…" Piers seemed faintly embarrassed as he polished his glasses. "I'm here as a sort of spectator, I suppose. I used to see spirits when I was a child, and now that I'm retired, I'd like to explore that some more. As far as hobbies go, it's more exciting than golf and cheaper than a yacht and will make a great icebreaker at parties."

Remy chuckled then turned to Taj. "You?"

"I'm a bit more mercenary than my friend," Taj said, inclining his head toward Piers. "I want to capture irrefutable proof of the supernatural. I produce documentaries featuring haunted locations, and I think Carrow will give me some phenomenal, potentially groundbreaking material."

"Documentaries?" Lucille perked up instantly. "You're a film producer?"

He nodded cheerfully. "An indie producer, that's right. I post to my YouTube channel. The pay is peanuts, but it's unbelievably gratifying."

The scowl returned as Lucille slumped back in her seat. Hoping that Taj hadn't noticed the dismissal, Remy quickly said, "I saw you brought equipment."

"Everything I owned or could borrow." His face lit up as he recounted them. "Cameras—both the plain and the motion-detection kind—EMF recorders, a surveillance system, black lights, a specially adjusted radio—"

Marjorie made a noise that was somewhere between a cough and a laugh. "I see you've embraced the twenty-first century, dear. That's good and all, and I'm sure those gadgets may pick up some residual effects from a spirit's presence, but the most effective results always come from connecting with the entities on an emotional, empathic level. That's the only reliable way to communicate with them."

Taj's smile tightened. "Yeah, it's a real tragedy that they won't admit *feelings* into scientific journals."

"Science!" Marjorie threw her hands up. "Why must everything be attached to science before it's believed? Open your eyes, boy—not everything in this world can be put inside a test tube."

Remy and Mark shot each other a quick, concerned glance. The evening's civility was unraveling rapidly. In an attempt to save it, Remy interjected, "From where I stand, you're not too different."

Both Taj and Marjorie looked incredulous. She hurried to continue. "You both want to touch, to see, to talk with a realm that the average person doesn't believe exists. Yeah, your methods are different, but I don't see them as conflicting. And if they both get results, who's complaining?"

Taj gave her a nod and leaned back in his seat.

Marjorie, on the other hand, continued to look righteously offended. "Those cameras, those nasty EMF readers and electrical devices—they just frustrate and upset the spirits. You're poking at a hornet's nest by bringing them here." She turned to Mark. "I was led to believe we were truly attempting to communicate with the dead. Not putting on some inane circus act in the hope of getting a few clips we can string together into a sensational video."

"We're not." Mark shifted forward with both hands spread on the table. "Be patient with me. I've never participated in this sort of event before. I hired both you and Taj specifically because your methods *are* different. Maybe one will work better than the other. I don't know that yet. But I'd rather try *too much* than *not enough*."

Marjorie leveled a searching glare at him. After several painfully long seconds, she exhaled and resumed her grandmotherly smile. "I believe that. You have a bright aura. You, at least, came here with good intentions." She sent a pointed look at Taj, but he pretended not to notice.

Remy cleared her throat. "I think that works as Marjorie's introduction, too. As our spirit medium, she'll be overseeing most of what we do here. And, uh, Bernard—"

"I'm here because she's paying me." Bernard's voice was as flat and emotionless as his expression and invited no further questioning.

Lucille raised her wine glass. "Ditto."

"So that leaves our host, April."

April flipped a lock of hair over her shoulder and flashed a wolfish grin. "I own this joint. I'm awesome. And I can't wait to see some crazy, messed-up stuff here."

Marjorie exhaled a small, affronted noise.

"Well, maybe we can save the crazy, messed-up stuff for tomorrow." Remy glanced at her watch; it was after ten. "Unless anyone here considers cleaning to be crazy and messed up, in which case there's plenty of that."

"One question." Bernard, whose long face had been growing steadily more morose as the evening progressed, rolled his head toward Remy and held up his cell phone. "I've been trying to get a signal since I arrived. Is anyone else having problems?"

"Oh…" Remy looked at Marjorie. "Sorry, weren't you told? Carrow doesn't get any signal. Anyone who wants to make a phone call or check their email will need to drive to town."

Bernard's lips twisted in disgust. "Tell me you're joking."

"Oh, don't make such a fuss, dear." Marjorie patted his arm.

69

"They brought a two-way radio in case of emergencies. You can listen to some tunes if you get bored."

He let his head drop back. Remy barely caught his mutter of, "Lovely."

"Are we done here?" Lucille downed the last of her wine and wiped a dribble off her lips with the back of her hand. The bottle next to her was half-empty. "I still don't know where we're sleeping."

"Yes, definitely." Remy rose and began gathering plates. "You can have your picks of the upstairs rooms. Mark kindly brought fresh sheets, pillows, and quilts, so collect yours from the foyer. The gentlemen might be kind enough to carry the new mattresses upstairs. I would recommend not taking Room 9 because of the water leak. And, uh…" She pulled up a brief mental tally of Carrow's history. "Rooms 2, 5, 11, and 14 are less haunted. If that's important to anyone."

"Less haunted?" Piers had been quiet through virtually all of the dinner but was cleaning his glasses aggressively. "I'll, uh, be the first to admit I came here hoping for some spooks, but, uh, I'd rather not meet them while I'm sleeping. Are any rooms…*not* haunted at all?"

Remy dearly wished she had different news. She gave him an apologetic smile. "I won't sugarcoat this. There has been at least one death in every bedroom in this building. There have been supernatural phenomena experienced in most of them, too. But 2, 5, 11, and 14 are the least awful."

"Least awful." Lucille sent April a sour look. "You spent a small fortune on this hole, and the very best it can offer is 'least awful.'"

April met her guardian's frown then turned to Remy with an expression of such ferocious stubbornness that it was almost laughable. "I want to stay in the most haunted room."

"Are you mad, child?" Marjorie laughed. "There'll be plenty of time to meet the spirits in the morning."

"I'm not mad, and I'm not joking." A cold smile curved the teen's lips. "Give me the most awful room. I'll spend all night in it."

Remy, feeling helpless, turned to Mark. Judging by his tight-lipped, wide-eyed expression, he didn't have any clue on how to handle the situation, either. *She owns the house, but on the other hand, she's not even an adult...* "Um..."

April leaned across the table, eyes narrowed. "The. *Most.* Awful."

Remy held both hands up to beg for mercy. "Okay, how about you pick? Do you want the room where Edgar bludgeoned a widow and her child to death and now she rattles the window-panes, or do you want the room where the guests mysteriously suffocated during the night and now their gasping last breaths can be heard at four in the morning?"

"Ooh, that's a tough one." April's eyes lost their squint. She turned to Lucille with a mischievous smile. "We're sharing. Which one do you want?"

"I don't care." Lucille scowled at the ceiling. "It's all nonsense, so you can have whatever you like. Just as you always do."

Color bled from April's face as cold, tight anger squeezed her lips together and flared her nostrils. When she finally turned back to Remy, a vicious, blazing determination lit her eyes. "Give us the bludgeon room."

"Room 6," Remy said weakly.

Piers leaned close so that he could whisper to her. "Sorry... I mean...would it be okay if I called dibs on one of the better ones?"

"Room 11," she whispered back. "Hardly anything happens there. Get some luggage in it before one of the others moves in."

Piers beamed at her, quickly rose, and trotted back to the foyer with April and a sniffling Lucille in his wake.

Marjorie stood slowly and gave the remaining guests a polite nod. "I'll rely on my empath abilities to choose a room. Good night, all. I'll see you nice and early for breakfast. Come, Bernard, I need you to make my bed for me."

Bernard's mouth curled, but he made no comment as he followed his employer. Taj stayed just long enough to thank them for dinner, then he hurried out, leaving Mark and Remy standing beside the stack of dirty dishes.

Remy raised an eyebrow. "Looks like I'm on dish duty tonight."

"I'll help." Mark hefted an armful of plates, grinning. "It'll give the others a chance to get settled. Theoretically."

CHAPTER 11
THE WOMAN IN THE HALL

IT WAS NEARLY AN hour later when Remy and Mark, their arms full of luggage and clean sheets, reached the top of the stairs. The time had passed faster than Remy had expected. Mark had been chatty and made her laugh easily. She found herself looking forward to getting to know him better during the following weeks.

Marjorie paced the second-floor hallway. Her eyes were half-closed, and her fingers stretched out so that they barely brushed the walls. She chuckled when she saw Remy and Mark. "Sorry, don't mind me. Just getting a feel for the place before bed."

Remy raised her eyebrows. "Are you having trouble choosing a room?"

"Oh, goodness no, dear. I've already staked out my territory. Room 11 was my first pick, but Piers had already slipped in there, darn him. I opted for Room 5, instead. Bernard's fixing it up for me."

"Glad you're settled." Remy passed Marjorie to check who had taken the other rooms. April, true to her word, had placed herself and Lucille in 6. The room only had a single bed, so Lucille's mattress had been dropped unceremoniously on the floor below the window. Her mouth scrunched into an unhappy grimace, Lucille hung her tailored clothes in the wardrobe. Taj's jacket dangled from the doorknob of Room 2, but Remy found him in Room 9, the room with the leaking pipe. He was focused on the screen of a camcorder he'd set up earlier.

"Find anything?"

"Nah." His smile was apologetic. "I got excited when it caught some motion from a few hours ago, but it was just the loose wallpaper moving in the wind. I'll leave it running overnight."

"All right, don't stay up late." Remy turned back to the hallway, where Mark waited politely. "Out of the remaining rooms, 14 is the best, historically speaking. It's yours if you want it."

"Which will you stay in?"

"Room 7," she answered easily. "It's got a ghastly backstory, but at least it's near the bathrooms."

That earned her a laugh. "Then I'll take 8. That's the one where the fellow was stuffed into his wardrobe, right? I can handle that. Have a good sleep."

"Good night." She waited until he'd closed his door, then turned the handle and entered Room 7.

The air tasted stale, so she pushed the window up to let a breeze in. She used her sleeve to rub the worst of the dust off her side table and put her linen bundle on it before switching on the room's lamps. Shadows bled away from the matching collection of dark-wood furniture and age-stained wallpaper. The room wasn't large, but it was plenty for one person.

She pulled the old mattress off the bed and replaced it with one of Mark's that had been left in the hallway. April had insisted on maintaining as much of Carrow's original furniture as possible, and that had included the mattresses from the building's last opening in the eighties. That was a long time for anything to sit dormant, and Remy was impressed the bed hadn't developed mildew in the interim.

The multiple renovations had erased every trace of death from her room, but they were all preserved in Remy's mind, cataloged by year. Five guests had disappeared from the space during Edgar's reign, including two sisters and a maid who had reported a dark stain in the carpet. The police investigations had turned up bloodstains on the bed's underside, where one of the victims had tried to hide and subsequently been stabbed to death. Remy tried not to think about it as she tucked fresh sheets into the mattress.

Quiet noises from up and down the hallway created a reassuring background melody. She hadn't chosen Room 7 just because of its proximity to the bathroom. It was also central to where everyone else was staying. While Room 14 had a less violent history, she was more concerned for the living than the dead. She wanted to be close if anything went wrong during the night.

April's and Lucille's voices rose above the background noises. From the snatches Remy caught, Lucille hated everything about the room and wanted them to drive back to town and stay in a "proper hotel." April threw around a handful of names, including *ungrateful whiny wretch* and *insipid killjoy*. Remy didn't want to eavesdrop, but it was hard not to when the words shook the walls.

At last, the bickering subsided. Remy shoved the original mattress and sheets into a pile near the wardrobe then retrieved her pajamas and toothbrush and went to the bathroom.

It was nearing midnight when Remy clambered into her bed. Despite how bone-tired she felt, sleep refused to visit her. She lay in the alien bed, staring at the peeling off-white ceiling six feet above her, as the house gradually settled. The other occupants turned off their lights and fell quiet, and soon, all she could hear was a faint rattle of plumbing and the mournful groan of flexing wood.

A series of niggling questions ran through her weary mind. At the forefront was concern for April and Lucille. Why were they together when they were so hostile toward each other? If April's parents were pliable enough to buy her a mansion, surely they would find her a new chaperone if she didn't like Lucille?

Frowning, Remy rolled over to see her bedside clock. The red digital numbers crept toward one in the morning.

Another question vied for attention. Mark had been nothing but pleasant and accommodating since they'd arrived at Carrow. He hadn't asked any questions, made any plans, or given them any tasks. And during the dinner, he'd implied that he didn't know much about ghosts or spirit mediums. *So why did he spend a small fortune renting Carrow for the fortnight?*

She groaned and flipped onto her other side, facing the door, hoping she could shake some of the buzzing thoughts out of her brain. Somewhere outside her window, a bird cried out in alarm then was silenced.

A low, agonizing creak reverberated through the dark. Remy sat up as her door drifted open.

"Hello?" She kept her voice to a whisper, but the word carried in the quiet house.

She slid her feet out of bed and felt them indent the rough rug. The only light in her room came from the LED clock, and it was barely enough to see the wall, let alone the hallway beyond.

Just the wind. You didn't close the door properly, and a breeze pushed it open.

The wood felt faintly cold under her hand as she pushed the door closed. She waited to feel the click of a latch catching then shuffled backward until her legs hit her bed.

Just the wind.

As she curled back under the blankets, she tried to force her breathing into a slow, steady rhythm. It was hard to stop her fingers curling into the corner of the pillow as though they needed to hold on to something.

You're being ridiculous, Remy. It's barely past one in the morning. The tours routinely keep you in Carrow much later than this.

Despite that, her fingers wouldn't relax. Spending the night in Carrow while fully dressed and busy with chores felt vastly different from spending the night in a bed, in the dark, listening to the crash of waves below her window and the creak of wood flexing as it cooled.

Wait...that's not just the wood relaxing. They're footsteps.

Remy's heart leaped painfully. She stayed curled in her bed, her eyes frozen on the barely visible door. *No, calm down. It's someone going to the bathroom, that's all.*

But that didn't make sense. The house was too dark to move through without some kind of light, and the space below her door was solid black.

The creaks grew closer. They were steady, rhythmic, almost hypnotic. Remy clenched her teeth and dug her fingers into her pillow as the presence neared then passed her door. A second later, a drawn-out groan sent shudders down her spine. Her door drifted open.

Remy's breaths were quick and tight. She slipped out of bed, crept toward the door, and turned on her light.

The lamp was dirty, and the light didn't spread as far as she would have liked. Remy leaned through the doorway, her heart fluttering, and looked down the hall.

Some kind of flowy white fabric disappeared around the corner. The glimpse was so brief that Remy couldn't give it any other attributes. She couldn't tell how large it was or how fast it was moving, only that it had turned down the opening that led to the stairs.

The night's cold was starting to seep through her pajamas and spread goose bumps over her skin, but the niggling worry urged her to step into the hallway. *What if one of the guests is sleepwalking?* The house was dangerous, and if they couldn't see, it would be too easy to step on unstable flooring or fall down the stairs.

Remy balled her hands into fists and folded her arms across her torso. She kept her footfalls light as she moved down the runner, past the row of closed doors, and toward the staircase. She wished she'd thought to bring a flashlight in her luggage. The house was loud around her. It seemed almost alive as its wood shifted and the wind whistled through tiny cracks in the stone.

She reached the landing and squinted down the staircase. The foyer was pitch-black. To light it, she would need to find the switches near the front door, on the other side of the room. Remy swallowed. She tried to pretend her shakes were from the cold alone as she descended the stairs, stretching bare toes into the darkness to feel for each new step. Unlike the hallway, the foyer seemed eerily still. Remy was almost certain she could hear her breaths echoed back at her as she passed the first landing and continued to the base of the stairs, one hand running along the cool wooden rail, the other stretched into the dark ahead of her.

The floor to her right creaked. Remy turned toward it, blind but straining to see, unsure of whether it was a presence or simply the house's normal noises. She'd lost count of how many steps she'd descended. Her feet touched carpet-covered stone, and she knew she'd arrived at the foyer.

She could visualize the vast space, but no moonlight made it through the windows to illuminate it. Remy felt swallowed by the dark, and the only audible noises were her quick, gasping breaths.

The lamp. Remy turned right, away from the front door and toward the entrance to the basement. She kept a lamp there for tours; it was closer and wouldn't have any furniture obstructing her path. Her outstretched hands touched a wall. She moved along it, using her fingertips to trace the rough stone until they brushed against the frame she knew belonged to the basement's entrance. The table was just to its left. She fumbled over its doily, found the lamp, found the matches, and worked to strike one.

The wick flared, and Remy sucked an icy breath into her aching lungs. She lifted the lamp, turned, and cried out.

Marjorie stood a pace behind her. The elderly woman's steel-gray hair fell over her shoulders like waterfalls, as loose and limp as her arms. Her white nightdress's hem dragged along the floor, already discoloring in the grime. Her face was a blank, emotion-less mask. Her eyes were wide and pure white; they had lost both iris and pupil.

Remy pressed her back to the wall, her heart hammering, one hand over her mouth to muffle her breathing. Marjorie stared at her, perfectly motionless, then twitched and turned away.

Is she sleepwalking? Remy's hand shook so badly that it rattled the lamp.

Marjorie walked slowly and deliberately across the foyer. She stopped underneath the massive portrait of Edgar Porter, lifted her chin to admire it with her sightless eyes, then turned again and began walking back toward the basement.

Remy moved out of the medium's path as Marjorie neared. Like before, the older woman came to a halt in front of the basement door, staring at the space Remy had occupied a moment before. She convulsed, turned, and began pacing back to the portrait.

Except for the twitches, Marjorie's movements were steady and slow, as though her limbs were heavy.

Could it be a trance? Either way, I need to get her back to bed. Remy cleared her throat and moved closer to the medium as she made another loop toward the picture. "Marjorie?"

The medium's head twitched to one side, making her long silver hair shimmer. Remy took a deep breath and stretched out a hand to touch Marjorie's shoulder. Her fingers had just grazed the fine white nightdress when something yanked her back.

CHAPTER 12
GUIDED

REMY TURNED AND FOUND Bernard looming over her. She opened her mouth but couldn't make a noise. Bernard held her wrist in a viselike grip, his eyes cold and his lips a hard line. Then he released her, and Remy stumbled back.

"Don't wake her." He turned his unforgiving eyes toward Marjorie, who stood under the portrait as she blindly admired the shadows. "Don't disturb her when she's sleepwalking."

"Why not?" Remy's voice shook, so she took a gulping breath. "Are you sure she's sleepwalking?"

"Yes. She reacts badly when she's disturbed. It's best not to touch or talk to her."

Remy clenched her hand into a fist so that Bernard wouldn't see the fingers shaking. "Why are her eyes like that?"

"They roll back." Bernard reached into his pocket. He pulled out a string with a series of small round bells tied to it.

"I—" Remy lowered her voice to a whisper as she looked back at the other woman, who was staring at the portrait once again. The words still felt too loud as they echoed around the foyer. "Marjorie can't stay down here. It's not safe."

Bernard's lip curled. "I know how to handle her. Go back to bed." He stretched his hand toward his employer and shook it to jingle the bells. The sound was faint but crisp. Marjorie's pacing ceased, and very slowly, she turned toward the tinkling melody, her pure-white eyes glowing in the lamplight.

"Go back to bed," Bernard said again. "I'll take care of her."

He backed away from Marjorie, still shaking the bells. She followed with hesitant, shuffling steps, as though magnetically attracted. Bernard turned as he reached the stairs and began climbing. Remy watched, afraid that Marjorie would trip over the barely visible steps, but the medium scaled them as though she'd known them her whole life.

Remy stayed in the foyer until the jingling bell faded from hearing and the distant clack of a door told her Marjorie was back in her room. Then, feeling faintly sick, Remy placed the lamp on the floor and braced her head in her hands.

I really could've done without that on the first night.

Now that she was alone, Remy realized she was freezing. Carrow's stone exterior insulated the building, but once its insides were chilled, it could take days to warm up again. A leak was letting cold air in and dropping the house's temperature.

A breeze skimmed over Remy's exposed neck, making her shudder. She turned toward the wall and caught the glitter of lamplight on glass. *That's right; Mark and I opened windows earlier today.*

It was hard to see what she was doing in the lamplight, but Remy managed to close both windows on one side of the house then crossed to the other. The final window—the one Mark had struggled with—was frozen in its frame, and she was afraid it might break if she strained on the handle too hard. It couldn't stay open, though—not unless they wanted to maintain permanent fires to ward off the icy ocean wind. She strained harder, trying to turn the handle and pull the window down at the same time without crushing her fingers. Lightning flashed outside. The window slammed closed, and Remy had a split-second glimpse of a long, thin face looking at her through the glass.

She stumbled back, but the vision was gone before she could even focus on it. She picked the lamp up off the ground and held it near the window, trying to see through, but the space outside was empty.

Angry thunder shook the air in the lightning's wake. The window was closed, but a long, thin crack now ran up its center. Remy swore under her breath. The windows were the house's originals—they were so old that the glass had become warped and blurred. April would be furious.

The rumbling thunder faded and gave way to the subtle ping of rain hitting the glass. Remy watched a drop run down the length of the crack and disappear into the sill. More soon followed.

She had a distinct, paranoid impression that she'd spent too long wandering the house's halls and inhaled as she turned back to the staircase.

The shock of meeting Marjorie and Bernard had chased away any desire for sleep, but she knew she had to try if she didn't want to be a walking disaster the following day. As she reached the top of the stairs, she caught faint snores coming from Piers's room. The sound was so mundane compared to her surroundings that Remy smiled. No light was visible under Marjorie's or Bernard's doors. Remy let herself back into her room, extinguished the lamp, curled up under the now-cold blankets, and stared at the cracked ceiling as she pleaded for sleep to take her.

Time passed in a dull blur. Remy fell into the twilight stage just before sleep and dreamed she heard a woman crying. The noise shocked her back awake, but when she sat up, the house was silent. Grimacing, she rolled over, squeezed her eyes closed, and waited for her heart to slow again.

When she next opened her eyes, her alarm clock showed it was after nine in the morning. The room was still dim. Steady rain beat against the window, and rolling, near-black clouds obscured the sun.

Muted noises came from deeper in the house. People seemed to be talking, and she caught what sounded like a scraping chair. She got up, dug fresh clothes out of her luggage, and changed into jeans and a simple comfortable blouse before going downstairs.

She found the entire group, minus Lucille, in the dining room, and the smell of warm toast, bacon, and scrambled eggs infused the room.

"Good morning!" Mark, seated near the door, waved to her. "We saved you food. Help yourself. Or I can make you an omelet if you feel like one."

"This is good." Remy fetched a plate, piled it with bacon and scrambled eggs, then made herself coffee from the machine set up on the end stand.

Instead of sitting at the vast dining table, her group had pulled their chairs into a messy half circle near the fireplace, which had been lit. Mark shuffled his seat to one side so that Remy could fit next to him.

"I wasn't sure if I should have woken you or not," he said. "But Bernard said you'd had a disturbed night, so we thought we'd let you sleep in."

"Thanks, it's definitely appreciated." Despite the patchy sleep, Remy didn't feel tired. She glanced at Marjorie. The medium looked serene as she sipped at her cup. If she was aware of her nighttime wandering, she didn't seem concerned by it. Remy stretched her legs toward the fireplace and glanced at the floor-to-ceiling windows behind them. Sheets of rain drenched the landscape, hiding most of the grounds from sight. "Good thing we arrived yesterday. I wouldn't want to be unpacking in this weather."

"You weren't joking when you said it was a rainy area," Mark agreed. He seemed to be in a good mood that morning, and Remy hoped it was a sign the house hadn't disturbed him during the night.

She glanced around the rest of the group. Most were either talking in subdued voices or focused on their food. "How did everyone sleep?"

"I'd say 'like a log,' but Bernard tells me I went for a wander last night," Marjorie said. "That was probably my empathic side tapping into the emotional needs in this house. I hope I didn't startle you too badly, dear."

Remy's mind flashed back to the white-eyed woman, her long hair and nightdress flowing behind her as she paced between Edgar's portrait and the basement door. She made a vague, noncommittal noise in response then cleared her throat. "While you were, uh, sleepwalking, you seemed especially interested in Edgar's portrait."

"Oh, did I?" Marjorie raised her eyebrows, but she didn't look too surprised. "I did pick up on some energy around the portrait yesterday. Occasionally, photographs and painted images can imbibe some of a person's essence, which could explain why I was drawn to it."

Remy turned to Taj. "That might make it a good location to investigate."

"Yes, absolutely." He ran his thumb over his lip as he thought. "I'll get some sensors and a camera set up there."

"Did anyone else wake during the night?" Remy hesitated, uncertain of how much of her experience she should share. Investigating the unexplained was their entire purpose at Carrow, but she didn't want to lead them down the path of reading something into every creak or shadow. Air pressure changes in the house or uneven hinges could have caused the door's movements, and she wasn't fully certain that what she'd seen in the window wasn't simply reflected lamplight.

"*I* would have slept fine, except for Lu." April spoke around a mouthful of scrambled eggs. "It was incessant. 'Oh, April, it's so dark… April, did you hear that? April, I think I saw a spider.' I was about ready to throw myself out the window by the time she fell asleep."

Remy noted Lucille was still missing. "Is she sleeping in?"

"Yuppers. She gets nasty when she's tired, so it's best to let her wake up on her own."

"Sorry to hear that," Piers said.

April waved her fork cheerfully. "She's the one who's suffering, not me. I didn't see any ghosts, though. Did anyone else have any luck?"

Taj broke into chuckles and ran a hand through his long, dark hair. "You're incorrigible. I used to think I was on the obsessive end of enthusiastic, but I've never been disappointed that a ghost didn't frighten me awake."

"Oy, remember, this is your career. My parents have a strict no-ghost-hunting-in-the-house rule. Staying here is like being in the world's best amusement park. I don't want to waste a second."

Remy cleared her throat. "On the subject of time limits, we should come up with a plan for today."

"I want to lay down some cameras and readers." Taj scraped the last forkful of food into his mouth and stretched to shove the plate back onto the table. "The sooner I get my equipment set up, the sooner I can actually use it."

"Do you need any help?"

"It's best if I do the setting up myself. A lot of my equipment is borrowed, and I promised the owners I'd be the only one to handle it. But it would be super helpful to know where to put it. Edgar's portrait is one good location, but I need to find out which rooms have the most activity, that sort of stuff."

"I can help with that." Remy noticed Marjorie was starting to look sour and quickly added, "I hope Marjorie will come with us. I can tell you where spirits have been sighted, but she'll be able to tap into the house's energy and give you up-to-date readings."

Marjorie nodded solemnly. "That dovetails nicely with my suggestion. I wanted to look through the house this morning—become acquainted with it, I suppose—and introduce myself to the lingering souls."

"Can I come?" April asked.

Piers cleared his throat. "If you're accepting spectators…"

Remy glanced at Mark, and he gave a quick nod. "How about we all go?" she asked. "Marjorie can feel out the house's energy, Taj can figure out where he'll set up his equipment, and the rest of us can get a crash course in Carrow's history."

"Brilliant," Piers said.

The dining room's door groaned open. Lucille, dark shadows under her eyes and her blond hair a disheveled mess, blinked against the room's lights as she entered. "What's brilliant? Are we going home?"

"We're going ghost hunting," April crowed.

Lucille's face contorted into a grimace that threatened tears, and Remy rose to put an arm around her shoulders.

"You don't have to come," she promised as she guided Lucille into a chair. "Now, do you want tea or coffee?"

"You're a saint. Coffee. Black. Enough sugar to give me cavities." Lucille pressed her fingertips against her temples, and Remy remembered how many glasses of wine the woman had downed the night before. She was likely nursing a hangover on top of a bad night's sleep, so Remy made the coffee extra strong and brought Lucille a plate of bacon and eggs along with it.

"Shall we leave once we're done with breakfast?" Marjorie asked.

"Once it's washed up, yes." Remy hurried to finish her own drink. "We need to devise a roster for food preparation and cleanup."

"Bernard doesn't have anything to do, so give it to him." Marjorie gave a dismissive wave in her companion's direction.

Bernard's lips twisted.

"Er, well, it's not fair to ask Bernard to do it all the time. If we split into teams of two, we'll only have to cook one day out of every four."

"Suit yourself. But he's being paid to work; don't be afraid of giving him jobs." Marjorie turned toward her assistant. "Mark did the cooking this morning, so you can do the dishes. You didn't want to be part of the tour party anyway, did you?"

"No." He rose, gathered an armful of plates, and strode out of the room.

Remy felt a rush of acute secondhand embarrassment for the man. She didn't know how he'd ended up in Marjorie's employment or why he didn't leave, but Marjorie treated him like a servant. Remy collected the remaining cups, mumbled something about being back soon, and hurried after him.

She found Bernard in the kitchen, running hot water into the sink. He glanced at her as she entered, then turned back to his task. The way the shadows fell across his face mimicked his appearance during the previous night. Back then, in the darkness, he'd looked wild—almost dangerous. In the light of day, the threat had melted away into tired, bored apathy.

"Hey," she said, placing the cups on the counter. His hostile exterior made it nearly impossible to find the words to express what she wanted to say. "We can leave this for later. I'd be really glad if you joined us for the tour—"

"I like being alone."

"Oh." Remy rubbed at the back of her neck. "Um, I just don't want you to feel like you're not an equal party here—"

"I don't." He flipped a tea towel over his shoulder and turned off the tap. After a second of silence, he added, "But thank you."

Remy shrugged. She'd kept her questions to herself during breakfast to avoid embarrassing Marjorie, but the words tumbled out of her before she could stop them. "And thanks for last night. For looking after Marjorie."

"It's my job."

"Does Marjorie, uh, sleepwalk often?"

"Every single night." He placed two plates on the draining board and dunked more in the sink.

"Oh." Remy hesitated, not sure if she could ask more without being rude, but to her surprise Bernard spoke without prompting.

"That's part of my job. To make sure she doesn't walk into a pond or in front of a train while she's asleep. She panics if she's woken and fights if you try to touch her. She follows the bells, though."

Remy raised her eyebrows. "Wow. She wanders that far?"

"Yes. And she's clever even when sleeping." Bernard's face was blank, as always, but a vein throbbed in his throat. "If I lock her in her room, she finds the key and lets herself out. If I take the key away, she breaks the lock. It's unnatural."

Remy chewed on her thumbnail. She'd heard of sleepwalkers who could hold conversations, even perform some simple tasks, but Marjorie's level of subconscious cognizance seemed to go beyond that. *Is it because of her medium abilities? Could she be following spirits?*

"I was serious when I said I like being alone," Bernard said, a hint of frustration in his tone.

"Oh. Right. Thanks. Uh, if you ever need help or—"

His mouth twisted into a sneer, and Remy beat a hasty retreat back to the dining room.

"All ready?" Marjorie asked. She stood by the dining room doors, and the others gathered around her like an audience, including, to Remy's surprise, Lucille. She'd placed herself close to Mark and kept shooting him glances as she patted her hair. Marjorie flipped her shawl around her shoulders. "Good, let's go."

CHAPTER 13
TURNED STONES

THE MORNING FELT SURREAL to Remy. In some ways, it was reminiscent of her regular tours—but with enough differences that she found it hard to fall into her usual flow. She recounted the house's history, from its fires to Edgar killing and replacing his employer to the prolonged string of murders and, finally, Edgar's death. April, Piers, and Mark had already heard the tour but listened politely as Remy led them through the upstairs rooms.

"One of Carrow's better-known spirits is a young, unidentified girl. People call her Red because of her crimson dress. Even when Carrow was still open as a hotel, many people heard quick, light footsteps disappearing down the hallway or caught glimpses of a brown-haired child in a red dress racing into a room.

"We don't know whether she was one of Edgar's victims or an unrelated death. Because Carrow House was originally a sanatorium, some of the ghosts may belong to patients who passed away in the original building. Either way, Red seems to have a mischievous streak, because it's common for visitors to lose one or two of their possessions after seeing her and later find them in a completely different room."

"She's friendly?" Piers kept close beside Remy, even though he was slightly breathless from the quick pace.

"I'd say more shy than friendly. She's certainly not malevolent—at least, we have no reason to suspect she is. Some of the other spirits in Carrow appear to be resentful or even aggressive, but Red only ever lets us glimpse her."

"Aggressive?" Lucille, who hung beside Mark, blinked quickly. "How do you mean?"

Remy hesitated. Her book of tour notes held photographs of researchers covered in bruises from thrown items, and an account from a man who had broken his leg after falling down the stairs, though he claimed he'd been pushed. But she hadn't personally experienced anything worse than faint noises or moving shadows, and it was always difficult to know which paranormal researchers could be trusted and who was spinning fiction to make a quick buck. Remy opted for a middle ground and only recounted events from researchers she trusted. "People have experienced patches of cold, a bitter taste to the air, heard voices that demand they get out, and even seen some poltergeist phenomenon where objects fall off tables. Some visitors report bad feelings, too, like they can tell they're unwelcome."

April rubbed her hands together. "Sounds like great fun."

Remy could only laugh. It took a certain kind of person to appreciate a malevolent supernatural entity.

She stopped at a set of huge double doors, one of her favorite parts of the tour, and rested her fingertips on the ornate handle. "We're at the master bedroom. As a physician, John Carrow insisted on being at the heart of the house so that he was never far from his patients in case of a midnight emergency. It's harder to be sure why Edgar continued to live in his predecessor's room. He might have thought it would look suspicious if he moved, or more likely, his ego liked it. Being in this room may have made him feel in control of the entire house."

The door hinges complained as they turned. The curtains were drawn, and the only light came from the hallway's lamps. Their glow shimmered off the furniture and caught on two pairs of eyes.

Remy turned the light switch, and the eyes resolved into a painting hung opposite the master bed. The picture depicted a couple: a wiry, gray-haired man and his dark-haired wife nestled close to each other, faint smiles hovering about their lips.

"John and Maria Carrow." Remy gestured to the portrait. "This was created a year before their deaths. You can see how closely John's appearance matches Edgar's. They're not quite perfect doppelgängers, but it was enough to fool an entire town."

She paused to let her group appreciate the portrait then revealed the part of the story that always turned her blood cold. "This portrait used to hang in John's private sitting room at the opposite end of the house. Edgar moved it into the bedroom sometime during the four months the hotel was closed after he murdered John. No one's sure why. If he was trying to hide it, he could have put it into storage or destroyed it. Instead, he made sure it had the place of honor in his own room."

April blew out her breath. "I would have gone mad. Imagine having a picture of your victims watching you while you sleep."

"For eight long years," Remy agreed. "It's baffling. Was this another way for him to establish dominance over his old employers? Did he relish the memory of killing them? Or had he started to think of himself as John—had his identity blended with his fake persona so thoroughly that he no longer recognized the man in this painting as a separate person?"

She took a few steps farther into the space, leading her little group with her. "When she bought the house, April took a lot of care to get the original furniture restored and returned to this room. This is the same bed both John and Edgar slept in, and it even has the original sheets and pillows. The clothes are all John's, as well." She opened the wardrobe door to show them the age-worn outfits. A dead moth tumbled out. "Edgar adopted all of John's clothing. He even used the same hairbrush. I won't say I'm sad, but it's almost a shame Edgar's death was so sudden—I would have loved for him to be put through a psychiatric evaluation."

Taj had been making notes on a small piece of paper, and he tapped his pencil against his teeth. "Is there any chance Edgar's ghost became trapped in Carrow?"

"It's a possibility," Remy said. "None of the reputable ghost sightings match Edgar's description, but he might not be showing himself. Some ghosts—such as Red and the Gray Lady—are seen frequently. Some are only seen once in a blue moon."

Remy closed the wardrobe doors and nodded for them to return to the hallway. "I'm going to show you something the regular tour guests don't get to see," she said as she led them back to the ground floor and toward the darkened area below the stairs. "It's my favorite room in the house, but sadly, it can't be appreciated at night."

She shoved against the heavy double doors, and their hinges groaned. Dulled light washed over them as they stepped into the recreation room.

"Wow," Mark said behind her.

Remy grinned. "I know, right?"

The room was designed to seat more than a dozen guests. A massive, empty fireplace had pride of place against the wall to their left, and to their right, bookcases were stacked with old novels. The most impressive feature was straight ahead: a massive floor-to-ceiling window filled the wall.

Piers moved toward it then stopped an arm's length from the glass. Remy didn't blame him. Her reaction had been exactly the same the first time she'd seen the view. Instead of looking out onto a yard, the recreational area's window was positioned against the cliff's edge and overlooked the ocean.

"I had no idea the house was so close to the water," Mark said.

Remy beckoned her group forward. "It doesn't look it from the front, does it? There's barely two feet separating parts of the house from the cliffs. Isn't it spectacular?"

The rain blurred the horizon ahead. As she drew closer to the glass, she could see the waves smashing over black rocks far below. A large wave gathered farther out from shore, and Remy watched it, knowing what was going to happen. The wave built as it neared then crashed against the cliff face. Spray burst up, drenching the window and making most of her companions jerk back.

"The waves only get this high during bad storms," she said as the seawater trickled away from the glass and was replaced with droplets of rain. "Normally, it's a much more serene view. Don't worry, though, the house was built to withstand the weather."

Lucille moved closer to Mark and placed one hand on his forearm. "Imagine it at sunset. I think it could be quite romantic, don't you?"

He made a vague noise in reply and carefully extracted his arm from her manicured fingers.

"This room has amazing energy." Marjorie had her eyes half-closed and her fingers stretched out as though caressing the air. "It doesn't have the sour taste that permeates other areas. This may be a good place for our séances."

"Yes!" April, hands on her hips, grinned at the large, overstuffed chairs and carved wood coffee tables dotting the space. "We can make this our headquarters. It's not as stuffy as the dining room."

"It'll be colder than the rest of the house," Remy said, nodding toward the window. "But shouldn't get too bad if we keep the fire going. Let's keep moving; I haven't shown you the basement yet."

She led them back into the foyer and toward the door near the kitchens. As she neared it, she saw the table beside the door was empty. "Damn, I left the lamp in my room."

"I've got a flashlight," Taj said. He dropped his backpack off his shoulders and rifled through it. "Hey, jackpot—I've got two."

Taj gave his spare to Remy, and they opened the door.

"Watch your step," she cautioned, just as she did with her tour groups. "The stairs are narrow and uneven. People have been seriously hurt falling down them."

"The air has a strange taste." Marjorie closed her eyes and stretched her hands out while continuing to descend the stairs, giving Remy a pang of terror that she would trip. Just like the night before, though, her steps were confident despite her blindness, and she reached the landing unharmed. "Something… something I've never felt before."

"This is where Edgar buried his victims," Remy said, shining her light across the open graves. "The police removed as much of the bodies as possible, but many were severely decayed and there are still bone fragments remaining."

"Yes, that certainly won't help a spirit's attitude." Marjorie opened her eyes and inhaled deeply. "There's at least one lost soul down here, possibly more, but I can't make contact. I don't think they want to talk."

"Maybe a camera…?" Taj's smile was hopeful.

Marjorie exhaled and shrugged begrudgingly. "If you must."

He unzipped his backpack and began setting up a mini-camcorder and tripod. The others gathered around the edge of the landing, where the cord divided the even ground from where slabs of stone had been dug up.

"How many did you say were buried here?" Piers asked.

"Twenty-nine. They were often buried on top of one another, which made separating the remains tricky."

Marjorie made a faint surprised noise, and Remy turned toward her. The older woman was in the corner beside the staircase, clutching her hands to her chest as though she'd been burnt. "Come here," she said. Excitement made her voice waver. "I want to know if you can feel it, too."

Remy stepped forward first. The rest of the group followed, except Lucille, who stood with her arms crossed and scowled at the darkness. At first Remy didn't understand what Marjorie wanted felt, but then she extended her hand and gasped. It was like her fingers had been plunged into freezing water. "A cold spot."

"Exactly, exactly!" Marjorie moved her arms in slow arcs, feeling out the area. "There's no breeze. In fact, the air here is unusually stagnant. Oh, it's big, too—it extends all the way over here."

Piers cleared his throat. "What causes cold spots?"

"It could be a specter," Marjorie said. "Or simply an imprint. Sometimes cold spots gather for no discernible reason except that an area's energy is elevated."

"Imprints?" By the sound of it, coffee hadn't dissolved Lucille's irritability. "Specters and energy? You're all starting to sound like you stepped out of a New Age cult."

Mark glanced between Remy and Marjorie. "Forgive my ignorance, but what's an imprint?"

Remy answered. "When people think of ghosts, they often

think of a see-through person floating around. But 'ghost' is actually an umbrella term for several different apparitions. A specter is an entity that can think—though often primitively— and react to changes to their surroundings. They may move from room to room and usually have some kind of impetus keeping them on earth. They're the closest to the pop culture concept of ghosts. Imprints, on the other hand, are a small amount of energy left behind at the point of death. They're not conscious. Most commonly, they replay their death, often at the same time each day or on the anniversary of when they died."

Remy motioned to the floors above them. "If you think about Carrow's ghosts, the girl in red would be a specter. She's shy. She's been glimpsed in various parts of the house. Sometimes, she hides guests' possessions. On the other hand, Louise Small, the woman who died in Room 19, seems to have left an imprint. If you turn the lights out, you can sometimes hear crunching glass. That would be a memory from her death, when the mirror was cracked in the struggle. She's not aware, and she can't be reasoned with—but her presence lingers."

"Don't forget about poltergeists," April interjected. Her eyes appeared huge and round in the dim room.

"You're right, poltergeists are the third classification. They're not an entity in their own right, though. They're altered versions of either specters or imprints. When a ghost becomes highly emotional—if a researcher taunts them, for instance, or if they see a scene strongly reminiscent of a powerful moment from their life—they can gather additional energy and start affecting the physical world. Usually, that manifests as objects being thrown or as gusts of wind. Sometimes, poltergeists will try to touch you, which I'm told feels like an ice cube being run over your skin."

Remy stopped to take a breath. Marjorie and April were still feeling around the cold spot, but the others had shifted back. "Ready to head upstairs?"

"Just a second." Taj had set up one camera to face the open graves and was fiddling with the settings on a second that had been turned toward the empty corner. "Aaand…okay. I'm done. On top of regular film, these babies can track heat levels, so we'll know what time the cold spot disappears—if it ever does."

Marjorie reluctantly stepped away from the corner. "It's phenomenal. I've felt small patches of cold before, but this is massive. It must be at least ten degrees cooler than the air. That confirms what I suspected: Carrow has immense energy stored here."

"You keep talking about energy." Lucille, arms folded around her torso and a wary glare leveled toward the empty corner, sniffed as she followed Remy up the stairs. "I don't think you realize how ridiculous you sound."

Remy kept her flashlight angled at the steps to light them for the people behind her. "Actually, Marjorie is right. Carrow is supposed to have unusually high energy levels. It's part of the reason its spirit activity is so elevated."

Marjorie's head bobbed with eager nods. "This whole island area is saturated."

They came out in the foyer and turned toward the nearest

room, the recreational area. Remy caught Lucille's skeptical look. "Humans, animals, and plants are made up of energy. It's what makes us aware and responsive to our environments compared to, say, dirt or dead wood. When a person dies, they can leave their energy behind. Under the right circumstances, it can form into a ghost."

"There's environmental energy, too." Marjorie settled into one of the recreation room's overstuffed armchairs. "It surrounds us constantly, but it's especially concentrated on ley lines or in places like Carrow, where the air has been infused by death and suffering."

"Exactly. Ghosts need energy to stay present, to stay powerful. They eat it like we eat food. Sometimes, they have their own energy; the more impactful or distressing the death, the stronger the energy their passing leaves behind. Those ghosts can subsist for decades or even centuries off of it. Weaker ghosts—especially imprints—consume environmental energy instead. That's one of the reasons Carrow is such a haunted building—a series of horrific, gruesome deaths charged the land and keeps its spirits restless."

Marjorie said, "Don't forget the landscape. Powerful weather can increase an area's energy. There's an aggressive easterly wind coming across the ocean, plus plenty of storms and lightning strikes. It's no wonder this place is hopping."

"Perfect," April crowed. "I knew I made a good investment in this building. It'll be the ideal place to learn how to be a spirit medium."

"Oh?" Marjorie's eyebrows rose. "Have you ever spoken to a ghost before?"

"I mean… I feel like I've been *close* a couple of times. And it's not like I've been able to spend much time at haunted locations. I keep asking Mum to take me to the Mary Celeste for our holidays, but she insists on dragging me to boring resorts instead."

Marjorie burst into heady, giggling laughter. She pressed her fingers over her lips to stifle the mirth then said, "Oh, you poor, sweet thing. Hotel resorts are some of the most spirit-heavy ground you could ever walk over. All of those depressed business-men throwing themselves out of windows… My dear, I'm afraid I have a better chance of winning the Olympic men's one-hundred-meter sprint than you do of being a spirit medium."

Remy cringed. It was the truth but delivered with the subtlety of a sledgehammer. April's cheerful smile had been a near-permanent fixture for the entire morning, but at Marjorie's words, it quivered, drooped, and disappeared into a tight-lipped mask of displeasure. The teen swallowed audibly. "You can't say that. The ability is like a muscle, right? It can get stronger with practice. I just haven't had much training."

"You can't exercise a muscle that doesn't exist, honey." Marjorie folded her hands in her lap. "Trust me, if you had any sort of gifting, you'd have felt it by now. I'm afraid you'll have to resign yourself to mediocrity, just like ninety-eight percent of the population." She gave a smile that she probably thought looked grandmotherly but came across as condescending. "There *are* worse fates."

"April—" Remy started but didn't know what to say.

The teen glowered at Marjorie, a vein pulsing in her temple, then stood. Her voice was a tight, barely audible whisper. "Excuse me. This room's too stuffy." She crossed the space in five long, fast steps, wrenched open one half of the double door, and slammed it behind herself.

Remy flinched at the noise.

No one spoke for a beat, then Lucille said, "About time someone knocked that nonsense out of her head."

Cold, bubbling frustration rose in Remy's stomach. *How can Lucille be so callous? April's dream just got crushed. It was an unrealistic dream, sure, but that doesn't stop it from hurting.*

"I'm going for a walk, too," she said as she stood.

Mark rose and followed. He stopped her just as she was about to open the door, his face tightened with concern. "Can I do anything to help?"

She smiled and patted his forearm. "I don't even know if there's anything *I* can do. But thanks."

They shared a brief smile, then Remy slipped through the opening and ventured into the house in search of April.

CHAPTER 14
MISTRUST

APRIL WAS NO LONGER in the foyer. As the recreation room door closed behind her, Remy wrapped her arms about herself and flicked her eyes across the space. To each side, the twin grand staircases rose to the second floor and its maze of bedrooms. Various carved doors set into the walls would take her to the dining room, the kitchens, a smoking room, and a ballroom. No footsteps or slamming doors reverberated through the house, so Remy chose to go straight ahead, toward the entrance that led outside.

Her hunch was right. She found April crouched on the top step of the porch, as close to the yard as she could get without sitting in the rain. Remy moved forward to join her.

"She's a stupid, fat windbag," April said as Remy settled at her side. "And I'm not going to apologize for calling her that. She doesn't know what she's talking about."

Marjorie had been a full-time spirit medium for close to forty years, but Remy suspected it wasn't a good time to share that with April. Instead, she let the silence draw over them as they stared at the drenched shrubs, the muddy gravel path, and the now-filled birdbath.

"She acts like she's an expert, but no one can be an expert in ghosts when there's so much about them we still don't understand." April wasn't crying, but her eyes were rimmed with red when she lifted them to beg for Remy's agreement. "So…so…just because I've never seen a ghost before doesn't mean I never will."

At least that was something Remy could agree with. "Exactly. And even if you never develop a gift to communicate with spirits, doesn't mean you can't work with them. Look at me. I'm not a medium—I've got about as much gifting as a potato—but I get to walk through the state's most haunted house every week. Marjorie hasn't even visited Carrow before this."

April wiped her nose on her sleeve. "No one thinks I can do it. Mum says it's a phase, Dad doesn't care, and even Lucille groans when I try to talk about it. But I'm going to prove them wrong."

Remy nudged April's shoulder. "You know, I suspect Taj doesn't have an affinity for ghosts, either. But it sounds like he's seen some amazing things on his equipment."

"Yeah." Fresh light appeared in April's eyes. "Maybe that's where I should focus myself. The science-y side. None of that stupid emotional empath nonsense. Who's to say she's gifted, anyway? She can't show us any evidence. She could be making it all up, and we wouldn't even know."

The brief bit of research Remy had done on Marjorie before the trip had convinced her the medium was the real deal. Marjorie could pick up on details about deceased parties no casual observer should be able to know, and she had even helped the police solve a high-profile murder case. Remy diverted the discussion. "You mentioned Lucille doesn't like talking about ghost stuff. Are you and her…okay? I mean, I don't want to pry, but if you'd like to stay in different rooms tonight…"

April laughed. The sound lasted only a moment then faded, swallowed by the drum of falling rain. The pause became so long that Remy was preparing to change the subject again when April said, "It's so stupid."

"What is?"

April's face twisted as she glared at the rain. "Lu and I were best friends. Like, best friends for life. We're polar opposites, but we got on so well. We'd stay up way past midnight, laughing. She covered my butt so many times when I got in trouble with my parents. I can't believe we fought over something so stupid."

Remy waited while April sniffed and scuffed her sneakers.

"My dad became friends with this small-time politician last year. He started visiting Lu and me. He'd bring flowers and presents and stay to talk with us for hours. Lu was smitten. She was sure he'd want to make it official—and soon. But, turns out, she wasn't the reason he visited."

"Oh boy," Remy murmured and propped her chin up in her hands.

"He was old enough to be my dad." April's face scrunched

up in revulsion. "I don't even want to get married, anyway. I'm going to be single my whole life. I'll have twelve cats and live in a haunted house and be the happiest spinster you've ever met. But he had to go and propose with a freakin' huge diamond ring in front of everyone. And he made such a big fuss when I laughed at him." For a moment, her face lit up with a vicious smile, but it died before it could reach her eyes. "Lu was crushed. She thinks I tried to steal him."

"That sucks."

"Like I said, it's stupid." She continued to scuff her shoes, her eyes gloomy and frustrated. "The more I think about it, the more I doubt he would've wanted Lu even if I hadn't been in the picture. But she's desperate. She's thirty-two."

"She wants to have a family?" Remy could sympathize with that. She'd let her work consume too much of her life and had found herself becoming increasingly lonely in the evenings.

"Hell, she just wants to have a husband." The glance April sent her held a hint of guilt. "Don't tell her I told you this, but she's destitute. She stays in our home and wears Mum's second-hand clothes and drives a car we lent her, but without us, she'd be living in a shelter. She always intended to marry well and be a stay-at-home wife, but no guy has proposed, and she's starting to get too old to be wanted for a trophy wife."

Remy didn't know what to say, except for "Jeez."

Once April started talking, she seemed incapable of stopping. Words rushed out of her in a torrent. "She's never had a proper job, unless you count being my au pair when I was a kid. No qualifications. No skills. No way to support herself. She thinks her only option is to marry well. And she knows time's running out, that she won't look young and pretty for much longer, so whenever she meets a rich guy, she flirts like crazy. It's embarrassing to watch her."

Images flashed through Remy's mind: Lucille perking up when she'd thought Taj might be a director, her overly warm attitude toward Mark on the first evening, and how she'd tried to get closer to him during the tour.

April's expression darkened. "And since we had that fight over that stupid politician who I didn't even want…I've started thinking. Maybe she never actually liked me. Maybe she's only pretended to be nice because she needs a home. We're rich. We have lots of rich friends. What if she's using us to get access to them?"

"Do you really believe that?"

April scowled then huffed out a breath. "I don't want to talk about this anymore. Can we go back inside?"

"Of course." Remy rose and extended a hand to help April up. Her head was buzzing with the revelations about Lucille, and she wasn't looking forward to returning to the stuffy house. "Are you okay to go in alone? I'd like to stay out here a bit longer and clear my head."

"Yeah, course. It sucks about the rain." April sent one last bitter glare toward the grounds then turned to the front doors. "It would be nice to go for a walk."

Remy watched the door grate close then sucked in a long, slow breath to savor the rain-cleaned air. She had a lot to process.

Poor Lucille. She puts on such a sophisticated, haughty act, like she's a class above the rest of us, but even her clothes are secondhand. That must burn her pride. I don't envy her.

It felt good to be out of the house. Remy stretched, relaxing her spine, and filled her lungs with the cold air. Something moved near the copse of pine trees that grew by the edge of the island. She frowned, stepped toward the porch's stone rail, and leaned so far over it that icy raindrops hit her arms and face.

A faint, barely visible figure skipped through the grass near the trees. The rain blurred it, but it seemed to be a boy, no older than five or six. It leaped over a log then turned in to the forest and vanished from sight. Remy pressed a hand to her thudding heart as shock and wonder rose inside her. "Wow."

CHAPTER 15
GLIMPSE BETWEEN THE TREES

REMY BURST INTO THE sitting room, too excited to care that she was interrupting conversation. "I saw a ghost!"

Someone had lit a fire, and the occupants—April, Taj, Marjorie, and Mark—were all gathered around it.

April pushed away from the wall she'd been lounging against. "You're joking. Is it still there?"

"No, it disappeared into the woods. It was a child, I think. I couldn't see it well, and it was only there for a second, but…" She laughed, giddy, and began shaking the rainwater off her arms.

Taj beamed at her. "First ghost of the season goes to Remy. Congrats!"

"First?" Marjorie sniffed. "We're surrounded by ghosts, you nitwit. You just can't see them."

Taj stoically ignored her. "We should make a list of the presences we find here. Start a diary or something with dates and times."

Mark touched Remy's arm. Something bright and urgent shone in his eyes. "You said it was a child. What did it look like?"

"It was so far away—and the rain was so thick—I'm pretty sure it was young, though. Maybe five or six."

"Hmm." He chewed on his lip as his gaze turned toward the window overlooking the ocean.

"I can't believe I missed it," April wailed. "I was *right there!*"

"Honestly, it was so brief and so faint, there wasn't much to see. But it's a good sign. Carrow's energy levels seem to be increasing with the rain. Today might be a good day to make contact with spirits."

"That's convenient." Taj nodded toward the corner of the room. "I just finished setting up a surveillance center. Check it out."

For the first time, Remy noticed a jumble of equipment tucked beside the bookcases at the rear corner of the room. Taj had co-opted the desks there and arranged four monitors into a tidy row, with multiple modems and cables connected to them. She moved forward to get a better look.

"Taj was just teaching me about them when you came in," April said, bounding up to join them. "Look, this is a live feed for the foyer, and this one's in the basement. He's going to set up more cameras later, too."

"Run some cables up to the bedrooms," Taj agreed, pride making him glow. "We'll be able to monitor a good part of the house without leaving our seats."

"Nice," Remy said.

"The best part is this." He tapped the fourth monitor, which was blank. "It's a custom setup one of my friends has. It's connected to a motion-sensor camera in the hallway and will only turn on when something moves. But it'll record whatever it captures, so we'll be able to review the event without having to fast-forward through hours of nothing."

"That will save a lot of time." Remy pointed to a black box on the table. "What's that?"

"EMF sensor. It's picking up signals from meters in different parts of the house." He grinned and rubbed at the back of his neck. "Well, it will, when I actually go around and put them there. It's a work in progress."

April leaned her hip against the table, beaming. "It's amazing, though, isn't it? He really knows what he's talking about." She glanced at Marjorie for a split second before fixing her adoring gaze back on Taj. "I'm so grateful we have a *real* researcher here."

Marjorie's expression had grown increasingly sour through the discussion. At the final barb, she huffed and adjusted her shawl. "Enjoy your gadgets and flashing lights, child. I'm sure you'll have great fun analyzing shadows and stray specks of dust."

Oh boy. The fragile civility was dissolving again. Remy looked for Mark to see if he had a way to salvage the situation, but he was no longer in the room. A sense of abandonment tightened her stomach. "It really is a good setup, Taj," she said, feeling as if she were treading on eggshells. "I'm looking forward to learning more when it's fully ready. Marjorie, what were your plans for the day?"

"Well." She pursed her lips and turned toward the windows.

"I was thinking of conducting a séance shortly after lunch, while the energy is still high."

April's eyes brightened, though she kept them fixed on the screens. Remy knew April had been dying to take part in a séance for years.

"I'm looking forward to it," Remy said. "Would you like to do it here? The table's large enough for all of us."

A tiny, cruel smile twitched at the corners of Marjorie's mouth. "Don't worry about that. I'm only inviting a limited group. It can distress or offend spirits if disrespectful, narrow-minded individuals try to take part."

Remy cringed. It seemed that Marjorie had found a way to get revenge for April's snubs. It was a harsh punishment. "Well, uh, how about we work out the details later? After lunch, maybe." *Some food might help calm tempers.*

"Very good. I'll retire to my room and meditate to prepare." Marjorie rose with great ceremony, wrapped her shawl about her shoulders, and stalked through the doors.

Remy turned back to April. "I'll talk to her."

"You don't need to." The teen's face would have looked calm except for the crease between her eyebrows. "I don't care about her silly séances. Taj and I have plenty of work to do without her."

Remy sighed. "Don't poke her too much, April. You don't have to agree with all of her beliefs to be civil. Remember, she's Mark's guest, not yours."

April's eyes narrowed a fraction, and she squeezed her lips together. Remy looked about the room, which felt unusually empty with only three of them left. "Do you know where Mark went? And Lucille, Piers, and Bernard, for that matter?"

"Bernard and Piers are cooking lunch," Taj supplied. "Lucille said she was going to have a nap. Not sure about Mark."

April shrugged. "He was here just a moment ago. Maybe he got tired of listening to that windbag, too."

"April," Remy said, a hint of warning in her tone, but the teen refused to look ashamed.

Taj stepped in and nudged April's shoulder. "C'mon, I'm going to lay down the EMF readers. You gonna help?"

"Yes!" Her irritability melted away as she took the armful of black brick-like objects he passed to her. "Bedrooms first?"

"You know it. Remy, want to come along?"

She waved them off. "Thanks, but I'll see you at lunch. I want to enjoy the quiet while I can." *As well as wanting to find out where Mark disappeared to.*

As the sound of their footsteps faded, Remy sighed and rubbed her hands though her still-damp hair. She hadn't anticipated it would be so hard to maintain peace.

Maybe it's inevitable in this house. It's oppressive. Like the air is thicker here. I can feel it weighing on me, and they must, as well. The pressure's making us edgy and hostile. It's especially bad with the rain locking us indoors.

She crossed to the vast windows as a wave swept up and sprayed foam across the glass. The storm wasn't easing like she'd hoped.

Where did Mark go? He'd been in the room one minute, asking about her ghost, then she'd turned around and he'd vanished. It sent uneasy prickles crawling up her arms, and she stepped back into the foyer. Taj and April's chatter echoed from the upstairs hallway, and the clang of cutlery and plates came from the kitchens, but the rest of the house was eerily silent.

On a hunch, Remy moved around the stack of supplies still piled in the foyer's center and went to the front doors. One was open a crack, but she could have sworn she'd closed it when she came inside.

"Mark?" She pushed on the wood, but the porch beyond was empty. She squinted through the rain, searching the front yard then the fields beyond, and saw a hint of dark color near the woods' edge. "Oh, damn it."

The cluster of pine trees grew against the edge of the cliffs. In the dim of the rain-darkened day, it would be all too easy for a distracted person to tumble over the bluffs and into the roiling, rock-dotted ocean below. The thought made Remy sick with fear, and she jogged down the stairs.

Mark was moving slowly, but he'd disappeared behind the tree line before Remy left the yard. She increased her pace, head bent to keep the rain out of her eyes as she dashed across the field.

She was breathless and gasping by the time she reached the edge of the small woods. Rain drenched her, trickling off her hair and seeping under her clothes. The dribbles stung as they sucked warmth out of her skin. She stepped between the trees, searching for the telltale gray of Mark's jacket. "Mark?"

There wasn't any response. She moved farther in. The trees were tightly packed and badly misshapen, forcing Remy to contort herself to fit among them. Pine needles littering the ground made her footing unsteady. The dim day combined with the thick branches left her nearly blind and only able to see hazy shapes. She stretched her hands out to feel her way through the maze. Her breathing was shallow, and each icy inhalation burned her lungs.

A crunch of dried leaves drew her to her right, and she caught sight of a figure between the branches. Mark stood in a small clearing, one hand braced against a tree, as he stared into the shadows.

Remy's breathing came a little easier as she stumbled toward him. "Mark!"

He finally turned to look at her. He appeared slightly dazed, as though she had interrupted some deep thoughts, but he moved to meet her halfway.

"What are you doing out here?" She grabbed his arm once he was in reach, to prevent him from disappearing back into the trees.

He looked about himself then gave her a sheepish grin. "Sorry. I wanted to see the ghost. I'm a bit of an idiot for coming out here in the rain, aren't I?"

"Little bit." She chuckled, half from relief, half to shake off the lingering anxiety. "C'mon, let's get back to the house. It's not safe out here. The cliffs start right where the trees end, so it's easy to fall over if you're not paying atten—"

A hint of motion flickered between the trees behind Mark. Remy caught her breath. She squinted as she tried to make out the shape, but it was gone before she could focus on it.

Mark's voice was a whisper. "Was that…?"

"I think so." Against her better judgment, Remy took a step toward it.

Mark followed. They crept around a tree, and a small, translucent shape darted through the trunks ahead of them.

Remy's heart thundered with nerves and wonder. She followed the ghost as it wove through the forest. It allowed them only split-second glimpses before vanishing again. She had the impression of cropped mousy hair, a fluttering jacket, and bright eyes, but it always hid behind a new tree before she could see more.

Remy, desperate to catch up to the pale figure, began moving faster, changing from a walk to a jog as she clambered between the tangled growths.

"Wait!" Mark's hand clamped onto Remy's shoulder and yanked her back.

She slammed into a tree and gasped as the impact jarred her. The trees had ended without her realizing, and barely two paces ahead, the ground disappeared. The thick clouds blocked out almost all natural light, but she could still see the cliff's edge like a jagged knife-edge ahead of her.

Remy lifted her eyes. A young child's laughter floated through the air then faded. Her whole body turned clammy.

"You okay?" Mark kept his grip on her shoulder.

She patted his hand as a weak laugh escaped her. "Yeah. Wow. Sorry. I should've listened to my own caution about the cliff edge, huh?"

"We both got caught up in the moment." Mark tugged her

back, and Remy followed as he led her back into the safety of the trees. "I don't think I'll ever forget that. It was a boy, wasn't it?"

"Yeah. I think I know him. Byron Christel. Four years old. His family stayed at the hotel during one of its reopenings in 1965." Remy turned to read Mark's expression, but it was too dark to make out anything except his outline. "He wandered into the trees while his family was picnicking on the lawn. When his nanny went to look for him, she couldn't find him. Byron's body turned up four days later, washed up on shore four kilometers away."

"Oh." Mark exhaled. "He fell over the cliff."

"Apparently so." *And he wanted me to follow.* The heavy rain dripped off Remy's nose and chin. She shivered. "Let's get back to the house."

They retraced their path through the pines, both of them weaving and ducking to get through the branches. Remy released a held breath once they were back on the clear lawn before the house.

It was easier to see Mark once they were out of the woods. Although his face was serene, shadows clouded his eyes. He was drenched, his dark hair stuck to his face, and his clothes were a sodden mess.

Remy suspected she didn't look any better and fought back a laugh. "C'mon. I'm freezing, and there's a fire in the recreation room."

Remy set a brisk, half-running pace back to the house. Mark matched her speed easily. Once they'd reached the foyer, they pulled off their jackets and slung them on the coatrack by the entrance, where they could drip without ruining the carpet. Faint voices echoed from the second floor, where Taj and April were setting up their cameras, and the sound of knives on chopping blocks echoed from the kitchen.

As they passed the pile of supplies, Remy stopped to dig out an armful of towels then followed Mark into the recreation room. It was empty, but the fire was starting to warm it. She pressed two of the towels into Mark's arms then turned so that her back was to the flames as she dried her hair.

"How many ghosts are in this house?"

Mark's question caught her by surprise, and she frowned as she thought. "Huh...depends on who you believe. A fellow called Carvarello claimed to sense over a hundred spirits, but he tends to exaggerate. Most estimates put them at between eight and twenty-five, but that's only based on the ghosts that show themselves. There could be others that are staying quiet."

Mark stared at the towels in his hands but made no move to dry himself. "What makes someone become a ghost?"

"Energy, mostly." Remy, finished on her hair, began rubbing her towel over her clothes to wring the water out. "Because ghosts are made from energy, there needs to be a lot present when they die. That can come from suffering, such as murders, suicides, and prolonged illnesses. Or energy can come from a powerful character. Someone with an exceptionally strong personality is more likely to leave a ghost than a passive person. It's a bit of a cliché, but unfinished business can create spirits and imprints, as well. If the person *refuses* to die—despite their physical body failing them—their spirit may linger."

"And…" He seemed to be phrasing himself carefully. "Are the ghosts unhappy? Are they distressed?"

Remy slowly lowered her towel. "You know, that's a really hard question." Mark was watching her, so she tried to think it through as she squeezed the towel between her fingers. "I guess it's not natural for ghosts to remain on earth. Most seem happy or relieved when they're finally cleared. But…there's debate about how much a ghost can feel, and whether they count as sentient beings."

He looked confused, so she brushed her hair away from her face as she tried to explain what she meant. "There are three parts to a person: a body, a spirit, and a soul. When the body dies, the soul goes into whatever is waiting for us after death. But the spirit can sometimes get stuck behind. That's what a ghost is: a spirit anchored to earth by residual energy. The soul, the part that goes to the afterlife, is our core person—the identity we were born with. The spirit is our emotions, our temperament, our intelligence—the parts of us that are created and changed by our time on earth. So, when a ghost is formed, it's missing both the soul and the body that it needs to be a full human. It's like an echo of what it once was." She shrugged. "That's how it was explained to me, anyway."

"Does that mean they can't feel?"

"I don't know. Many ghosts appear distressed. But I don't know if they're actually suffering or just mimicking the emotion."

Mark was staring through the window at the raging ocean. He looked older, Remy thought. Tireder.

He still held the folded towel, so she gently took it out of his hands and stretched onto her toes to dry his hair. "What's wrong?"

"I…" He sighed, then after a second, he said, "It's just a lot to process."

"You're not alone there."

He finally smiled. Remy hadn't realized how much she'd missed the expression until it created a little bubble of joy in her chest. He looked nearly comical with his damp hair poking out from under the towel and his clothes still dripping onto the carpet, but at the same time, his eyes riveted her.

She'd stood close to him to dry his hair, and the contact was more intimate than she'd intended. For a split second, the crazy part of her mind wondered what it would feel like to move even closer, take away the space between them, lean up to kiss the droplet of water off the tip of his nose…

"You'd better get into some dry clothes." Remy let the towel drop around his shoulders and stepped back. "We both should. Lunch must be ready by now, and Marjorie said she wanted to conduct a séance after. She won't be happy if we make her late."

CHAPTER 16
SÉANCE

PIERS AND BERNARD HAD prepared sandwiches, and Remy almost laughed when she saw the plates. Bernard's were perfectly aligned and evenly filled, and the cuts were so immaculately centered that she thought he must have used a ruler. Piers's were uneven and crammed full of every type of filling, so generous that it was impossible to hold them without dropping bits of lettuce or tomato.

They ate in the main dining room, once again gathered around the fire. Because Carrow's insulated design held its temperature for a long time, it also took ages to warm up. They'd started fires in several rooms, but the temperature was still a few degrees too cold for all of their comfort. Between bites, Remy filled the group in on what they'd seen in the woods. She finished by saying, "Be careful if you're going outside. The cliffs are hard to see, especially in the rain, and not every ghost is going to have your best interests at heart."

April blinked her owlish eyes. "It was trying to kill you?"

"I don't think so. Not deliberately, at least." Remy glanced at Mark for confirmation, and he gave a small nod. "It was more like he was trying to lead us to the place he had died—which happened to be at the base of the cliffs. Sometimes that's all ghosts want—to not be forgotten."

Taj frowned as he picked lettuce out of his sandwich. "I brought four boxes of equipment, but not a single waterproof plastic cover. That forest would probably be a brilliant place to set up a camcorder if it wasn't raining."

"It sounds like a harrowing experience." Lucille scraped her chair a few inches closer to Mark's. "You poor thing."

"Actually, it was exhilarating." Mark avoided her eyes as he took another bite of his sandwich. "I can see why people dedicate their lives to catching glimpses like that."

Lucille's expression tightened. Remy tried to smother a smile as the woman scraped her chair back to its original position.

"On the subject of glimpsing ghosts, I've begun preparations for our séance," Marjorie said as she stretched her slippered feet toward the fire. "We will conduct it in the recreation room after lunch. Piers, Remy, Mark—would you do me the honor of joining me?"

Remy glanced toward April. The girl refused to speak or look up from her meal, but her face scrunched up, and her eyes looked watery.

"Thank you." Remy chose her words carefully. "Since this is our first séance, I was hoping we could all take part."

Marjorie made a happy humming noise in the back of her throat. "No, I don't think so."

Remy licked her lips. "What if some of us sit at the back of the room and just watch?"

"Not this time, dear."

April stuffed an entire half of a sandwich into her mouth, apparently to stop words from coming out. Lucille gaped at her bulging cheeks, her expression equal parts horrified and revolted.

"I'm going to get a cup of tea." Mark rose. "Anyone else want one?"

A couple of muted replies followed him as he crossed to the thermos. He set up the cups then called, "Marjorie, you know how to use this thing, don't you? I can't get the water to come out."

"How do you mean?" Marjorie's eyebrows rose. "You press the lever. It's quite simple."

"Which lever?"

She exhaled a frustrated sigh and rose. "Have you lost your brain, dear boy? It's *your* machine." She joined him at the other side of the room, and they leaned over the drinks together. The discussion was hushed and lasted far longer than Remy would have thought a thermos warranted. When Marjorie finally returned to her seat, she wore an odd expression.

"Now that I think about it..." She spoke slowly as Mark passed around the steaming cups. "It might be best to have a fifth party at the séance. April, would you like to join us?"

The teen's eyes bulged, and the words tumbled out of her. "Yes. Yes, please."

"Very good." Marjorie blew on her drink, her face serene.

Remy glanced at Mark, eyebrows raised, and he gave her a small, secretive smile.

Taj cleared his throat, his hands clasped as he turned a polite, wide-eyed expression toward Marjorie. "Is there the chance that a table of six might be even better than a table of five?"

"Oh, fine, all right. You can come, too. To heck with it, you can *all* come. But be respectful and don't talk too much."

Marjorie's tone was full of exasperation, but Remy thought she saw a glow of satisfaction in the woman's cheeks. She was pleased to be the center of attention again.

Bernard collected their plates and disappeared into the kitchen, and the rest of them filed through the foyer and toward the recreation room. Remy hurried to catch up to Mark. She leaned close and whispered so that the others wouldn't overhear. "How did you manage that?"

He placed one hand on his chest, his expression intensely serious. "You should know by now that I'm an extremely talented negotiator."

Remy lifted her eyebrows, and Mark's serious act crumbled into a laugh.

"I said I'd double her fee if she let April sit in."

"Ha!" Remy jostled him. "That's really sweet of you. I know April will appreciate it."

They stepped through the double doors of the recreation room. Marjorie had moved a large round table to the center of the space and shifted the comfy couches and lounges out of the way. An unlit candle, a box of matches, and a pen waited in the center of the table, surrounded by sprigs of herbs.

"I must ask for a respectful silence during this process," Marjorie said. She wandered among them, grasping their shoulders and dragging them to the seats she wanted them to take. "And please remember, this isn't some parlor trick or cheap spectacle for you to gawk at. We're handling lost souls, some who may be afraid or angry or confused. Treat them with compassion."

Remy found herself between Mark and Piers. She took her seat, trying to look suitably polite. April sat opposite. The girl's eyes were huge, and she was nearly trembling from anticipation.

"I'd rather not be included," Bernard said, refusing to sink into the chair Marjorie pushed him toward.

"Very well. Sit in the corner and stay quiet."

Lucille shot the table a wary glance then followed Bernard to the back of the room.

Remy had barely gotten settled when Marjorie's sharp bark made her startle. "No, absolutely not!"

Taj, camcorder in one hand, gave her a sheepish smile. "Just one! Please!"

"Were you listening at all, boy? Respect! Compassion! Stop trying to monetize my ghosts!"

"I'm not, I swear! I want to record your, uh, methods. For scholarly purposes."

The twist to Marjorie's lips suggested she didn't believe him.

Remy cleared her throat then chose her words carefully. "It may be helpful to have a record of this. If we manage to make contact with a spirit, what they tell us could be important for our work in Carrow. It would be good to have a way to review the session once it's over."

Marjorie's stare was frosty, but after a long pause, she made a grumbling noise. "Very well. One camera. But I swear, if I find any trace of this on your VideoTube contraption, I will send a plague of vengeful spirits to your house."

"YouTube," Taj mumbled but fell silent at the medium's scowl. He hurried to set up the camera on one of the bookcase shelves, beside the radio, and checked its viewfinder to make sure the entire table was in the screen.

April leaned forward, her curiosity outweighing any lingering resentment. "Can you really do that? Send angry ghosts after people?"

"No." Marjorie exhaled a regretful sigh as she settled at the end of the table. "But regardless, it's bad karma to cross the dead. Bernard, get the lights, please."

The medium struck a match and lit the candle as Bernard turned out the lights. With the door closed and the sky heavily overcast, the room was plunged into shadows. Remy had the unnerving sensation that the rest of the world had dissolved away, and all that remained was the little table and the six faces lit by the candlelight.

Marjorie took the pen and placed it upright so that it was balanced on its end. She then reached out, and the others followed her lead to clasp hands. Piers's fingers were a little clammy, but Mark's were warm and firm.

Their table was enveloped in silence for a moment, then

Marjorie took a slow, deep breath. "Are there any spirits present who wish to speak with us?"

Remy strained both her eyes and her ears to detect anything. The faces around her were all serious and intent. April's lips were clamped together, and Taj's eyes shone in the candlelight.

"We wish to help you. My name is Marjorie, and these are my friends. We will be staying in your house for a few days. I would be glad to meet anyone who wishes to speak with me."

A large wave came up outside the window, coating the panes with spray. Remy's chest was tight, but she kept her breathing slow and quiet so as not to interrupt the medium's work.

"If there is anyone present, please let me know by tipping my pen over."

All eyes fixed on the pen that stood on its end. Seconds ticked by. Remy could feel Mark's fingers tighten around hers.

The pen hit the tablecloth with a dull thud.

Remy drew a breath. Part of her mind argued the movement could have come from a natural cause. Someone might have bumped the table, or a strong exhale might have been enough to tip the instrument. The rest of her mind had frozen, convinced that they had a seventh guest at the table.

"Thank you." Marjorie's voice was slow and soothing. "My mind is open and welcoming if you would like to speak." She closed her eyes and tilted her head back. The silence stretched. Outside, the wind picked up, roaring against the house as it drove the rain at a steep angle. The candle flickered. Mark's thumb twitched where it rested on Remy's knuckles.

Marjorie spoke in a whisper. "It's a woman. Young…in her twenties, I think. She wears a gray dress. She's frightened."

More silence. A frown settled over Marjorie's features, and her voice dropped lower. "She was visiting her father. He was sick… She wanted to see him before he passed…"

Remy bit her tongue to keep quiet. She didn't realize she was holding her companions too tightly until Piers tried to squirm his hand free.

"I see it…" Marjorie's frown grew. "Weight. Cold metal. There was blood. And then…and then dark and cold. She's still afraid. Afraid of a man. Who?"

The wind was faster, harsher, rattling the windows. The icy air seemed to seep into the room. Goose bumps rose across Remy's arms. She wished she'd brought a warmer jacket. Opposite her, April was breathing through her mouth, sending up small plumes of condensation with each exhale.

"Don't leave," Marjorie said. "You don't need to be afraid."

The flame flickered. A wave hit the window. Noises ran through the house—groans and shudders as the building strained, its supports bending, the shingles on its roof rattling. Fear pulsed through Remy's chest, squeezing her heart in its chilled grip. She saw the same emotion reflected in her friends' faces. Then the flame went out.

The room was pitch-black. That wasn't natural. Even without the candle, there should have been enough ambient light to see her friends' faces. Remy squeezed Mark's hand, looking for some kind of reassurance that she wasn't alone, and he squeezed back.

Lightning flashed, bathing the room in a second of harsh light, then the black swallowed them again. Remy heard a soft *thud* come from the wall near the door.

Marjorie spoke. "Bernard, lights."

They heard the tall man shift out of his seat at the back of the room. Remy was freezing. Piers's fingers were like ice. Her heart felt as though it might explode.

Then a muted click accompanied the room's lights coming on, and the world returned to normal.

"Wow," Piers muttered.

They released each other's hands as Marjorie rose, looking displeased. "Did anyone do something to frighten her away?"

Taj shook his head. "No. I don't think so. What sort of thing?"

Instead of answering, Marjorie adjusted her shawl around her shoulders. "She was happy to talk. Eager, even. Then all of a sudden, I felt her withdrawing, and she wouldn't come back."

"I think I know who she is." Remy's mouth was dry. She clasped her hands together to keep her fingers from trembling. "Eva Spiers. Twenty-three years old. Traveling across the country to see her sick father. She was one of Edgar's last victims. He went to her room in the middle of the night, knelt on her chest to pin her down, and cut her throat. She was buried in the basement."

"Steel and blood, then cold and dark. That sounds correct." Marjorie was gazing about the room as though she might see the woman hiding in a corner. "I'll try to make contact with her again later, perhaps in calmer circumstances. I'd like to help her move on."

I'd like that, too. Remy watched as Marjorie collected her pen and candle. *It would be good to not just observe the spirits here, but to help some of them, if possible. They should have peace.*

April had her elbows braced on the table and both hands pressed over her mouth. Her shoulders were trembling, but when she dropped her hands, a grin stretched across her face. "That was amazing. Really, really, really amazing."

A flash of pride softened the creases on Marjorie's face. She chuckled and patted April's shoulder. "We're just getting started, my dear. Wait until you see what I have planned next."

Piers rose from the table and stepped toward the shelves near the door. He picked up their radio off the floor and turned it over. "I thought I heard something fall when the lights were out. Did one of the ghosts knock our radio off the shelf?"

"Very likely." Marjorie flexed her shoulders. "It may have been a poltergeist manifestation… What a shame it happened when the lights were out."

"Shame," April agreed, and Remy stifled nervous laughter.

Piers frowned as he fiddled with the switches. "Mark, this has batteries in it, doesn't it?"

"Yes. I made sure it worked before I packed it." Mark crossed to the other man and took the radio. He pressed the same switches Piers had then opened up the back to check the batteries. He gave the radio a sharp knock, pressed more switches, then looked at the table, his expression equal parts confused and concerned. "It's broken."

CHAPTER 17
THE RECORDING

"REALLY?" TAJ TOOK THE radio. He tried the same tricks, removing and replacing the batteries and rapping on its side, but without any response. "It could have been an electromagnetic pulse. Strong ghosts can create them. Sometimes they jam electronics."

A sense of prickly foreboding rolled through Remy. "That's our only way to contact the outside world, isn't it?"

"Unless we drive to land, yes." Mark frowned. "I brought the radio as a backup. I never thought we'd need a backup for the backup. Sorry."

"Can't be helped." Remy brushed stray strands of hair behind her ears. She kept her voice light, despite the lingering unease. "Come on, Marjorie, I'll help you pack up."

Bernard left, muttering something about starting dinner. Taj snatched up his camera and took it to his station in the room's corner. The others gathered into a loose group, discussing the séance and the radio in hushed voices.

"It's a shame Eva left so quickly," Remy said as she folded the tablecloth. "Did she cause the lights to go out, or was it another ghost that frightened her away?"

"Who knows?" Marjorie returned the herbs to a little Tupperware container and gave Remy an indulgent smile. "I'm actually quite happy with how that went. Any kind of contact is a success as far as I'm concerned. Sometimes, spirits are shy. Sometimes, there's no spirit at all. Sometimes, there isn't enough energy, and they can't speak even though they may want to. Have you been in many other séances, dear?"

"This was my first," Remy admitted. "I guess I'm more of a historian than a ghost hunter. Most of my job is recounting other peoples' encounters."

"Well, you may have a tale or two of your own by the end of this." Marjorie tucked her herbs into her bag and sighed. "I could do with a cup of tea. Where did Bernard scurry off to? He's so antisocial."

"He's making dinner, I think." Remy cleared her throat. "Please tell me if this is none of my business, but—"

"Why am I employing him when he's such a miserable wretch?"

Remy cringed. She'd been planning to phrase her question in gentler terms, but that was the essence of it.

Marjorie settled into one of the chairs beside the fireplace. "Be a dear and relight the fire, please. My feet are cold."

"Oh, sure." Remy knelt by the hearth to stack kindling.

Marjorie watched her for a moment before speaking. "Part of being an empath is the ability to read people. I can see beneath the masks we wear and uncover the vulnerable, raw humans underneath. And, unlike many people, Bernard's insides are quite a bit nicer than his external disguise."

"Oh?" Remy lit a firelighter and waited for it to catch.

"He always had trouble getting and keeping jobs because no one liked him. But I've employed him for six years now, and I can honestly say my empath abilities haven't misled me. He's one of the most honest, hardworking individuals I've had the pleasure of encountering."

Remy remembered the night before, how Bernard had come downstairs to retrieve his sleepwalking employer. He'd said it was a frequent occurrence. Remy wasn't sure she would have the fortitude to coax Marjorie back to bed every night. "Do you ever… tell him that? Sometimes you can sound a bit, uh…" She hunted for a word that wouldn't hurt the medium. "Unconcerned."

Marjorie exhaled a laugh through her nose. "We have an understanding. I don't baby him, and he doesn't censor his opinions."

"Oh."

"You can stop trying to look after him, too." Marjorie stretched her slippers toward the infant fire. "He prefers being alone. Cooking is a relief compared to having to sustain conversation. I'm not being cruel to him. This is a system that suits both of us."

Remy chuckled and pushed new pieces of wood into the fire. "I'll keep that in mind."

The door at the back of the room groaned open, and Bernard entered. He carried a cup of tea, which he dropped unceremoniously on the table next to Marjorie's chair.

She beamed at him. "Thank you, dear. I didn't even have to ask."

He grunted and disappeared back through the door.

Remy watched him go in mild fascination. *Is Marjorie right? Is he happier when he's being a solitary grouch?*

"You have quite a nice aura, dear," Marjorie continued. "A little too quick to step into business that doesn't concern you. A little too eager to fix others' problems. But generally nice."

"Thanks...I think?"

"That Mark has a nice aura, too. But it's not clear like yours. He's keeping secrets."

Remy shot a glance toward Mark, who was deep in conversation with Piers. "What about?"

"That's the problem with secrets, my dear. They're secret." Marjorie winked then sobered. "Sometimes, I see people as threads. And your thread is starting to tangle with his, which is why I'm saying this. Be careful. I can't promise he's wholly good."

Marjorie picked up her tea and sipped it, leaving Remy to wallow in confusion and faint embarrassment. *What does that mean?*

Before she could ask any more questions, Marjorie waved toward her. "Off you go, now. I need to meditate to clear my mind, and I can't focus when you're being so persistently anxious."

"Sorry." Remy threw a final log onto the fire then rose. Instead of joining Mark and Piers in conversation, she crossed to the window. What pale light managed to claw its way through the clouds was fading as the sun set. She folded her arms and watched flecks of sea spray mix with the raindrops. *What sort of secrets is Mark keeping? Can I even trust Marjorie on this? Empaths aren't infallible…*

A loud, strangled swear word made her turn. Taj jerked away from his computer, knocking the chair over with a clatter. He choked out a laugh then waved to them without taking his wide eyes off the screen.

"What is it?" Remy jogged between the chairs. "Did something happen?"

"I got something!" Near-hysterical laughter cracked through his shock. "I got something on the tape! Look!"

He pressed several buttons, and the image on the screen rewound. The others gathered around, bumping shoulders to get close. The video showed their table, angled so that Marjorie was facing the screen and the window behind her filled the background.

"I didn't manage to get the falling pencil," Taj apologized. "Piers's head was blocking it. But I got the flickering candle. And then watch this. It's just after the candle goes out."

He tapped a button, moving the recording forward one frame at a time. They watched as the room was plunged into darkness.

For several beats, nothing was visible except for black, then the room fluttered back into view as the lightning's glow poured through the window. The light's angle and color were unnatural and lit strange planes on their faces and created heavy shadows across the table.

"Look there." Taj tapped the button again to progress one more frame. "See that?" He pointed to a space behind Marjorie.

"Oh." Remy pressed her fingers over her mouth. The light was harsher in the new frame. It revealed a seventh figure standing at the end of the table, just behind Marjorie's shoulder. His features were indistinct, and his tall form nothing more than a black blur, but his eyes were clear. They glowed white.

For a moment, no one spoke. Then Lucille, at the back of the group, made a faint choking noise and stepped away. "It's a mistake. The camera couldn't cope with all of the light and glitched."

"It's not very clear," Piers said. "But I don't think it's a glitch, either."

"No," Marjorie agreed. She seemed calm as she stared at the images.

Remy bent forward, squinting as she tried to make out details. "What's in the next frame?"

Taj tapped forward again, but the image returned to darkness as the lightning faded. He kept tapping until the lights came on, but the scene had returned to showing just the six of them.

One by one, they looked from the screen to the round table, scanning the place where the man had stood.

"Do you think he's still there?" Piers asked.

Remy folded her arms around herself. She hoped not. She hadn't been able to make out anything of his face except that it was long and gaunt, but it was a shade too familiar for comfort. *It couldn't be Edgar Porter…could it?*

Marjorie rubbed her thumb over her lower lip. "He must be the reason the girl, Eva, left."

"He didn't speak to you?" Remy asked.

"I didn't sense any other presences, which means he didn't want to be felt."

But he approached us, which means he's interested. We'll need to try to contact him again, one way or another. Remy sent one last lingering glance at the area where the man had stood. She didn't like how empty it looked.

CHAPTER 18
SECRETS AND STAIRCASES

MARJORIE INSISTED THAT SHE needed to meditate for the rest of the evening, and she did so by the fireplace with a steady stream of tea supplied by Bernard. Remy suspected meditation was just an excuse to let her relax uninterrupted, but she wasn't about to complain. Lucille took the other fireside seat, her face stony. Glass in hand, she gradually emptied the bottle of wine at her side.

Taj had found a notebook, and he, Remy, Piers, and April sat around one of the smaller tables and documented the three spiritual contacts that had occurred.

"Keeping good records is vital," Taj said when April whined about how fussy he was being. "If a spirit has a system—if they appear at the same time each day or go through the same routine—we need to know. It will make it easier to identify and communicate with them."

Remy glanced up to look for Mark, but he'd left the room while she was distracted. She frowned. *He's keeping secrets.*

"Remy?" Taj's voice shook her out of her fugue.

She blinked at him. "Sorry?"

"The first time you saw the ghost boy outside. I didn't get the exact time, but I'm estimating quarter past twelve. Would you agree?"

She thought back. "Yeah. That sounds right."

He made a note and flipped the journal closed. "I'll leave this here. If any of you see another spirit, make sure to fill out all the data."

Remy nodded, but her mind was still with Mark. He'd left without telling any of them. He wasn't stupid, and she knew he didn't need her following him to keep him safe, but part of her worried that he'd returned to the forest to search for the ghost. She muttered an excuse and left the room.

You need to stop worrying. He probably just went to his room. Even so, she couldn't stop herself from going to the front door. Outside was still and quiet except for the falling rain. She scanned the field and the woods' edge, but there were no signs of human motion.

There, see? Maybe Marjorie was right about you. You try to fix problems before they even need it. Remy closed the door and turned back to the foyer, glancing from the stern-faced portrait above the fireplace to the windows. The glass she'd accidentally broken the night before caught her eye, and Remy frowned as she approached it.

When the window had slammed closed, a single crack had run up its length. Three new branches had grown from it, dividing the pane. *How did this happen? Did someone else touch it, or did the temperature changes break it?*

Remy ran a finger along the crack. Freezing-cold droplets of water seeped through, and she pulled her hand back.

The floor above groaned. Remy turned her eyes toward the ceiling, listening to footsteps move through the house. It had to be Mark, but he didn't seem to be going to his room. The team had occupied the rooms on the left-hand side of the house, but the groans reverberated to the right.

He's indoors, at least. Leave well enough alone, Remy.

She'd gotten halfway back to the recreation room when a scraping sound came from the second floor, like heavy pieces of wood being rubbed together. Her mind scrambled to identify the noise, but she couldn't place it. *Leave well enough alone.*

But he's keeping secrets…

She was already climbing the stairs before her mind caught up with her body. The grating sound had fallen quiet, but the silence felt immeasurably more awful. She moved quickly but carefully, keeping her feet light, and turned right at the top of the staircase.

The hallway felt deeply neglected. Specks of dust, nearly invisible in the windowless space's dark, rose around her shoes with every step. At the end of the hallway, she turned right and found the source of the noise. The retracting staircase that led into the attic had been lowered. It created a dark, gaping hole, inviting her into the uppermost section of the house—the servants' quarters.

So many awful things had happened in that area, and not all were Edgar's doing. Staff had murdered each other over small sums of money. They had died from diseases, from pneumonia, and from cuts that had become infected. Even after Edgar's reign ended, the highest level had seen tragedies each time the hotel reopened.

Remy licked at dry lips. The attic wasn't safe. Its floor was rotting, and it didn't have any lights to reveal the jumble of discarded junk that filled the space. She opened her mouth to call out, but before she could make a sound, a figure appeared in the opening at the top of the stairs.

"Oh, hello." Mark blinked in surprise then turned to climb down. His hair and jacket had collected dust, but his eyes were bright as he smiled. Despite his carefree tone, perspiration dotted his forehead.

"It's not safe up there." Remy tried to return his smile, but her face wouldn't create the right shape.

"Sorry. I didn't go far. You said this place had an attic, and it occurred to me that I hadn't seen it yet." He dusted his hands on his jeans then pulled the cord to retract the ladder back into the ceiling. It made the same scraping noise she'd heard before. "I thought it would be smart to see more of the house before we settled in for the evening."

That didn't make sense to Remy. He hadn't seen many parts of the house. Why seek out the attic—the entrance to which had been concealed—above the others?

Instead of voicing the questions that lay unspoken on her

tongue, she forced brightness into her voice. "It's probably a good idea to let someone know before you explore on your own. Just in case you go missing or something."

He laughed and began leading the way back to the stairs. "You're right, of course. I'll be more careful next time."

Quiet enveloped them. Mark seemed happy to walk in silence, and Remy didn't know what to say. When they arrived at the recreation room, she speared away from Mark and gravitated to the hearth, where a heated discussion was underway. Marjorie and Taj were debating the advantages of their individual methods, but that evening's discussion lacked the venom of their previous spars. Remy guessed that the séance had given them a small measure of respect for each other.

"But remember," Marjorie said, "nothing's infallible. Gadgets break."

"They do. And empaths can be wrong, can't they?"

"I will admit to that, dear boy."

Remy took one of the spare seats a little back from the flames. The room's atmosphere was pleasant; everyone seemed inclined to relax that evening. Lucille had finished her bottle of wine and opened a second, but if she was drunk, she didn't act like it. April sat cross-legged on the rug between Taj and Marjorie, a subtle signal that she wanted hostilities to cease.

Marjorie noticed Remy and raised her teacup in greeting. "Good, you're back, dear. Shall we devise a plan for tomorrow? I think it would be wise to rest tonight but have an early start in the morning."

"Yes." Remy still felt unsettled and faintly numb. She glanced toward Mark, who stood by the window, his hands folded behind his back. *He's keeping secrets.* Remy licked her lips. "Mark, maybe you can weigh in here. You invited us to Carrow, after all, but you haven't given us any kind of task yet. What would you like us to focus on?"

He smiled at her, but it didn't fill her with warmth as it had earlier that day. "Actually, I'd be happy to leave the planning and orchestrating to you, Taj, and Marjorie. You know more about this business than I do, so I'll trust your good judgment."

That answer didn't sit well with Remy. She was searching for a way to express her thoughts when Marjorie stepped in, saving her the effort. "But surely you have a goal in mind, dear boy. Why are we here? What do you want us to achieve?"

He shrugged and crossed to take a seat by the fire. "Contact the spirits here. Learn about them. If you want to help them to move on—and if April doesn't mind—that would be fine by me, too."

Marjorie stared at him then laughed. "You're an odd duckling. You spend goodness knows how many hours and thousands of dollars preparing for this operation, just so you can turn us loose and watch what we do? I don't believe it."

"Well, it's the truth. I don't have any talent in the psychic or spiritual realm, but I am curious about it. I'll follow your lead."

"Remarkable." The crease between the medium's eyebrows told Remy that Marjorie didn't buy Mark's story, either. "You don't want any evidence? You don't want to write a book about the house or be admitted to a paranormal society or become famous from what you find here?"

"Sorry to disappoint."

"Oh, don't worry; I'm not disappointed." Marjorie sipped at her tea without moving her gaze from Mark. "Only very, very curious."

Remy studied their sponsor out of the corner of her eye. He looked relaxed with his long legs stretched ahead of him and his head artlessly tilted to one side, but a distant intensity in his eyes made her think his nonchalance was an act. She cleared her throat. "If Mark has no preference, that means you can do whatever you like, Marjorie. What's on the cards?"

"I would like to contact Eva again." She looked at the ceiling as she thought. "Plus any other spirits I can convince to join us for a séance. And…and…" She pursed her lips. "Perhaps Taj would indulge me and set up some of his equipment at our next session. To record any significant events."

"I'd be glad to." He raised his cup in cheers.

"I'll also visit the basement again. I sensed something odd down there and would like to know more about it. Other than that…we'll remain open to Carrow and its denizens and see what it wants to show us."

At her final word, a door slammed closed above them.

CHAPTER 19
POLTERGEIST

REMY STOOD, HER EYES fixed on the ceiling. One at a time, the others rose beside her.

"The wind?" Piers suggested.

Remy tried to think back to whether any of the bedroom doors had been open when she'd retrieved Mark. She didn't think so, but then memories from the night before made her hesitate. "My bedroom door's latch doesn't seem to catch. Last night, it opened on its own. It could've been that."

"Did you leave your window open?" Taj asked.

She shook her head.

They were silent for a moment, listening to the house shift around them.

Then April turned toward the door. "We gonna check it out or what?"

"Incorrigible thing," Taj laughed. "But I'm game if you are."

"I am, as well." Mark stood, and Piers followed suit.

Marjorie wrapped her shawl more tightly around her shoulders. "Let's all go. If it's a distressed spirit, I'll try to make contact."

"No." Lucille's eyes were wide and her lips frozen in a thin line. "I'm not going up there. And you shouldn't, either."

"Lu, you're drunk," April said as she rolled her eyes. "Alcohol's meant to *lower* your inhibitions, you know."

"What if it's dangerous? Stay here. The fire's warm. This room is safe."

"You can stay if you want, but I'm going to check it out." April marched to the door. "C'mon, gang. Last one up there's forever a chicken."

Remy felt her laughter loosen some of the tightness that had built up across her chest. "Please don't rush. No one ever got hurt by being careful."

"Hold on one second." Taj scrabbled through his equipment. He came up with a camera and a black box with a clear light in its end. He passed the box to Remy. "You're in charge of the EMF reader."

"What should I do with it?"

He grinned. "Wave it around a bit. If there's a ghost present, it'll light up."

Marjorie led the party through the foyer and up the stairs, with April close at her heels. As they passed the staircase's first landing, their pace slowed as they looked and listened for signs of movement.

"Anything?" Remy asked when Marjorie stopped at the top of the stairs.

The medium glanced down both paths, her eyes heavy-lidded and head held slightly forward as though she were trying to pick up on a quiet noise. She frowned. "Nothing that I can sense. It may have just been the wind, after all."

Except there's no breeze. They spilled into the hallway. Remy held the EMF meter ahead of herself, but it stayed dead as she moved toward her room and opened the door.

As Remy had suspected, the window was closed, and she couldn't detect any sort of draft. She left the door partially open then stepped back, waiting to see if it moved. It didn't.

"Check other windows," she suggested. "See if you can find a breeze or anything that would slam a door."

Taj paced the hallway, camera held ahead of him as he watched the area through the viewfinder. The others all opened doors— not just of their own rooms, but the uninhabited ones, as well.

"Guys, look at this." April had come to a halt on the threshold of Room 9. A wondering smile twitched at her lips, but she hesitated on the threshold, seeming reluctant to step into the room.

Remy hurried to her side. The wallpaper Mark had cut away from the plaster the previous day still lay on the ground in long shreds, slightly damp from the leaking water. The stains had spread across a wider, splotchy oval area, and the liquid was just as vividly red as before.

"It'll keep getting worse with the rain," Remy said.

"Don't you see it?" The teen waved a hand at the shape. "Can't you see what it's becoming?"

Remy could, but her mind revolted against the image. The

distinct spots had merged together to form an ill-defined, impressionistic face. Its eyes cast upward, its mouth open in a voiceless scream. The red liquid glistened as it continued to trickle from the effigy. "It's pareidolia. The human mind is constantly looking for patterns in chaos. Just because we see a face doesn't mean one's there."

"You don't believe that," April retorted, looking petulant.

Remy could only manage a very small smile. "No, not really."

"Out of the way." Marjorie shoved between them, closely followed by Taj. He already had a camera in the room—the one he'd set up the day before—but he moved closer with the handheld camcorder, zooming in on the liquid.

Marjorie stretched her hands toward the shape, her eyes half-closed, her jaw slack. She swayed, her fingers making strange little patterns in the air, then sucked in a deep breath before retreating. "There's no presence here now, but there was one within the last day. Probably an imprint, though the energy has faded so much that it's hard to be sure."

April frowned. "Is it going to come back?"

"Truly, I have no idea, child. Obviously, these marks aren't old, so something must have happened to rouse the spirit. Our arrival, possibly."

Remy felt faintly queasy. "Does this mean it's not just water like we first thought?"

"Oh, no, not necessarily. Spirits will use their environment to make a mark on the physical. The ghost may have taken advantage of the burst water pipe to form this shape. Or it could even have poltergeist abilities and be *responsible* for the pipe's breaking. Either way, the ghost isn't here at the present."

Although Taj continued to film, Marjorie adjusted her shawl and left the room. Remy, feeling uncomfortable with the image, followed. She found Mark and Piers not far outside, gesturing down the hall as they talked.

Piers turned toward Remy as she neared. "Marjorie can't find any spirits, and we can't find any breezes. Are there any other possibilities?"

Remy scratched at the back of her neck. "No one came up here, did they? Everyone was in the recreation room except for Bernard, and he was in the kitchen."

"Just because I haven't sensed a spirit yet doesn't mean there's not one here," Marjorie called over her shoulder as she continued to pace the hall. "In fact, I'd appreciate a little silence while I do my work."

The other five obediently gathered in the center of the hallway to wait. Taj continued to film, keeping his camera on Marjorie. She strode down the center of the runner, her fingers extended toward the walls, her steps slow and measured. At the end of the hall, she stopped and turned, and Remy saw a mix of confusion and fascination on her face.

"My name is Marjorie." She used the same steady voice from the séance, her eyes unfocused. "I would like to speak with any spirits who inhabit this house. If you can hear me, give me a sign."

The black box in Remy's hand whined, making her jump. The light lit up green then faded. April squeaked, and a smile grew over Marjorie's cheeks as Remy held the box forward.

"Thank you," Marjorie said. "I appreciate your answer. Tell me, have we encountered you before?"

They waited expectantly, but the seconds stretched by without any response from the box.

"Have you been in Carrow for long?"

The light flickered green again. Remy swallowed and focused on keeping her extended hand as still as possible.

"Were you one of Edgar's victims?"

The box stayed dead. Marjorie tried again. "Did the owner of this house kill you?"

Again, there was no response. She tried a different tactic. "Are you a woman?" And after a nonresponsive pause, she asked, "Are you a man?"

The light flashed green, and Remy drew an excited breath. Both April and Piers stood behind her, leaning over her shoulder as they watched the light eagerly, and Taj had taken several steps back to keep both the EMF reader and Marjorie in the camera's frame.

"I would like to help you move on, if I can. Do you linger in Carrow because of some regret?"

No response.

"Is it because you don't feel ready to face the next life?"

The box stayed quiet, and a small frown settled around Marjorie's eyes. She licked her lips before asking the next question in a slow, cautious tone. "Is it because you're trapped here?"

The light flashed a dozen times over a few short seconds, making Remy twitch. Marjorie's frown intensified, and she took her eyes off the box to look around the hallway. Her lips pursed, and her hands came up to grip her shawl. "Something's not right here."

As if in response, low, grating creaks filled the hallway as every door drew open at once. Remy's mouth felt too dry to make a sound. The group shuffled inward, trying to get as far from the doors as the narrow passageway would allow. The doors moved slowly, languidly, and finally came to rest once they were fully open. For a beat, the house was perfectly silent. Then the doors started slamming.

They crashed closed so fiercely that Remy was surprised the wood didn't fracture. The noise was deafening, making them all cringe, and the force seemed to shake the building down to its foundations. The slamming doors started at one end of the hallway, banging closed one after another, passing the huddled group and continuing into the other end of the hallway. The light in Remy's EMF reader made a popping noise as its bulb burned out.

Then silence returned.

Remy's shoulders were pressed against Piers and April. The group had huddled into a tight, defensive circle, and she could feel their ragged breathing against her back. They held that pose as they glanced from the doors to the empty hall.

Marjorie was the first to move. She shook herself a little and lifted her chin. "Well. A poltergeist. A strong one, too."

April's laugh was shaky. "I'm not sure I want to sleep up here anymore."

"Really, dear. It's quite safe. I felt his presence. He wasn't angry, only frustrated and frightened. Most spirits are."

Remy didn't find that as comforting as Marjorie seemed to think it should have been.

"I wish I could have gotten a stronger read on him," the medium continued. "He was old, maybe sixty, and said he felt trapped here and that he didn't die at Edgar Porter's hands. Does that narrow it down at all, my dear?"

Remy shook her head. "Sorry. Edgar's era was the most violent, but not the end of Carrow's bloodshed. That spirit could have been a construction worker, a guest who died of natural causes, or even one of the staff."

"I'll give him some time to calm, then, and try to make contact again tomorrow. He likely used up most of his energy in that little show."

Piers pulled out a handkerchief and mopped at his face. "I need a drink."

Remy could empathize and was about to suggest they return downstairs when a high-pitched scream interrupted her. It stretched out into a raw wail full of terror, then it broke. *Lucille.*

CHAPTER 20
HER BLACK HAIR

REMY RAN FOR THE stairs, her pulse jumping through her like electricity. Choking, miserable cries echoed from the recreation room. Remy leaped the last two stairs, hit the ground too hard, and slammed through the heavy double doors.

Lucille had pressed herself into a corner of the room. Her hands were clutched around her throat, and tears washed mascara down her cheeks as she sobbed.

"What's wrong?" Remy scanned the room as she crossed it to reach Lucille. The space seemed unchanged from when they'd left it. Mark was just behind her, but she could hear the others still clambering down the stairs. "Are you okay?"

"Hair—hair—*hair*—"

Remy gripped the woman's shoulders. She could feel Lucille shaking and pulled her into a hug. "C'mon, talk to me. What happened?"

Lucille buried her face into Remy's shoulder. Her hands held on hard enough to leave bruises, and she spoke in abortive little gasps. "There was hair. In my glass. In my wine."

Remy twisted to look behind them. Lucille's wine glass had smashed on the fire's hearth, spilling its red liquid across the stones. She frowned. "There was a hair in it?"

The other woman pulled back, her face white, her lips shaking. "Not *a* hair. *Clumps* of it. The glass was full with it—" She closed her eyes to draw a breath. "Woman's hair. Long. Black. I felt it—I was taking a sip, and I *felt it*!"

"Okay. Take deep breaths. You're okay now." Remy rubbed Lucille's back. April, her normally cheerful face dark, stepped up to Lucille's other side and wrapped an arm around her.

"I want to go home," Lucille mumbled.

"You can," Remy said. "You don't have to stay here."

Lucille nodded. Tears continued to leak from her puffy eyelids, and Remy and April half led, half carried her to a nearby chair. The others had gone to the fireside to examine the shattered wineglass. Remy shot another glance at it, but she couldn't see any sign of hair.

"I want to go right now." Lucille turned to April and grasped her hands. "Please come. I don't want to leave you here. I don't want… I don't want—"

April squeezed her lips together. Her eyes were watery. "I'll be okay, Lu."

"I don't want to *lose* you—"

"Shh."

Remy, realizing she was intruding on a private moment, stepped back. She kept shuffling away until she'd joined the others near the fire. Taj had his camera focused on the glass, but the others had given up examining it.

"No sign of hair," Mark whispered. "She's had a bit to drink, but I don't think she's intoxicated enough to hallucinate things."

"It was likely a momentary apparition," Marjorie said. "The sort of thing that appears for a second but vanishes as soon as you look at it closely."

"Either way, she wants to leave," Remy said.

Mark nodded. "Yes, of course."

Remy looked back at April and Lucille. They'd shuffled close together so that they both fit on the one chair and had their arms around each other as their heads rested together. For the first time, they reminded Remy of sisters. She wondered if that was what their relationship had been like before the fight.

She went to the window. A wave crashed, washing seawater past her eyes. She folded her arms and exhaled deeply. The storm was still in full force and showed no sign of abating.

Mark appeared behind her. "I could help pack Lucille's luggage. That way, she wouldn't need to go back upstairs."

"Thanks, but it will have to wait until tomorrow. The storm's too strong."

"What?" April's head jerked up. "No, she wants to leave tonight."

Remy gave a helpless shrug as she turned back to the room. "I'm really, really sorry. But the storm's awful. It wouldn't be safe."

Stubbornness froze April's face into hard angles. "Well, tough. Lu's a good driver. And I got my license, so I can take over if she gets fatigued."

"I wouldn't trust the world's best driver on Carrow's road tonight." Remy grabbed the back of a chair and pulled it close so that she could sit opposite the pair. "Do you remember how the road dips into that bridge to cross the chasm between Carrow and the mainland? During storms, waves crash over it. It's like how they hit this room's window, but worse. The bridge doesn't have any guardrails; your car could be swept over and into the ocean."

"Well, it's only waves. It's not like the bridge is submerged." The teen's eyes were flashing. "We'll just wait for a good moment and—"

"*Eight* people have died on that passage." The words left Remy more harshly than she'd intended. She squeezed her hands together. "Eight people, all sober, all experienced drivers, who thought they could handle the bridge during a storm."

April's lips pulled together. She looked livid but didn't reply as Remy took a slow breath to calm her voice.

"It's not safe to leave during a storm. It's the sole reason why my winter tours are subject to the weather. The risk is too great."

They were both quiet for a moment. Mark began pacing while Piers settled into a seat. April still had her arm around Lucille, whose expression had slackened, possibly from shock.

Then April said, "We can leave tomorrow morning?"

"As long as the rain has cleared, yes."

The girl nodded then cleared her throat. "Are any of the nice rooms still free? You know, the not awful ones?"

"Uh—yes. Room 14." Remy tried to smile, but the expression didn't come out right. "It's a really calm room. I can help you move your things over."

"Nah, I'll handle it. Are you okay with that, Lu? We'll stay one more night, but we can leave first thing tomorrow."

The woman blinked then gave a slow nod as she leaned against April's shoulder. "Thank you."

"Did anyone else want to leave with them?" Remy ran a hand through her hair as she glanced about the small group. "No one is expected to stay for the full two weeks if things have become too intense for you."

Piers cleared his throat. He looked nervous, but his eyes were bright. "In all honesty, I'm having a terrific time. There's zero chance my grandchildren will think I'm boring after this."

"No offense to Lucille," Taj said, "but wild horses couldn't drag me out of here."

"Okay." Remy looked at her watch. It was already late. What had started out as a relaxing evening had gone disastrously awry, but they would need to return to the upstairs rooms with their slamming doors before long. She just hoped Carrow had expended some of its excess energy and would stay dormant until morning. *Like how a minor tremor can stave off an earthquake.*

They huddled around the fire in the sitting room for a while longer, talking in soft voices. Mark cleaned up the smashed glass, and Bernard wandered in and out of the room, occasionally bringing cups of tea. By the time Lucille started to fall asleep on April's shoulder, Remy called it quits and went upstairs to shower.

She washed quickly, skipping the conditioner and braiding her wet hair without drying it, then she sat in her room with the light on and door open while the others took turns in the bathrooms and got ready for bed. She didn't dare drop her guard until every other door was closed and the lights were turned off, then she reluctantly shut her own door and crept into bed.

Like the night before, she lay on her back, facing the ceiling, as her eyes picked out patterns in the cracked plaster by the light of her alarm clock. It was nearly one in the morning when her bedroom door creaked open.

CHAPTER 21
THE ATTIC

REMY STAYED IN BED, highly conscious of the open door but not willing to play games by getting up to shut it. A crawling, creeping sensation made her feel as though a person or a presence stood just beyond the doorway, past the reach of her alarm's glow, watching her. She squeezed her eyes closed.

There's nothing to be afraid of.

A floorboard creaked. It was moving away from her, toward the other end of the house.

Good. Let it go.

Remy didn't want to listen, but her ears strained for any more noises. In the middle of the night, the house seemed eerily loud. The structure groaned. Wind whistled through the multitude of tiny holes, and the storm refused to abate, buffeting the building with unyielding aggression.

Then came the slow, drawn-out scraping sound as the attic's staircase was lowered.

Remy's eyes popped open. She held her breath, fear gnawing at her. It was faint, but she could hear the stairs groan as someone ascended them.

Is it Mark? Is he going into the attic again? I warned him—

The noises fell quiet as the unseen person finished climbing. Dread filled Remy's mouth with a sour taste. The attic was a maze of ropes, metal implements, and collapsing furniture. Whoever was up there hadn't taken a light, which meant they would be blind to the hazards in their path.

It's got to be either Marjorie or Mark. I can't just ignore them.

Remy rose, shivering against the cold, and crossed to her bedroom door. She would need light to see inside the attic, and the area didn't have any electricity run through it. A glint of glass caught Remy's eye, and she saw the lamp she'd left on her bedside table from the previous night's outing.

She fumbled through her bag and found the lighter she kept in a pocket of useful tools. She lit the lamp's wick, waited for the flame to stabilize, and stepped into the hallway.

For a moment, she seriously considered waking some of the other occupants, but eventually settled against it. She didn't want to risk disturbing Lucille, who had shown signs of shock. The others were all exhausted from the day. Besides, she told herself, the attic wasn't too far from the occupied rooms. If something went seriously wrong, she could yell to wake them.

The carpet muffled her footsteps but didn't stop the floorboards from groaning as she followed the hall to its end. The retractable stairs created a gaping black hole that not even her lamp could penetrate. Remy cleared her throat and stage-whispered Mark's name. She didn't get a reply.

Don't panic. He's probably fine. She squeezed her lips together and took the first stair. The wood felt flimsy under her shoe, but it held her weight. She climbed the second step and called, slightly louder than before, "Mark?"

A muted sound echoed back to her. Remy couldn't tell if it was a response or ambient noise from the storm. She blinked watery eyes and continued climbing.

The attic was freezing. As she moved through the square opening in the ceiling, she felt as if she were immersing herself in a different world. The smell of decay and mildew tickled her nose and made her squint. The second floor's ceiling and the attic's floor didn't line up, but had a two-foot interstitial space between them. Remy was surprised at how much difference the gap made. The subtle sounds from the lower levels faded out of hearing, and the noises from the external storm magnified. As she stood on the top step and blinked at the dim space, Remy felt wholly separated from the rest of the party.

"Mark?"

Although the attic only covered half of Carrow's floor space, it felt immense. It had been used to store some of the old furniture during renovations, and the space was still cluttered with old mattresses, broken furniture, burnt relics from the first fire, and dozens of empty crates. By the light of her lamp, they were barely recognizable. Long shadows stretched out behind them, creating a mosaic of light and dark on the slanted ceiling and dull windows.

She took a step forward, testing the floor before she trusted her weight to it. The roof leaked and had rotted sections of the floor, so she moved carefully, keeping to the parts she knew were solid.

"Mark?" She couldn't see him. The attic seemed to stretch forever, its contents offering infinite hiding spaces. Loops of rope hung from the ceiling like nooses, and a mess of construction supplies blocked part of the room. She licked her lips. "Marjorie?"

A clattering, scraping sound made her twist to her right. She took a hesitant step in its direction. The sound repeated, and this time, she saw motion.

A large mahogany wardrobe, one of the house's originals, stood among a heap of broken furniture. Its doors were closed, but glints of light reflected off the handle as it jiggled.

Fear coursed through Remy's veins. She tried to call out, but her voice felt awfully quiet in her own ears. The storm's roar increased, and the rumble of shaken roof tiles made her flinch. A drop of water landed on her arm, and she wiped it away.

"Hello?"

The handle rattled again, more urgently. Remy's throat felt too tight to even swallow as she moved closer. The wardrobe was locked, but the glittering key hung off the handle by a ribbon. Remy reached toward it, her heartbeat loud. The lamp's light wavered as her hand shook. She thought she could hear breathing coming from inside the wardrobe—low, panicked gasps infused with fear and claustrophobia. She took the key, feeling how cold the metal was, then slotted it into the hole and turned it.

A quiet click announced the door was unlocked. The breathing fell quiet. Remy drew back and waited for the door to open, but it didn't. She turned the handle, and the door opened in a slow arc, its hinges wailing. Inside was empty.

Remy stepped away from the wardrobe as clammy sweat rose across her skin. She looked toward the attic floor. Her shoes had left clear impressions in the dust, but only one pair led toward the wardrobe. She looked back toward the stairs and saw two pairs there—her own, and another, which took three paces into the attic before returning to the lower level. *My own, and Mark's from yesterday. No one is up here.*

No one living, at least.

She began backing toward the ladder, but a muted crack froze her. Remy turned back to the open wardrobe, her nerves taut. The back of the structure had a split in it. As she watched, the split widened, and fragments of wood poked away from it. Remy's mouth opened, but she couldn't make a sound, couldn't move, couldn't do anything but stare in horror as the false back of the wardrobe fractured open, widening to expose the secret cavity behind.

A jumble of shapes had been hidden inside. Some were cloth. Others were off-white lumps.

Her mind revolted against the image, trying to block it out, although she already knew what she was looking at. The wood decayed, crumbling before her eyes, then with a final, loud crack, the skull tumbled out of the secret compartment and rolled toward Remy.

She screamed and scrambled back. Her feet hit a soft part of the flooring. She had a fraction of a second to realize what was happening, then the boards gave way. She plunged through the floor.

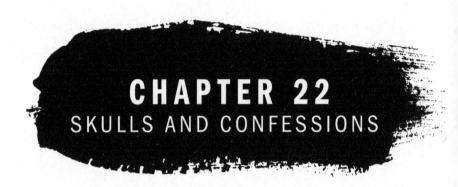

CHAPTER 22
SKULLS AND CONFESSIONS

REMY THREW HER ARMS out, fingers grasping for any kind of hold, and managed to grab on to the floor as her torso dropped past it.

The edges of the rotten boards dug into her, and she gasped but didn't loosen her hold. She came to a halt with her head and shoulders in the attic, her hands planted on the dusty floor and straining to keep her from falling farther. Her legs kicked at darkness. Terror flooded her, the adrenaline lending her strength, and she tried to pull herself up, but froze as the wood under her arms splintered.

Her legs hunted for purchase but found none. She couldn't understand that—the interstitial space was only two feet deep, so she should have been able to push against the second floor's ceiling, but there wasn't anything underneath her.

The lamp, its wick still burning, had fallen on its side. Remy risked a glance over her shoulder and saw nothing but darkness below, as though the hole opened into a void. As though the house intended to swallow her.

"Remy."

The voice was familiar. Remy looked up and saw a lopsided face leering at her. The skull had come to rest not far from her fingertips. The shock sent tremors through her limbs. She was slipping into the darkness, sucked into the house's gullet, as her fingers lost their tenuous grip. She squeezed her eyes closed as terror churned her stomach and clouded her mind.

Then something warm touched her arms. Fingers wormed under her shoulders and pulled, dragging her out of the hole. Remy opened her eyes and saw Mark, on his knees, his eyes wide as he pulled on her.

"Careful." She didn't have enough breath, and the words came out as choked gasps. "The floor—rotten—"

"I know." He shifted backward a fraction as the wood splintered under their combined weight. "Hold on."

He leaned back, using his body weight to help pull her up. The ragged wood hurt as Remy was dragged over it, but she bit her tongue to keep silent and focused on holding Mark's arms. The wood fractured. Mark jerked them both back, pulling them clear of the hole as boards fell silently into the darkness below.

They collapsed into a pile, their limbs tangling, their breathing heavy. Remy's heart felt like a caged bird fluttering frantically. Mark kept his arm around her, his fingers gripping as though ready to pull her farther back, but they'd landed on one of the solid parts of the attic.

Remy propped herself up, swaying slightly as the adrenaline drained from her limbs and left weakness in its place. The hole, although lit by her lamp, looked impossibly dark. She glanced to her right. The skull was barely visible in the edge of the lamp's light, and the dark hollows of its eyes seemed to watch her.

"We need to go back down," Mark said. "Can you stand?"

"Yeah." He hadn't loosened his grip, so Remy let him help her to her feet. Now that the fear was fading, she was aware of the pain of cuts and unformed bruises. Mark ushered her down the stairs before he retrieved the lamp. As she stepped into the hallway, she found Piers waiting for her, wearing pajamas with a cartoon duck patterned over them, his graying hair a mess. Not far behind him was Marjorie, who looked immensely annoyed.

"What was that hullaballoo about?" The medium adjusted a bandanna, which hid her long gray hair. "Were you sleepwalking? Heaven forbid Bernard has a second night wanderer to follow."

"Not quite." Remy swayed, and Piers kindly took her arm to keep her steady. "I heard something in the attic—"

"You're hurt," Piers said.

Remy glanced down and saw a gash on the side of her upper arm. It didn't hurt beyond a throbbing sting but was dripping blood. She pressed her other hand over it. "Oh, damn, sorry. I'll clean it up."

Piers, looking agitated, scratched at his scalp. "It looks bad. Might need stitches. Someone should take you to the hospital."

Remy tried, and failed, to pull away from his supporting arm.

"We can't leave while there's a storm. It's not bad, really. It barely even hurts."

"You're in shock. You're not thinking clearly." Mark took her other arm and nodded to Piers. "Help me get her downstairs. I have a first-aid kit."

She tried to argue, saying it wasn't serious and could wait until morning, only to be shushed by Marjorie.

"The others are still sleeping. Go clean up, for goodness' sake, and keep the noise down."

Mark and Piers, one on each side, led Remy down the stairs and into the recreation room. They put her into one of the chairs beside the dying fire, then both disappeared into different parts of the building. Once she was alone, Remy's head started to clear. She closed her eyes and saw the image of the skull rolling toward her, its hollowed eyes staring, its detached jaw falling away from the cranium.

Was that a real skeleton or just a spirit's manifestation?

She tried to think back through Carrow's history. Edgar had hidden at least one body inside a wardrobe. Following his demise, the police had searched the other wardrobes but hadn't found any victims.

But what if a wardrobe had been moved into the attic before Edgar's death? The police probably would have opened it, but would they have thought to look inside the hidden compartment?

Her head throbbed, so she rested it against the chair's back.

If the skull was real, it would need to be referred to the police. It was so old that a positive identification would be nearly impossible unless it was accompanied by clothing or jewelry with the victim's name on them, but either way, the remains would be given a proper burial.

A blanket dropped over her lap. Mark had returned, carrying a bundle of towels. He knelt beside her, gently eased her hand away from her arm, and placed a cloth underneath to catch the drips.

She tried to smile. "Don't worry about that. I can clean it up in a minute."

Mark shot her a dark look.

Piers trotted through the doorway, holding a steaming kettle. "Is this okay?"

"Thanks." Mark opened his first-aid kit and rummaged through it. "Hold still, Remy. This will hurt a bit."

She gritted her teeth and fixed her eyes on the dying embers while Mark washed, disinfected, and stitched the cut. He worked quickly and with steady hands. She guessed his father, the surgeon, must have taught him some tricks. Piers hovered nearby, alternately putting more wood on the fire, fetching them both cups of coffee, and offering to get more towels.

"There." Mark tied off the bandages and took away the towel. "It's not as bad as it looked, thankfully. But you should probably catch a ride to the mainland with Lucille tomorrow and get it checked by a hospital. Some antibiotics wouldn't go astray."

"Told you it was fine," she retorted then grinned to let him know she was joking. She didn't want to leave Carrow while the others were still inside. It felt like abandoning a tour. A panic started to rise in her. After what had happened that night, she knew she wasn't being irrational when she worried about her group's safety.

The disinfectant and stitches had woken up the nerves in her arm, leaving a constant, throbbing ache. She tested it by moving her hand and managed to hide her flinch.

"Would you like to go back upstairs?" Mark asked. "Or stay here tonight?"

For a moment, she imagined her bedroom door gliding open once more, followed by the scrape of the retractable staircase being pulled down, and felt chills crawl along her spine. "I'll stay here. It's warmer."

"Good thought." Mark stood, folding up the bloodied towels, and nodded to Piers. "Thanks for the help. Go get some sleep. I'll stay."

"Are you sure?"

"Yeah."

Piers gave Remy a smile and a wave then left the recreation room. The neon-yellow ducks on his pajamas were last to disappear from her sight. Remy wrapped the blanket around herself as she watched Mark pace the room. "You should go to bed, too. You must be exhausted."

He chuckled and shook his head. "I don't think I'll sleep any more tonight. Let me keep you company."

She watched out of the corners of her eyes. He moved with quick, efficient motions as he packed away the first-aid kit and bagged the towels. But underneath the steady demeanor, she saw a tightness in his muscles and a sheen of perspiration over his face. He'd been frightened.

"Hey, Mark?"

He turned toward her, eyebrows raised.

"Thanks for saving me."

"Of course." He smiled and ducked his head again. "I wasn't about to leave you up there."

"How did you know where I was, anyway?"

"I had a bad dream. It unnerved me enough that I got up to check on the other rooms, but your door was open, and I couldn't find you. I was about to go downstairs when I heard a noise above my head." He shot her a quick look. "If you don't mind the question, why were *you* up there? Did you say you heard something?"

"Yeah. A ghost wanted its body found. I think." She rubbed at the corners of her eyes. "Or maybe it just wanted to mess with me. If the bones are still there tomorrow—if it wasn't just an illusion—we'll have to call the police about it once we get back to the mainland."

Mark left the kit and towels on one of the tables by the door then pulled up an armchair next to Remy. The logs Piers had put on the fire had caught and spread heat across her legs. If she'd been less frightened of the building, it would have been enough to make her sleepy.

Instead, she watched the man at her side. His pose looked relaxed, but his muscles were still tense. *He's keeping secrets…*

"Mark?"

"Hmm?"

"Why did you come to Carrow? And please, please don't give me any more of the vague excuses you've been feeding us. I've trusted you so far, but I need some trust in return. Why did you *really* come?"

He stared at her for a moment, and she saw a deep, unyielding sadness in his eyes. When he spoke, his voice was raspy, as though the words hurt him. "Sometimes, people can be afraid of things. Horribly, permanently afraid. And the fear takes root in their lives and twists them and controls them. And they know it will haunt them to their grave unless they confront the thing they're frightened of. Meet it, feel it, then immerse themselves in it."

Remy shifted closer. "You're afraid?"

He held out his hand. The fingers trembled. "Of houses like Carrow. Of attics like Carrow's."

"Oh." That explained why he'd ventured into the attic alone the previous night. Remy brushed loose hair away from her face. "Have you always been afraid?"

"Since I was eight." His eyes fixed on the fire. "I'd prefer not to talk about the whys, please."

"Right. I'm sorry for prying."

He's keeping secrets. Marjorie's warning now felt strangely hollow. The barrier it had put up between her and Mark melted away and left Remy feeling embarrassed for being so wary of him. "If you don't like haunted houses, Carrow's about as far in the deep end as you can get. I don't know if it's any consolation, but you're holding together remarkably well."

"Ha! That's why I went on your tour first: to see if I could handle it." His expression softened as the haunted sadness left his eyes. "I'd expected it to be one of the worst nights of my life, but *you* were there. You were so bright and full of enthusiasm, and you made it fun and easy, and I thought, *I wouldn't be frightened of anything if I had this woman with me.* I knew that if I wanted to spend a longer stretch of time at Carrow, I'd need you there, as well."

"Oh." Remy hoped he wouldn't see the color spreading over her face. "Wow, that's a lot of pressure. I hope I'm not a disappointment—"

"No, the opposite."

His eyes were enthralling. The way his lips twitched into a smile made her want to touch them. Instead, she leaned toward him, resting her head on his shoulder. He shifted closer to hold her, and they let silence absorb them as the fireplace crackled and popped.

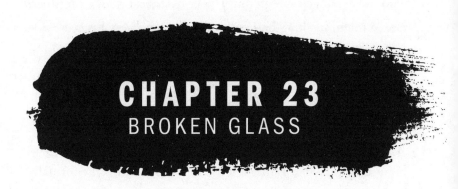

CHAPTER 23
BROKEN GLASS

REMY HADN'T EXPECTED TO sleep that night, so she was surprised to wake up and see the fire was dead and her lamp had burned out. A muscle in her neck felt sore, and she rotated her head to loosen it.

Mark stirred beside her and rubbed sleep out of his eyes. "What was that?"

"Hmm?" She blinked at him, then the noise—the one that had woken her—repeated. It was a cry of "Piers!"

Remy bolted out of her chair, remembering too late that her arm was hurt, and flinched as she used it to wrench open the door. Mark followed close behind as they ran into the foyer.

The sun had risen, but it was hard to tell through the overcast sky. The air was frosty as the storm continued to beat at the house. A small group had gathered on the rug in the center of the foyer, and Remy shambled toward them, trying to pick out the source of the distress while her mind was still half-asleep.

April and Lucille were at the head of the group, April holding her guardian back with one arm. The cry had come from Lucille, who was reduced to gasping, near-hysterical sobs. Taj stood beside them, his long hair still mussed from sleep, his eyes wide and jaw slack. He looked strangely lonely without a camera in his hand. Marjorie came down the stairs, wrapping a shawl about her shoulders, with Bernard on her heels.

And Piers lay on the ground.

Confusion clogged Remy's mind. Had Piers fallen asleep there? He didn't look like himself. His skin was ashen. His normally lively face was slack and blank, and his open eyes stared at the ceiling. The remains of a smashed glass lay at his side. She almost wouldn't have recognized him except for the duck-print pajamas.

"Piers?" She dropped to her knees beside him and shook his shoulder. His head lolled. He felt cold—far colder than any person should be—and Remy withdrew her hand.

Mark gripped Remy's shoulders and turned her to face him. His voice was brisk and tight. "Listen. I need your help. Can you think?"

Numbness was creeping over her, but she nodded.

"Take April and Lucille into the recreation room. Look after them. I'll be in as soon as I can."

"Okay. Yes." Remy rose and moved toward the two other women, but she couldn't keep her eyes off Piers. He looked so wrong, lying there like that, like a wax sculpture or some awful impressionist painting that had gone awry.

She glimpsed a pale face out of the corner of her eye and turned toward the fireplace. Edgar's portrait hung above the mantel. The small smile curling his lips looked nearly triumphant as he watched over the scene.

Remy grabbed April's shoulders with one hand and Lucille's with the other and began pulling them toward the recreation room. Lucille was hysterical. April looked stunned, as though she couldn't understand what was happening. Remy felt somewhere between the two extremes but bottled up the emotions as she urged her friends into the room. Marjorie passed them, dragging her fingers through her gray hair as she approached Piers, a tight-lipped Bernard close behind. Remy turned at the door, and the last thing she saw was Mark kneeling on the rug, pressing his fingers to Piers's neck as he searched for a pulse.

"He's going to be okay, right?" April whispered.

Remy closed the door firmly, willing herself not to watch any longer. She knew the answer but didn't want to speak it into being, so she kept her lips fixed firmly together.

April took Lucille's hand in one of hers and led the older woman toward the chairs. They sat, and Lucille's sobs finally ebbed into muted hiccups as they waited.

They weren't left alone for long. Mark, his face wan, opened the doors and stepped inside, followed by Marjorie, Taj, and Bernard. He hesitated, opening his mouth and then closing it again, as he hunted for words. At last, he said simply, "Piers is dead."

Remy had known it since she'd first seen the man's face, but the words still felt like knives gouging her insides. She folded her arms across her torso in an attempt to keep herself together. "Do you know how?"

"Heart attack, I think." Mark stayed standing but braced himself against the back of one of the chairs. Harsh shadows played over his features. "There's a broken glass beside him. He was probably getting a drink from the kitchens."

Bernard crossed to the serving table at the back of the room and poured a mug full of wine, which he began consuming in gulps.

Lucille watched for a moment then beckoned to him. "Give me some of that."

Bernard poured her a cup of her own then held the bottle out toward the others with a questioning look. They all shook their heads, so he refilled his cup and put the bottle back.

"If it's any comfort," Marjorie said, "I searched for a spirit but was unable to find anything. Piers has moved on."

Remy looked up. "He didn't leave a ghost?"

"No, thank mercy. Considering the environment's abnormally high energy levels, I was afraid he would have been trapped here. But it seems he was at peace with this life and able to move on to the next."

Frowning, April still clasped Lucille's hand tightly in her own. "Heart attack… You don't think he saw something that frightened him, do you?"

"I have no idea," Mark said.

Taj cleared his throat. He had his arms folded, and his face looked haggard, but his voice still kept its crisp edge. "I had a camera set up in the foyer. It should have filmed whatever happened. I can review it and—"

Marjorie made a faint, disgusted exclamation. "Do you have no respect? A man is dead, and you want to watch his final moments?"

"I only thought—"

"Shall I get you some popcorn, too? We can make a movie night out of it!"

"Enough." Mark's voice took on a steely edge. "I won't tolerate bickering right now. Whether we view the film or not is an issue for later. Right now, our friend's body is in the foyer. We need to decide on a course of action." He looked to Remy, a hint of pleading in his expression. "Can we leave the house?"

She licked her lips and glanced toward the window. The storm raged against the building, gale-force winds driving torrents of rain into the glass. She turned back to Mark and opened her mouth, feeling helpless, but words refused to come.

"That's a no, I take it?" He closed his eyes, a muscle twitching in his neck. "Without the radio, we have no way to contact anyone for assistance. We'll wait until it's safe to leave."

Taj spoke. "What will we do with the body?"

"Treat it as respectfully as possible. Remy, how long do these storms normally last?"

Her tongue was dry, but she made it move. "It varies. Sometimes half a day. Sometimes as long as a week."

"Then we will need to move Piers somewhere cold to prevent decomposition. Just in case it takes that long."

"Where?" Taj asked. "The freezer unit?"

Lucille made a gagging noise and doubled over.

Remy tried to imagine folding the man into the freezer. It was horrific and inhumane, and the thought made her feel queasy. "We can't do that to him."

"I feel the same way," Mark said. "Are there any other options?"

An unpleasant silence flooded the room. Then April spoke. "There's the cold spot in the basement. I bet that would keep him chilled."

Lucille's body lurched as she gagged again.

"Really, dear," Marjorie said.

April blinked watery eyes as she scowled at the ground. "Do you have any other suggestions?"

Again, the question was answered by silence. Mark blew out a breath through his nose. "Okay. It's not a pretty choice, but we need to decide. Freezer or basement?"

"Basement," Remy said after a moment. "Wrap him in a blanket. It will be like he's resting."

Marjorie pursed her lips. "I…I suppose it's the more dignified out of the two. Which isn't saying much."

"All right." Mark pushed away from the chair he'd been resting on. "Let's take care of him now. I don't like leaving him in the foyer like that. I'd appreciate any volunteers who want to help."

"I'll come," Taj said.

Bernard drained his mug of wine, placed it back on the table, and followed the other men to the door. Marjorie trailed in their wake. After a moment, Remy stood and followed, as well.

Mark and Taj did almost all of the work. Remy appreciated seeing how much care they took with Piers; they folded his hands over his chest and placed his spectacles back on his nose then wrapped his body in one of the clean sheets before carrying him to the basement. Remy stood at the top of the stairs, watching helplessly as her friend was lowered into the dark and placed in the basement's corner, where the cold spot persisted.

She didn't realize April had joined them until the teenager touched her arm. "Will it be okay leaving him down there? I mean, with the heightened energy—"

"Don't you worry, child," Marjorie said. "He didn't leave a ghost. All that remains is the human flesh, which will ultimately be returned to the earth, where it came from. The spiritual realm cannot touch him now."

Mark and Taj returned from the basement. Taj cradled two cameras under his arm. He nodded at them sheepishly. "Seemed a bit disrespectful to leave them on."

Mark touched the door. "Open or closed?"

"Closed," April said. "I don't think I could stand looking down the stairs at him every time I went through the foyer."

He shut the door with a soft click, then as a group they returned to the recreation room. Unlike the previous day, they didn't gather around the fire together, but broke off into small groups. Remy found herself sitting next to Mark near the window. She suspected he wanted to watch the weather, too, and together, they searched for anything that might indicate it was clearing.

It was one of the worst mornings of her life. She couldn't

stop her mind from going back to Piers and how he would have collapsed in the foyer, his glass shattering, so close to help but unable to call for it. She and Mark had slept through his death, just a room away.

And what if April is right, and the heart attack was brought on by something he saw? Would he still be alive if he hadn't come to Carrow? Am I indirectly responsible?

"This isn't your fault," Mark said.

Remy startled and stared at him. "Was I talking out loud?"

His smile was weary. "No. But your face speaks volumes."

They fell back into silence. Bernard moved through the room, passing around plates of fruit and toast with jam.

Remy took hers with muted thanks and added, "I'll help with food for the rest of today."

"Don't bother. I don't want company." He moved away before she could say anything else. Despite the snippy tone, Remy sensed he was doing what he could to help the group, and she was grateful for it.

Midday arrived with no change in the weather. Lucille continued to drink while April paced the room, occasionally stopping to look at the antique books on the shelves. Taj quietly returned to his computers. Remy wondered if he was looking at the tapes from the previous night despite Marjorie's chastisement. If he was, he didn't say anything.

Marjorie sighed loudly and stood. "Well, I'm going to conduct another séance. I need at least two assistants to create a circle. Who'll help?"

"What?" Taj swiveled in his seat to look at her. "Piers is *dead*, and you want to have a séance?"

Marjorie bristled and adjusted her shawl. "Piers has moved on. He'll neither hear nor appreciate our tears. Meanwhile, I have a very limited window during which I can help those who *do* need it. The trapped spirits. If I can assist even just one of them to pass over, our time here won't have been a waste."

Taj mumbled something that sounded like "tasteless" then turned back to his screens.

"Well, what about you, Remy? You'll help, won't you?"

Remy cringed at the medium's tone. "Thank you for the invitation. But I don't feel like I can right now—"

"Honestly." The medium puffed her chest out as she scowled at them. "You're a miserable bunch. It's toxic to wallow, and it won't help any soul one whit. We came here to do a job, and right now, we have time to burn. I say we do what we promised to."

After a moment, April spoke. "I'll help." She sat cross-legged on a sofa, staring at her hands, and shrugged when Marjorie looked at her. "There's nothing better to do."

"That's the spirit. I need one or two more. Come on, who'll it be? Mark?"

"Uh—" He sent a questioning look toward Remy, and she knew what he was asking. He didn't want to take part in a séance without her.

"Okay," she whispered back then added more loudly, "Mark and I will help."

"Good, good," Marjorie said as they stood. "Everyone else, clear out."

"I'm staying here," Taj snapped from his corner.

Lucille only pulled a face then picked up her wine glass and downed it in one go.

Remy cleared her throat. "Marjorie, can we do it in another room? That way we won't have to disturb the others."

"The atmosphere's really best here…" Marjorie saw the look on Remy's face and sighed. "All right. I saw a lovely little smoking room not far from here. Take a few minutes to center yourself and clear your mind while I prepare, then meet me there. If we're very lucky, one of the spirits may be able to tell us what happened to Piers."

CHAPTER 24
THE SMOKING ROOM

REMY TRIED HER HARDEST not to look at the basement's door as she passed it, but the discreet wooden shape was impossible to ignore. She went to the nearest bathroom, turned on the tap, and dunked her face under the icy water.

She'd started to feel more human by the time she came up. Her skin was sallow and blotchy, she noticed in the cracked mirror, and she tried to brighten it with a smile. The result was a grimace.

Marjorie's right...in a way. Crying won't bring Piers back. The best I can do is hold things together until the storm clears.

Thunder rumbled outside. Remy shuddered, knowing the storm was nowhere near done, and dried her face on the hem of her shirt before leaving the bathroom.

She found Marjorie, Mark, and April in the smoking room. It was a small, dim area with too much furniture and not enough ventilation. Even though no one had smoked in it in decades, the musty, sour smell remained. Close to a dozen paintings of landscapes and people cluttered the walls. Its fireplace hadn't been lit, which made it feel cold and unwelcoming.

Marjorie had cleared a space around one of the circular tables and was covering it with a tablecloth. Remy helped light a candle while Marjorie placed her pen and the herb sprigs on the table.

"What're the plants for?" April asked from where she'd perched in an armchair.

"Herbs, dear. They attract the spirits. A candle for those who are trapped in the dark, fragrant food for those who are hungry." Marjorie turned off the lights, set the pen upright, then beckoned them close.

They pulled up their seats and held hands. Remy closed her eyes and felt Marjorie's papery, aged skin in her left hand and Mark's warm fingers in her right. She took a deep breath and tried to ground herself.

"My name is Marjorie," the medium began. "I would be glad to speak to any spirits who are present and willing to communicate."

The smoking room had no windows, but Remy could still hear the storm outside. She tried to block out the environmental noise and focus on what was happening in their circle.

Marjorie's eyebrows pulled together, and she spoke again, maintaining the same steady tone. "I wish to communicate with any who are present. If you can hear me, please tip my pen over."

All eyes turned to the little implement standing on its end. Remy held her breath, ready for it to fall. It stayed still.

Marjorie let the quiet stretch for several minutes then spoke again. "I feel your presence. I wish to communicate. If you are able to, please tip my pen over."

The pen refused to move. Remy swallowed and adjusted her grip on her companions' hands.

"It's strange," Marjorie whispered. "I can feel *someone* here. But they're not replying. Usually, spirits are eager to communicate."

"Maybe they're too weak?" Remy asked.

As soon as the words left her mouth, the pen clattered to the table. A smile lit Marjorie's face. "Ah, thank you. My mind is open if—"

The candle hissed and died. The windowless room was plunged into darkness. Remy blinked against the black as anxiety rose in her chest. It was the same deep, permanent dark that had swallowed them the day before. She could feel the icy cold creeping across her skin and seeping into her, chilling her core.

Marjorie's fingers tightened around hers. They pinched to the point of hurting. Then Marjorie exhaled. The noise was guttural, rasping, and unnatural. True fear coiled through Remy's insides. "Light the candle," she begged. "Someone light the candle."

"We're not supposed to break the circle," April said. Remy could hear the fear in the girl's voice.

"Something's wrong. Light the candle!"

At her words, the candle hissed, and its flame flickered back into life. None of them had touched it. Remy stared at the flame then turned to look at Marjorie.

The woman sat pin-straight, her shoulders squared and head facing forward. Her features were slack, but her eyes had rolled back, showing only the whites.

Remy tried to shy away, but Marjorie's hand tightened around hers. Very slowly, as though the motion was unfamiliar, the medium's head rotated to stare at Remy. Her lips peeled back into an inhumanly wide smile.

"Please," Remy begged. She was no longer maintaining the circle, but pulling her hand, trying to escape Marjorie's grip. She may as well have been struggling against manacles.

Marjorie twitched. The skin around her throat darkened into a grisly bruised shade of red. She twitched again, the too-wide smile stretched over her features, her eyes sightless. The room was impossibly cold. Remy didn't know she was crying until she felt the tears freeze on her cheeks.

The medium twitched again, convulsing, spittle dribbling over her gaping lips. A gurgling cry rose from her throat.

"Marjorie!" Mark yelled. He'd let go of Remy's hand and threw himself over the table to reach the medium. He grabbed her shoulders and shook her. The candle spluttered then stabilized again, and Marjorie slumped back in the chair, breathing heavily and pressing her hands to her chest.

"Oh… Oh my…" she gasped.

Remy wrapped her hand around her sore wrist. Her head throbbed, and her lungs were starved for oxygen.

Mark, his face sheet-white, eased back into his chair. "What the hell was that?"

"Oh, my dears, I'm so sorry." Marjorie wiped the spit away from her chin. "I allowed it into me."

"Allowed what?" April's voice had risen to the point of being near hysterical. She'd frozen in her seat and was staring about the room with wide eyes.

Marjorie drew a slow breath then rose to turn on the lights. "I could feel a spirit in this room, but when it didn't tip the pen over, I thought it was weak. I opened my mind too far—invited it in too willingly—and it took control."

She returned to her chair and eased herself into it, looking nearly a decade older. "It possessed me. There's nothing inherently wrong with that—it's a common tactic mediums use to let spirits speak directly through them—but I wasn't planning on it and so didn't warn you about what to expect. He took charge before I could close my mind against him."

Remy swallowed an unpleasant taste. "It looked…horrific. Did he hurt you?"

"Oh, goodness no, dear. I'm a little tired, that's all." Marjorie scratched at her neck. The bruises had vanished, but the skin looked faintly darker, as though it held on to a memory of the injury.

Mark touched Remy's shoulder, a question in his eyes. She mouthed, "I'm fine," as she hid the bruised wrist under the table.

April sucked in a hiccupping little gasp. "I don't think I want to be a spirit medium anymore."

"Ha! You poor thing." Marjorie seemed to have recovered. "Possessions are normally much more gentle than that. A spirit enters you and uses your body to speak to the living. My guest tonight was…rather exceptional."

Remy swallowed. "Did he tell you anything?"

"No thoughts, only feelings." Strands of hair had come loose when Mark shook her, and Marjorie brushed them behind her ears. "He was… Oh, I can't even explain it. He was awful. So angry. So bitter. One of the worst spirits I've ever had the misfortune of contacting."

"It was the same ghost that chased the spirit away during the first séance," Remy said. "The one Taj saw standing behind you. When the lights went out, I felt the cold. I felt his presence—"

"Yes, I believe you're right. This spirit, whoever he is, seems to be following us."

"I think I know who it is." It was difficult to express what she'd seen—and felt—but she tried. "When you were…possessed, bruises appeared on your throat. They looked like the sort of marks that would come from a rope. As though you'd been hung."

"Oh…" April pressed a hand over her mouth.

"And you were convulsing, too. I think he was reliving his final moments alive. This spirit—I think it belongs to Edgar Porter."

CHAPTER 25
WHAT LITTLE WAS CAPTURED

"DON'T LET IT ALARM you," Marjorie said as the small group crossed the foyer toward the recreation room. "We always knew there was a chance Edgar's spirit had become trapped here. But remember—he's no more dangerous than any other ghost."

April's laugh was hollow. "I dunno, the regular ones have gotten pretty violent when they put their mind to it."

"Don't go thinking like that. Spirits in their normal form cannot touch us. Usually, they can't even be seen. The only time a spirit can affect the physical world is when their energy gets out of control and they become a poltergeist. But even poltergeists are largely harmless. They can slide things along tables, sometimes throw small objects or knock chairs over, but they expend energy quickly and return to their regular, harmless state. Let me be very clear in this: no matter what Edgar was in life, he is not dangerous now."

They'd come to a stop outside the recreation room's doors. Remy frowned and rubbed at her neck, imagining the welts that had appeared on Marjorie's. Her wrist was still sore.

"I know what you're thinking," Marjorie said. "But that was a possession. It only happened because I willingly opened my mind to him and welcomed him inside. Ghosts can't go around possessing people willy-nilly. They have to be invited in, and it's near impossible to do if you're not an adept spirit medium. Now stop being such silly geese, all of you. Have some coffee and an aspirin. I'm going to change into warmer clothes and meditate for a spot."

She stalked toward the staircase, and Remy managed a chuckle.

"What is it?" Mark asked.

"Oh, just thinking how nice life would be if I was as unconcerned about things as Marjorie is. Spirit possesses you? Not a problem. Your friend dies? Well, that's life. Trapped in the state's most haunted house? What a bore! I'm going to take a nap."

He laughed, too, though his voice was still tight with stress. "Maybe that's what being a medium does to you. Her life is consumed by contacting and communicating with the deceased. It probably does a good job of erasing any fear of death."

Remy glanced over Mark's features. His cheeks were pale and his eyes shadowed. Even though he'd admitted to being afraid of Carrow, he'd responded quickly and with conviction when the séance turned sour. She'd begun to develop a lot of respect for him.

They entered the recreation room. Lucille and Taj were both in the same chairs as when Remy had left. As far as Remy could tell, they hadn't heard the commotion in the smoking room. It felt vaguely surreal, as though she'd taken a brief detour into a different dimension.

April took up her place beside Lucille, who looked half-asleep.

Mark exhaled and said, "I'm going to take Marjorie's advice and brew a very, very, very strong cup of coffee. Did you want some?"

"Thanks, but I'll wait for lunch."

Remy watched him leave then turned toward her space by the window so that she could watch the storm. She'd only taken two steps when movement caught her eye. Taj was motioning to her, casting furtive glances at the open door as he tried to get her attention. She approached him and bent close.

"So," he began, seeming uncertain about how to phrase himself. "I know Marjorie said not to watch the tapes from last night…"

"But you wanted to know," Remy finished.

He gave her an apologetic nod. "I thought you would understand."

"Of course I do. What did you see?"

"That's the thing—I'm not sure. Do you have a moment?"

Remy settled into the spare seat beside his desk. The table had four computer screens set up; three were live feeds from various parts of the house. Remy could see Marjorie entering her room on the upstairs floor and Mark turning toward the kitchen. The final one was blank.

"I haven't gone through everything yet, but last night was eventful for more than one person. I saw you going down the hallway shortly after midnight, then Mark, Piers, and Marjorie following you. Marjorie told me about what happened last night. You and Mark stayed downstairs until morning, didn't you?"

Remy nodded.

"Well, the cameras caught Marjorie and, a little later, Piers going back to bed. Around three in the morning, Piers gets back up and goes to the kitchen." Taj pressed some buttons, fast-forwarding through a tape.

The camera had been set onto the top of one of the display units in the foyer and had a bird's-eye view of the lower half of the stairs, most of the foyer's floor, and the doors to the kitchens, recreation room, and dining room. Remy caught a glimpse of Piers's duck-print pajamas coming down the stairs. She turned away, suddenly feeling shameful for watching the man's last moments.

"Sorry," Taj said and sped the film up further. "What comes next is important. He goes to the kitchen, gets a glass of water… and then look at this."

The tape slowed down to normal speed. The kitchen door opened, and Piers stepped out, glass in hand, looking toward the opposite side of the room, the side where Edgar's painting hung. He stepped forward, his movements slow and careful, and just as he was nearing the rug in the center of the room, the screen cut to black.

"Did you pause it?"

"No," Taj said. "The cameras malfunctioned. Not just the one overlooking the foyer and the portrait, but the upstairs ones, as well. It's like the power was cut."

Remy chewed on her thumb. "A power surge? The storm got pretty nasty last night."

"That's what I thought at first, too. But they all resumed playing at six thirty this morning, just in time for April and Lucille to come downstairs." Taj pressed several more buttons, and the screen lit up again to show the two women descending the staircase. Piers's body lay on the rug, his glass smashed beside him.

Remy shuddered, and Taj turned off the screen. "Sorry to show you that, but I needed to share it with someone. Not just because the cameras spontaneously died, but because of how Piers was acting. It struck me as odd this morning that he'd brought his glass into the foyer with him. Normally, I'd expect someone to finish their drink in the kitchen and leave the glass there. But it looks like something interrupted him."

"Like he heard something," Remy agreed. "The recording wasn't clear. What was he looking at? The painting or one of the lower doors?"

"I can't tell. He's looking toward that side of the house, though. From my best guess, the cameras cut out barely seconds before he collapsed."

"Jeez." Remy ran her hands through her hair. Her mind was moving in so many directions that it made her light-headed. It seemed too great of a coincidence that the cameras would fail so close to Piers's death. "Could this be a result of human tampering?"

Taj shrugged. "I suppose. Someone could have come in here and erased the missing hours. But why would anyone do that?"

"Yeah." Remy frowned at the screen. "Spirits can affect technology but not normally to that degree."

"Not all the cameras at once," Taj agreed. "And especially not these cameras. They were designed to withstand the energy pulses spirits can emit. I've never had them fail on me before."

Remy shook her head as she rose. "Keep looking through them. See if you can find anything else unusual."

If a human edited the tapes, which of us would have a reason to? Marjorie didn't want Taj to watch the film, but I'd be surprised if she knew the technology well enough to erase it. Unless Bernard helped her. But I can't imagine any reason for the others to tamper with it...

The door creaked as it was nudged open, and Mark entered, carrying two mugs. He flashed Remy a smile as he handed her one. "I know you said you'd wait for lunch, but you looked like you could use something warm. Besides, Bernard very graciously informed me that he's setting the table, so it's a moot point either way."

She laughed and took the cup. "All right, thanks. I might go and see if he needs any help."

"You can try. But I have this weird premonition that he'd prefer to be alone."

"Oh no, did he snap at you, too?"

"Only a little." Mark offered a hand to Lucille, who had slumped over the couch's armrest. "Hey, Lu, time for lunch. Come on, you'll feel better after some food."

She looked ghastly. Her blond hair was becoming matted, and day-old makeup had smudged around her eyes. She stared at Mark's hand for a second then grudgingly took it and let him pull her toward the foyer with April on her other side for support.

"When can we leave?" Her words were slurred.

"Soon." April spoke soothingly. "When the rain stops."

"I can't stay here for much longer. It's killing me."

"Shh, you'll be okay. Have some food, then you can go and take a nap."

Remy quietly excused herself as the others moved into the dining room. She speared off to the kitchen, her mind still buzzing with Taj's videos.

Bernard was stacking sandwiches and fruit onto trays. He glanced up when Remy entered, then grunted as he returned to his work. "I don't want help."

"Who said I wanted to help you? Maybe I'm here to be a nuisance."

He frowned, but she caught a sliver of a smile under his frosty demeanor.

Remy scooted up a chair behind the counter and sat, mug clasped between her hands. "Actually, I wanted to ask you about last night."

He didn't encourage her, but he also didn't tell her to leave, so Remy tried her question. "Did Marjorie sleepwalk?"

"Yes." His voice was crisp. "She always does."

"Do you remember what time?"

"Shortly before four."

That was after Piers died. "Did she…go downstairs?"

"No. I found her looking at the staircase into the attic."

Remy squeezed her hands tighter around the mug as she tried to phrase herself gently. "She didn't ask you to make any changes to the tapes, did she? I won't be angry if she did, but—"

Bernard's lip curled. "What? I wouldn't have touched that equipment, even if she *had* asked me. I don't tamper with other people's property. You must have a poor impression of me if you think I would."

"It's not that. It's just—part of the tapes were erased, and there are only so many people in the house—"

"I suggest you ask one of them instead of me." He cut the final sandwich and passed one of the trays to Remy. "You can help now."

Remy tried not to let her frustration show as she followed Bernard back to the dining room. *If Marjorie or Bernard wasn't responsible, is it possible it really was a supernatural event? A large enough pulse could have broken through Taj's precautions. But it would have to be powerful.*

She'd been working on a theory that Marjorie might have been the reason Piers had left the kitchen—possibly even the cause behind the heart attack—but the times didn't line up. If Bernard was being truthful, there was at least half an hour between the cameras cutting out and Marjorie leaving her room.

She followed Bernard into the dining room and set her tray on the table. Bernard disappeared back toward the kitchens, and Remy settled into a seat and picked up one of the sandwiches. They were evenly filled and cut with Bernard's trademark precision, and the sight created an emptiness in Remy's chest as she remembered Piers's messy masterpieces.

The doors slammed open, and Marjorie stormed in, breathing heavily and her cheeks flushed. "Who did it?" she demanded, glaring at each of them in turn. "Who vandalized my room? I'll not tolerate this kind of disrespect."

Remy stood. "What happened?"

"Someone cut up my door—that's what happened!" She pointed at Taj. "It was you, wasn't it? You were nagging about that séance."

The party turned their attention to Taj, who held up his hands. "I haven't touched your room, I swear."

"Well, someone did. Someone went in there while we were in the smoking room. Who?"

No one responded. After a second, Remy said, "Can I see it?"

Marjorie sniffed, adjusted her shawl, and turned on her heel. "Come. See. It's blatant harassment."

CHAPTER 26
THE NEXT STEP

REMY FOLLOWED MARJORIE UP the grand staircase, with the others close behind her. Even Lucille showed enough curiosity to leave her seat and trail after them.

The house was gradually growing colder, and Remy didn't think it was her imagination. On their arrival, Carrow had been a cool but comfortable temperature. But despite three days of fires lit in the major rooms, a deep chill was invading. She wore her heaviest jacket and still would have liked to be warmer.

She hadn't been upstairs since being woken the night before, and the long hallway felt strangely foreign. She'd walked the faded carpet dozens of times and welcomed guests into each of the rooms, but that day, she felt like a stranger.

"Here," Marjorie said, knocking open the door to her room and ushering them inside. "I want to know who wrote it."

On the back of her door, gouged into the dark wood, were the words DEATH IS THE NEXT STEP.

Remy reached forward to touch the marks. They were jagged and uncoordinated, as though carved in a hurry. The phrase felt vaguely familiar, but she couldn't place it.

"What does it mean?" April asked. "Next step? Like, the afterlife?"

"It's nonsense to me, child." Marjorie sniffed again. "Taj, I know you did it. You may as well admit it."

"I swear I didn't." He looked honestly insulted. "I was in the recreation room the entire time you were having your séance. Lucille can vouch for that."

Lucille hiccupped and rubbed at red eyes, smearing her mascara even further.

"Well, if it wasn't you, who did it? It wasn't there this morning."

"Maybe…" April cleared her throat. "Maybe one of the ghosts?"

"Nonsense. I've already told you that spirits can't affect the physical world unless they're poltergeists, and poltergeists don't have anywhere near this level of control. Asking a poltergeist to write on a door is like asking a tornado to vacuum your carpet."

Taj shrugged. "Well, it wasn't me. I didn't budge from my corner all morning."

Marjorie scowled and massaged her temples. "Who else could it have been? Did anyone slip away from the group, even for just a couple of minutes? Bernard was in the kitchen, but I trust him implicitly. Remy, Mark, and April were with me for the séance. That leaves… Lucille, did you do this?"

Lucille hiccupped again and shook her head.

"I have a camera filming the hallway," Taj said. "I could check it, if you like."

She sent him a shrewd look. "Yes. I'll review the film with you. As long as you haven't done anything to tamper with it—"

"Of course I didn't," he snapped. "Honestly, woman. What sort of person do you think I am?"

"That's enough." Remy stepped between them and spread her arms to quiet the argument. "Go review the film, if you want. But I'm finishing my lunch. I'm starving, and I have the feeling we could all benefit from some food."

A sullen silence fell over the group, then one at a time, they began shuffling back into the hallway. Remy left last, brushing her fingertips over the markings on the way out. "Death is the next step…" she breathed.

Mark, looking weary, waited for her in the hallway and matched her pace as they moved toward the stairs. "Any theory on who or what did it?"

"No, but I could swear I've heard the words before. If this place had an Internet connection, I would look it up."

"It sounds vaguely poetic, but I have the feeling whatever poem it came from is one of the depressing, existential ones."

They reached the base of the stairs. Taj and Marjorie continued toward the recreation room, both stubbornly keeping an awkward distance from each other, as the rest of the group returned to the dining room.

Remy knew something was amiss before she reached the door.

A faint hum was audible, and the atmosphere felt imperceptibly wrong. She pushed open the door and gagged.

The platters of food Bernard had laid on the table were rotten. Massive plumes of green and gray mold grew out from the sandwiches. Hundreds of flies buzzed around the mess, their wings filling the place with a disquieting whirr. Maggots coiled through the bread, spilling out in writhing piles.

Remy pressed a hand over her mouth as the smell and the sight combined to fill her with dizzying nausea. April gagged beside her, doubled over, and was sick.

"Shut the doors." Mark grabbed both Remy's and April's arms and pulled them back. Remy slammed the door, shutting in the flies and the stench, and stumbled away from it. The nauseating odor lingered on her tongue. She dragged in deep breaths, desperate for clean air as she waited for her stomach to settle.

"How…" April began. Her face was sweaty and pale, and her eyes watered. "We were just there—"

"Did anyone eat the food?" Remy asked, dreading the answer.

Mark and April shook their heads.

She glanced toward the recreation room, where Marjorie and Taj were debating over the screens in muted voices, then looked toward the kitchen. "Where's Bernard?"

At the sound of his name, he appeared in the kitchen doorway and raised an eyebrow in a silent question. Remy, feeling helpless and ridiculous, motioned toward the dining room. "Did you… know? Did you see it?"

He frowned at her, crossed to the door, and opened it. Remy

was prepared for the smell and took several steps back to keep her stomach steady.

Bernard stood in the door for a second then turned to look at Remy, confusion and irritability warring for dominance on his face. "What am I supposed to see?"

Remy and Mark glanced at each other then stepped nearer to the door. The buzzing hum had disappeared, and Remy couldn't detect the rotting stench except for what lingered at the back of her throat.

The room had returned to normal. The sandwiches, fresh and impeccably neat, waited on the trays. She looked at the floor where April had been sick, but it was clean.

"I…I…" She gave Bernard a helpless look. "They were rotting. Maggots and…"

His lip curled. "If you don't like my food, just say so."

"No, it's not that—"

Bernard was already returning to the kitchen.

Remy swallowed and said to April and Mark, "I'm not going crazy, am I? You both saw it, too, didn't you?"

"Yes," Mark said.

April didn't speak, but her green tinge was all the answer Remy needed. She gave the room a final glance, searching the shadows, but it looked no different from how it had before they went upstairs. "It looks so…normal. I never thought normalcy would unnerve me."

"Well, I'm not eating it," April said, finding her voice. "Not after that."

"Seconded," Mark said.

A single fly buzzed past Remy then spiraled up toward the ceiling. She slammed the door closed.

Marjorie and Taj were both hunched over the desk by the computers. Marjorie looked far more composed than she had before, and she even smiled at them as they entered the room. "My friend Taj's reputation has been cleared. This is really the most amazing thing—we've watched the tapes from the moment I left my room this morning to when I returned to it, and no one else even came up the stairs."

Remy pulled up a seat next to them.

Marjorie saw the look on her face and tilted her head. "What is it, dear?"

She told Marjorie about what they'd seen in the dining room.

The medium nodded slowly, fascination lighting up her face. "Sounds like a slip in time."

"I read about those." April was still pallid, but her voice had regained some of its energy. "Wasn't there a house where one of the rooms would alternate between a modern style and being decorated like it was the '60s, and you wouldn't know what to expect until you opened the door?"

"Embrey House, yes. Slips almost always take you back in time, but it sounds like you encountered one of the very rare forward slips."

Remy pulled a face. "Lucky us."

"Don't worry, they're quite harmless. They only play with your perception of an area. I'm starting to feel like I underestimated this house." Marjorie propped her chin on her fingers. "I always knew its energy was abnormally high, but a few little things are making me suspect we haven't seen all it's capable of. Excuse me, dears. I'd like to do a little research."

She left the room at a quick trot.

Taj stretched back in his chair and grinned. "It sucks about lunch. But did you hear what she said? I've been acquitted of my vandalism charges. She made me go through the film *twice* before she admitted it."

"It still leaves the question of where the marks came from," Mark said.

"Maybe someone put them there yesterday, but she didn't see them this morning. Remember, she came downstairs after she heard Lucille's scream. She probably wasn't paying attention to what her door looked like."

"Maybe," Remy agreed.

Taj scratched at his chin, and his eyes wandered toward the foyer. "So…lunch. You said it's back to normal. Does that mean it's edible?"

That was enough to make Remy laugh. "Anything's edible if you're brave enough. Personally, I don't think I could eat it without getting sick. But you're welcome to it if you want it."

"Oh good, that means I get seconds." Taj was out of his chair before Remy could blink, leaving her with Mark and April.

Mark sighed. "I admire his enthusiasm, but I won't be joining him. There's plenty of other food, though, including nonperishables such as cereal and canned fruit. I'd like to see a slip in time try to ruin those. Should I bring you two some?"

"Yes, please," Remy said then frowned as she looked around the room. "Where's Lucille?"

"Huh—" Mark sat up a little straighter. "I remember her being in Marjorie's room with us. Did she come down the stairs?"

"She probably decided to skip lunch and cut straight to the nap." April moved to follow Taj out the door. "I'd better bring her some water, or she'll get a headache, and it'll be constant complaining this evening."

"Thanks," Remy said. Both Mark and April left, leaving her to her thoughts.

She crossed to the window and pressed near to the glass. The sky remained an ominous black, and the wind roared. Remy shivered and wrapped her arms around herself as a wave swept up and hit the glass.

This seemed like such a good idea when we were planning it. Now I wish I'd never come.

Something clicked in her mind, and she gasped. "I wish I'd never started, but I cannot stop…"

She recalled leaving her little black book of Carrow's history on one of the recreation room's side tables and jogged to retrieve it. She had to hunt for several minutes, but she found the photocopy she was looking for.

Shortly following Edgar's death, his room had been searched. On his writing desk was a mess of scribbled messages. Most were illegible, and almost none of them made sense, but a handful had been kept. Remy found the one she was looking for, unfolded it, and squinted to read the messy handwriting by the dim lights.

The paper held nothing but a few lines of seemingly meaning-less text. It was written at an angle, as though scribbled late at night, and blotches of ink indicated a shaky hand. *I wish I'd never started, but I cannot stop. Death is the next step. Heaven owes me no mercy, so I will make my own.*

She reread the phrase several times, but it offered no additional clues. It was clear, though, that whoever had written the message on Marjorie's door had read the note, which was boggling. It was an obscure message. Remy, who had always found Edgar a fasci-nating character, had kept copies of his letters, but the average person wouldn't even know they existed.

Has someone been reading through my book? I left it out in the open so that they could...but I never saw anyone touch it.

Remy's eyes drifted toward the window. The storm raged, waves crashed against the cliffs below the house, and lightning crackled through the black clouds like broken fingers.

A figure fell past the window.

CHAPTER 27
HUNT

REMY'S MOUTH DROPPED OPEN. Her mind seized up as panic washed through her, then she was running toward the window, moving so quickly that the cut on her arm burned. She hit the pane hard enough to rattle the glass and leave herself breathless. Pressing her face against it, she tried to see the water below. The storm hid the environment as it pummeled the cliff wall.

I saw someone fall...

She screamed for help.

But was it a person, or was it a spirit reliving its death?

She pressed even closer to the glass, hunting for any flash of color in the spray-veiled waves below. Footsteps thundered toward her, and Mark burst into the room.

He seized Remy's shoulders and swung her around. "What happened? Are you okay?"

"I saw—someone fell—I think—past the window—or a

spirit—" She knew she wasn't making sense, but her brain couldn't piece the phrases together. "I-I…"

"You saw someone fall?" His brows pulled together as he ran a hand over his mouth.

"I think so. Maybe. It was so fast—"

"We need to account for the group," he said, turning toward the door. "Call them together. Make sure we're not missing anyone."

"Yes." Purpose gave Remy focus, and she ran into the foyer with Mark. They began calling for their friends. Remy turned in a circle and counted the guests as they arrived. Bernard came out of the kitchens, followed by Taj from the dining room. Marjorie appeared at the top of the stairs, scowling.

"Excuse my language," she said, adjusting her shawl as she paced down the stairs, "but what the hell is this hullaballoo about? Has the food gone rotten again?"

Remy couldn't spare time or breath on an answer. She pushed past Marjorie and dashed up the stairs in search of April and Lucille.

She'd only reached the halfway landing when April appeared at the top of the staircase, her eyes huge. "What's happening? Is it Lucille?"

"Lucille?" Remy's mouth was so dry that the words escaped as a rasp. "Is she with you?"

April shook her head. "I can't find her. I've been looking everywh—"

Remy swore. She turned to Mark, but he only stared back at her, his face a mask of growing horror.

"Search the house," Remy said, then she spoke louder so that the others could hear her. "I think I saw someone fall into the ocean. We need to look for Lucille. Look *everywhere*."

April made an awful choking noise and ran down the stairs, past Remy, and into the lower rooms.

They scattered, all moving into different parts of the building. Carrow's air was saturated with the sound of banging doors and calls of "Lucille! *Lucille!*"

Remy tried to hold on to hope. Lucille had been drunk. She could have passed out in a shadowy corner where she couldn't hear their calls. But her mind kept revisiting the memory of the falling figure and imagining Lucille's features on it. She could picture the woman's blond hair whipping around her face, her hand stretched toward the window beseechingly, her eyes huge with terror…

April screamed Lucille's name louder than anyone else, but her voice kept cracking. She was frantic, racing from room to room without seeming to know what she was doing. It tore at Remy's heart.

Remy was the most familiar with Carrow, so she automatically took on the task of looking in the less-traveled parts of the house. She started in the basement, only sparing a brief glance at Piers's ashen face before leaning over the barrier. She looked in the nearest row of holes in case Lucille had stumbled down there and fallen in one, but they were empty except for puddles of water and old slime. She panned her light across the ground farther into the space, but its dust was undisturbed.

From the basement, she went into the servants' passages at the back of the house. She hunted through the narrow rooms, being careful to search each one thoroughly before moving on. Her voice was growing hoarse from calling for Lucille by the time she returned to the foyer.

Mark met her in the center of the room, under Edgar's gaze. His face was coated with perspiration, but Remy thought it was more from fear than exertion.

"Where did you look?" she asked.

"The upstairs bedrooms and part of the attic. I didn't go far into it, but I couldn't see her, and she didn't answer when I called."

Remy ran her hands through her hair. She felt sick. "I've looked in all of the back parts of the house. The others have gone through the main rooms multiple times. She's not here."

Mark swore quietly.

Doors continued to bang as the others searched. Remy was struggling to think straight. Quickly becoming more imagination than actual recollection, the memory of the figure plunging past the window replayed over and over in her mind.

April dashed past them to the front doors. Mark called out and ran after her, catching her as she wrenched open the doors. Rain poured in, drenching them both, and wind howled through the opening to buffet Remy and knock one of the antique photographs off the wall.

"Lucille!" the girl screamed, struggling against Mark's arms as she tried to run into the storm. "Lu! Lu!"

"Calm down," he barked. "This won't help her!"

April slumped, her shoulders shaking, her face twisted as the downpour plastered her hair to her face.

Mark kept an arm around her to hold her upright. "Remy, is there any way to get down to the ocean?"

She hesitated. "Yes. But it's dangerous—"

"I've got to try. Stay here with April. I'll be back soon."

"I'm coming with you." Remy turned back to the foyer and its stack of supplies. "Help me find some rope."

"No, you're not. Not with your arm hurt."

"You don't know the way down," she retorted. "The path is hidden. You'll miss it if you don't know where to look. Besides, it will be safer with two people. Help me here. We need rope and torches."

Mark grimaced, then he hustled April back into the foyer and joined Remy at the boxes. "They're in one of the larger crates."

Taj and Marjorie came from different parts of the house, both breathless and pale.

Remy pointed to Marjorie. "Keep April with you. Take care of her."

"I'm coming, too," the girl said.

As Remy dragged one of the crates off its stack to look in the one below, she said, "No. I need you to keep searching for Lucille here. You know her best, so you need to go through the rooms again, thoroughly. Look in closets, under beds, behind curtains." April opened her mouth to argue, and Remy cut her off. "If you come with us, I'll worry about you. I need to focus on looking for Lucille, not keeping you safe."

Taj stared from them to the open door. "You're going down the cliffs?"

"Yes."

"Isn't it dangerous?"

"Yes."

He swallowed and pulled off his jacket. "Then I'll help. Just tell me what to do."

"Got them." Mark rose, a bundle of rope and two flashlights in his hands. He threw the flashlights to Taj and Remy and slung the rope over his shoulder. "Let's go."

"Everyone else stays here." Remy put force into her voice as they jogged to the door. "No one is to leave the house until we return. Understood?"

Marjorie placed one arm around April's shoulders. The teen's face was blotchy with tears. Bernard stood at the back of the room, his long face exceptionally grave. Remy gave them a final parting glance then stepped out into the storm.

CHAPTER 28
BITTER OCEAN

REMY LED HER GROUP toward the copse of pine trees at a run. She was already exhausted from searching the house but couldn't bring herself to slow down when every second might be precious. Freezing rain poured over them. Within seconds, it had soaked Remy's clothes, turning the bandages on her arm into a sodden mess.

Their flashlight beams jittered over the landscape, catching glimpses of muddy ground and gnarled trees. Remy was surprised by how strong the wind was; she had to fight against it, leaning heavily to one side to keep herself from being blown off course. It snatched her words away as she yelled instructions over her shoulder. "We're going to climb down to the beach. Then I'll tie the rope around myself and go down to the ocean's edge. The pair of you stay on higher ground and keep a hold of the rope's other end. Make sure I don't get caught in a wave."

"I'll go to the water," Mark offered.

"No. It's got to be me. I'm the lightest. I'll need your muscles keeping me grounded."

He called something back, sounding unhappy, but the words were drowned out in a thunderclap.

Remy reached the woods and slowed her pace to a walk. The trees, knotted and twisted, were nearly impossible to walk through. Remy struggled between them until she found the overgrown path she knew led to the cliff's edge.

"Rope," she called, and Mark tossed one end to her. She wrapped it tightly around her unhurt hand. "Both of you, hold on to it. The stairs down are steep and slippery. Lean into the rocks so the wind can't get behind you."

The path ended a dozen paces ahead. Lightning flashed across the sky, highlighting the cliff's edge and the ocean's great, crashing waves below them. Remy slowed even further as she approached the cliffs, tightening her grip on the rope. She did her best to swallow her fear as she stepped over the edge.

The staircase had been carved into the cliff side for access to the water when Carrow was a health resort. An outcropping of rock sheltered it from the waves. That didn't keep bursts of spray from frothing over it, though. Salty water filled Remy's mouth, and she spat it back out.

They moved single file, clinging to the rope with one hand and the rocks with the other. The stairs were uneven and coated in slime. Twice, Remy lost her footing but managed to regain it. Sharp tugs on the rope told her the others were struggling, too.

She fought to find a balance between preserving their own safety and hurrying as much as possible for Lucille's sake.

More lightning flashed, highlighting the wet rock and the waves' crests. She couldn't see any color among them.

Remy couldn't stop her mind from replaying all of the deaths that had stained the stairs and the rock pools below. Two drunk guests had slipped and fallen over the edge of the stairs, cracking their skulls open on the rocks below. A family had gone down to bathe, only to be trapped there by a sudden storm. Men and women had been caught in riptides and drowned.

Her hands were numb, and her whole body was shaking by the time they reached the shielded pool Carrow's guests had once bathed in. The area stood just above sea level but was protected from the worst of the storm by a row of tall, rough rocks. Waves poured over them, sweeping around Remy's feet and nearly tipping her over before retreating again. Remy unraveled the rope from her hand and quickly tied it under her arms, double knotting it for security. She beckoned the other two forward, toward the edge of the rock.

"The waves come from that direction," she said, pointing away from them. "You won't be caught up in them as long as you stay behind this rock. Keep a tight hold on the rope. A slow pull means I need more tether. If you feel me give two hard tugs, it means I need to be pulled back in. Okay?"

Mark took her arm, his expression tight with anxiety. Knowing he was going to ask to switch places again, she slipped out of his grip before he could speak. If she were stopped for even a second, her courage would fail. She crept to the rock's edge and looked around.

From that vantage point, she could see the sheer cliff side leading up to Carrow. The house's lights were on, turning it into a steady beacon at the top of the bluff. She waited, watching, as a massive wave swept in. It hit the rocks, bursting upward as its spray drenched the building. Remy ducked back behind the rock to shield herself, but she still had to hold her breath as overflow poured over her. The ocean was cold enough to make her feel as though she had been encased in ice. As soon as the water retreated, she stepped around the barrier and faced the cliffs.

The waves came in cycles: three to four small swells then a large one. The small waves would sweep over the rocks, but she thought she could endure them. The large ones were the danger-ous ones.

The space was a mess of rock pools and uneven boulders. Remy moved across them as quickly as she dared, leaping from one rise to another, desperately hoping Lucille might have managed to swim to the rocks or even become trapped between them. "Lucille!"

A wave swept forward, and Remy dropped down, wrapping her arms around one of the jagged shapes. The water rushed around her, filling her ears with its roar and pulling furiously as it tried to loosen her grip. She held on, waiting until the water abated, then rose and continued moving forward. The rope tugged at her as the men meted it out.

The rock pools lasted only briefly then dropped away. The

water directly below Carrow was deep. If Lucille had fallen, she would have plunged into the ocean rather than hit the rocks. Remy bent over the edge of a boulder. She hunted among the waves, her flashlight beam picking out frothing water and nothing more. "Lucille!"

She already knew it was hopeless, but she couldn't stop herself from looking. She ran her flashlight across the ocean, up the steep cliff side, then over the rock pools. A wave caught her off guard, and Remy had to jam her foot into the crevice between two rocks to brace against it. The water swept around her, filling her with fresh panic. Her heart beat so furiously that she worried she might pass out. Then the wave passed, and Remy began searching again. She shut her mind against the fear and against the pain of a dozen little nicks growing over her arms and legs. She began stepping among the rock pools again, looking for any sign of color.

There! A flash of pale skin moved in one of the holes. Remy gasped Lucille's name and ran forward, reckless in her hope. The woman lay facedown in a pool, fully submerged, and Remy dropped onto her knees and thrust both arms into the water to pull her out. Her fingers passed through what felt like ice but didn't touch the figure.

The submerged woman rolled over languidly, apparently moving in the swell, and her face turned toward the sky. Remy tried to muffle a scream. The woman in the pool was a stranger. Brown hair and a long white dress billowed around her as the body rolled. The face turned upward, exposing empty eye sockets, a gaping, toothless mouth, and mottled green skin. Remy barely had a second to feel sick, then a new wave rushed onto her ledge. She was unprepared. It swept her back, scraping her across the rock, and she grasped at the stone to keep herself from being dragged over the edge and into the ocean. Her cut arm burned, and her numb fingers struggled to find purchase. Then the rope became taut and started pulling. Remy sucked in a breath as her head cleared from the water, and she yelled, "I'm okay!"

They either didn't hear or didn't trust her. She had to stumble to keep up with the rope as it reeled her back in. As she passed the rock pool, she looked into the dark bowl of water, but the dead woman had vanished.

A specter, then.

Mark and Taj didn't stop pulling until Remy was back around the sheltered side of the rock. Mark wrapped his arms around her, and Remy leaned against his shoulder as she sucked in quick breaths to fill her hungry lungs. His grip was tight, and she felt him shaking. Taj rubbed her shoulder, silent but sharing in her emotions. One of the larger waves hit, crashing up the cliff side and drenching the three friends.

"We're not going to find her," Mark said after a moment.

Remy, incapable of speaking, nodded. She'd known finding the woman alive was a slim hope, but feeling the waves' force had removed even that.

Lucille was gone.

CHAPTER 29
REGRET

THE CLIMB BACK UP the cliff side was excruciating. They'd lost the urgency that had driven them going down, but the storm continued to batter them, taxing already-exhausted muscles. Remy's mind slipped into a fugue.

As they reached the top of the stairs and reentered the safety of the woods, Mark took the rope back and wrapped it around his shoulder. He then gripped Remy's hand in his own and led her through the trees. She could feel his fingers still shaking and squeezed back to tell him it was okay.

Except it's not okay.

Lucille was gone. Remy had told April to search the house again, but she already knew they wouldn't find the missing woman. She had been taken by the ocean—and would likely have been dead before they'd even started searching for her.

Tears mixed with the saltwater and rain on Remy's cheeks,

but she didn't try to stop them. It was her fault Lucille was gone. After Piers's death, she'd vowed to watch over all of Carrow's guests, but she hadn't noticed when Lucille split from their party. And that moment of inattention had cost her dearly.

They stepped out of the woods and were assaulted with fresh sheets of rain. A figure pacing along the trees' edge turned and jogged toward them. Even from a distance, Remy recognized the blue highlights in April's hair.

They met halfway. Neither spoke. Then April pressed her hands to her face and broke into sobs. Remy put her arm around the girl and held her close as they walked slowly back to the house.

The following moments were a blur. Remy and April were separated, and Remy found herself back in the recreation room, staring at the fire while Mark pressed towels into her hands and urged her to dry herself.

She felt mentally and emotionally dead. Cold had filled her insides, and the fire wasn't doing much to remove it.

"Here." Mark spoke softly as he dabbed a towel over her dripping hair. "I got some clothes from your luggage. Will you be okay if I leave the room while you change?"

"Hmm." She blinked, shook her head, and tried to collect herself. "Where's April?"

"Upstairs. Marjorie's looking after her." When she didn't take the bundle of clothes he held toward her, Mark placed them on the nearby table. "I'm going to make you a hot drink. Please change. I don't want you to get sick."

Remy's mind felt full of salt water, and it was a struggle to assess what needed to be done. She held a hand toward Mark as he began to leave. "Someone needs to search Lucille's room. For a note or an open window or any other clue for why she…" Remy didn't want to say *jumped*, so she cleared her throat. "For why she fell."

"I'll do that." Mark took Remy's outstretched hand, gave it a squeeze, then disappeared through the door.

Remy had never minded solitude before, but as she dripped on the rug and stared at the fire, she felt desperately lonely. Faint noises floated through the house, but she couldn't distinguish the human sounds from the creaks the weather wrung out of the ancient building.

When the chills set in, Remy was finally motivated to change. She did so quickly, toweling herself off and hopping into the clothes Mark had brought her. She left the wet clothes on the stone hearth, where they wouldn't damage the carpet. She was drying her hair when a knock startled her. "Come in."

Bernard entered, carrying a steaming mug. He didn't speak—or even look at her—before setting the cup on the table and turning back to the door. He hesitated with his fingers resting on the handle then spoke in an uncharacteristically hushed tone. "That was a brave thing you did."

"Oh." Rather than brave, she felt scattered, useless, and helpless. "Not really. It didn't actually *help*."

He shrugged and left as silently as he'd arrived. Remy slumped into a chair and let the solitude consume her once more.

The cup of tea was nearly cold by the time Marjorie came down the stairs. The older woman exhaled heavily as she slid into the chair opposite Remy. "The child's asleep, poor thing. Exhausted. I'll check in on her later in case she wakes up."

"Thanks." Remy gazed at her folded hands. "How bad is she?"

"Oh, pretty bad, I suppose. She didn't want to talk." Marjorie stretched her feet toward the flames. The light played across her face and made her eyes look unusually bright. "This is always the worst part of death. The people left behind have to suffer so much more."

"April was incredibly close to Lucille," Remy said. "They'd had that fight, but you could tell they were like sisters."

The door creaked, and Remy glanced over her shoulder. Mark and Taj entered, both wearing dry clothes. They took up seats next to Remy and Marjorie, creating a semicircle around the fire. Mark sat on the edge of his seat, hands braced on his knees, and Remy instantly knew something was wrong.

"What is it?"

He cleared his throat. "I looked through the upstairs rooms like you suggested. No note that I could find, and I was pretty thorough. I also tried to find the window she fell through—but they're all shut, and most of them are frozen in place."

Remy frowned. "That's...bizarre. How else could she get outside on this side of the house?"

Mark nodded to Taj.

The researcher looked wrung out. He rubbed a hand over the back of his neck. "While we were in Room 8, I felt a drop of water hit my arm. It was coming through the ceiling, so I went into the attic. One of the windows was open and letting water into the house."

"Oh." Remy pressed a hand over her mouth. She hadn't thought of the attic. Lucille had been heavily drunk and so uncoordinated that Remy was amazed she'd been able to climb the stairs.

"But this is the weird bit," Taj continued. "There were three sets of shoe prints in the dust. Two pairs going to the window, one coming back."

Remy blinked at Taj then Mark. Uneasiness wormed its way through the shock. "Someone was up there with her?"

Mark held up a hand. "Not necessarily. It's possible all three sets belong to Lucille. She could have gone to the window, changed her mind and returned to the stairs, then changed her mind again and leaped."

"Whoever the prints belong to was shuffling," Taj said. "It made the marks too smudged to see clearly."

Remy stood, ignoring her sore muscles, and began pacing. "There's a chance Lucille was up there alone. But there's a chance someone was with her, too. And if someone was with her, they either saw her jump or…"

"Pushed her," Marjorie finished, scowling.

"Yes. And if they didn't push her, if they were innocent, why didn't they say something?" Remy exhaled and ran her hands through her damp hair. "We've got to wake April and get her down here. Bernard, too. I don't think it's a wise idea for us to be scattered through the house any longer."

Lightning flashed through the window, sending a sharp burst of light across the furniture. Thunder cracked in its wake, and Remy shuddered. She'd only known the people in the room for a handful of days, but she'd grown to trust them. In fact, they'd become her friends. The idea that one of them might have caused a death was unimaginable. At the same time, she needed to consider and prepare against the possibility. She couldn't let anyone else in her group be hurt.

The door's hinges creaked as they turned. April stepped through the opening. Her hair was disheveled, and dark circles hung around her eyes, but she'd stopped crying. Without saying a word, she crossed the room and curled herself into one of the couches in the corner.

"Couldn't sleep, dear?" Marjorie asked. When April didn't reply, the medium exhaled and rose. "I'll fetch Bernard. If we're lucky, he might have started on some kind of dinner we can bring back with us."

Remy couldn't stop pacing. The shock of losing Lucille still lingered, but her brain had caught up and was furiously working through the puzzle. The last time they'd seen Lucille was while examining the cuts on Marjorie's door. They'd then gone downstairs while Lucille presumably stayed on the second floor. Remy, Mark, and April had discovered the rotten food in the dining room while Taj and Marjorie had gone into the sitting room to review the cameras.

After that, they'd split up. Mark had gone to look for food. April was going to take Lucille water. Marjorie had said something about research, and Taj had gone to eat the no-longer-rotten lunch. Bernard was in the kitchen. Any of them could have gone to the upper floor. The task would have needed to be completed quickly—the time between separating and Remy seeing the falling body had been no more than ten minutes—but it would have been manageable for any of them.

The person with the easiest opportunity was April; she'd said she was going to visit Lucille, after all. But Remy couldn't believe the teen would willingly hurt her guardian, despite the fight. After Lucille's breakdown, April had been nothing but caring.

Remy turned toward Taj. "You still have your camera set up in the hallway, right? You'd be able to see if someone followed Lucille up the stairs?"

"Yes." His eyes lit up, and he pushed out of his chair. "I would indeed."

Remy followed him to the computer. Various images flashed across the screen, followed by black.

Taj's eyebrows gradually lowered, and he pressed his lips together. "The cameras are cutting out again."

"How much of the recordings have you lost?"

He pressed more buttons, typed in commands, then swore. "Most of them. The hallway camera has been dead since eleven this morning. The foyer died shortly after midday, came on for five minutes, then crashed again."

Remy blew a frustrated breath out through her teeth. "What's causing it?"

"Hell if I know." He sat back in the chair, his mouth twisted in frustration. "No one's been tampering with this computer, have they?"

"Not that I've seen."

"I guess someone could be pulling the plugs directly out of the cameras. Or the cameras themselves could be malfunctioning—except, if that's the case, why's it happening to all of them? They're meant to be resistant against EMF emissions and energy pulses."

Remy folded her arms and moved back to the fireplace, deep in thought. As much as she didn't like considering the possibility, Taj seemed to believe someone was tampering with the footage. And that meant one of them had something to hide.

Marjorie and Bernard returned to the room, carrying trays of food, which they set on the same table they'd used for the séance. Remy waited for them all to take a plate, then she said, "I'm imposing a curfew. There'll be a few new rules until we leave this house."

CHAPTER 30
CURFEW

REMY FILLED APRIL AND Bernard in on the extra footprints Taj had found in the attic. April's face steadily darkened, though she stayed perfectly still.

Remy finished by saying, "It's still my belief that no one is to blame for Lucille's death. But there's enough doubt that we're going to tread very, very carefully until the storm clears and we can get to the police. Okay?"

"She didn't kill herself." April's voice was raw but steady, and she sat a little straighter as she spoke. "She wasn't that kind of person. Someone pushed her. And I swear, when I find out which of you—"

"I understand." Remy spoke quickly to cut April off. The teen's stony expression was morphing into something ferocious, and it frightened her. "I'm not saying Lucille's death was intentional. She might have been looking for some cool air, and when she found the bedroom windows were sealed, went into the attic. The wind is brutal. It's possible she fell by accident."

April didn't respond, but the anger lingered in her eyes.

"Still." Taj folded his hands over one knee and averted his gaze. "I don't mean to be insensitive, but we know how unlikely that is. Lucille was distressed. Intoxicated. When we were helping her into the dining room, she actually said that the house was killing her." He licked his lips. "Is it possible that was meant literally? Could one of the spirits have done something to her?"

Marjorie snorted. "I've already said, multiple times, that ghosts can't affect the physical realm unless they're poltergeists."

"Yes, but it's still possible. What if one chased her into the attic?"

"And what? Scared her so badly that she unlatched the window and stepped through?"

Taj shrugged. "Weirder things have been known to happen. We're assuming something scared Piers into having a heart attack."

The discussion was spiraling into a debate over opinions, so Remy tried to pull it back to the facts. "Lucille's death may have been accidental. It may have been deliberate. It may have been forced on her. And it's because of the third possibility that we have to start taking precautions."

"What are you suggesting, dear?" Marjorie asked.

"We don't travel through the house alone. If you need to go somewhere, take at least two other people with you." Remy made eye contact with each guest to ensure they understood and agreed with her. "Communication is important. We should all know where everyone else is at any given moment. And, finally, I'd like to suggest we sleep in this room tonight."

Mark nodded slowly. "It keeps us together and near Taj's surveillance setup. I think that's a good idea. We can bring the mattresses and blankets down here and sleep around the fire."

"Everyone okay with that?" Remy waited until she had a yes from every party. "Good." She settled back into her chair with her plate of food.

The room was quiet except for the scrape of cutlery over ceramic. Remy's thoughts whirled, but they were all directionless. The storm battered at the windows, its mournful wail trailing through the house. She didn't want to watch it, so she turned away from the window to look over the room's furniture and shelves of books instead. The little black diary lying open on the table caught her eye, and she put down her plate. "As an aside— has anyone been reading through the black book I left on the desk back there?"

Some mumbled no; others shook their heads.

"Well, I found the source for the quote in Marjorie's door. It's one of the letters Edgar wrote shortly before his death."

Marjorie's plate clattered as she dropped it onto the table. She retrieved the diary, pulled a pair of glasses out of her pocket, put them on, and squinted to read the words as she returned to her chair. "I wish I'd never started, but I cannot stop. Death is the next step. Heaven owes me no mercy, so I will make my own."

"Does it mean anything to you?" Remy asked.

Marjorie settled into her chair, a frown growing over her eyes as she turned the page and read more of the scrawled messages. Mark and Taj were watching intently. April hadn't stirred, and Bernard's face was enveloped in harsh shadows as he stared at the window. Thunder crackled outside. The medium blew a breath out through her nose and turned another page. "How dangerous is it to leave?"

"Uh…" Remy glanced toward the window. "Really, really, stupidly dangerous. The waves sweep over the road—"

"Yes, you explained all of that." Marjorie still hadn't taken her eyes off the book. She turned the page. "If we tried to cross, what are our odds? Certain death?"

"Uh, no, not quite that severe. But it's not a tiny chance, either. Maybe…I want to say…thirty or forty percent we'd end up in the ocean?"

"They're not good odds." Marjorie turned another page and made a faint, unhappy noise in the back of her throat before snapping the book closed. "But I'm starting to think our odds here aren't so peachy, either."

Remy stared at her. "In what way?"

"Earlier today, shortly before Lucille went missing, I had the strange idea that something about this house was wrong. Carrow's energy levels are far higher than I would expect from a building that's been dormant for decades. I went to search Edgar's room to see if I could find any evidence supporting my hunch but was, of course, interrupted." She lifted the book. "Little did I know that the proof was under my nose this whole time."

"Proof of what?" Uneasiness made Remy rub at the backs of her arms. "Do those messages mean something?"

"They read an awful lot like the writings of a certain cult that had its heyday in the late nineteenth century, dear. You're stretching my memory, but I believe they were called something like The Red Crows of Salisbury. They wore bird skull masks and had a main base only a few towns away. The Red Crows were composed of gifted spirit mediums who manipulated and tormented the dead for their own purposes."

Mark shifted forward in his chair, his face tense. "What purposes?"

"Placing curses on their enemies. Gaining power and influence. Black magic rituals. Extending their lifespans." Marjorie held up a hand to halt questions. "I'm not saying they *succeeded* in these attempts. It's my personal belief that magic as the common person thinks of it is fictional. But energy, especially spiritual energy, can certainly affect the physical world, as we've seen during our time at Carrow.

"One part of their work was attempting to trap spirits on earth. They needed the spirits' energy for their black magic and couldn't very well have their batteries evaporated into the ether, could they? So they worked in highly charged areas, kidnapped and sacrificed people to further their cause, and marked both the bodies and graves with symbols that were supposed to tether the spirit to earth."

Taj asked, "Were there many of these Red Crow people? I haven't heard of them before."

"Oh, not many at all, dear. I only learned about them after encountering a spirit who had been kidnapped by them during life. There were fourteen in the core cult, I believe, and several wives, children, and associates on the fringe of the group. They only operated for eight years before being caught and executed for their crimes."

"And you think Edgar Porter followed their beliefs?" Remy asked. "There aren't any records of him leaving the house for meetings."

"He would have been a young child when the cult was active, and Carrow House hadn't even been built. But based on the writings in this book, I suspect he may have somehow picked up their teachings. He's recorded phrases that were used as part of their rituals."

"Ah." Remy chewed on the corner of her thumb. "All those victims—all those people who died in Carrow—does this mean he wasn't killing them because he was a sociopath, but for a cause?"

"Oh, I'd place money on him being a sociopath, as well, dear." Marjorie smiled. "Now this brings me to the crux of our problem. I doubt the Red Crows had anywhere near as much power as they pretended to. But one thing they were adept at was recognizing environments that could gather energy, then trapping it and building on it. They set their base on ley lines, sacrificed their victims to charge the ground, then worked to hold the spirits at that location. Do you remember the gentleman we met in the upstairs hallway, the one who communicated through the EMF reader? I asked if he had a reason for lingering, and he said he was trapped here. I suspect he isn't the only one."

Mark looked from Remy to Marjorie, his brows pulled tight over his dark eyes. "Is that bad?"

"It means that Carrow may be far more volatile than I had anticipated. Instead of its energy mellowing through all of the years it's been abandoned, it's grown worse. Now, high energy isn't necessarily a bad thing. But it has some…shall we say, repercussions. Carrow has always been prone to storms, but this one has lasted abnormally long for being this early in the season, hasn't it, dear?"

Remy opened her mouth, closed it, and mutely nodded. A wave sprayed up the window, showering it with seawater. Carrow's storms could last for up to a week, but most fizzled out overnight—especially in the early winter months.

"Taj's recordings are being erased," Marjorie continued, listing the points off on her fingers. "The time slip. Spirits are transforming into poltergeists with abnormal ease. Two deaths—even if they were both accidental, that's a bad sign. It's my opinion that this house was charging the entire time it lay dormant, and now that it has guests, it's waking up."

"Waking?" Remy felt faintly sick. "Not woken? As in, it's going to get worse?"

"Oh, almost certainly, dear. I don't know how strong this building is, but I suspect we haven't tasted its full power yet."

Taj swore under his breath. "How bad is it going to get? What…what would peak power look like?"

"I have no clue, dear boy. I only know I'd prefer not to be here to see it." Marjorie pursed her lips as she looked around the gathering. "I don't mean to frighten you all. Please remember, spirits, even in poltergeist form, are largely harmless. What I'm more concerned about is the energy. It can affect humans as much as spirits, often by elevating negative emotions or reducing a person's ability to think calmly and rationally. I don't mean to say Piers's and Lucille's deaths directly resulted from the energy, but I'm sure it didn't help."

"What are we going to do?"

They all turned toward April. The teen's voice was raw and croaky, and she hadn't bothered to brush her disheveled hair away from her face. Strands stuck to her wet lips and eyelids as she spoke. "Two people are dead. It's this house's fault. Are we just going to sit here and wait for it to squeeze the life out of the rest of us?"

Marjorie's smile was gentle, though the expression wasn't returned. "That was my next consideration. We have a few options. We can attempt to cross the bridge to the mainland. As Remy points out, it would be a large risk, but it's still a choice." She swept her hand toward the rest of them. "Or we could conduct a third séance. I'm certain Edgar is the instigator of all of this. If we can communicate with him—possibly even clear his spirit—it may be enough to discharge the worst of the house's energy. Or, finally, we can keep doing what we're doing now—and wait. The storm won't last forever, no matter how much energy goes into prolonging it. Though it will likely endure for another couple of days."

None of the options appealed to Remy. She chewed on her lip. "Let's put it to a vote."

"Bridge," April said without hesitation. "To hell with bad odds. I just want to get out of here."

"While I admire your, uh, nihilistic tendencies, I'm actually pretty invested in staying alive," Taj said. "I say we wait it out."

"Even if it means another week in Carrow?" Marjorie pressed. "That's the potential we're facing. If one of us is a murderer, can we protect ourselves for that long? And I don't mean to get too morbid, but our friend in the basement won't retain his shape much longer, cold spot or no."

They all grimaced.

"How dangerous would a séance be?" Mark massaged the bridge of his nose. "If the energy is high, would it pose a risk to the people participating?"

"Oh, almost none, dear boy. I don't mean to say there's *no* risk, but I've been doing this for nearly forty years. If a spirit became aggressive, I'd be able to handle them."

Remy wished she could believe in Marjorie's words as much as the medium evidently did. She glanced at her wrist. Faint bruises circled where the medium had squeezed her earlier. She drew a long, slow breath. "I'm strongly opposed to leaving while the storm's active. But I don't think I could stay here much longer, either. I'd be willing to try the séance."

"Me too," Mark said.

"All right." Taj clapped his hands on his knees. "That's a majority. I'll join, as well."

April's lips tightened, but she didn't argue.

Looking pleased, Marjorie rose. "I'll prepare the table. Spend a few minutes clearing your minds, my dears. We're going to push further than before, and it would be best if you can approach this experience with a calm disposition."

CHAPTER 31
THE FINAL SÉANCE

REMY TRIED TO FOLLOW Marjorie's advice and relax, but it was impossible. April sat close to the fire, her normally bright face flat and her eyes dead. Taj worked quickly and quietly to set up a camera on the shelf facing the table. Mark stared at his folded hands, saying nothing. Bernard, who had refused to participate in their discussion, hung near the back of the room and glared at the window.

The atmosphere was tense and miserable, and Remy found herself thinking about the small café near her home. If that evening had been a regular tour, she would have been in the middle of cleaning up and only a few hours away from enjoying a warm croissant while the sun rose. Then a comfortable, familiar bed would welcome her home.

I wish I'd never come here. If I hadn't, Piers would still be alive. And if Piers hadn't died, Lucille might not have, either. I'll have to carry that with me forever.

"Right, gather around, everyone," Marjorie called from the table near the center of the room. When the group was sluggish to rise, she clapped her hands. "Come on, don't dally. This is important."

Remy took her place next to Mark, with Marjorie to her left and Taj and April opposite. A chair waited for Bernard, but he lingered by the door, long fingers poised over the light switch. The table had its usual candle, bouquet of shriveling herbs, and the pen. It also held two small condiment bowls. One was filled with a fine white substance, and the other contained a gritty dark mixture. They reminded Remy of salt and pepper.

Instead of reaching out for their hands as she normally did, Marjorie shifted forward in her chair. "I'm going to try a few different things tonight, depending on who gets in touch. If we speak with one of Carrow's more friendly spirits, I'll conduct the séance as normal and ask if they know what's holding them here. If Edgar comes—and I hope he will—I'll first talk with him, then if he's not compliant, I'll attempt to break his hold on this house and forcefully dissipate his energy. If it comes to that, you might see and hear things that alarm you. But don't be frightened. Remember, the dead have very little power in this realm."

She set her pen on its end, lit the candle, then turned to Bernard. "Please turn out the lights above this table, but keep on the ones at the back of the room. I would appreciate some ambient light in case the candle is extinguished."

The switch clicked, and their table fell into muted shadow. The sconces along the back wall and the warm fireplace helped prevent Remy from feeling as though the rest of the world had been erased. She inhaled and took Marjorie's and Mark's hands as Bernard took the chair opposite her.

"Spirits, we wish to communicate with you." Marjorie's drawl was confident and soothing. "Please make yourself known. If you can hear me, tip my pen over."

The pen fell before Marjorie had even finished speaking. She smiled. "I'm glad to meet you, spirit. Can you tell me about yourself? My mind is open."

A spike of horror hit Remy at those words, but Marjorie's soft smile didn't falter. She tilted her head back and closed her eyes, and after a moment, she spoke in hushed tones. "Oh, she's coming through wonderfully clear. A woman. Middle-aged, graying brown hair, Edwardian dress. Her name...her name...I believe it begins with an A."

Realizing the details were meant for her, Remy frowned as she tried to remember the victims who might match that profile.

"Pain across her throat," Marjorie continued. "Then pain in her chest. A knife. She was asleep when he attacked her. I see a number... Sixteen?"

"Anne Pail-Luther," Remy said, a small thrill of triumph battling back some of the fear. "Widowed with adult children. She was traveling to visit her sister and stayed in Room 16 when she went missing. A maid vanished along with her."

Marjorie asked, "Anne?" then smiled widely. "Thank you for speaking with me tonight, Anne. Is Edgar Porter present, as well? No? In that case, can you tell me why you linger in Carrow?"

Marjorie's fingers twitched inside Remy's. The medium had fallen silent, her mouth slightly slack and her eyes barely closed. The peace held for a long moment, then she said, "I don't understand. She's trying to show me, but it's so confused, I can't see…"

Marjorie's eyebrows drew closer together, then she pulled Remy's hand across the table and joined it with Bernard's, effectively cutting herself out of the circle. She took up the pen and snapped its lid off. "Show me, Anne."

Remy felt a small thrill despite her anxiety. She'd read about psychography but had never actually witnessed it before. Marjorie held her hand out and began swirling it in circles, the pen's tip held an inch above the table. The motion continued for several seconds, then she lowered the pen, drawing directly onto the cloth.

The medium's eyelids fluttered as her eyes swiveled from side to side. She drew blindly. The ink began to build up on the cloth in a rough shape. They all leaned forward. It appeared to be some kind of symbol: a circle with an hourglass shape over the top. The lines thickened as Marjorie's hands continued to move, bleeding ink into the white fabric, and her breathing deepened. "What does it do to you?"

The movement stopped, and Marjorie lifted her hand from the table, her eyes still shut. "Anne? Why are you leaving? I want to communicate more if—"

The room's double doors shifted apart. The hinges creaked, creating a slow, grating whine that grew louder until they were fully open. They held that position for a beat then slammed closed, crashing together with such force that Remy's ears hurt.

"Don't break the circle," Marjorie said, taking Remy and Bernard's hands to resume her place. "Keep your minds clear and calm."

Lightning flashed. In that second of blinding illumination, Remy saw the man, tall and gaunt and wearing his old master's clothes, standing behind Marjorie. His eyes flashed as they fixed on Remy, and she tried to shrink away from him.

"Don't break the circle!" Marjorie's fingers were tight. Remy felt a tremor run through them.

"He's here," she gasped. "He's behind you."

"Edgar." Marjorie closed her eyes and lifted her chin high. "We wish to speak with you. Why do you stay at Carrow? Why do you trap these other souls?"

Lightning flooded over them once more. The room's bulbs all lit up, growing impossibly bright, then died in a series of hissing, fizzing pops. The light above their heads burst, raining sparks over them. April cried out, and someone's chair fell over.

"Don't break the circle!" Marjorie barked. "Stay calm!"

The lights were gone—and not just the ones in their room. No glow came from under the doors, either. The fire had died. All that remained was their single candle. Its glow felt impossibly dim. Remy could see the round, shining eyes of her companions, hear their ragged breathing, and feel the hands gripping hers. Her throat had constricted and choked any noise she tried to make. Cold sweat trickled down her back.

Something paced around them. It moved just beyond the circle of light, but she could hear its heavy, thudding footsteps and the groaning floorboards as it circled like a shark. It passed behind Marjorie and encroached on Remy's space, and she felt a wave of chilled air drift over the back of her neck.

"Edgar Porter, your time on earth is finished," Marjorie said.

Remy wasn't sure if it was excitement or fear that introduced a waver to the woman's voice.

"You are dead and have been dead for more than a hundred years. Do not linger. Do not torment the living."

A sound crackled through the room. It was like dead leaves scraping over dirt, like shoes crunching in gravel, like nails being drawn across rough wood. It was Edgar's laugh.

"Why are you holding the other spirits here?" Marjorie pressed. "They cannot help you! They cannot save your soul! Release them and beg for forgiveness. It may not be too late."

The unseen figure continued to circle. April drew a sharp breath as it passed behind her, then Remy felt Marjorie's fingers shudder. A second later, she understood why.

As Edgar passed behind her, the air's temperature dropped horrifically. Remy gasped and felt her lips burn as the moisture on them turned to frost. More than just the cold, she could feel Edgar's *essence*. Pure evil rolled off him, so tangible and repulsive that her stomach flipped. He seemed to charge the air with electricity that raised the hairs on her arms.

"You are not welcome in this realm." Marjorie's voice boomed. She no longer sounded like an elderly woman as she forced authority and assuredness into her words. "Your time on earth is finished, and you will pass over whether you wish to or not."

She dropped Remy's hand to snatch at the bowls on the table. Remy hunted for Bernard's fingers in the dark, found them, and held tight. Marjorie seized a fistful of the white substance and threw it in an arc. Remy watched the grains glitter in the candlelight before vanishing into the shadows as they scattered through the room.

A furious hissing, spitting sound rose from Edgar, growing in volume and intensity.

"You are no longer welcome here!" Marjorie took up a handful of the dark grains and threw it. "Leave now!"

The hiss became a roar. Thunder, louder than ever before, shook through them, jangling Remy's bones. Something—a wave, she thought—impacted the side of the building. The candle flared, its flame shooting upward, then dropped back, fainter than before. The room's doors banged open. Someone grabbed Remy's chair and pulled it out from under her. At the same time, Mark, to her right, lurched. They kept their hands connected, but Remy fell, banging her chin against the table's edge. Taj cried out, then April screamed.

The storm shook the house. The bowls on the table rattled. Something hit one wall, then another, accompanied by harsh smashing noises.

"April!" Taj called. "Where are you? Find my hand!"

"Don't break the circle!" Marjorie yelled.

Bernard barked a cry of alarm. Remy tried to stand. Another wave hit the building. The effect was like an earthquake, and Remy dropped back to the ground, pulling Mark with her.

Then all fell quiet.

The storm softened. The candle, still upright in the center of the table, hissed and flickered back to life. Remy kept her hold on Mark's and Bernard's hands as she rose to her knees.

For a second, they all held still, barely able to see each other in the dim light but too afraid to move. Marjorie's breaths came in quick gasps. Then Bernard released Remy's hand and jogged to the wall. He pressed the light switch. The fixture above their table hissed and sparked then died again, but some of the sconces along the wall lit up.

Remy stared at the pale, shaken faces around her. She counted five, including herself. April was missing.

CHAPTER 32
NEW VOTES

"APRIL!" REMY STAGGERED TO her feet. Terror choked her voice. "April! Answer me!"

A crunching noise came through the open doors, and Remy jogged toward it. The foyer was deeply shadowed. Only the recreation room's patchy light battled the dark. A shape moved on the rug beneath Edgar's portrait. Remy recognized the streak of blue and ran toward April. The teen had coiled into a ball, but she rolled onto her side and propped herself up as Remy reached her.

"Where are you hurt?"

"Ugh." April pressed a hand to her head. "I'm fine."

"Are you sure?" Remy embraced her, pulling her close, as Mark and Taj appeared on her other side. "Are you *certain*?"

"I'll probably have a couple of bruises, but I'm not dying, if that's what you want to know." April had lost the emotionlessness that had dogged her throughout the evening. Her face contorted in mingled shock and fury. "He *dragged* me. Grabbed my ankle and just pulled me out like I weighed nothing."

"You're okay now. You're safe." Remy couldn't have let go of the girl if she'd wanted to. She was shaking. Her limbs felt like jelly, and her heart jumped painfully. She glanced over April's black hair to see Mark and Taj crouched beside her. Bernard and Marjorie were emerging from the recreation room. "Is everyone else okay? Did he hurt anyone?"

Marjorie snorted. "Don't give him too much credit. He's only a spirit. He can't actually harm anyone."

Anger bubbled in Remy's stomach. She embraced it, glad to feel something other than fear. "Really? You keep saying that, and each time I'm stupid enough to believe you, someone gets hurt. April just got dragged along the floor like a rag doll!"

"He was manifesting poltergeist abilities," the medium said, her voice rising. "A brief burst of almost mindless power—"

Taj held out his arm. Three scratches ran over the soft underside, six inches long and reminiscent of marks left by animal claws. They seeped blood.

Marjorie blinked at him, momentarily speechless, then cleared her throat. "That was probably caused by shards of broken light bulb glass. Things were flying everywhere. Poltergeists aren't conscious enough to target people. Edgar wasn't aiming specifically to hurt you—"

"Oh really? Because the end result is the same." Taj turned to Remy. "I change my vote. I want to leave right now."

April cracked a bitter smile. "Embracing your nihilistic tendencies at last, eh, Taj?"

"The opposite." He pulled the cut wrist close to his chest. "I think our chances on the bridge are better than our chances here."

"You're all being ridiculous." Marjorie's shawl had dropped down her shoulders, and she pulled it back into place. "That was a show. It was all lights and smoke. Edgar knows as well as we do that he's ultimately powerless. He wants to scare you, and you're letting him. For all we know, he could be trying to *make* us cross the bridge."

For a second, Remy's conviction wavered. Then she looked at April, who trembled despite her hard expression, and Taj's bleeding arm. She licked her lips. "We should put it to another vote. I'm assuming the séance didn't work, so our options are now to stay and wait it out or risk the bridge."

"Bridge," April said and was echoed by Taj.

Marjorie sniffed. "We should stay. Bernard agrees, don't you, Bernard?"

He made a noncommittal grunting noise.

Remy glanced toward Mark and found him watching her. He inclined his head, indicating that he was waiting for her answer.

She licked her lips. "If anyone stays in the house, I'll remain here, as well. I'm not going to leave them alone with Edgar. But my preference would be for us to leave together."

"Fine." Marjorie threw her hands up. "If you're all fixed on being frightened little rabbits, I'll leave with you, too. But hear this: I will be extremely displeased if I drown tonight."

Remy felt as though a weight had been lifted from her back. She tested her legs, was relieved that they were stable enough to stand, and helped April up. "We'll go, then. It's night, but the sky is so heavily overcast that I don't think waiting for day would make much of a difference. Will we, uh, pack our things?"

"Don't bother." Purpose had brought light to April's eyes. "I want to leave *right now*, not wander through this monster's house for another hour while we gather up our scarves. I'll send you all money to pay for whatever you leave here, okay?"

"Thanks. That might be wise," Remy agreed. "We'll grab some flashlights, but I've seen enough that I don't feel comfortable with any of us staying for longer than absolutely necessary. We'll be safe once we're on the other side of the bridge. It's only an hour drive to town. The police can come back for Piers and Lucille once the storm has calmed."

Mark fished flashlights from the stack of supplies. "Should I go ahead and drive a car up to the house, or will we brave the rain together?"

Taj was already moving toward the door. "Together. There's not going to be any separating until we're well and truly off Carrow's land. When was the last time you watched a horror movie, Mark? Separation means instant death. *Instant. Death.*"

It was enough to make Remy laugh. Taj pushed on the front doors. The rain's heavy drone became louder. As she stepped over the threshold, Remy found she didn't care that she was getting wet or that she'd left half her clothes in Carrow. She didn't even care about the risk of crossing the bridge. She was leaving the house, and that knowledge released something tight and painful that had been growing through her chest over the previous days without her realizing.

They kept to a tight group as they jogged across the lawn. The shed loomed out of the rain ahead of them. Mark reached it first, pulling open the huge sliding doors. Then he stepped back so that they could move inside.

Remy shook the excess water off as soon as she was over the threshold. The shed, which had been intended as a stable before being converted to a garage, was huge. Taj's light glittered over a loft above them, scraps of ancient, damp hay scattered about the dirt floor, and their six vehicles.

"Can I suggest we share a car?" Mark said. "A single trip will probably be safer than multiple."

"Definitely." Remy began pacing between the vehicles as she tried to guess which would have the best traction and speed. "We can return once the storm's over to collect our own cars."

April nodded. "And I'll cover you all for rental vehicles in the meantime."

Remy came to a halt in front of a four-wheel off-roader and patted its side. "This is yours, isn't it, Taj?"

"I borrowed it from a friend, but basically, yeah."

"Great. It's the heaviest. Let's use it. Taj, it's probably best you don't drive while your arm's hurt. Are you a fast driver, Mark?"

He grinned. "Like a bat out of hell."

"Sounds like you just volunteered as designated driver." Remy opened the back door and ushered her companions inside.

Mark took the driver's seat with Marjorie shotgun, and the remaining four squeezed in behind. Remy positioned herself in the center so that she could see through the front windshield. "We're going to have to time this really, really carefully. The waves come in a pattern: one big wave, followed by either three or four small ones. We'll get as close to the bridge as we can, wait for a large wave to sweep over, then start crossing as soon as the water recedes. The bridge isn't short, so speed is important. But it's also going to be slippery, so keep control of the car."

"Gotcha," Mark said. "Drive like a Formula One racer with his judgmental in-laws in the backseat. I can do that."

Remy squeezed her hands together in her lap to keep them from shaking. "All right. Let's get out of here."

CHAPTER 33
SABOTAGE

MARK FITTED THE KEY into the ignition and turned it. The car didn't start.

They all kept silent as they listened to the engine turn over without catching. Remy could see the energy drain from Mark's face. Awful apprehension took its place as he tried again, and again, and again.

"Edgar's not going to let us leave," April said at last.

Mark swore, jumped out of the car, and went around to open the hood. Taj followed, and the two of them bent over the car, talking in quiet voices as they hunted through its insides. They were only there for a minute before Mark came back to lean through the open car door, his face grim. "Someone cut the fuel line."

Nauseating dread rose through Remy as she slid out of the car. Taj was already examining underneath Remy's vehicle while Mark moved on to April's.

"This one's cut, as well," Taj said.

"April's, too."

"And Marjorie's."

Remy looked inside her own car. She found the fuel line and traced it to where it had been cut. A four-inch segment had been removed. She returned to the group that had clustered in the center of the shed, shivering and blinking in the light from Taj's flashlight. Remy couldn't keep the quiver out of her voice. "So none of the cars will work?"

"No, none." Mark's expression was murderous. "They've been sabotaged. Anyone going to confess?"

No one spoke. Remy glanced at their faces, hunting for signs of guilt, but all she saw was fear and frustration.

"Can they be fixed?" April asked.

"Not without equipment we don't have."

Remy muttered a swear word and wiped strands of her soaked hair away from her face.

"Could we run across the bridge?" Taj asked. "I know it would mean walking half a day to get to town, but I'd be willing to do that."

"I don't think there's enough time." Remy's voice was tight. The pressure in her chest was coming back, and she hated it. "The waves come too often—really, the only way we even have a decent chance is with a car—"

"Then it's back to the house," he said.

There was nothing she could do except nod.

The group that left the shed and crossed the field toward

Carrow was very different from the one they'd been minutes before. Their footsteps were sluggish, their heads bowed against the rain, and their silence came from frustration and despondency rather than anticipation. Remy turned her eyes toward the building. The house rose out of its dead grounds like a massive, elaborate tombstone.

I used to love this building. Now, I would gladly burn it to the ground.

The doors no longer appeared mysteriously enticing, but were ominous. The foyer, its furniture still bearing ax marks, didn't fascinate her anymore. She knew in her bones that if she got out of Carrow, she would never return to it.

They came to a halt in the foyer, dripping over the marble floor, and glanced from one to another.

Mark cleared his throat. "I suppose our options have been narrowed to waiting the storm out."

"We're going to be as safe as possible," Remy said. "The curfew is still in place. No one goes anywhere on their own. Even if you have a companion with you, don't leave the group without telling people where you're going. We're sleeping in the same room. And…" She felt sick just saying the words. "If anyone has evidence that one of our party has been erasing the tapes or tampering with the cars, please speak to me. Okay?"

"Where will we stay?" Taj asked. "I'm not sure I want to be in the recreation room after what happened there."

Remy ran through the other options in her mind. "There's the dining room, but it's massive and hasn't had a fire in the last day, so it'll be cold. Same goes for the ballroom. We could bunch into one of the upstairs bedrooms, but it'll be cramped and a long way from any exit if…" *If things get bad,* she silently finished. She cleared her throat. "I'm vetoing the smoking room, the kitchens, the servants' quarters, and the foyer for the same reasons. Most of the other rooms are pretty small."

"So what you're saying is the Room of Ultimate Summoning is still our best option?" April asked.

She shrugged. "I don't like it much, either."

"I vote for the recreation room," Marjorie said. "Despite the séances, it still has the best energy out of the house. And remember—just because he appeared there doesn't mean Edgar is limited to that room. He's capable of following us no matter where we sleep." She hesitated then shrugged. "I can perform some cleanses to keep bad energy out of the room, too, if it helps anyone."

Taj gave a resigned, tight-lipped smile and mutely led them to the doors under the stairs.

Remy hadn't seen the room since April was dragged out of it. The damage was worse than she'd expected. The chairs that had been pulled out from under them had been flung about the room, leaving dents in the walls, and one of the chairs was broken. Nearby furniture, including some of the massive stuffed lounges, were overturned. The two bowls containing the white and black grains had been smashed against the walls. And nearly half of the room's lights had blown during the power surge.

Remy scratched the back of her neck as she blew out a breath.

"This'll need cleaning before bed. Let's get the fire started first thing and then grab some dry clothes and bedding material."

It was easy to shut off the frightened part of her mind while there was work to do. Remy ensured that her group stayed together as they went upstairs and split into their separate rooms, doors open, to change. Then she, Mark, Bernard, and April dragged mattresses downstairs while Taj and Marjorie carried pillows and quilts.

Back in the recreation room, Mark pulled Taj to a seat by the fire and worked on washing and bandaging his cuts. Remy joined Marjorie to clean up from the séance. As Remy picked up shards of the smashed bowls, she looked over her shoulder at Marjorie. "What was in these, by the way? The black and white substances?"

Marjorie laughed. "Oh, those. The white stuff is salt. It's commonly used to remove evil spirits and cleanse areas. The black dirt is something I've been trialing recently: soil taken from around the front step of a church. It was wonderfully effective when I used it for some recent cleanses."

Marjorie shook out the tablecloth. The mark she'd drawn on it stood out clearly against the white, and she hung it over the back of a chair where they could all see it. "Is anyone familiar with this symbol?"

They all shook their heads, and Marjorie pursed her lips. "If our theory about the Red Crows is correct, it could be one of the cult's markings or even their emblem. I can't really do much with it until I know what it was used for. If you find any other instances of it around the house, I'd be very grateful if you let me know."

With the remains of their séance packed up, Remy worked on

shifting some of the other furniture away from the fireplace then laid down their mattresses and threw the blankets and pillows about. Mark finished bandaging Taj's arm and shut his kit, then he helped Remy make the beds.

As she worked, Remy's mind returned to the car's cut fuel lines. It was hard not to feel wary about the people she'd grown to accept as her friends. The most obvious suspect would be April. At the beginning of their stay, Lucille wouldn't stop nagging her to leave. Remy could imagine the teen sneaking out to the cars to remove Lucille's choice in the matter. If she felt embarrassed about it, she might be reluctant to confess. On the other hand, she'd led the recent campaign to leave the house. Remy couldn't believe the teen would be so set on it if she'd known the cars wouldn't work.

Another option would be the spirits. Remy didn't voice the idea because she knew how Marjorie would respond. But the marks on Taj's arm made Remy question the medium's belief.

The final theory was the worst: one of the party didn't want them to leave for malevolent reasons. As she watched her companions, Remy found it hard to believe any one of them would want to trap and harm the others. But the possibility still existed, and she couldn't expunge it from her mind. Bernard was a dark horse who had ample opportunity to sneak out to the shed. Mark kept disappearing without telling anyone where he was going. Marjorie had been reluctant to leave the house. And Taj was practical enough to know how car engines worked and make quick work of breaking them.

"Who—" April started out of her chair, staring toward the open doors as shock spread over her face. Remy crossed to her side.

"What is it?"

"I saw someone out there. A girl."

Remy jogged to the door. She was just in time to see the faint outline of a red dress disappear into the dining room. Mesmerized, she followed, crossing the foyer with quick steps, but she knew before she even entered the room that it would be empty.

"Was it a ghost?" Mark asked. The others had followed her.

"Yeah. Pretty sure we just saw Red. Keep an eye on your possessions. She likes to borrow things." She spared one last, lingering glance around the dining room, scanning the shadows and the spaces below the vast drapes, but it was empty. She returned to the foyer but paused as a small, glittering shape caught her eye.

A gold necklace had been hung on the stair's banister. Remy reached toward it but was interrupted by April's cry.

"That's Lucille's." The teen snatched up the necklace, held it reverently, then looked up the stairs as she yelled, "Lucille! *Lucille!*"

"April, I'm sorry." Remy gently touched the teen's shoulder. "I think it's just one of Red's tricks."

The girl's hopeful smile cracked and melted. Her shoulders dropped. Then she surprised Remy by laughing. "Of course. I'm being stupid. It's late. I probably just need sleep."

"April…"

"I'm fine." The teen shook Remy's hand off her shoulder, gave

261

her a dead-eyed smile, then returned to their room, necklace clutched close to her chest. Remy could only follow.

They settled in for the night. No one seemed to want to turn the lights out and go to sleep, so they huddled near the fireplace, occasionally feeding it new wood. Marjorie paced around the area, burning a bouquet of sage and sprinkling salt around the doors and windows to protect them.

At one point, the men left and returned with trays stacked with tea and coffee, plus snacks from the kitchen. Remy took one of the muesli bars and chewed on it as she crossed to the window. She'd hoped to see some sign that the storm was easing, but as she neared the glass, a wave washed up to mock her.

Remy raised her eyes and caught sight of a strange shape near the top of the window. It was small but oddly colored. Frowning, she took a step closer to the glass, close enough to feel the chill rolling off it. Remy sucked in a breath as lightning flashed. The shape came into focus during that brief second of illumination, and fear, sickness, and horror collided in Remy's stomach.

She fought to keep her face calm as she turned back to the room. She wet her lips and said, "Marjorie, it would make me feel easier if you burned some of that sage in other parts of the house, too."

"I don't really see the point. This is only a precaution for while we're asleep." She wafted the herb's smoke around Taj's desk at the back of the room.

"Please." Remy's voice wavered a fraction, but she hoped it wasn't too noticeable.

The medium raised her eyebrows. "Well, all right, if it's that important to you."

"Thanks. April, why don't you help Marjorie?"

The teen rose without objection and followed the medium to the door. Bernard, unasked, went with them.

Remy waited until the door was closed and their footsteps had faded, then she drew a shaking breath. "Mark, Taj, come here, but keep your voices quiet. I don't want April to have to see this."

She took her flashlight out of her pocket, turned it on, and angled its beam at the limp hand hanging outside the window.

CHAPTER 34
SALVAGE

"OH," TAJ MUTTERED WHILE Mark pressed a hand over his mouth. "That's Lucille, isn't it?"

"I think so."

"We need to bring her inside." Mark's voice was low but quick. "What's the best way to get to her?"

Remy's shaking fingers made the flashlight's beam jitter. "My guess is that her body is caught on something outside. Maybe a windowsill or a pipe. I can't see a way to get to her through this window, but we might be able to through one of the upstairs ones."

"Let's go, then," Mark said. "We should hurry. A wave could pull her loose."

The three of them left the recreation room, checked the others weren't within earshot, then crossed to the stairs. Remy knew she was going against her own instructions by leaving without telling the other group where they were going, but she couldn't risk April seeing what had happened to her companion.

They jogged up the stairs, using their flashlights instead of turning on the hallway light. Remy tried to guess which bedroom would be positioned over the recreational area's window and chose Room 9.

They turned on the light. The red-stained wall glistened opposite. The marks had developed further, becoming larger and sharper, making the painted face far more realistic than Remy wanted it to be. She tried not to look at it as they went to the window.

Mark tried pulling the pane up, but it was frozen in place. He strained against it, then shifted back, breathing heavily. "It opened on the first day we were here."

"The water might have swollen the wood," Taj said.

Mark ran his fingers through his hair. "I'll need to break it."

"Do it."

He took off his jacket, wrapped it around his hand, and punched through the glass. The shattering sound made both Remy and Taj flinch, even though it was partially masked under the storm's roar. They moved closer as Mark scraped stray shards of glass out of the frame then bent his torso through the opening.

"Someone get a sheet," he said, and Taj ran out of the room. Mark began moving back, shifting and wiggling his way through the window.

Remy saw the woman's pale, limp hands first. They were followed by her mottled arms, and finally, her dead, gray face appeared in the window's frame as Mark dragged Lucille inside.

Taj returned, his arms full with a sheet and a blanket from one of the other bedrooms, and swore when he saw Lucille. Her eyes were wide, bloodshot, and staring blankly. Water dribbled from her open mouth. Her dress was shredded, and the exposed flesh was so horribly discolored that Remy was afraid she might be sick.

She and Taj hurried to spread the sheet, and Mark lowered Lucille's body onto it then wrapped the blanket about her. He was shaking, his mouth in a hard line, but Remy couldn't tell if it was from revulsion, grief, or anger.

"How did she get up there?" Taj asked. "Did she not fall into the ocean after all?"

"No, I think she did." Remy reached out to brush a strand of sea grass out of Lucille's blond hair. "I think… I think one of the big waves washed her back onto the house. Maybe that huge one from the séance, when the lights went out."

Taj buried his face in his hands. "That's got to be a crazy coincidence."

"I don't think coincidence has anything to do with it. Not with Edgar in this house, and not with so much energy buzzing around us."

Mark sat back, his eyes skimming the room, looking everywhere except at the dead woman. "There's something else. Look through the window, and you'll see why the wall is stained. It's what Lucille was caught on."

Remy rose and leaned through the window. Icy rain hit her face, running down her neck and under her clothes. She squinted against it and looked to the side.

A hole, at least four feet wide and six high, had been gouged into the building's exterior, and jagged pieces of stone and wood poked out of it. A thick, dark-red liquid dribbled down the building's outside to be washed into the ocean. Remy, struggling to understand what she was looking at, lingered in the window until she was drenched and shivering.

She pulled back inside and stared at Mark while Taj moved to take her place. Her own confusion was reflected back in his eyes.

"It's like…" She struggled to find the words, but Mark finished for her.

"Like the house is injured. It's like it's bleeding."

"Yeah."

Taj came back through the opening, rainwater sticking his long hair to his face. "It wasn't like that when we checked it on our first day here. Maybe one of the waves damaged the house. It could have swept up some flotsam or something."

"Maybe." Remy sat next to Mark, facing Lucille, and watched water trickle off her dead friend's face. "But why's it bleeding? I thought it was a rusty pipe, but it can't be. Not with that much red liquid. It's almost like this house is alive."

They were silent. Remy couldn't stand seeing Lucille's open, staring eyes and gently, reverently pressed the lids closed. Her friend's skin was cold and faintly slimy.

A noise came from the doorway. They looked up to see that Marjorie, Bernard, and April had found them.

The teen sucked in a deep, slow breath, a muscle twitching in her temple, then exhaled. Her voice was tight and high. "You found her. That's good. Stops me from wondering. Stops me from worrying."

Remy didn't know what to say. "I'm so sorry, April."

"Will we put her in the basement, too?" April's swallow was audible. "Piers can keep her company. She liked Piers."

"Yeah." Mark spoke softly. "We'll do that."

He and Taj rose and each took one end of the sheet. The others moved out of the way as they carried Lucille out of the room. They created a slow procession down the stairs, across the foyer, and to the basement door. Remy went with them to the house's lowest level, partially out of respect for Lucille and partially because she didn't want to leave her group alone in the basement. She was dreading seeing what Piers looked like but was surprised that he'd barely changed in the last two days. His skin remained horribly gray, but he hadn't yet started to decay.

As they placed Lucille at Taj's side, her head lolled. Marjorie made a faint noise of surprise and bustled forward. She pushed Lucille's hair to one side to expose the back of her neck.

"Oh," Remy whispered and knelt to see it more clearly.

Scored into the back of Lucille's neck was the same symbol Marjorie had drawn on the tablecloth: a circle surrounding an hourglass design. It was small and seemed to have been caused by something sharp, leaving red marks on her skin but not quite cutting through.

Marjorie reached across Lucille's body and pushed on Piers's head. It tilted to the side to expose an identical mark on the back of his neck.

"What's he done to her?" April's voice shook as she clenched her fists at her side. "What's that Edgar bastard done to her?"

Marjorie gently adjusted the bodies so that their heads faced upward again, then she rose and dusted her hands on her skirt. "I'm afraid I don't know, my dear. I can't sense any presence. I can't promise Lucille's spirit has moved on—it might linger in the place of death, the ocean—but at least it's not tethered to her body."

April sucked in a quick breath, turned, and ran up the stairs. Remy followed, moving as quickly as she dared on the narrow steps, and kept pace with the teen as she stalked toward Edgar's portrait. She came to a halt below the image and stared up, meeting the man's cold gray eyes and subtle smirk with a glower.

"He killed her," April said.

It was a statement, but it begged for confirmation. Remy stopped at April's side and wrapped an arm around her narrow shoulders. She pulled April close, hugging her, as the others returned from the basement.

"It's late," Marjorie said. She exhaled, sounding older and tireder than ever. "We need to sleep. Perhaps the storm will end tomorrow."

April nodded and let herself be pulled back to the recreation room.

CHAPTER 35
A STRING OF BELLS

NOISE ROUSED REMY FROM sleep. The fog clouding her brain told her that it was still the middle of the night. She pulled her eyebrows together as she tried to identify the sound. It was a shuffling, scuffing noise, punctuated by quick breathing.

She rolled over and opened her eyes. The fire was nearly dead, but before going to bed they'd turned on the sconces at the back of the room. The ambient glow lit a tall, thin shape digging through the bags beside the door.

"Bernard?"

He turned, his long face pinched with frustration. "I can't find the bells."

"Wha?" Remy wriggled to sit up. She tried to keep her voice quiet so as not to disturb the others. "Bells?"

"The bells for Marjorie. She's sleepwalking, and she won't come back without them."

Remy clambered out of her bed and crossed to Bernard, keeping her footsteps light. She scanned the beds as she passed them and saw that Marjorie's was, indeed, empty. *I forgot that she sleepwalks. We should have taken some kind of precaution.* "Did you leave them upstairs?"

"No. They were in this bag." He scratched at his scalp. It was an anxious motion that suggested the stress had been wearing on him.

Remy rubbed at the inside corners of her eyes as she tried to think. "Okay. We can't let Marjorie walk through the house alone. Do you know where she went?"

"No, only that she's gone."

"Keep looking for the bells." Remy went to Mark's bed. She shook his shoulder, and he startled awake. "Sorry," she whispered. "Can you help? Marjorie's gone. We need to find her."

He blinked as sleep cleared from his eyes, then sat up. "Yes. Of course."

They slipped their shoes on, trying not to disturb April or Taj, and went to the door. It was already open a crack, so they crept through and turned on their flashlights.

"Bernard needs the bells to bring her back," Remy whispered. "He's searching for them now. We just need to find Marjorie and make sure she's not in any danger."

As the words left her, a prickling, anxious feeling crept up her spine. Remy swallowed, but it was hard not to feel the panic coiling through her stomach. The last time people from their group had gone missing, they'd ended up dead.

Marjorie is an experienced medium, she reminded herself. *Out of all of us, she's the best equipped to handle this house. Even while sleepwalking. Probably.*

The foyer was freezing, and Remy's breath plumed on each exhale. She turned her flashlight toward the windows and saw the pane she'd accidentally cracked had broken open. Glass shards glittered across the floor. *Did one of the ghosts do this? I didn't hear it—but then, it could have happened during a thunderclap.*

"Where should we start looking?" Mark asked. "Upstairs? Outside?"

Remy had been listening for any shuffling footsteps or creaking floorboards that might give away the medium's position, but the house was eerily silent. She chewed on her lip then said, "Let's start upstairs."

They moved toward the stairs, and Remy stepped on something soft. She gasped and leaped back from it. The light from Mark's flashlight revealed one of Marjorie's slippers discarded on the floor. Remy swung her flashlight in a wider arc but couldn't see any other signs of the woman.

"How'd she lose a slipper?" she whispered.

Hearing a very soft, very low creak above her, Remy lifted her flashlight and her eyes. A shape hovered above her, shadowed but horribly familiar, and a scream built in Remy's throat.

She staggered back as the recreation room doors burst open. Bernard made a choked, horrified noise and dashed toward the staircase. Someone else ran across the foyer to the lights by the door and turned them on. Even after the bulbs lit the room,

Remy kept her flashlight's beam on Marjorie's body as horror and shock froze her in place.

Hanging from the banister, Marjorie's body dangled over the open area ahead of the recreation room, her toes lingering above the path Remy had just walked. She'd been hanged with her shawl. The fabric was twisted around her throat and knotted to the wooden rail above.

"Cut her down!" Taj yelled from beside the lights.

Bernard was already at the top of the stairs and tearing along the landing, but Remy knew he would be too late. Marjorie's eyes were open but sightless. Her face was blotchy, her limbs limp, her expression unexpectedly serene.

Bernard struggled to undo the shawl's knot. Remy fought back her horror and fear to step under the body and raise her arms. Taj joined her, but Mark hung back. His face was pallid, and his eyes glazed over.

"Mark!" Remy barked. "Help us!"

He didn't move.

A ripping noise told her Bernard was cutting through the shawl. A second later, Marjorie dropped, and Remy and Taj braced themselves to catch her. She was heavy, and they collapsed to the ground before laying her back and scrambling away. Remy pressed her hand to her injured arm, which burned from where the healing cuts had retorn.

"Mark?" Taj's fingers scrabbled at the shawl around Marjorie's throat, struggling to undo the knots. "Mark, what should I do?"

"Uh—" Mark finally seemed to come back to awareness and

staggered forward. He gently pushed Remy back and knelt at Marjorie's side, his hands joining Taj's as they tried to unravel the fabric.

Bernard came down the stairs with unsteady, halting steps. He stopped beside a shivering April in the recreation room's doorway, breathing in quick, short breaths.

Remy turned to him. "How long was she gone?"

"I—" He swallowed thickly, perspiration shining on his long face. "I don't know."

"You didn't see her leave?"

"No. I woke, and she was gone." He wiped the back of his hand across his lips. "Why—who—"

Remy turned back to the medium. She'd felt Marjorie's skin when she'd caught her. It had been cool; Marjorie must have been hanging from the banister for hours.

Mark took his fingers away from the medium's throat, where he'd been searching for a pulse. He sat back and shook his head. "She's gone."

"This wasn't an accident." Taj dropped the remains of the woman's shawl. "Her hands were tied together. Look."

A quiet jingling made Remy press her hands over her face. She didn't want to see the string of bells—the bells the medium would follow, the bells Bernard had lost—knotted around Marjorie's wrists.

Bernard spat unintelligible, bitter words and began pacing.

"Why didn't we hear her?" April was shaking. "She was just outside the door. Wouldn't she have yelled or struggled? Why didn't we wake up?"

"The storm is loud," Mark said. "And Marjorie was sleepwalking. She might not have known what was happening until it was too late."

"But even so…she was *right there*…"

"Taj, get a blanket." Remy lowered her hands and forced herself to look at the body. She wanted to scream, but a deep, aching bleakness had begun to grow in her and squash down the frantic emotions. "We'll take her to the basement. Then we're going back to the recreation room."

"But—" April started then fell quiet when Remy sent her a hard look.

Taj retrieved the blanket from the pile of supplies. In a ritual that was becoming surreally familiar, he and Mark wrapped Marjorie's body and carried it to the basement door. Remy followed them to the entrance to keep them both in sight. Once they had returned, she mutely indicated to the recreation room's door. They filed inside, turning on the lights as they passed. Remy made sure she was the last to enter, then she took a deep, slow breath and spoke.

"Taj is right. This wasn't an accident. And I'm now convinced that neither Piers's nor Lucille's deaths were, either."

"I told you," April said, her expression fierce. "It's the house. It's Edgar."

"No." Remy's mouth was bone dry. She folded her hands behind herself so that the others wouldn't see them shaking. "It's one of us."

"We don't know that," Mark said. "Marjorie was sleepwalking—"

"Marjorie didn't sleepwalk to her death." Remy paused to see if he would argue, but he didn't. "Marjorie wasn't unhappy or suicidal. Someone lured her out while she was asleep, bound her hands, and hung her. Someone human. Someone in this room."

She looked over the pale faces surrounding her: Mark, April, Taj, and Bernard. There were so few left. Her throat threatened to constrict, so she spoke quickly. "I don't know what their motive is. They may have come to the house with the intention to murder, or the building's negative energy could have pushed them into homicide. That doesn't matter right now. What matters is that no one else is going to die." She extended a hand toward the furniture. "Slowly, making no sudden moves and without trying to hide anything, we're going to throw every potential weapon out of this room. Anything that can cut, strangle, or bludgeon is going into the foyer. Is that clear?"

April looked like she was trying not to cry. "That's half the stuff in the room."

"Yes." Remy nudged the door open. "Get started."

CHAPTER 36
BURIED HISTORY

THIS IS SURREAL. REMY lifted a small wooden chair, brought it to the door, and placed it in the foyer, all while being careful not to expose her back to anyone else in the room. April, her lips scrunched up, and her eyes wet, carried a vase past her. *These people are my friends. Can I really believe one of them is capable of murder? Can I really treat them so coldly?*

Yes, she answered herself. *Because if I don't, the rest of us will die.*

Mark had relit the fire but was shifting the spare logs of wood outside. They were large enough and heavy enough to use as a weapon, which meant they couldn't remain in the recreation room.

Taj had argued against his monitoring system being moved out, and Remy had eventually relented under the condition that the screens be tied together with duct tape. They were already attached to a nest of cables and would be hard to lift at short notice. The tape made it virtually impossible. His cameras stayed, but the EMF sensors were heavy enough that Remy had them expelled.

The mattresses were left inside the room, but the remaining sheets were tossed out. Remy doubted they could strangle a person without a lot of effort, but it was still a risk she didn't want to take. The larger furniture—including tables and the overstuffed chairs—remained. Anything light enough to lift went.

Bookcases lined the walls. Remy tested one and was relieved to find it had been bolted to the stone. With Taj's help, she ran strips of duct tape along the shelves, sealing the books inside. Finally, the fire pokers were thrown out, then Remy searched each of her friends for hidden weapons. She found none.

"Okay," she said at last. "Thanks, everyone, for the cooperation. If you want to go back to sleep, you're welcome to. We just have to make sure at least two people are awake at a time to act as guards."

"This is it, huh?" April settled onto one of the mattresses but didn't lie down. "We're just going to camp here, knowing one of us is a murderer, and wait for the storm to break?"

Remy settled into one of the chairs. "I'm open to alternatives."

"Well, what if we knew who did it? We could tie them up or lock them in the basement or something."

Despite the exhaustion, grief, and fear, Remy had to smile. "That would be easier, yeah. But I doubt a killer is going to readily confess, and I'm not prepared to waterboard any of you."

"No. I already have a pretty good idea of who it is." At Remy's questioning look, April tilted her head toward Mark.

"Whoa, no. Definitely not." Mark held up both hands, palms out.

April's expression twisted. "Yeah, just keep playing innocent."

Remy felt sick to her stomach. She glanced at Mark, half-afraid of what she would see, as Marjorie's words echoed through the back of her mind. *He's keeping secrets.* "April, what's your evidence?"

"He organized this whole shebang, didn't he? Seven guests, all strangers, locked up in a house with him. He knew Carrow was prone to storms. He knew that if he planned the stay for two weeks, there was a good chance we'd be trapped for at least a couple of days. Plenty of time for him to bump us off one by one and frame the deaths as accidents."

Mark was starting to look nauseated. "I can understand your logic, but I swear I invited you all here for benign reasons."

"*Benign reasons.*" Her eyes rolled as she imitated his voice. "Oh, yeah, those benign reasons which are so clear to us all. You know nothing about ghost hunting. You couldn't give us any kind of task, even when we asked for one. As far as I can tell, you'd never even seen a ghost before coming here. You've been lying about this trip's purpose since the day you planned it, and you're still lying, even now."

His lips were in a tight line, his eyes wide, his skin blanched white. "It's not like that."

"Oh, isn't it?"

Remy squeezed her hands together. Her palms were sweaty. It was hard to forget how Mark had gone into the woods and the attic without telling the group, but she didn't want to believe he'd been preparing to kill.

Taj's face had taken on a dark expression, and he rubbed a finger over his lips. "You're being awfully quick to accuse, April."

"Yeah, because he's all but red-handed!"

"But, like you said, he knows almost nothing about spirits or Carrow's history. You, on the other hand…"

"What are you saying?"

Taj shrugged. "Someone had to carve those words into Marjorie's door. Someone had to know about that symbol to cut it into Lucille's and Piers's necks."

"That doesn't mean anything! If knowledge makes you suspicious, you should be pointing the finger at Remy!"

"Except Remy isn't obsessed with this building." He leaned forward, his eyes hard. "Whereas I could see *you* wanting to be a significant part of Carrow's history. Even if it meant getting blood on your hands."

"Are you stupid? Lucille is dead! I loved her, and she's dead!"

"You loved her, huh? Could've fooled me, what with all the arguing and screaming."

April's jaw dropped. Bright patches of color built on her cheeks, then she spasmed, and tears ran over her lids to drip down her face.

"Oh, April." Remy reached a hand toward the girl but pulled back as April threw a punch at her.

"Don't touch me! Don't any of you bastards touch me!" She was breathing in hysterical gasps, the tears flowing unchecked, and scooted away from the rest of them. Mark had half-risen out of his chair, and she pointed at him. "Stay away from me! *Murderer!*"

A loud clap startled them all. Bernard stood, using his impressive height to tower over them, and glowered at April. "Stop screeching. The truth is that you could build a case against any of us." He paused to let that sink in as he scanned the gathering. "Remy has the knowledge to cut the message into Marjorie's door. Mark is suspicious for inviting us here without any apparent cause. April, you're obsessed with this house and more than a little spoiled. And the argument could be made that the footage caught in this building could lift Taj's career out of the dregs and make him a millionaire."

"I don't care about being famous," Taj interjected. "I'm looking for the truth, nothing more, nothing less."

"That's easy to say, but can you prove it? Any evidence has been erased from the tapes—which you have the easiest access to."

Taj shrugged, conceding the point.

"And a case could even be built against me," Bernard said. "Maybe I hated my employer and saw this as an opportunity to get rid of her. Or maybe I'm crazy. None of you know me well, and there's nothing I can do to prove my innocence." He slumped back into his seat, suddenly looking exhausted, and massaged the bridge of his nose. "No one has any kind of alibi. Both Piers and Marjorie died during the night, when we were asleep, and we'd split up when Lucille went missing. The cars could have been tampered with at any point since our arrival. There's no way to be sure about any of us. Not until we get out of this house...or the killer slips up."

For a moment, the only noise came from the crackling fire and the wind beating against the house. Remy flicked her eyes between her companions, trying to read their expressions, and found they were all watching each other.

Then Mark cleared his throat. "Bernard's right. There's no way I can clear myself. But I would like to share my reason for coming to Carrow, even if just for my own sanity."

He sat hunched forward in his chair, his hands clasped around his knees. The haunted expression lingered in his eyes. Remy shifted forward a fraction. He'd already told her he'd come to Carrow to face his fears, but she knew there was something more he wanted to share—something he'd been keeping from her.

"Remy..." He hesitated and licked his lips. "When I gave you my business card, you thought my name was familiar. You assumed you must have heard of my father, the surgeon, but there's another connection you missed. This isn't my first time in Carrow. The building was last open twenty years ago, as a hotel. I was eight at the time. My father, mother, twin brother, and I stayed here for the night."

Remy covered her mouth as an awful realization rushed through her. "Oh no...not Luke Sulligent—"

He exhaled a mirthless laugh. "Yes. Luke. We shared a room separate from our parents. We were supposed to be asleep, but he wanted to explore."

Remy already knew how the story went. She felt sick but kept quiet, understanding that Mark needed to share his history with the group.

"We'd never been in such a big house before. We snuck through the kitchens, the servants' quarters, and finally found the stairs to the attic. He said it was like a genie's cave. So much treasure hidden everywhere…" For a second Mark's mouth twitched into the ghost of a smile, then the expression vanished. "The floor was rotten. He was jumping between the ropes suspended from the ceiling. The boards broke, he fell through, a rope became caught around his neck—"

Taj muttered a swear word under his breath, but Mark didn't seem to hear. His expression was distant, the same dazed, horrified look he'd worn when they'd found Marjorie hanging from the banister. "I tried to pull him up. I wasn't strong enough. I could feel the rope twitching in my hands. I was screaming—my parents tried to get to him, but he'd fallen into one of the rooms, and it was locked." He pulled in a slow, rattling breath and squeezed his eyes closed. He didn't speak for a moment. When he continued, his voice was raw. "The rope finally stopped moving. I looked up and saw a man standing at the back of the attic, smiling at me. He seemed impossibly tall. Wide gray eyes. Rope burns around his throat. Edgar had been watching my brother die." Mark pressed his palms into his closed eyelids.

Remy gave him a moment then continued the story in a muted voice. "Luke Sulligent's death was Carrow's last…until this week, at least. The hotel closed the following day and stayed shut until April bought it two years ago."

After a moment of quiet, Taj said simply, "That sucks, man."

"Ha." The laughter was forced, but Mark dropped his hands. His expression became more present. "I'm not trying to prove my innocence or buy sympathy or anything. But after what's happened, I think it's fair for you all to know the real reason why we're here."

April had stopped crying and no longer stared at him with blatant loathing. "So why did you come back? Did you want revenge on Edgar?"

"No. But I wanted to know that Luke wasn't here. What if his ghost became trapped? What if he's been stuck in this house, alone, frightened?"

Remy closed her eyes. So many things made sense. She now understood why Mark had run into the forest when Remy saw a child's spirit there. Why he'd gone into the attic alone. Why he knew so little about the paranormal but had hired both Marjorie and Taj—two sides of the ghost communication coin—and asked that they make contact with as many spirits in the house as possible. He was in a building filled with ghosts, but he only cared about finding one. Even throwaway comments, such as how his father had made him take first-aid courses every year since he was eight, took on new significance.

Mark met each of their gazes. "I never intended anyone to be hurt. But this operation was my plan, and so I'm responsible for the consequences. Three good people have passed away during this trip, and it's destroying me."

Remy felt her guardedness toward him melt. At the same time, caution begged her to be wary. Her instincts trusted him, but her logic said she was courting danger.

Thunder crackled outside the window, and somewhere upstairs, a door slammed. They all looked toward the ceiling, but no one suggested they investigate. The time for chasing ghosts was over.

Minutes bled into hours. The fire began to die, so Remy excused herself to fetch new pieces of wood from the foyer. She kept the doors open so that she never left her companions' sight, but the atmosphere made the hairs on her arms rise. The house was crackling with energy. She retreated to their room, shoved both pieces of wood into the fireplace, and hoped the others wouldn't see her trembling.

Marjorie said the house was still waking up. How much more active will it get? We're already having to protect ourselves against a killer. I don't know if we can keep ourselves safe from the spirits, as well.

She couldn't discount the idea that the killer was feeding off the house's energy in some way. It was common that haunted houses could influence the occupants' moods, especially when there were evil presences. If someone in the group had socio-pathic tendencies, they would only be exacerbated at Carrow.

We just need to wait until the storm breaks. Remy lingered by the fire, absorbing its warmth and wishing it would reach her cold core. *As long as we stay as a group, the killer won't have a chance to strike again. We'll go to the bathroom as groups. We'll rotate guard duty when people need to sleep. We won't take any more chances until the storm passes.*

As though he could hear her thoughts, Taj cleared his throat. "I want to leave."

"The bridge isn't safe." She felt as though she'd said the phrase a dozen times over the previous days.

"I know. But I want to try."

She turned away from the fire to stare at him.

He spread his hands. "You said it's dangerous to run across the bridge. But I'm fast. I was in track during high school. I could have gotten into national competitions if my parents had let me. I want to try running across the bridge."

Remy returned to her chair, feeling the unconquerable fear rising in her again. "Taj—"

"I know. It's dangerous. But so is this place. I want to get out. And if I'm successful, you lot won't have to wait for the storm to clear. I'll run to the town and bring the police back."

April narrowed her eyes at him, though the expression didn't have the loathing she'd given Mark. "Or you could be the bad guy trying to escape."

Taj grinned at her. "It's a win-win either way. If I'm the killer, you guys will be safe with me out of the house. If I'm not, the police will be here within eight hours."

Remy glanced toward Mark. He had his eyebrows raised. "It's a good point."

"I just—" Remy struggled to find the words. "I don't think I could cope if we lost you, as well."

"I'm going to make it." Taj's expression was firm. "But even if I don't, it wouldn't be your fault. This is a calculated risk. I've been thinking about it all evening, and I'm certain that I want to leave. You have no authority to stop me."

"Okay." Remy folded her arms around her chest in an attempt to keep from feeling as though she were falling apart. "Good luck."

CHAPTER 37
RECEDE AND UNCOVER

TAJ SAID THEY DIDN'T need to accompany him to the bridge, but Remy insisted on it. She thought he looked relieved by the decision. He spoke confidently, but perspiration coated his forehead.

They moved as one through the foyer, shivering against the cold air coming in through the broken window and the energy prickling at their skin. Remy took a bracing breath before stepping into the storm.

Being drenched had become something like a habit since arriving at Carrow, but practice didn't make the sensation any more pleasant. Remy kept her pace quick and her head down as they left the grounds and crossed the field. More than once, her flashlight's beam picked up faint, translucent shapes near the woods' edge. Carrow's spirits were restless.

The hike to the bridge did nothing to warm Remy, and she

folded her arms around herself as they came to a halt at the place where the dirt path gave way to stone.

"Are you sure about this?" She had to yell to be heard over the wind's roar. "You can come back with us."

"Thanks, but I'm certain." Taj's face was set. He scuffed his sneakers on the dirt and flexed his shoulders. "So I wait for a big wave and then run, right?"

"Yes, but you'll have less than a minute to get across. And it's not a short dash."

The rail-less bridge, suspended barely above the water, was washed with spray each time the smaller waves hit the rocks. Remy watched as one of the massive swells crashed over it, blocking the stone structure out of sight. Salty spray flicked over the group, and Remy clenched her hands at her sides to keep them from shaking. "Taj—"

He laughed. "Yes, I'm sure."

Remy couldn't keep her face stoic anymore. She wrapped her arms around Taj's torso in a fierce hug, willing him to be strong, praying that he would be fast enough. When she released him, both Mark and Bernard shook his hand and clapped his shoulder.

"Good luck," Mark said.

Taj approached the start of the bridge, just far enough back that the swell couldn't reach his feet. He shed his jacket, squinting against the rain, and fixed his gaze on the barely visible shrubs marking the opposite side of the bridge.

Remy moved forward to stand at his side and lifted the

flashlight so that it would light his path. "Do you want me to tell you when to go?"

"Thanks."

Remy fixed her attention on the waves. A large one was coming, and she waited for it to hit before speaking.

"Get ready." The swell coursed over the path, fully submerging it and blotting it from sight. "Nearly…" The wave receded, creating frothing white waterfalls over both sides of the stone. "Go!"

Taj shot forward. They'd timed it perfectly; the water had barely drained enough for him to have a steady footing. Seawater splashed up with each pounding step, and he bent his head low, arms swinging in long arcs as he raced for the mainland.

Remy squeezed both hands around the flashlight to keep it steady. She bit her lip so hard that she tasted blood through the salty spray. Every fiber of her being urged him on, urged him to be faster than the wind. One of the smaller waves hit the side of the bridge, showering him with spray, but he didn't even slow. He was nearly halfway across. He was going to make it—

A large wave built not far away from shore. Remy's lips parted with dawning horror. They should have had at least two more smaller waves before another large one hit. She sucked in a breath to scream a warning, but the words died in her throat. Taj had passed the bridge's halfway mark. He had no chance of escaping the water, no matter which direction he ran.

The wave washed over Taj. Remy clamped her hands over her head, her too-tight throat choking a wail. The water seemed endless. Its brute force shook the bridge, and the swell licked at Remy's shoes. Then it began to recede.

Taj was gone.

Remy stumbled forward. An insane hope had lodged itself in her that Taj might have somehow caught himself on the bridge's side. Mark yelled her name, but she didn't slow as she staggered along the stone path, even though water continued to flow off the bridge and threatened to drag her with it. She stumbled, collapsed onto her hands and knees, and leaned over the side of the bridge. The black stone stretched down for what seemed like forever as the water ebbed away. She moved her light over it, not daring to breathe, blinking back the tears that blinded her. She couldn't see him—not on the bridge's side and not in the rolling, foamy water below.

Someone wrapped their arms around her torso and dragged her back. She tried to writhe free but fell still a second later when spray gushed over them. The hands held her tightly as they hauled her along the bridge and back to solid ground. She blinked water out of her eyes and saw another massive wave building farther out from shore.

When they reached the muddy field, Mark let them drop to their knees, though he still didn't relax his arms around her. His body shook. She thought he might be crying, but it was hard to tell.

"He should have made it," Remy moaned. "He was fast enough."

"It's the house's energy." Mark rocked her and ran a hand over her wet hair. "It's not your fault. It's no one's fault except this damn building's."

April came up beside Remy, arm held out. Remy pulled her close, then to her surprise, Bernard pressed a heavy hand on her shoulder. They stayed like that for several long minutes, kneeling on Carrow's lawn, ignoring the rain as they shared in their grief. The idea that she was absorbing comfort from a murderer passed through her mind, but she couldn't bring herself to pull away.

The heartache was unbearable. Remy couldn't stand to think of Taj's body, trapped in the water, being rolled, dragged, and beaten against the rocks in the relentless swell. She wanted to scream but had no energy. Instead, she clung to her friends, tears mixing with the rain, and her heart burning as though someone had driven a spike through it.

An angry streak of lightning moved across the sky, and the following thunder was close enough to shake the air in Remy's lungs. She swallowed around a painful lump in her throat. "We need to go back to the house."

Mark wordlessly helped her to her feet.

Four left.

One by one, her friends were being consumed by the building. She didn't think she could survive losing any more of them. They moved back toward the house in a tight clump, hands resting on each other's shoulders.

Remy reluctantly lifted her eyes toward the building. She'd grown to loathe it. The tall windows, dark-slate roof, and dramatic facade no longer held any fascination for her. All she felt was bitter resentment.

Something dark moved in one of the windows. She pulled up short. "Do you see that?"

April squinted at the house. "What?"

"In the upstairs window, the one with the light on. There's a person in there." As Remy spoke, the figure turned and disappeared behind the curtains. She shifted her eyes to the next window along, but the silhouette didn't reappear.

"Was it a ghost?" Mark asked.

Remy shook her head. A rushing noise filled her ears, and she couldn't breathe. "No. It was a silhouette, which means it was blocking the light. Ghosts can't do that."

"But..." Mark frowned as he looked between Remy and the house. "But it's got to be a spirit, surely? What else could it be?"

Remy refused to take her eyes off the building. She ran her hands through her hair then rubbed at tense, sore shoulders. "It can't be a ghost. They're intangible. Even if they look like they're solid, they can't be touched—not by us, not by air, not by light. They don't create shadows, let alone silhouettes. There's more than ghosts living in Carrow."

No one spoke for a beat. Then April said, "I'm pretty sure that second-floor light was turned off when we left, too."

Bernard's long face was stiff. "So we have an intruder living in Carrow."

"I..." Remy struggled with the concept and let her hands sag at her side. "I can't see any other explanation."

"They must have been here since before the storm set in," Mark said. "Probably since before we arrived. Have you ever encountered squatters here before?"

Remy shook her head. "As far as I know, no one comes inside the house except for the tours. I never found any signs of habitation, at least. April, did you give a key to anyone else?"

"Nope. I gave one to you and kept the other for myself." The teen's face was scrunched up from barely contained rage. "How'd they get in? The house is locked up super tight."

Remy kept her fingers kneading at her neck. Her mind was spiraling out with possibilities. "The foyer window is broken. I thought it was either from temperature changes or a spirit's influence, but what if someone's been getting in and out through it?"

"The windows are large enough for a grown man to fit through," Mark agreed. "And the front door creaks. The window might be the only way for someone to come and go without being heard."

Remy dearly wanted to sit down. The sight of the figure wove a string of awful possibilities. "What if they've been following us this whole time? What if they're responsible for the deaths?"

"They could've deleted Taj's missing footage," April said. "Slammed those doors we keep hearing. Led Lucille into the attic. Stolen Marjorie's bells."

"Someone paced around us during the last séance," Remy said. "It was after the lights went out. We assumed it was Edgar, but what if...what if it was a person who scratched Taj and dragged April out?"

April's expression darkened into something murderous. "I'm going to beat his face in."

"Slow down." Remy pressed a hand to April's shoulder to keep her grounded. "If we're right, this is someone who must know the house and its quirks very well. They've already killed three people. They probably intend to kill us, too. Rushing into a confrontation is one of the riskiest things we could do."

Mark muttered several frustrated words as he paced. "Going inside will be dangerous. But we can't stay out here forever. The downpour's so heavy, I feel like I'm half a moment away from drowning. Could we stay in the shed with the cars?"

"We'd freeze during the night and have nothing to eat tomorrow." Remy licked rain off her lips. "The house is more dangerous but has more resources, too. There's four of us left. That's a lot for a single person to take down at once, but I don't want to leap to conclusions by thinking we're only up against one person."

"You mean there might be more?"

"It's not likely. Every additional person hiding inside the house makes it increasingly difficult for them to conceal their presence. But we can't discount it." Remy took a step toward the building as she tried to cobble together a plan. "We'll make a run for the foyer. Grab whatever weapon you can find as quickly as you can, then get inside the recreation room. We stick together—no matter what. We can't let them separate us. Once we're in the recreation room, we'll try to use the cameras to see who, and where, the stranger is."

Mark caught Remy's hand in his. It seemed to be a reflexive

motion. His fingers were icy from the rain, but she squeezed him back, glad for human contact.

More, she was glad to have her friends again. The doubt, the fear, and the mistrust that had dogged her were erased. She didn't have to imagine any of them committing murder or know that she was sitting next to a serial killer. Instead, they were united against an enemy. No matter what else happened that day, Remy was grateful for that relief.

They moved to the house quickly, pushing tired legs and aching lungs to carry them up the stairs to the porch. There was no chance to have the element of surprise, so Mark kicked the front door open. Its hinges shrieked as they turned, and Remy sucked in a breath. Bodies lay on the foyer floor.

CHAPTER 38
FIGHT OR FLIGHT

PIERS, LUCILLE, AND MARJORIE had been placed on the rug beneath Edgar's portrait. They were on their backs, arms crossed over their chests, heads tilted back as though to admire the painting above them.

The sight made Remy's stomach turn, but it also eradicated the last of her doubt. They were facing a human enemy, and humans could be defeated. Trying not to think of how much of an advantage the unseen stalker might have, Remy nodded toward the recreation room's doors. "Hurry. Find a weapon and get into the room."

She felt awful passing her fallen friends without stopping, but the foyer was too exposed for them to linger there. She only prayed the stalker didn't have a gun.

Edgar's eyes seemed to follow them as they moved past his painting. The small, mysterious smirk felt larger, and his eyes colder, than before. Remy refused to acknowledge him with anything more than a passing glance as she sifted through the items they'd expelled from the room. She came up with a fire poker. Bernard found a knife left over from their last meal. Mark applied pressure to one of the already-cracked chairs to break it and tore off two of the carved legs. He gave one to April and took the second for his own.

Remy rotated in a circle as they shuffled back to their haven. She scanned the stairs, the landing, and every door that opened into the foyer, but she caught no sign of motion. If their stalker was watching, he was well concealed.

Inside the room, April bolted the door. Remy, without dropping her weapon, paced around the space and searched any area that a person could hide. She looked under tables, behind the curtains, and in every nook and cranny she passed. She even tugged on each of the bookcases to ensure none hid any form of secret passage.

One of the huge waves hit the window, rattling its panes. Remy lowered her weapon and turned back to the room. Mark, Bernard, and April stood in a loose semicircle. Their hair was plastered to pale faces, but they watched her, all waiting for her lead.

She licked her lips. "Okay. We're inside. We think we're safe… for now. But we're trapped in a room without food or water, and we don't know how long the storm will last. That gives us some tough choices to make."

April shivered and moved to huddle by what remained of the fire. "I've had enough water for a lifetime. And I doubt I could eat anything today."

"Ha! I feel the same way, but that sensation's not going to last for more than, say, six or seven hours." Remy's smile faded. "We'll need access to different parts of the house. The bathrooms, the kitchens. And, of course, the front door for when the storm clears. Our intruder must know that. If any parts of the house are riskier than others, it will be those."

"We've got Taj's system," Mark said. He stripped off his wet jacket, hung it over the back of a chair, and tried to shake some of the excess water off. None of them seemed to care anymore that they were damaging the carpet.

Remy turned toward the screens and bent close. She was comfortable with computers, but she didn't know the system Taj's equipment operated on. Three of the screens showed empty bedrooms; the fourth screen was set to the EMF readers' feed. It took her several minutes to figure out how to switch the view. She chose the foyer's camera.

A black screen appeared. Remy swore under her breath and selected another option. The second-floor hallway appeared. Remy was just in time to see a shape disappear down the stairs. Her blood turned cold.

"That was them, wasn't it?"

April's breath tickled Remy's cheeks, making her jump. She pressed a hand to her leaping heart and straightened. "It's got to be. They were too solid to be a spirit."

"Did you see what they looked like?" Mark asked.

"No. Only their back. They were wearing some kind of flowy clothes—like a cloak." Remy quickly changed the settings, hoping to catch the stranger on one of the other cameras, but they'd been traveling toward the foyer, and its image was still black. "They've cut the feed to the main camera. They know what they're doing."

She fiddled with the settings and options to find the recordings. The files were all blank. Everything had been erased.

"I have an unpopular opinion," Bernard said. He'd approached the window and was looking out over the ocean, his face gaunt but set. "I say we go on the offensive. Hunt them out before they have a chance to catch us with our guard down."

April pursed her lips. "Yeah, I'll back that motion. That storm's not even close to settling, and like Remy said, we're going to need food and whatnot soon. Without the foyer camera, we wouldn't know if they were lurking on the other side of the door. The longer we wait, the more time they have to prepare."

That was an unsettling thought. Remy glanced toward the large, carved wood barrier. It was bolted, but it didn't feel as secure as she would have liked.

"Mark?" she asked.

He took a slow breath as he swung his makeshift bat. "It's dangerous. But maybe it's better than the alternative—waiting."

"Yeah." Remy felt slightly queasy, but the decision also filled her with exhilaration. "They might not be expecting us to move against them so quickly."

"Let's go, then." April was halfway to the door before Remy caught up and grabbed her arm.

"Wait—" Words caught in her throat, and she had to swallow. "We've got to be careful. Crazy, obsessively careful. Whoever we're up against must know the house well. Carrow is a maze of back passageways and hard-to-access areas, but it's still difficult to believe we didn't find any sign of the intruder while searching for Lucille. Wherever they're hiding must be well concealed."

"All the more reason to move now, before they have time to hide. You saw the video! They're probably in the foyer right now!"

Remy swallowed, wrapped both hands around her fire poker, and straightened her back. "You're right. If we find them, don't hesitate—not even for a second. Try to knock their feet out from under them and subdue them in any way you can. Are you all ready?"

She had three nods in answer.

"No matter what happens, don't split up. If we become divided, we lose by default. Worst-case scenario—if things go disastrously wrong, everyone meet back in this room, okay?"

She approached the door and pressed her ear to the wood. As far as she could hear, everything was peaceful outside. That was enough to make her skin crawl. In the days they'd been at Carrow, the house had never been silent. But there was no trace of the groaning wood, the whistling wind, or the heavy, hollow echoes. Even the rain seemed to be holding its breath. Remy lifted her poker in preparation, drew the bolt, and nudged the door open.

The three bodies still lay on the rug, lined up like statues. Rain poured through the broken window and created a large, slowly spreading puddle across the floor. The portrait smirked across the scene, its gaze knowing and bleak.

She couldn't see any sign of the invader. Remy motioned for the group to move forward, and they slunk toward the nearest door, the one belonging to the dining room. Remy felt a small swell of pride for her little party. They moved in a tight bunch, Mark and Bernard sweeping their gazes over their sides and back, and their footfalls were so soft that they barely disturbed the unnatural peace.

Remy pressed the dining room door open and clicked its light on. Their sandwiches still waited on the table. She was suddenly struck by the idea that the slip in time might not have been showing an illusion but the literal future. It was hard to imagine a scenario where they stayed long enough to throw out the wasted food.

"Stay in the doorway," Remy whispered to Bernard. "Yell if you see movement."

She, Mark, and April spread through the room, weapons raised, to search it. Remy held herself tense, prepared to bring her poker down at the first sign of motion. The constant anxiety had started to build a headache through her skull, but she pushed it back, ignoring it, as they examined around and behind the room's furniture.

When they circled back to Bernard, she felt sure that the dining area was empty. By silent agreement, they progressed to the overcrowded smoking room. Again, Bernard stayed in the door, watching the foyer, while they searched. The taxidermied animals' black eyes glittered in the light as they hunted around the huge wingback chairs and felt the sconces and walls for any sign of secret compartments. They found none.

April nudged Remy's arm and silently nodded toward the opposite wall. It took Remy a second to notice what had bothered the teen. One of the paintings showed a stately, plump gentleman. His necktie had been undone, and red bruises circled his neck.

"It wasn't like that before, was it?" April whispered.

Remy mutely shook her head. The smoking room wasn't part of the official tour, so she rarely visited it, but she was certain she'd never seen the noose's marks before. *It might be a spectral illusion. Possibly that man died in Carrow and his spirit wants his death avenged—or at least recognized.*

Creaks echoed above them, and they all looked toward the ceiling. April opened her mouth to speak, but Remy pressed her hand over the girl's lips. They listened as footsteps shifted along the upstairs hallway. Then a low, grinding noise told them the attic's stairs were being lowered.

"Ghost or human?" Mark asked.

Remy bit her lip. "Marjorie would probably know…if she was still with us. We've already heard a spirit slam doors in a poltergeist state, and I suspect a ghost lowered the stairs that night I went into the attic."

April's eyes shone in the room's dim lights as she flexed her fingers over her bat. "Do we keep looking down here or go upstairs?"

Remy hated the idea of moving farther from their sanctuary, but the footsteps had sounded solid. She tried to suppress her shivers as she said, "I think upstairs." She glanced at Mark. "Will you be okay going into the attic?"

His face was blanched but resolute as he nodded. "Yes."

"Let's go, quickly," Bernard said.

Together, they crossed to the staircase. Although they kept their footsteps light and hung along the stairs' edge, the boards still creaked. Remy could only pray the intruder didn't hear.

They reached the hallway and looked down its length. The lights flickered then settled. Remy nodded toward the stairs hidden in the shadowed end of the hall. Bernard climbed them first, followed by Mark, with Remy and April bringing up the rear. As she emerged into the attic, Remy couldn't suppress a shudder. The air was icy and damp, and it stuck in her throat. They turned on their flashlights and scanned the beams across the area.

The open window Lucille had fallen through allowed water to drench and soak into the wooden floorboards. Some had swollen and bulged up unnaturally, creating a disorienting warp to the ground. The wardrobe, cloistered in shadows, still stood open, its offering of bones scattered over the floor.

"Be careful," Remy whispered. "The floor's rotten. There's a hole over there. And don't step on any of the discolored patches."

She turned in a circle to examine the dusty floor. Several sets of tracks led away from the trapdoor. Three went to the window—*those would be from Lucille's death*—but an area had been scuffed clean leading in the opposite direction, deeper into the attic. Remy thought she may have created the path on the night she'd discovered the skeleton in the wardrobe, but she wasn't completely certain. She took an experimental step down the clear patch, and the boards groaned.

Her companions' breaths were low and quick. Remy strained to hear a fifth presence, but between the drumming rain and the echoes that coursed through the attic, it was impossible to be certain what she was hearing. Her flashlight's beam landed on the skull she'd uncovered. She let the light linger there, unnerved by how deep the shadows in its eye sockets appeared.

Something moved farther in the attic. Remy swiveled toward it. Her flashlight's beam was joined by three others. They picked out a tangle of discarded, broken furniture, vast spans of cobwebs, and a swirl of disturbed dust.

"We see you!" April yelled.

The sudden noise made Remy jump. The teen ran forward before anyone could stop her, crossing the space in ten quick steps, and skidded to a halt beside a stack of broken chairs. She spun her flashlight over the area behind the pile, frowned, and turned back to Remy. "There's no one here."

Remy couldn't speak. Her light had caught on a figure behind April. A man, tall and bone thin, stared at April, his fingers twitching over the area where his jaw had once existed.

CHAPTER 39
DARK OF DEEP NIGHT

"BEHIND YOU!" MARK BARKED.

April's eyes widened. She turned and gasped, stumbling backward in the same motion. The specter took a step toward the teen, clawing at the gore that dribbled from his broken face. His fingernails made faint clicking noises as they bumped the teeth protruding from his upper jaw. Then he faded, dissolving like a puff of vapor on a hot day.

April backed into the stack of chairs, her eyes huge and the makeshift bat raised above her head. Her voice escaped as a squeak. "Where'd he go?"

"It was only a spirit." Remy tried to force oxygen into her lungs as she stepped forward. "He was strong to appear as a corporeal specter. He probably lowered the stairs, too. We should get out of here. It's not safe, and I don't think any other human has been here in a long time."

April sucked in a hiccupping breath then, keeping her eyes on the space where the man had stood, backed toward the group.

Two long, thick ropes fell out of the rafters, their loops shifting to block April's path. The teen's attention stayed fixed on the space behind her as she backed into the cords. A sickened gasp escaped Mark.

Panic spiked Remy's heart rate. Leaping forward, she yelled, "April, watch out!"

April turned as she bumped the ropes. They reacted like living things, shivering and coiling up, but the teen's reflexes were faster. She twisted backward and ducked away from the cords before they could loop around her throat. Momentum carried her stumbling back, and her sneaker landed on one of the darkened areas of the floor. A sharp crack was all the warning they had, then April plunged through the floor.

"No!" Remy skidded to her knees beside the hole. The floorboards groaned under her weight, threatening to send her down, as well, but she ignored them as she leaned forward and extended her flashlight into the pit. Bernard followed closely behind her, his flashlight beam joining hers.

Remy couldn't see anything except black. The interstitial space between the attic and the floor below swallowed every ounce of light. Icy air radiated out of it, billowing over her face as though she'd opened a freezer door. "April!"

There was no reply.

Did she land on the floor below? How far would that be to fall? It must be at least twelve feet...enough to break bones. Or crack a skull.

"April, answer me!"

A hand touched her shoulder. Mark was pale and shaking, but his voice held conviction. "Do you know where she would have landed? The hall or one of the rooms?"

Remy glanced at each of the attic's nearest walls then closed her eyes as she tried to picture the house's blueprint. "I-I think... Room 21."

"Then we'll go downstairs and get to her that way. Come on."

As Remy backed away from the hole, she caught a hint of motion behind the jumble of chairs. The specter crouched there, his fingers spasming at his missing jaw, his bulging eyes following them. Remy raised her poker as she moved away. He made no attempt to follow, but his unblinking eyes didn't leave them as they rushed to the trapdoor.

Remy took the stairs faster than was safe and dropped into the hallway. The two lights set into the ceiling flickered, and in the fluttering semiseconds of illumination, Remy thought she caught sight of a woman in a dark-gray dress pacing along the runner. She pointed her flashlight toward the figure, and the woman vanished.

"I saw it, too," Mark whispered. "But we can't hesitate. We need to find April."

Remy nodded and moved forward. She knew the house's layout so well that she could have found Room 21 with her eyes closed. It wasn't part of the official tour, but its history was far from pleasant. Three guests, all poor travelers, had vanished while staying in it. During the police investigation, bloodstains had been found on the carpet, and a bureau had been positioned to hide tears in the wallpaper that looked suspiciously like fingernail markings.

During the subsequent questioning, several staff claimed to have heard hollow wails coming from the space late at night, usually when the room was empty. They said Edgar had told them to ignore it. He'd claimed that it was only the wind.

Remy twisted the handle, but it stuck. She rattled it then beat her fist against the door. "April! April, can you hear me?"

None of these rooms were locked when we arrived.

"We need to break it down," Bernard said.

The lights flickered. A faint, broken laugh echoed down the hallway. Jagged like a scratched record, it set Remy's teeth on edge. Bernard turned and scanned the empty space.

Mark kicked at the door. It bowed inward but didn't budge. He kicked again, leaving a small crack in the frame.

"No—" Remy staggered away from the room. A dark liquid seeped out under the door, staining the carpet black. The sickening, metallic tang saturating the air told her it was blood. "April!"

Mark raised his foot again, his teeth clenched, but then the flickering lights burst. Darkness rushed around them. The kick never landed. Instead, Remy heard a grunt and felt something large and heavy fall past her. She pressed the button on her flashlight, but the bulb had burned out. She stretched out her hands, her wide eyes futilely trying to see through the dark. "Mark? Bernard?"

Bernard spoke. "Watch ou—"

A thud, a groan. The scrape of fingernails being drawn across wallpaper. A picture hung on the wall rattled as it was bumped. The floorboards creaked.

Something icy brushed across Remy's cheek. She swung toward it, bringing her fire poker down on the unseen entity, but it touched only air. Her breaths came in ragged gasps. She could no longer hear her companions. She couldn't see anything except darkness or feel anything except the metal between her hands.

Then a low, scraping noise made her turn. Something heavy was being dragged across the floor.

Her heart felt ready to explode. She couldn't draw enough breath to make any noise but stretched her hand forward, searching for the entity making the awful noise.

Cold fingers fixed around her ankle and tugged. She fell, hit her shoulder against the wall, and rolled. Remy swung her poker toward the hand and felt the metal impact something spongy and fleshy. It made a sucking noise as she pulled it free, but the fingers didn't release her. A second hand wrapped around her forearm. The flesh was scabby and sticky, and cold enough to sting. *Corpses' hands,* her mind screamed.

Another hand grabbed her other leg. Two more scrabbled at her back. She swung her weapon at them, wild in her terror. She twisted, rolling onto her stomach, and felt another hand touch her face. Its fingernails scraped across her throat. She kicked one leg free, rolled again, and found the wall. She used it to drag herself up. The final hand released her other leg, and she staggered back.

Her body was starved for oxygen. Dizziness and nausea made

her double over, but she didn't dare stay near the hands. She staggered down the hallway, clinging to the walls to keep upright. "Mark?" Her voice escaped as a croak. "Bernard?"

Silence flowed around her, and she knew she was alone.

Her foot bumped something small and solid. She bent and felt one of the flashlights. Its metal was still warm from being held. *How did it get over here?* The button clicked, but the light wouldn't turn on. She discarded it and searched around the area, praying she might still find one of her companions. Her hands brushed over carpet, over the plaster, over cloistering dust, but couldn't find the touch of warm skin she desperately searched for.

A choked cry startled her. She recognized Mark's voice, but the sound had come from below her—from downstairs. The yell broke off partway through. Fresh fear hit Remy, and she desperately tried to orient herself.

Her fingertips found a door, and she felt over its surface until she touched the bronze numbers hung on its front: *14.* That put her nearly halfway down the hallway. She turned toward the staircase and began moving forward, her fingers extended just far enough to brush along the wall and count the ridges that signaled each doorframe. She knew the house well enough to stop opposite the staircase, turn, and place her hand on the dusty railing.

Moving down the stairs in the dark was a terrifying experience. Remy felt like she was always a step away from walking into the killer hunting them or into one of the grasping hands. She was blind but didn't dare close her eyes, instead staring into the void.

Her fingers were numb from shock and cold. Adrenaline kept her jumpy, and fear for her companions kept her alert. They'd agreed to meet in the recreation room if anything went seriously bad. Remy prayed the others had found their way there, but Mark's cry frightened her.

I can't lose any more of my friends. I can't be alone in this house.

She counted thirty-five stairs until her feet touched the foyer floor. She could hear the rain rushing through the broken window, the dull echo of her gasping breaths, and the groans of slowly flexing wooden supports. No sounds from other humans.

"Mark? Bernard?"

Speaking was a risk, but the awful quiet was unbearable. She took a step toward the recreation room, and her foot caught on something hard.

She stumbled and caught herself before she fell. Blind groping revealed that she'd walked into a chair.

I forgot—we piled everything from the recreation room out here. That includes the lamp.

Thin hope sparked in her heart. She dropped to her knees and began feeling over the shapes, her fingers searching for the cool touch of glass and metal. She remembered carrying the lamp outside—she'd put the box of matches inside it and left it near the door.

Something shifted in the foyer behind her. Remy froze, bent at an awkward angle but too frightened to straighten. The unseen entity moved again. Its steps were heavy and shuffling, and it didn't move far before halting again. A rattling exhale sent goose bumps rising over Remy's skin.

It's probably a spirit. It can't hurt you. Marjorie said it a hundred times: spirits are harmless. Oh, please, please, let it only be a spirit.

Remy kept feeling forward, caution keeping her movements slow and careful, as she sought the precious lamp.

The figure turned and took two shuffling steps in Remy's direction. At the same time, she touched glass. Remy continued to probe, feeling around the shape, and relief hit her as she found the lamp's handle. She tugged it toward herself.

Heavy objects tumbled to the foyer floor. Remy had forgotten Taj's EMF recorders were stacked on top of the lamp. The clattering racket seemed impossibly loud, and Remy flinched. No longer cautious, the unseen being staggered in Remy's direction.

The impulse to run overwhelmed her, but the foyer was too dark to see where to go. Instead, she wrenched open the lamp's door, found the box of matches inside, and tried to light one blind.

The being was nearly on top of her. She could hear its rattling breath as it mimicked drawing air into damaged lungs. The foyer's atmosphere suddenly felt much colder and much thicker.

She struck a match—it didn't light. She fumbled, dropped the box, caught it, and shook a fresh match out.

Unbearably cold fingers touched Remy's shoulder. *It can't hurt you... It can't hurt you... It can't hurt—*

The hand squeezed, and she gasped against the pain. The match lit. Somehow, it didn't go out, despite how badly her hand shook. She looked over her shoulder. A man stared back. The right side of his face appeared human; a scraggly gray beard grew over his chin, partially hiding blood-caked lips. The blue eye was wide and intent. A cleaver was embedded in the temple on the other side of his face. Blood hid his left eye and saturated his beard. He leaned closer to Remy, his breath growing frost over her tear-dampened cheek.

"You're a ghost." The words were a whisper. "You can't hurt me."

His lips twitched into something like a grin. His hand tightened further, the nails biting into Remy's skin, pinching hard enough to make her cry out against the pain, then the match burned out.

CHAPTER 40
GRAVES FOR THE DEAD

REMY TRIED TO PICK up the spilled matches, but terror and pain made her shake too badly. The pressure left her shoulder. She drew a sharp breath, clenched her fingers into fists to still them, and tried again. She found a match, struck it on the box, and lifted the light.

The dead man had vanished. Remy, not daring to believe it, swiveled to look across the room. She couldn't see far in the tiny light.

She held the match to the lamp's wick before it could die again and waited for the small flame to stabilize. Her shoulder still hurt, and she touched her fingers to the bruises as awful significance hit her.

The house is waking up. Marjorie had insisted spirits couldn't harm humans. *But what if they were only limited by how much energy they had access to? Would an overload of energy allow them not only to take on corporeal forms, but also to affect the physical world?*

She'd never heard of a case like that before—but then, she'd never known a house like Carrow before, either. Remy bent close to her lamp, cherishing the precious light, and tried to take in enough air to quell the dizziness.

I need to find the others.

The recreation room doors weren't far to her right. She stood shakily, approached them, and held the lamp ahead of herself as she looked inside.

The space was exactly how they'd left it. The fireplace, its embers dead, radiated faint warmth, but it was the only welcoming part of the room. Without the ceiling lights, the collection of overstuffed armchairs took on a sinister appearance, looking almost like hulking giants.

Remy barely dared whispering. "Mark? Bernard? Please answer me."

A hiss drew her attention to Taj's screens on the opposite side of the room. They showed only a tangle of static. Remy started to see screaming faces among the white noise and turned away.

Lightning flashed, bathing the room in harsh whites and impenetrable shadows. In that split second, she saw unfamiliar figures standing in the area: women in heavy black mourning dresses, men in work clothes, even a child, her hair wet and limp. They all stared at Remy. She swallowed the lump in her throat and backed out of the room.

The house is waking up…

She was starting to recognize that her friends either wouldn't or couldn't return. Remy turned toward the stairs and prepared to climb to the second floor and search for her companions. She tried to convince herself that things would be different because she had a lamp, but it was hard to forget how easily Edgar's spirit had snuffed out other flames.

She took a step toward the stairs but stopped. Something dark and sticky was smeared on the floor. Remy shifted back and held out her lamp to examine it. A line of blood led away from her, across the tiles, and disappeared under the basement's door.

No... Oh, please, mercy, no...

She had to bite her cheek to stay quiet as she crossed to the door. Dread clenched her stomach, but Mark had called for help only minutes before. If there was a chance he was still alive—even a slim one—she couldn't abandon him.

She nudged the door open with her foot. The darkness inside was unnaturally intense. It blocked her lamp's attempts to pierce it. She could see eight steps down, but everything beyond that was hidden.

"Mark?"

She already knew he wouldn't respond. She extended one foot into the stairwell then followed it with the other, unwilling to stop moving once she had momentum. Her little sphere of light moved with her, brightening the rough stone wall at one side and the thin metal rails protecting her from the drop on the other. The farther she descended, the harder it became to see the doorway behind her. Eventually, it faded into black.

Her feet hit the compacted-dirt floor. She tried not to let the fear rule her, but that was hard when so much awful potential was hidden in the space.

She could feel the chill rolling off the cold spot that lingered in the landing's corner, and could even see a patch of dampness where Lucille's wet body had rested. She turned back to the room, took a shuddering breath, and ducked under the cordon that separated her from the open graves.

She'd never been so far into the area, not even when exploring the house on her own. It had partially been from the danger posed by the unstable strips of ground between the holes and partially out of respect for the victims who had been buried in the space. Now, though, she had to not only walk among the dozen graves, but look inside them, too.

She bent over the nearest hole and held her lamp out to light it. Shadows played over a jumble of limbs in its base, and she bit down on a gasp. The translucent man twisted his head and shoulders to stare up at her, his lips pulling back into a grimace to expose rotting teeth. Then his form faded, rolling away like smoke.

Remy stumbled away from him, misjudged her footing, and cried out as her leg dropped into the hole behind her. The lamp and fire poker clattered to the floor as she threw out her hands to catch herself. The flame spluttered but, by some miracle, stabilized. The poker spiraled out of her reach and tumbled into the grave.

She kept still just long enough to assure herself that the ground wasn't going to collapse any further, then she pulled herself back up to a steady footing. She was shaking but not hurt, and still had her light. Afraid of what she might see, Remy looked into the grave her poker had fallen into.

It held a maid. The girl's eyes were bloodshot, and she had both hands pressed over her cut throat. Her mouth opened, but no noise came out. Nestled at her side was Remy's weapon.

Remy's fingers itched for some kind of defense, but she couldn't bring herself to descend into the girl's bed. Instead, she held her lamp close as she pressed deeper into the graveyard. The black holes were filled with the restless ghosts. Her sanity continued to unravel with each tormented gaze she met.

The basement extended under most of the house. Support beams loomed out of the darkness and blocked her sight, giving her the awful impression that someone or something might be hiding behind them and waiting for her to move too close to their trap. The dirt, long dried and crumbling, shifted under her feet, and Remy moved back to more solid ground. She turned and saw a flash of skin inside a grave near the back wall.

It had a different color from that of the spirits. Although they appeared solid, the ghosts all held a faint, translucent aura about them. But the person in this final grave was human. Remy dropped to her knees as her heart threatened to crack. The dark hair was familiar. The angular face had smiled at her countless times during the past days. His hand had held hers when she was frightened. Only the stain of blood painted across his face was new.

"Mark!" She set the lamp on the ground and slipped into the

grave. Her feet sank ankle-deep into the water that had collected there, but she didn't care. She knelt in the cramped space by Mark's side and felt around his neck.

He was cool but not deathly cold. She pressed her fingers to his throat as she hunted for a pulse. The task was impossible; her fingers were numb and shaking uncontrollably.

"Mark, please wake up—please." She shook his shoulder. His head rolled, his hair dragging through the water, but his eyes remained closed. He looked peaceful. Unpleasantly so.

She sized up the grave's sides. It was only four feet high, but Mark was heavy. Still, she couldn't leave him there. If he was still alive, he would freeze in the water.

Remy reached her arms under his shoulders and pulled him up. Pain arced through her injured arm. Slimy water and blood dripped off Mark's form and trickled over Remy as she raised him. She heaved, using every inch of her remaining strength to get his torso over the grave's lip, then managed to push his legs over.

The effort left her exhausted, but she still smiled at her triumph. She braced her forearms on the dirt and pulled herself out, as well, then collapsed next to Mark. For a moment, she focused solely on breathing.

We can't stay in this basement. It's a toxic area. But I don't know if I can get him up the stairs.

She wasn't given the chance to try. The basement door slammed closed.

CHAPTER 41
GAMES

REMY JOLTED AS THE door crashed shut. She reflexively reached toward Mark. A mad idea that she needed to put out the lamp's light flashed through her, but she dismissed it quickly. Whoever had shut the door already knew she was there. Blinding herself wouldn't help.

I can't let them get to Mark.

She didn't have a weapon, but the fire poker wasn't far away. She looked toward the grave it had fallen into—halfway between her and the stairs. The lamp highlighted its edge, but its glow didn't reach much farther.

If I'm fast, I might be able to get it before...

A crunch echoed through the still, cold air as the unseen figure stepped off the stairs. Remy bolted for the grave. She'd taken three half-running steps before a faint noise froze her.

Bells.

Their jingling rhythm was familiar. Her mouth dried as her heart did an unpleasant skip. A match hissed, then a halo of brightness appeared at the base of the stairs as a candle was lit. The light lifted to reveal Marjorie's wrinkled face as it shifted into a smile. She had both hands clasped around the candle, with the string of bells looped around one of her wrists. Her head tilted to the side as she regarded Remy. She would have looked perfectly normal except for the circle of reddish bruises around her throat and the way her blue irises flashed black.

"Hello, Remy."

The voice didn't belong to Marjorie. It was deep and heavy, the guttural growl of a man whose throat had been damaged. Remy fought to stay upright as her legs turned to jelly. "Edgar."

"You're not completely stupid. It took the others longer to figure it out." Edgar flexed his host's neck, eyes fluttering closed as the vertebrae cracked.

"The others?" Remy was already starting to suspect the truth, but she wanted to hear the words. Her eyes flicked to the grave before returning to her companion's face. Edgar was too close for her to make a run for it, but if she could keep him distracted long enough—

The black eyes smiled at Remy. "Piers and Lucille. Though, to be fair, Lucille was drunk out of her mind. I had to bodily carry her into the attic."

Remy slid a foot closer to her target, trying to move slowly enough that it wouldn't attract attention. Terror had sunk its teeth into her, clouding her mind, but she focused on keeping the conversation going. "You were using Marjorie's body this whole time, weren't you?"

"Good girl," he purred. "Poor sweet Marjorie was so eager to make contact with the spirits that she left the doors to her mind wide open. I infiltrated during that first night while she wandered my house asleep, and made a little room for myself inside. It took some care to ensure she didn't find my presence, but it wasn't challenging."

"I'm assuming you were responsible for everything else we didn't have an answer for. The words on Marjorie's door. The erased tapes. Tampering with the cars." Another foot closer. Sweat beaded over Remy's skin.

"Of course. All I had to do was take control for a handful of minutes then erase her memories. You would think a skilled medium would be better at identifying possession, wouldn't you? Blocks of missing time are a classic symptom. But, of course, vanity was her downfall, as it is for so many people. She wouldn't even consider that she'd made such a great error."

Another few inches closer to her weapon, Remy could see the candlelight flickering on the medium's dead, black eyes. "I don't understand—if you were using her, why did you kill her?"

"Really, what a question to ask after I complimented your mind. You were growing suspicious of your party. Keeping tabs. Not letting them wander off alone. The only ones not under your scrutiny were the dead. I can just as easily puppet a corpse as a live body, so it was convenient to lead the cow out and have her hung."

Remy flinched at the words but continued her slow progress. She was nearly at the grave. "So there never was an intruder."

"No, little Remy." The smile widened. "Just an old friend who has been watching you for a very long time."

"Can I ask one last question?" *Almost...* "What's your end game? Do you just love killing so much that you refused to stop after death?"

"Ha!" Edgar threw back the medium's head in a rasping laugh. "I do obtain some significant satisfaction from it; you're right. But it is hardly my motivation. So much of life is about games. Have you noticed? We fake emotions. Lie about our intentions. Pretend innocence. For example, you're pretending not to be slinking closer to that fire poker. And I am pretending not to notice."

Remy froze. Her heart dropped as she stared into Marjorie's coldly smiling face. Then she lunged toward the grave, desperation pushing her to be faster than the medium.

Marjorie's hand rose, splayed fingers curled toward the ground, then jerked up. Five gray, decaying hands burst out of the packed earth. The limbs curled toward Remy and caught around her legs. The fingers tightened their grip then pulled her down so harshly that it forced her breath out. More arms grew out of the floor and wrapped around her shoulders and back to pin her. Their spongy, scabbed flesh was sickeningly cold and unrelenting.

Remy cried out and thrashed, but the hands only tightened. The touch of rotting flesh made her nausea swell, and only the pressing terror kept her stomach where it belonged.

Marjorie released a heavy exhale and moved forward. Her extended fingers twitched, controlling the dead hands like a puppet master, as she knelt at Remy's side.

"I'm so glad I get to have you, little Remy. I've been watching you lead your tours through my home these last two years. I fascinated you—I could feel it. And, in a way, you fascinate me. That's why I saved you for last."

"Stop it," Remy gasped.

Marjorie set the candle on the floor and gripped a fistful of Remy's hair. The bells jingled as Remy's head was jerked to the side.

"Oh, don't worry. I'm not going to kill you. Not just yet. You wanted to know my end game, didn't you?"

Despite the rasp, his voice had a smooth, enchanting ease to it. Remy understood how he'd fooled an entire town for eight years; a dangerous charisma seeped out of every pore.

"You already guessed at it when Marjorie spoke of my old order, the Red Crows. Ah, but you would be amazed by the tests we conducted. We were still training for our greatest experiment when the church persecuted and killed my kin. I was a child then, and spared, but never forgot my teachings."

Something sharp pierced the back of her neck. Remy tried to squirm away, but the holds on her hair and her body constricted like a straitjacket.

"All beings on earth are made up of energy. Humans. Animals. Ghosts. With enough energy, almost anything is possible."

The scratching, stinging pain grew over the back of Remy's neck. Edgar was using one of Marjorie's fingernails, and Remy felt sick when she realized he must be carving the symbol into her neck.

"With enough energy, a ghost could restore his mortal form. He could *live* again. *Immortal.*" Edgar exhaled a laugh. "That is Carrow's purpose, my dear. This emblem binds souls to me. They cannot escape—not as long as the house stands. And so they have been gathering energy these past decades. It has slowly built, accumulating to phenomenal levels, leading us to this night. At the height of my storm and with you and your friends as living sacrifices, I shall walk this earth aga—"

The words cut off with a low, cracking *thwock*. Marjorie's head jerked back. A look of surprise widened her eyes and slackened her jaw. Her body was still for a moment, then she collapsed onto the ground.

In the space behind her stood Bernard, his features gray with dust, Mark's bloodied bat held high.

CHAPTER 42
REVELRY

BERNARD STAGGERED THEN REACHED a hand toward Remy. "Quick. We need to run."

Shock made Remy sluggish to respond. She blinked at Marjorie's fallen body then at Bernard. Finally, awareness clicked into place, and she began squirming. The cold corpse hands holding her down had gone limp and sloughed away. "How did you—"

"Later. We need to move." Breathless, he pulled Remy to her feet then snatched up Marjorie's candle and turned toward the stairs.

Remy turned back to Mark. His face was paper white, save for where blood stained it. "We need to help—"

"There's no time, damn it! We'll come back for him later."

Motion at Remy's side made her stagger back. Bernard's blow had cracked a hole in Marjorie's skull, but the plates were shifting back into place like a jigsaw puzzle. The black eyes swiveled toward Remy.

"Oh—" Remy sent a final, desperate look toward Mark, but she understood Bernard's urgency. If she stayed to help him, they were all dead. The best she could hope for was to lead Marjorie away from him.

She ran for the exit, leaping around the open graves, no longer worried about the unstable earth. Bernard was already climbing the stairs, one hand holding the candle ahead and the other pulling on the rail to lengthen his strides. Remy, lighter and still riding on adrenaline, caught up near the top of the steps.

"What are we doing?"

"Winging it." Sweat soaked into the powder that coated his face, and his eyes were frantic as he burst through the basement door.

The foyer was filled with people. Ladies in elegant silk gowns and gentlemen in dark suits mingled, laughing and talking as a band played a soothing waltz in the space below the stairs. Maids wove through the crowd, ferrying plates of food and alcohol to the guests with light steps and deferential bows.

Remy came to a halt, confusion and wonder freezing her mind. She glanced toward the place where they had piled the recreation room's furniture and found it replaced with a buffet table. The lights were bright and warm. A fire crackled in the grate.

"It's a slip in time," she said.

Bernard took a quick breath as he nodded. "He's trying to distract us. We need to get to the kitchens."

"Why—" Remy started, but Bernard was already moving.

They merged into the crowd. The bodies felt warm and real.

Remy's hands brushed over feathers, silk, chiffon, and furs as she pushed between them, but none of the guests paid her any attention.

"He's here," Bernard said, real fear infusing his tone. Remy followed his gaze toward the fireplace. The wingback chairs, so old and dusty in her world, were new and free from ax marks in this version. They had been pushed aside to increase the floor space, and standing in front of the fire with one hand in his pocket and a glass of brandy in the other was Edgar.

He looked immaculate. His gray eyes sparkled, his sooty hair slicked back, and his suit—rather, John Carrow's suit—was sleek and crease-free. He truly looked like the ruler of the house, holding court where he could benevolently smile over his guests.

Except he wasn't looking at the crowd. His gaze was fixed on Remy.

Her stomach lurched. The social elite seemed ignorant of her presence, but Edgar's dispassionate eyes didn't blink as they tracked her movements. He placed his glass on the mantelpiece below his own portrait and began stalking toward them.

"Can he hurt us?" Bernard whispered to Remy.

"No idea. Don't want to find out."

They veered away from Edgar to take a more circular course to the kitchen and broke into a run. Remy had to fight her way through the bodies. The guests were not only unaware of her, but unyielding, and roving maids repeatedly blocked her path. Edgar, on the other hand, cut through the crowd. Guests shifted aside as he neared them. He broke into a jog, his previously congenial face cracking into the harsh, wide-eyed grin of a predator closing in on its prey.

Bernard made a quick, barking noise. Remy turned, but they'd become separated in the throng, and she couldn't see him. Another familiar figure loomed out of the crowd of strangers, and the tinkle of bells surrounded her.

Marjorie.

The medium's wild smile perfectly mimicked the man's. While Remy had been distracted by the phantom, incorporeal Edgar from the time slip, the real Edgar within Marjorie's body had moved to block her path and stood, arms extended, to catch her.

Remy jumped backward. She slipped on the waxed floor and fell. In a split second, Marjorie was on her, pinning her to the cold tile.

The world suddenly felt much colder. Remy blinked, and the illusion—the guests, the warm lighting, the chatter, the music, and the bobbing maids—melted away. All that remained was Marjorie and the lamp she'd dropped onto the floor in the dusty, dilapidated house.

"You're a greater fool than I suspected," Edgar's voice purred. He seemed to be holding in laughter. "You can beat the cow's head in. You can stab her. You can burn her to soot. But none of that will harm *me*. You cannot kill the dead."

Remy landed a kick on Marjorie's thigh. She didn't even flinch.

"What was *your* end game, Remy? Hide out in the house? Take your chances on the bridge? Both are certain death. You are past any hope of winning. Lie still, now, and I won't prolong this part any more than necessary."

The hand gripped her hair and twisted her head to the side as Marjorie's weight pinned her to the floor. The fingernails found the still-sore patch at the back of her neck. No amount of kicking and punching could shift the medium.

Where's Bernard? Did he get away?

Remy glimpsed a figure moving toward them out of the corner of her eyes. The lamp's light was so thin that she couldn't see his features, but the walk was familiar. Dread filled her. He was moving toward them. She couldn't let Edgar catch him, too. "No, don't!"

"Shush, now," Edgar whispered, leaning closer while Remy struggled. "I told you to keep still."

The figure broke into a run. As he drew closer, Remy could see the blood shining on Mark's face. His teeth were bared in a snarl, and his eyes flashed dangerously. Marjorie's head turned a second too late. Mark's boot collided with her face, knocking her across the floor.

"Run," Remy begged.

Mark grabbed her arms and dragged her away from the medium. His hands were strong and warm, and only fear for his safety kept her from crying with relief.

"It's Edgar. He can't be killed."

Marjorie sat up, her neck making unnatural cracking noises as its vertebrae reconnected. The smile had vanished as she glared death at Mark. She extended one hand, fingers twitching toward the floor, and Remy, knowing what was about to happen, threw herself at the medium.

Decaying hands cracked through the tiles. The limbs thrashed as Remy and the medium tumbled to the floor. Mark was at her side, alternately trying to hold Marjorie down and pull Remy away, as the medium's face contorted into a roar of rage.

A door slammed open. Bernard's voice boomed through the foyer. "Hold her down!"

He ran out of the kitchens, something small clasped in his hand. Remy grunted as Marjorie's hand fastened around her neck and squeezed.

"You cannot win," Edgar snarled.

Remy gagged as the fingers tightened, but she leaned her weight into the medium. The cold, rotting hands were slinking up her legs and around her torso to scrabble at and grip her skin. Spittle flew from Marjorie's mouth as Edgar laughed.

"Hold her!" Bernard repeated.

He skidded to a halt above Marjorie's head. Both Remy and Mark applied their weight to keep the medium down. Bernard held up the object he'd fetched and poised it over her head.

A saltshaker. Remy would have laughed if she hadn't been so frantic. *Why on earth did he fetch a saltshaker?*

Marjorie's eyes bulged, and the laughter became a snarl. Bernard shook the salt, pouring grains onto the medium's head, and a memory hit Remy. During her séance, Marjorie had used salt to attack the spirit circling them. She'd called it a cleansing element that she'd often used in cases of hauntings and possessions. It hadn't removed him, but the wailing shriek suggested it had hurt him.

At least during the séance, her salt had been kept in an elegant bowl and treated reverently. Even amid the oxygen deprivation, panic, and horror, Remy was acutely aware of how ridiculous Bernard looked shaking salt over the medium as though he were seasoning his dinner.

It was working, though. The hand around Remy's throat loosened. Smoke rose from Marjorie's forehead and cheeks, the tiny plumes popping up anywhere the salt hit her, and the snarl grew into an earsplitting howl.

The scabbed, dead hands attempting to hold Remy twitched. Their fingers scrabbled erratically, then they turned limp. One by one, they slithered back through the holes in the tiles.

Remy felt electricity buzzing around her, so dense that it stung her skin. A deep rumble shook the building. Marjorie writhed, and Remy applied her whole weight to the medium's torso to keep her grounded as Bernard continued to thump the saltshaker's base.

A wave of immense pressure threw them back. Remy skidded across the floor then curled into a ball, winded and with her ears ringing. The rattling earthquake subsided, and the prickling electricity faded. Remy gingerly sat up and turned toward the foyer's center. Marjorie lay limp and silent.

CHAPTER 43
DIRT AND SALT

BERNARD AND MARK HAD both been thrown back by the shock wave. They shuffled toward Remy, wiping at sweat-blinded eyes and fresh scrapes.

"You okay?" Mark gripped Remy's shoulders, his dark, anxious eyes glancing over her.

"Yeah, but I don't think you can say the same." She reached toward his bloodied face but didn't touch him for fear of hurting him more. "That's a nasty cut."

"I'm sure it looks worse than it actually is. And even if it's not, it's better than it could be." He exhaled heavily. "At least you're all right. I woke in the basement and heard you yell. I thought—"

He bent forward, exhaustion dropping his shoulders, and Remy pulled him closer. She rested her head against his shoulder and felt him lean into her warmth. His ragged breaths ghosted over her ear.

Unable to deny herself any longer, she pressed a soft, feather-light kiss to his neck. His breath caught. He pulled back, and Remy felt the ache of loss as he separated himself from her, but he didn't go far. His lips grazed over her cheek, seeking her mouth, and she tilted her head up to meet the kiss.

It was warm and hungry and gentle all at the same time. Not even the tang of blood and dirt could make her want to pull back. Mark's hands moved over her shoulders in a caress. His finger grazed the cut at the back of her neck, and Remy twitched back.

"Sorry," he said.

A giddy, shocked laugh escaped her, and she leaned her forehead back against his shoulder. "I'm not."

"Don't mind me." Bernard's tone dripped irritable sarcasm. He sat facing Marjorie, his elbows resting on his bent knees. "Take your time. It's not like we're in a dire, life-or-death situation or anything."

Remy shuffled around so that she sat beside Mark, instead of leaning into him, and brushed stray hair away from her face. "Sorry, Bernard. Are you all right?"

"I suppose." His face twitched into something that was probably meant to be a smile, then it collapsed into grief. "I never thought I'd have to kill my employer."

Remy's gaze drifted toward Marjorie. The older woman's body lay on its back, arms spread, eyes closed. "You didn't. That was all Edgar."

He scratched at his wrist. "The end result's the same, isn't it?"

Remy glanced between the two men. "What happened in the

hallway? Hands grabbed me, and when I got away, I couldn't find you."

"I was knocked out, I guess," Mark said. "I don't remember anything until I woke up in the basement."

"And I fell through the hallway wall," Bernard said. When Remy stared at him, he grudgingly elaborated. "It sort of…opened up and sucked me in. It took a while to break my way out. I came downstairs to see if either of you had made it to the recreation room, but heard you arguing with Edgar in the basement."

That explained the layer of plaster dust coating him. Remy turned toward Marjorie's still form. She was still reeling from the revelation that their intruder hadn't been an intruder at all. Marjorie's hand twitched, and Remy felt her heart plunge.

"Ah—"

"I saw it." Mark's smile disappeared as he rose and picked up Bernard's makeshift bat. "Get the salt."

"Wait." Remy scrambled to her feet and caught at Mark's sleeve.

He came to a halt as they watched Marjorie. Her face scrunched up into a frown, then she lifted one hand to rub at the bridge of her nose and opened her eyes. The black irises had vanished, leaving bright blue in their place.

The medium groaned and propped herself upright. She blinked at Mark, Remy, and Bernard. "I've made such a mess of this."

The voice belonged to Marjorie. Remy pressed a hand over her mouth. Tears overflowed as she crossed the room, dropped to her knees, and wrapped her arms around the medium.

"You're alive." The words came out as tight gasps. "I can't believe it."

"Oh, don't fuss, dear." Marjorie patted her hair. "I have a ghastly headache. And we can't afford to relax just yet."

Bernard looked faintly sick. "I don't understand. You were dead. We couldn't find a pulse. I knocked a hole in your skull—"

"Yes, thank you for that." Marjorie sighed. "I'm sure being bludgeoned has nothing to do with this migraine."

Remy drew back. Marjorie looked older. Her wrinkled skin had lost its color, and the hand that patted Remy didn't have its usual strength, but at least she was smiling. Remy wrapped an arm around the medium's back to keep her upright.

Bernard dragged his fingers through his hair. Plaster dust rained over his shoulders. "But…"

"I believe Edgar put me into some kind of stasis before— ahem—hanging me." Marjorie's hand fluttered to where her shawl normally draped around her shoulders, then flopped back into her lap when she couldn't find it. Dark bruises from the hanging still circled her neck. "I caught glimpses of what he was doing, like during a dream, but was powerless to control my own body. It was an experience I'd rather not repeat."

Mark crouched at her side. "So he deliberately kept you alive? Wouldn't it have been easier to kill you outright?"

"Certainly. But I suspect he needed living sacrifices for what he planned for tonight. So he put me into a coma, for lack of a better word, and repaired my body when my loyal friend gave me the Judas treatment and put a hole in my head."

Bernard laughed weakly. He still looked sick.

"In all seriousness, I don't blame you, dear. You did what you had to." Marjorie dropped her head and exhaled. "This mess is my fault. I owe you all my deepest apologies. My foolishness has caused a great deal of misery for us all. And the night's not over, I'm afraid."

Mark, half smiling, fidgeted with the bat. "Please don't say that. I just want to get as far from Carrow as I can."

"As do we all, my dear boy. Edgar has been expelled from my body, but he hasn't left the house. He's hurt, and he's angry—and he can kill us a lot more easily than we can kill him." Her lips tightened as she glanced around at them. "Where are my other friends? Where are Taj and April?"

"Taj is dead," Bernard said. "April is missing."

A door above their heads slammed, quickly followed by a second then a third. They stared at the ceiling as the implications hit them.

"He's going to hurt April," Remy breathed. "He has her trapped up there, and he can't attack us, so he's going after her instead."

Marjorie's expression darkened. She braced herself on Remy's shoulder and tried to rise, but her legs collapsed out from under her. Her face ashen, she sat back down, breathing heavily.

"Are you all right?" Remy kept her hand around Marjorie to hold her upright. "You don't look good."

"Ha. I don't feel good, to be honest." Marjorie swallowed, and her face scrunched up. "You need to find the girl. Save her. Bernard, fetch my kit."

Anxiety churned Remy's stomach as she watched Bernard disappear into the recreation room. "We'll need to go upstairs. Bernard can stay with you—"

"No, it will be safer if all three of you go." Marjorie sucked in a pained breath. "Mark, would you be a dear and get me something to lean against?"

Remy licked dry lips as Mark dragged a crate over and arranged it behind Marjorie's back. "We can't leave you down here alone."

"Don't you worry, my dear. I'm still quite capable of holding my own." She smiled with bloodless lips as Bernard returned and placed a small black leather bag at her side. She opened it and began digging through the contents. "My mind is closed to Edgar now, so he's not going to exploit that weakness again. He can't possess a body unless he is invited in. You must go to April. And hurry. Take these."

Marjorie pressed two small bottles into Remy's hands. She recognized them from the final séance.

"Salt and holy ground," Marjorie said. "They may give you some protection and can combat any supernatural tricks."

Mark had retrieved blankets from the supplies, and he draped them over Marjorie's legs. "Will you be all right like this?"

"Yes, fine." Marjorie clicked her tongue. "This week has been a disaster. I'm sorry I didn't see the signs earlier. I'm sorry I let him in."

Remy didn't know how to answer, but she squeezed Marjorie's hand to let her know she wasn't angry. It was easy to point fingers and delegate blame, but the truth was they had all knowingly, willingly stepped into a monster's lair.

"Hurry, my dears." Marjorie glanced above them. "I can feel energy growing. Heaven help that girl."

Remy clutched the bottles close to her chest as Mark retrieved the lamp. Then, with Mark at her right and Bernard at her left, they jogged toward the staircase.

The house continued to groan under the storm's pressure. Thin tendrils of cold air worked their way into Remy's still-damp clothes, making her teeth chatter and her breath plume. Two more doors slammed above them.

"Room 21, right?" Mark asked.

"Hopefully." Remy remembered Bernard's story of being sucked into a wall. She prayed nothing like that had happened to April.

As they neared the top of the stairs, a tall, gray-clad figure drifted past the landing and down the hallway. The light was too weak to catch its features, but Remy thought the dress was stained.

"It's not Edgar," Bernard said. "She's probably harmless."

Remy made her aching legs move a little faster. When they reached the hallway, she reflexively looked down the direction the figure had gone, but wasn't surprised to find it had vanished. She led them right, toward Room 21, and stopped in front of the door.

Bernard took hold of the handle and twisted it. Remy stared in shock as the knob turned. Whatever had been locking it earlier was gone. The door drew open, and her shock turned to dread.

Dusty furniture waited exactly where it always sat. Shadows

quivered across the wallpaper. Except for the rain pounding at the window, the room was almost unnervingly serene. April wasn't there.

Mark frowned. "This is the same room we were trying to get into earlier, isn't it?"

"I—" Remy looked upward, to where a jagged hole had been punched through the ceiling, and swallowed. "Yes."

The hole was directly above the bed, and shards of splintered wood littered the quilt. That was a hopeful sign, at least; the mattress would have broken April's fall.

Remy stepped back and faced the hallway. A spirit watched them. Recognition made Remy catch her breath. *The Gray Lady.* The ghost stood proud and tall, her hair fastened into a bun above her head and translucent drops of blood glistening on her long neck. Her elegant, stained Edwardian gown swished silently as she turned to point at a door.

Edgar's room.

The spirit lingered for a moment, a single finger extended toward the door, then vanished like smoke dispelled by a breeze.

"Thank you," Remy murmured as she hurried forward. She gripped the master bedroom's door handle and twisted it, but it was locked. She frowned and pressed a hand to her throat, where her pulse throbbed. "It's sealed. He must have moved April here."

"Give me some space," Mark said. He backed up a step then lunged forward, throwing his shoulder against the door. The wood shivered but didn't budge. Mark was pale, and his jaw clenched as he backed up for a second try. He'd been seriously hurt, and the continuing physical exertion was draining him quickly.

She put a hand on his arm. "Wait, let me try something." She used her teeth to pull the corks out of the bottles Marjorie had given her, and tipped an equal amount of each substance into her palm. She rubbed them together to blend the black soil with the white crystals then pressed the mixture against the wood. It hissed, and the mixture grew warm in her palm.

Marjorie said it would combat supernatural tricks. I hope that includes a sealed door. She started in a space just above her head and rubbed the substance across the door in gradually lowering arcs, grinding it into the wood, then stepped back once she'd reached just below her knees.

For a second, nothing seemed to happen. Then the wood began to shrink. It was like watching heat melt plastic. The dark mahogany shriveled, coiling in on itself, and dripped to the floor in thick black clumps. Dark smoke billowed out from the mess, accompanied by the repulsive smell of fungus and decay.

Remy pressed a hand over her nose. The door continued to melt until it completely sloughed away from the frame. She stepped up to the entrance, but before she could move through, a figure shot out.

"Thank you," April gasped, colliding with Remy and clinging to her jacket like a safety blanket. She spoke so quickly that the words ran together. "Thankyou-thankyou-thankyou."

Remy, weak from relief, pulled her into a quick hug then held her at arms' length. "Are you hurt?"

"That's a stupid question. I'd like to see you fall through a house and be fine." Small scrapes over April's arms and face glistened with drying blood. When April turned her head, Remy saw part of the symbol had been carved into the back of her neck. The flesh looked raw and painful, but April moved quickly, and her voice was strong. She tugged on Remy's arm. "We need to get out. Right now. Edgar's here. He's fighting that other guy, but I don't know how long they can keep it up."

"Other guy?" Remy turned back to the room as a massive impact shook the wall. Two figures wrestled, lurching across the room, punching and snarling as they battled for the upper hand. Both had gray hair. Both had long, thin faces. Both had gray eyes. The only differences were an inch in height and a few pounds of weight.

"Oh," Remy murmured, her heart dropping. "I didn't think John's ghost was trapped here."

John Carrow and Edgar Porter's spirits battled with an all-consuming vehemence. Everything Remy had read about the old doctor said he was a gentle, patient man, but he didn't look it as he clawed at Edgar's transparent form. Spending a century trapped in Carrow seemed to have woken a sharp ferocity in him. He was fighting against harsh odds, though. Edgar was crueler, more practiced, and far more vicious.

The painting hung opposite the bed—the portrait of John and Maria—had been scorched black. The idea occurred to Remy that their sprits had been held in the painting, kept there through the decades as they watched their home be turned into a graveyard.

Edgar broke free and tried to run for the door, only to be dragged back to the ground by John. The doctor's fist rose and fell at a near-blinding speed. Although the blows jerked Edgar's face back, they didn't damage it. Edgar kicked John in the chest, breaking free from his hold.

Remy tipped the last of the salt and dirt into her hand then hurled it toward Edgar. Plumes of dark smoke rose from his form as it hit him, and his back arched as he shrieked. John was on him in a second, forcing him to the ground, and they tumbled across the floor. The salt had hurt Edgar, but Remy knew it wasn't enough to defeat him.

You can't kill what's already dead.

"Back downstairs." Remy pushed April ahead of herself. "John's energy is going to be limited. He won't be able to hold Edgar for long."

April squinted up at her as they ran for the stairs. "What are we going to do?"

"Hope Marjorie has an idea."

"Marjorie? But she's—"

A roar echoed out of Edgar's bedroom. Something heavy hit the wall, shaking flecks of dust and plaster loose from the ceiling. April put her head down and focused on running.

They skidded onto the stairs and stumbled down them. Marjorie sat where they'd left her, her back propped against one of Mark's cases, and her hands sat limply on her blanket-covered lap. Her chin rested on her neck, and her eyes were closed.

Dread created a bitter taste in Remy's mouth. She ran ahead

of the group and dropped to the medium's side. The woman's shoulder felt cold when she shook it. "Marjorie?"

"Just resting, dear. Stop sounding so anxious." Marjorie opened her eyes and lifted her head with obvious difficulty. "Is she safe?"

"Yes, April's here. John's fighting Edgar, but he won't be able to hold him for long." Remy swallowed around a lump in her throat. "I don't know what to do, though. How can you kill the unkillable?"

Instead of answering, Marjorie turned to Mark. "Do you have any sort of liquid fuel, dear boy?"

"Ah—yes. Gasoline for a generator in case the power went out."

"Find it. Bernard will help you." She turned back to April and Remy. "You two will stay with me and help set up a final séance."

Remy made an unhappy noise, but Marjorie raised a hand to silence her. "Yes, I know. I have made nearly every mistake in the book while working here. But please trust me. I can't promise this idea will work, but it is our best chance."

Something crashed upstairs. It sounded like furniture being thrown. Remy prayed Edgar hadn't managed to break free.

Mark and Bernard speared off toward the stack of equipment in the foyer's center. Marjorie pointed Remy and April toward the jumble of furniture from the recreation room. "Find a table and three chairs. Set it up there, in that clear area. Quickly, my dears."

Remy hauled a round table out of the mess and dragged it to the indicated space. April followed with her arms hooked around wooden stools. Marjorie had rolled onto her side and was trying to get to her feet, so Remy called on her energy reserves to lift the woman. April appeared at Marjorie's other side, and together, they helped her to the table.

"Thank you." Marjorie was breathless as they eased her into the seat. She held out a hand. "My bag, please. And someone fetch that tablecloth."

Remy threw the cloth over the table as April retrieved the black bag. Marjorie fished out handfuls of equipment and placed the candle in the table's center. A door banged open on the second floor.

"No time for niceties." She dumped the container of herbs into a heap near the candle and tossed the container over her shoulder. "The spirits will have to make do with this."

"Found it!" Mark was perched on one of the crates partway up the stack, with Bernard at his side. They held up jugs of gasoline.

"Spread it everywhere," Marjorie said. "We're going to burn this house to the ground."

CHAPTER 44
ENERGY

"BURN IT?" MARK'S ENTHUSIASM faded into uncertainty. He looked around the dim room. "I don't think that's possible. Carrow doesn't have enough wood. Most of it is stone and plaster."

"Never mind that. The house will burn."

"But humidity and rainwater has soaked into all of the wooden supports and flammable cloth." His frown cracked the drying blood on his face. "And even if we can start a fire, as soon as the roof collapses, the storm will douse the flames—"

"My dear boy." Marjorie pounded a fist on the table, making them all jolt. "You think far too much. Spread the fuel. Let me handle the rest."

Remy squeezed her eyes closed then took a breath. "Do it, Mark."

Bernard had already unscrewed the lid from one of the cans. He lifted it to splash the gasoline over the walls. With a stressed, anxious grumble, Mark followed his lead.

"Oh yeah, sure, burn the house down," April muttered. "Don't worry about asking the owner's permission. I'm sure she won't mind."

"April—" Remy didn't know what to say.

The teen met Remy's eyes, and her face hardened. "You know what? Yes, *let's* burn it down. We'll burn it into hell, where it belongs."

"That's the spirit, my dear." Marjorie lit the candle then reached out to Remy and April. They sat at the table and joined hands to form a circle. "Red visited me while you were upstairs. I asked the poor child to gather all of the friends that she could. Let's see how many have answered our call. Calm your minds. Be respectful. Follow my lead."

Remy wished she could laugh. She doubted a week of meditating would be enough to calm her mind after what she'd been through in Carrow. She did her best, though, pushing back the fear for her remaining friends, her guilt over the lost, the awareness that Edgar was only a flight of stairs away from them, and the growing panic that they might never escape Carrow. She took a slow breath, felt her bruised ribs ache, and bowed her head as she tightened her grip on the hands to either side of her.

"Denizens of Carrow." Marjorie's smooth, loud voice boomed through the foyer. Her grip was frighteningly weak, but she managed to put immense force into her words. "We call on you tonight. With your aid, we will expel Edgar Porter, the parasite that plagues this building. With your power, we will have justice."

Remy drew a shocked breath. Energy prickled her skin and made her hairs stand on end. She opened her eyes.

348

The room was filled with figures: men in suits, women in gowns, and travelers in rags. She saw the girl in the red dress, the gray-clad lady who had shown them where to find April, and the man with the cleaver embedded in his skull. They moved toward the table, watching Marjorie.

Mark had frozen near the recreation room, a carton of fuel clasped in each hand, his eyes wide as he stared at the spirits. Then he shook himself and kept moving, splashing the fuel across the wall, floor, and any furniture he passed.

More spirits gathered with every second. The dead maid stepped out of the basement, and the man with the missing jaw descended the staircase. The drowned woman she'd mistaken for Lucille in the rock pools glided through the closed front door. There were others, too—spirits she'd never seen or heard of before. Some nursed lacerations or cracked skulls; others dripped translucent water from a drowning death. All were Edgar's victims, all trapped in his house, denied the right of moving on to their next life, used as batteries for his selfish purposes. Remy tried to find Lucille's and Piers's spirits, but there were too many ghosts. They formed a circle around the table, their eyes fixed on Marjorie as they waited for her to speak.

A shaky smile brightened Marjorie's face. "Thank you for heeding my call, dear friends. Tonight, Edgar's arrogance will be his end. He thought he could control the energy he hoarded here. But he forgot that his power fuels you equally. Look at how strong you are! Look how bright you shine! Carrow is a feast. Tap into its energy, and consume it for one single purpose. *Fire.*"

Marjorie broke the circle to hold the candle high above her head. The flame spluttered then flared, growing so large and bright that wax dribbled over Marjorie's hand and onto the table. If the wax burned her, the medium didn't show it. She lifted the candle even higher, inviting the heat.

The flame hissed as it grew. Sparks shot out of the wick and fizzled across the room in a long arc. One touched the ground where gasoline had been spread, and within seconds, a blaze circled the room.

"Yes!" Marjorie crowed as another spark left the candle and floated into the foyer's other corner. "Consume it all. Purge this ground. Burn your cage, and be free!"

The spirits moved in a blur, their individual forms and faces no longer clear. As they passed through the flames, the fire merged with their bodies. They blazed brighter and brighter as they spread through the building.

"Stop!"

The guttural, furious roar pulled Remy's attention toward the staircase. Edgar raced toward them, his face contorting unnaturally and his gray eyes blazing. The fight with John had left three long cuts across his face. Black energy coiled around him, and a sickening coldness spread through the area. The growing flames started to flicker and die as heat was sucked out of them.

"Do not be afraid!" Marjorie screamed. "Edgar cannot chain you any longer!"

Dozens of flaming spirits rushed Edgar. They twisted around him, their fire tangling with his black energy as his roar changed into a shriek. Remy, shocked and horrified, rose out of her seat.

They were consuming him. Teeth and fingers dug into his form, tearing off chunks of his translucent flesh. The fire spread over the marks, hissing and fizzling while burning deep into his body.

"Yes!" Marjorie dropped the candle and held both hands toward the ceiling as triumph lit her face. "He cannot hurt you anymore, my dears! Taste justice! Have your revenge!"

Edgar had disappeared beneath a swarm of the spirits. His scream rose then broke into a horrific gurgle. The fire grew and spread. It consumed anything it touched—not just the fabric lounges and wooden tables, but the stones, as well. Flames climbed the walls toward the second floor. Immense heat rolled off it, and Remy went from shaking with cold to gasping for breath in a matter of seconds.

Bernard and Mark joined them back at the table. Perspiration poured down their faces, but Mark grinned. "It's working."

"Edgar was a fool to store so much energy in one place." Marjorie panted as she slumped back in her chair, her eyes bright. "Look at how fast the flames are spreading."

April pressed a hand over her mouth as she began coughing, and Remy wrapped an arm around the girl's shoulder. "We need to move. The fire will block the exit soon."

"Oh." Marjorie blinked as though the thought hadn't occurred to her then glanced toward where the flames were licking close to the main doors. "Yes, you need to go! Quickly, get outside!"

"*We* need to go." Remy hooked an arm under Marjorie's shoulder. Bernard was at the medium's other side in an instant, and they dragged her to her feet.

The séance had clearly drained Marjorie's strength. She tried to shuffle her feet, but Remy and Bernard had to carry her weight as they struggled toward the escape. A flaming beam tumbled from the ceiling and smashed on the floor ahead of them, sending up a plume of sparks and smoke.

"Keep moving!" Mark snatched up one of the chairs from the séance table and ran ahead. He pressed the chair's legs against the beam and leaned into it. Flames spread over the wood, but he didn't seem to notice as he forced the smoldering board back far enough to clear a path for them.

Remy ducked her head and quickened her pace. April was already at the door, hauling it open for them. She squeaked as flames spread dangerously close, and darted outside into the rain.

As they neared the exit, Remy glanced behind them a final time. The fire had grown exponentially, and its crackle became a near-deafening roar. Parts of the upper level crumbled and showered embers across the room.

At the top of the stairs stood a familiar figure. Remy stared. For a moment, she thought Edgar had escaped the writhing pile of spirits bent on dismantling him, but then she realized she wasn't seeing Edgar. It was John Carrow, standing tall and with his hands clasped behind his back. He gazed over the scene, a smile lifting his lips, then he raised a hand in farewell toward Remy. She waved back, feeling both grief for the state he'd been trapped in and relief that his suffering would be over. Then she stepped through the blazing doors and into the rain.

The storm continued to drench the house. Moving from overwhelming heat into icy water was a bizarre sensation, and even Marjorie released a displeased choking noise.

"Into the yard," Remy said, adjusting her grip on the medium. "The house will collapse on us if we stay on the porch."

Thick mud sucked at their boots as they marched away from the building and through the dead grounds. When Remy decided they were safe enough, they stopped by a group of stone benches. She and Bernard set Marjorie on one of the chairs, and she slumped back, sheet-white and her breathing thin, to rest against Bernard's shoulder.

A section of Carrow's roof crumbled, sending up a pillar of glowing flames and sparks. Despite the storm's ferocity, the fire refused to die. It was consuming the entire building, collapsing walls and sucking the ceiling toward the ground. Embers flew over their heads like a million fireflies, and when Remy looked behind them, she saw the massive barn housing their cars was also burning.

"So much energy," Marjorie whispered. "I've never seen such a strong concentration in my life."

Mark had come up beside Remy, and she slipped her hand into his. His fingers were warm from the blaze, and he rubbed his thumb over her knuckles. "Will the ghosts be free after this?"

"Yes, they should be," Marjorie said. "Fire has a cleansing effect, a bit like salt. Burning an area can purge evil out of it—and hopefully do away with the bindings Edgar used to trap the house's victims." She tilted her head back and sighed. "Poor Piers and Lucille. They didn't deserve to die in there."

Didn't deserve to die... Remy's eyes widened, and her breath hitched. Horror rushed through her and turned her heart cold. "They're not dead."

April shot her a suspicious glance. "What?"

"He needed live sacrifices." Remy pulled her hand free from Mark's and began running. She called over her shoulder, even though she didn't think the words would reach her friends through the rain's drum and the fire's roar. "He didn't kill them. He put them in a frozen state, like what he did to Marjorie."

Heaven have mercy on me. I left them inside to burn.

The house was crumbling. The entire right-hand side had turned to blazing rubble, and the left looked close to following. *The heat must be phenomenal. Even if I can get inside, the fire might have already claimed them.*

She thought she heard a voice calling her but didn't waste precious time glancing over her shoulder. The doorway was clear. She could see inside the house's glowing maw.

A dozen ghosts had gathered around the carpet below Edgar's blazing portrait, some dripping water, others dripping blood, and one was missing half of his face. They paced in circles around Piers's and Lucille's prone forms. When flames licked too close, the spirits beckoned the heat toward themselves, and seemed to absorb it into their bodies. A spark of hope lit Remy's insides. *They're shielding the bodies.*

She tried to call to the spirits, but a section of the roof above the staircase collapsed, and a wave of heat hit her face, snatching her breath away. She staggered back, but then the scorching warmth abated in a rush. She opened her eyes. The young, transparent girl dressed all in red stood in her path. The spirit's large, baleful eyes blinked at her as it extended a gloved hand. Remy didn't hesitate to take it. The fingers were cold and only barely tangible. It was like trying to hold a wisp of mist. Red smiled then turned and guided Remy into the building.

Remy knew the house should be hot enough to scorch the hair from her skin and burn her lungs, but she couldn't feel it. The air was thin, and she had to gasp to get the oxygen she needed, but the rippling heat vanished before it touched her.

They made a beeline for the space below the portrait. The spirits that gathered around the bodies parted to let Remy through. She could barely breathe but whispered a reverential "Thank you" as she dropped to her knees.

Lucille was closest. Her skin was a ghastly gray shade, and she didn't show any response to the inferno surrounding them. Remy hooked her arms under the woman's shoulders and began dragging her toward the exit.

A warm hand on Remy's shoulder startled her. She turned to see Mark, sweat and rain mingling with the blood on his face, at her side. He took Lucille out of Remy's arms and lifted her body over his shoulder. His eyes squinted with the effort, but he set his jaw. "Get to the exit."

She turned back to Piers. Bernard had appeared, unseen and

unheard through the roar of the fire, and was already dragging the man by his torso. Remy lifted Piers's legs to share the weight, and the two of them staggered toward the doors.

The tiles below Remy's feet cracked. Fissures of hot air burst out from them, and she was forced to drop Piers's legs as she leaped away from the scorching heat. The ghosts pressed closer to her, sucking the fire away. The sensation was bizarre. Freezing air slid over fresh burns, leaving Remy shaking and overheated at the same time.

"Remy!" Mark's voice was hard to hear over the crackle, even when he yelled. "It's going to collapse. Get to the door!"

Bernard held more strength in his wiry frame than Remy had imagined. He leaned back as he hauled his cargo to the door, and Piers's bare feet jiggled over the tiles. Remy moved forward to help, but the ground shook. She dropped to her hands and knees, and the tiles ahead of her fingertips broke in half as a fissure grew across the room. Remy barely had enough time to take a breath, then the foyer's floor collapsed.

CHAPTER 45
RUINS

TILES POKED UP IN vicious fragments as the floor dipped. Remy threw herself prostrate and scrabbled for a hold. Dust billowed around her, choking her and turning the flaming blocks of wood and cinders falling from the ceiling into indistinct golden lights arcing through the haze. Remy felt herself falling and scrambled to reach the higher ground. Then a sudden drop plunged her out of view of the front doors, and the rumbling, sucking motion ground to a halt.

Remy blinked through the dust. Her patch of the floor had been sucked into the basement. She'd come to rest partway down the crater, nearly six feet below the main floor, and at an alarming angle. One of the basement's support beams poked through the chaos at her side, and Remy wrapped her arm around it to keep from slipping farther into the basement.

Mark's voice sounded worlds away. "Remy!"

He's still on the ground floor, thank mercy. Remy called back through a painfully tight throat. "I'm fine! Get Lucille outside. I'll follow!"

Flames licked out of the basement where embers had caught on the wooden supports. Ghosts darted around Remy, protecting her from the heat, but she could feel their effects waning. Their forms were growing fainter, and the fire licked closer as Carrow's energy was consumed. She had minutes, at most, to get to the door.

Remy turned to the slope and hunted for a handhold. A rasping, gasping noise came from the basement, and she twisted to look over her shoulder.

A figure crawled across the smashed foyer tiles and basement dirt below. Remy's insides turned cold. The shape was familiar but horribly distorted. The ghosts had torn chunks of flesh out of his arms and face, leaving scorched, smoldering lines across his features. His eyes seemed to glow as he crawled toward Remy.

"You're dying," Remy said as realization hit her. Edgar's form was too bright and too sharp—he was consuming Carrow's energy at a phenomenal rate. When it was gone—when the last of his batteries expired—he would lose his tether to the physical world.

He seemed to know it. His jaws opened, but only a rasping gurgle escaped the tattered remains of his throat. And yet, he continued to crawl toward her, dragging nearer to her perch with each extension of his tattered limbs. Remy didn't want to find out what would happen if he reached her. She turned and began scrambling up the incline.

The broken tiles nicked her fingertips, but she tried to block the pain out of her mind as she clambered higher. The foyer was only a few feet above her. If she could just get a good purchase—

A rock hit her thigh. Remy flinched, then the support beam she'd been leaning on lurched to the side, taking her balance with it. Another rock clipped her ear, and Remy clung to the slope with one hand and lifted the other to protect her head.

Poltergeist.

She threw a glance over her shoulder. Edgar's face distorted, the skin pulling apart horrifically and the muscles below vibrating as he screamed at her. He was close, and the ground shifted around him as the poltergeist phenomenon lifted the broken rocks and flaming wood, throwing them at the surroundings like a hurricane.

The ghosts flitting around Remy were so faint, they were nearly invisible. The house was drained; Edgar and his victims were snatching at the last dregs of its energy to stay alight. Roof tiles dropped past Remy, flames tangled around them, as the ceiling crumbled. She made a final leap for the ground floor. Pain cut across her arms and stomach as the fractured marble cut into her, but the lip of the hole was still a few inches out of reach.

"Remy!" A hand appeared through the dust and choking smoke. Remy stretched and grasped its fingers. It pulled on her, hard, and she kicked against the slope to help.

Freezing fingers dug into Remy's ankle. She screamed; the cold touch burned like fire. Edgar pulled on her, half dragging her down to him and half clawing his way up her body. His expression was demented with anger and fear. Remy kicked, but the grip was unbreakable.

Salt. Holy ground. She wormed her hand out of the man's grip and reached into her jacket pocket, where she'd stashed Marjorie's bottles. They were empty, but she prayed the residue inside the glass would be enough to hurt the spirit. She looked over her shoulder just long enough to see Edgar's twisted, insane features, then she threw the bottles at him. They passed through his form, just below his shredded throat, and his strangled snarl turned into a scream. The hand released her ankle. Remy threw her arm up to grab the hand offered to her and scrambled against the slope to get over the crater's lip and back into the foyer.

Mark pulled her close as they tumbled away from the hole. Shaking fingers brushed over her hair and touched her face, checking her. The arm around her shoulders was tight enough to ache. Remy clutched him back. She wanted to never let him go. Mark bent close to her ear. "Can you stand? We need to get out. Quickly."

"Yes." Her legs ached and shook, but she willed them to hold her for a few more seconds. Mark pulled her up then held his arm around her as they ducked their heads and stumbled toward the exit. Wisps of translucent light, the last of the ghosts, flitted around them, a poor filter for the phenomenal heat that surrounded them. Then they burst through the door and into the freezing yard.

Remy paused at the base of the steps and struggled to draw breath through her coughing. An immense rumble shook the ground under her feet, and a gust of heat on her back told her Carrow's roof had come down. Bernard appeared at her other side, and he and Mark half helped, half carried Remy into the yard. As they neared the rest of their party, Remy blinked against the rain to make out the faces.

Lucille sat on one of the stone benches with April at her side. Both were crying, though April smiled through her tears. Lucille was still a sickening shade of gray, and flecks of vomit stuck in her wet hair. She leaned against her ward, shaking and dazed but clearly alive.

Piers had been laid on the bench next to Marjorie. The medium had her fingertips pressed to his throat. As Remy, Mark, and Bernard neared, she gave them a thin smile. "He has a pulse, but it's not strong."

Mark frowned. "I still can't believe it. There wasn't any sign of a pulse when we found him in the foyer—"

"No, of course not. Their bodies were frozen. No pulse. No brain activity. No decay. They were simply kept immobilized until they were needed. Like a slip in time."

"I'm glad one of us understands." Mark carefully lowered Remy onto the third bench. Her leg throbbed, and her lungs burned, but she sighed as she took the pressure off her aching limbs.

Mark gave Remy's shoulder a squeeze then crossed to Piers. He tilted the man's head back and pushed his eyelid up to check the pupil. Piers still looked unpleasantly limp.

Lucille rubbed a hand over the tip of her nose. Her eyes were red-rimmed and her cheeks blotchy. "I want to go home."

"Me too." April held her friend closer.

"That's easier said than done." Bernard eased himself onto the seat next to Remy. The creases around his face looked deeper than normal. "We need the storm to clear before we can cross the bridge. And without the house, we have no shelter or food."

"I don't think we'll need to wait much longer." Marjorie nodded toward the sky. "Look at that."

They followed her gaze. A gap had broken through the clouds, allowing a thin spear of light through. The rain already felt lighter. They had spent so long trapped in darkness that Remy had lost track of the time of day. She couldn't hold back a smile at the sight of late-afternoon light.

"Edgar was influencing the storm, after all," Mark said. "Now that he's gone, the rain—"

Piers tumbled off his stone bench and hit the ground with a heavy thud. Remy darted forward and helped Mark roll the man onto his side so that he wouldn't drown in the mud. "Piers?"

He groaned, then his body convulsed as he threw up. Remy blinked stinging eyes as she rubbed Piers's shoulder. "You're okay. Just breathe."

They stayed in the yard as they watched the house burn to the ground. The flames and the storm faded together. By the time Carrow was reduced to rubble, the rain had eased to a sprinkle, and natural light poured through gaps in the clouds. Massive billows of smoke spread from the wreckage, pluming high into the sky. When Remy inhaled, she could taste the difference—the unpleasant taint saturating the area had evaporated.

A thought occurred. She reached for Mark and tugged on his sleeve. "Your brother—"

"Yeah." He continued to smile, though his voice was raw. "He led me through the fire to find you. He disappeared as we left the house…but I think he'll be free now."

Mark moved between Piers, Lucille, and Marjorie, checking on them and offering comfort when he could. Remy lifted her face toward the sky. As afternoon drew toward evening the golden embers that marked Carrow's corpse faded and died, and her mind turned to their freedom. Everything they'd brought was lost inside the collapsed building. Their cars were buried in the shed's rubble, and they'd lost their phones and the two-way radio. "The bridge should be safe by now. But we still need to reach civilization, and it's a long walk."

"It won't be pleasant, but we'll have to get home on foot. No one's coming to look for us, are they?" Marjorie sat with her back against one of the low stone fences. Her eyes were closed, and her hands were limp in her lap, but her tone was crisp. Although the storm had ended, the rain continued to drizzle, and her wet hair stuck to her face.

Remy glanced at Lucille, who was lying on the stone bench and using April's lap as a pillow, then at Piers, who was walking in slow, awkward circles, apparently to loosen stiff joints. "Maybe just one or two of us should go, so the others can rest here."

"Yes," Mark agreed. "Lucille, Piers, and Marjorie all need medical attention. And, Remy, I'm worried about your leg."

She shifted the burnt foot behind the other. It still throbbed but not as badly as before. "I'm fine. I can walk, but I'll be slow."

"I'd like to come, please." Piers shot her a tight smile. "All I really want right now is a warm bath, an aspirin, and some coffee, and I'll get that faster if I don't wait around here."

"I'll second that," Marjorie said. "But add a bottle of whiskey to my list of desired comforts."

Remy said, "How about you, Lucille?"

The woman squinted her eyes open. "How far is it?"

"If we can't hail a car, about four hours."

She made a choking noise and pressed her hands to her damp face. "Not a chance."

"C'mon, Lu." April prodded her shoulder. "You don't want to sit here for four hours, do you?"

Lucille was silent for a moment, then groaned. "I'm not going to enjoy it."

"None of us are," Remy promised with a thin chuckle. "But we'll do better if we start moving now, before night sets in and the temperature drops."

They all stood and shuffled toward Carrow's lawns. Remy's joints were stiff from sitting in the wet, but Lucille, Marjorie, and Piers had it worse. Being frozen for days hadn't done their bodies any favors. Remy took one of Lucille's sides with April at her other, and Bernard supported Marjorie while Mark helped Piers.

Spray still drenched the stones, but without the storm beating at it, the ocean no longer flowed over the bridge. They stayed in a tight group as they crossed the structure. Remy tried not to glance down at the sickening drops to either side, and instead focused on the spindly shrubs and sparse trees ahead.

She released a held breath as they stepped onto the mainland. It felt good to stand on ground that didn't belong to Carrow. She turned toward the driveway that led to the main road, then frowned. "Does anyone else hear that?"

"Yes," Mark said. "It's a motor, isn't it?"

Cars were uncommon in that part of the country. Remy craned her neck to see over the hill. *It's too much to hope that someone might be coming to Carrow. But I didn't think we were close enough to the main road to hear any traffic...*

Headlights cut through the misting rain. Three vehicles crested the hill and rolled toward Carrow's island. Remy caught sight of police markings on one of the cars. "How...?"

"You don't think..." Mark started, then caught himself. He met Remy's look and frowned. "No one else knew we were trapped except for Taj."

Hope billowed through Remy. She quickened her pace and raised her hands to hail the cars. Two police cruisers drew up on the side of the road, followed by an ambulance. The closest car's doors opened, and a familiar figure stepped out.

"Is everyone alright?" Taj called.

Remy burst into hysterical, crying laughter. She met Taj halfway to the car and hugged him tightly enough to make him grunt.

"Steady on, I've got some cracked ribs."

"Sorry, sorry." She pulled back and covered her mouth with a hand. "I just—I thought you were—"

"Yeah, me too." He wore a thermal blanket around his shoulders and his hair was still damp, though his grin was as broad as ever. "I'm still not sure what happened. I woke up on a beach about two miles away from here. Some huge, bearded guy was dragging me out of the ocean. He was gone by the time I stopped coughing up water."

"It couldn't be…" Remy bit her lip. "Sailors often drowned in the waters around Carrow. It couldn't have been a spirit, could it?"

"A spirit, a guardian angel, or maybe some random drunk guy who got lost going home—it doesn't matter to me."

The others had all gathered around Taj. Bernard ran his hands through his hair. "I can't tell you how happy I am to see you. And not just for your sake. You brought transportation."

"As promised." Taj nodded toward the police, who were waiting with arms folded by their cars. "I told them there had been deaths at Carrow and the survivors were trapped by a storm. Now I get here and, first, there's no storm. Second, no one's trapped. Third, no one's dead. And fourth, there's not even a house anymore." He waved a hand toward the black patch that marked where Carrow had once stood. "What the hell happened while I was gone?"

"I'll tell you everything later." Remy clapped his shoulder. "Right now, I just want to go home."

EPILOGUE

One Year Later

THE GRANDFATHER CLOCK'S PATIENT ticking matched Remy's footsteps as she hurried along the hall. Rain came down in sheets, masking the windows, and her guest's knocks were bordering on frantic.

She unbolted and opened the front door, and Marjorie barreled inside, dripping with water despite her umbrella. "Thank you, my dear. It's an abysmal day. Sorry we're late."

Remy laughed as she took Marjorie's coat and moved back so that Bernard could step inside. "You're always late. Did you pass another crash site?"

"We did indeed." Marjorie checked her hair in the hallway mirror then took her shawl from Bernard and wrapped it around her shoulders. "Motorcycle crash eight years ago. Poor soul was still wandering around in a daze. We got him moved on, didn't we, Bernard?"

Bernard grunted and shed his coat. "Stop sending me invitations," he said to Remy. "You know I only come because she's paying me."

"Psh. I know you'd feel sad if you didn't get an invite." Remy hung the dripping coats on the hooks by the door and indicated toward the sitting room. "You know the way."

She followed the pair down the hallway. Marjorie's limp was still pronounced, even though she tried to hide it, and she'd developed a frailty she'd never had before Carrow House. But her tongue was as sharp as ever, and the white hair suited her better than the gray had.

The large, cozy living room was full of light and chatter. Mark poured drinks while Piers and April eagerly talked at the same time. Taj waved to Marjorie as she entered, and the medium joined him by the fire. Lucille, her hair grown out, and wearing a business suit, lounged in one of the couches and sipped wine. Like it had Marjorie, Carrow had aged her prematurely. Light wrinkles around her eyes and mouth had taken her glamour but replaced it with an air of dignity, and she hadn't yet dyed the gray streaks in her blond hair.

"It's good to see everyone together," Piers said as Remy resumed her seat. "It's been a couple of months, hasn't it?"

"Yeah. We have plenty to catch up on." Remy inclined her head toward April. "I heard you joined Taj and Marjorie on a clearing last month. How did it go? Did you like it?"

"Loved it." April, recently eighteen, had added electric-green highlights to her hair. Remy couldn't decide whether they complemented or clashed with the blue streaks. "Most of it was pretty boring," April continued, swishing her glass of sparkling cider. "But Taj got some stuff on tape and Marjorie says we cleared something, so they're both happy."

"How do they get along, by the way?" Remy glanced toward Marjorie, who was in a heated discussion with Bernard. He was trying to drape a blanket over her legs to stop them from getting cold, but she insisted he was coddling her and that she didn't approve of it. Taj sat beside her, chuckling as he sipped his coffee. "Do they bicker as much as they did in Carrow?"

"It's way, way worse. 'Taj, you're being disrespectful.' 'Marjorie, stop standing in the way of progress.'" She laughed. "They bring out the best and the worst in each other. Oh—and did I tell you? Lucille joined on as our manager."

"Really?" Remy shot a quick look at Lucille, who was chatting with Piers. "Is she good at it?"

"Rubbish. She keeps double-booking us and invoicing the wrong clients. But I've never seen her so happy. And that makes me happy."

Lucille certainly was glowing. Instead of giving off the impression that she thought she was better than her company, she seemed to have found real confidence. Remy was happy for her.

"Oh, Remy dear." Marjorie waved Bernard away and leaned over the armrest of her seat. "You and Mark should consider becoming members of our little outfit. We're becoming quite a team with April and Lucille joining us."

"Thank you," Remy laughed, "but I'm happy sticking to graphic design. Carrow was enough to turn me off haunted houses forever."

"You say that now, but the bug never dies." Marjorie winked. "You'll call us one day, I'm sure of it."

Remy turned to Piers. "What about you? Any lingering desire to explore the secrets of the next life?"

He held up both hands. "None whatsoever. I decided that golf isn't such a boring pastime, after all. I'm getting quite good at it."

Mark emerged from their kitchen, carrying a tray of finger food, which he set on the coffee table between the chairs. Remy held her hands out toward him, and he resumed his place next to her, his long arms wrapping around her.

"Storm clouds always have a silver lining," Marjorie said, stretching back in her seat and folding her hands over her stomach. "Look how much we've all grown in this last year. If not for Carrow, we would never have become friends."

Remy looked up at Mark and matched his smile. "Yes, I can thank Carrow for a few good things in my life."

"Me too," he said.

She leaned a fraction closer and lowered her voice to a stage whisper. "They still haven't noticed."

He grinned and kissed the top of her head.

"Haven't noticed what?" Marjorie's bright eyes fixed them with a scrutinizing stare. "What am I missing?"

"That's for you to figure out." Remy's thumb tapped on her new engagement ring. April noticed it first and gave a cry of delight. Remy laughed as she was peppered with congratulations from her friends, punctuated with an "about time" from Bernard.

As she fielded their questions, she rubbed at the back of her neck. The scar there itched, the way it sometimes did when it rained. The rest of her scrapes and cuts had faded, but the insignia Edgar had carved into her never had. She, Mark, Marjorie, Piers, Lucille, and April all wore the mark, and although Marjorie insisted the cuts wouldn't cause them any harm now that Edgar was gone, Remy knew it would never let her forget her time at Carrow.

She didn't mind. As horrific as the stay there had been, she agreed with Marjorie's sentiment. Carrow had not only given her friends, but also left her with many cherished memories: Taj's enthusiasm, and his willingness to risk his life for them. Marjorie's resourcefulness under extreme stress. April's loyalty. Bernard's quiet strength during their final night. The way Mark had run back into the burning building to save her. Every time she looked at their living room fire, she remembered Carrow, blazing bright and scattering embers into the sky as its evil was finally erased and its spirits released. That alone was worth everything.

She closed her eyes, pressed a little closer to Mark, and smiled.

Keep reading for a sneak peek at the first book
in Darcy Coates's chilling new Black Winter series

VOICES

IN THE

SNOW

Available now from Poisoned Pen Press

CHAPTER 1

"EVERYTHING WILL BE OKAY." Clare leaned forward, hunched against the steering wheel as she fought to see through the snow pelting her windshield. "Don't worry about me."

The phone, nestled in the cup holder between the front seats, crackled. Thin scraps of Bethany's voice made it through the static, not enough for Clare to hear the words, but enough to let her know she wasn't alone.

"Beth? Can you hear me? It's all right."

The windshield wipers made a rhythmic thumping noise as they fought to keep her front window clear. They were on the fastest setting and still weren't helping much.

Clare had never seen such intense snow. It rushed around her, unrelenting. Wind forced it to a sharp angle. Even with snow tires and four-wheel drive, the car was struggling to get through the mounting drifts.

The weather forecast hadn't predicted the storm. Clare had been miles from home by the time the snow began. She couldn't stop. It was too dangerous to turn back. Her only choice was to press forward.

"Mar—alr—safe—"

"Beth, I can barely hear you."

"Marnie—safe—"

Even through the static, Clare could hear the panic in her sister's voice. She tightened her fingers on the steering wheel and forced a little more speed into the accelerator. "Yes. I'm on my way to get her. I'll be there soon."

That had been the plan: collect Marnie then drive to her sister's house. Beth's property had a bunker. They would be safe there, even as the world collapsed around them.

Clare had been asleep when the first confused, incoherent stories appeared on social media. She'd been in her kitchen, waiting for the coffeepot to finish brewing when the reports made it to an emergency news broadcast. She kept her TV off on Sundays. If not for Beth, Clare might have remained oblivious, curled up with a good book, and trying to pretend that Monday would never arrive.

But Beth watched the news. She'd seen the blurry, shaky footage taken just outside of London, and she had started rallying their small family. "We'll be safer together," she'd said. "We'll look after each other."

That included not just the sisters, but their aunt, Marnie. She lived on a farm an hour from Clare's house. Her only transportation was a tractor. Clare and Beth made time to visit her regularly, checking that she was all right and bringing her extra supplies when she needed them. She was the closest family they had. Now that the world was crumbling, there was no way Clare could leave their aunt alone to fend for herself.

"Op—stop—stop!" The static faded, and Beth's voice became clear. She sounded like she was crying. "Stop! Please!"

"Beth?" Clare didn't move her eyes from the road. Soon, she would be at the forest. The trees would block out the worst of the snow and give her some respite. Until then, she just had to focus on moving forward and staying on the road.

"It's too danger—s—turn ba—"

"I'm picking up Aunt Marnie." Clare flicked her eyes away from the road just long enough to check the dashboard clock. "I'll be there before noon, as long as none of the roads are closed. We'll phone you and make a new plan then."

She'd thrown supplies into the back of her car before leaving: canned food, jugs of water, and spare clothes. Worst-case scenario, she could stay at Marnie's place for a few days until the snow cleared. Marnie might not have a bunker, but Clare wanted to believe they would be safe—in spite of what the news said.

The storm seemed to be growing worse. She could barely see ten feet ahead of her car. Massive snowdrifts were forming against ditches and hills, but the wind was vicious enough to keep the powder from growing too deep on the road. Even so, her car was struggling. Clare forced it to move a fraction quicker.

She couldn't see the forest but knew it wasn't far away. Once she was inside, she would be able to speed up.

A massive, dark shape appeared out of the shroud of white. It sat on the left side of the road, long and hulking, and Clare squinted as she tried to make it out. It was only when she was nearly beside it that she realized she was looking at two cars, parked almost end to end, with their doors open.

"Dangerous—" The static was growing worse again. "Don't—as—safe!"

Clare slowed to a crawl and leaned across the passenger's seat as she tried to see inside the cars' open doors. Snow had built up on the seats. The internal lights were on, creating a soft glow over the flecks of white. In the first car, children's toys were scattered around the rear seat. A cloth caterpillar hung above the window, its dangling feet tipped with snow.

Clare frowned. There was nothing but barren fields and patchy trees to either side of the road. The owners couldn't have gone far in the snow. She hoped a passing traveler had picked them up.

Or maybe they hadn't left willingly. A surreal, unpleasant sensation crawled through her stomach. The cars' doors hung open, and the keys were still in the ignition.

She pressed down on the accelerator to get back up to speed. The steady *thd thd thd* of the windshield wipers matched her heart rate.

The abandoned cars had absorbed her attention, and she hadn't realized the static had fallen quiet. She felt for the phone without taking her eyes off the road then held it ahead of herself so that she could watch both at the same time.

The call had dropped off. Clare tried redialing. The phone hung in suspense, refusing to even try to place the call.

"Come on," Clare whispered. She pushed her car to go a little faster, even though she knew she was testing the limits of safety. Reception was bad in that area, and the storm had to be making it worse, but Beth would panic if she couldn't reconnect.

Clare tried to place the call again. And again. And again. The phone wouldn't even ring. She muttered and dropped it back into the cup holder so that she could give the road her full attention. As long as she made it to Marnie's, everything else would be all right. They would find some way to contact Beth and put her mind at rest. And if it came to it, she and Marnie could hide in her rural farm until some kind of rescue arrived.

Something small and dark darted past her car. Reflexively, she jerked the steering wheel and only just managed to correct it before the car began to spin. Clare pressed one hand to her racing heart and clenched the wheel with the other.

What was that? A fox?

It had looked too large for a fox, closer to a wolf, really, and there were no wolves in the area. It had nearly stranded her, whatever it was. She needed to focus more and not let her mind wander, no matter how much it wanted to. The family had stuck together like glue her whole life. They would find a way to stick together now.

A bank of shadow grew out of the snowstorm ahead, and

Clare sucked in a tight breath as she recognized what it meant. The forest. Safety. Shelter. She resisted the urge to go full throttle and instead let her car coast in under the massive pines.

Banksy Forest was a local curiosity. Rumors said the growth had started out as a pine plantation. Even two centuries later, from the right angle, the neat rows were visible. But no one had come to cut the trees down once they reached maturity, so they had been allowed to grow and die as they wished, only to be replaced by more pines and any other plants that managed to have their seeds blown or dropped among them.

The forest held an air of mystery and neglect in almost equal parts. It covered nearly forty square kilometers, dividing the countryside. The oldest trees were massive. Lichen crusted the crevices in their bark. The weary branches seemed to droop with age, and organic litter had built up across the ground in banks almost as deep as the fallen snow.

Clare could still hear the storm raging. But entering the forest was like driving into an untouched world. Snow made it through the treetops, but with no wind to whip at it, the flakes fell gently. The temperature seemed a few degrees warmer, and the car's heater worked a little better. Instead of looking at a screen of white, Clare could see far along the path, as if she were staring into a tunnel. The forest was deeply shaded, and she kept her high beams on but turned the windshield wipers off. She breathed a sigh of relief as the rhythmic *thd thd thd* noise fell quiet.

The government maintained the road that ran through Banksy Forest. It was a simple two-lane highway that connected

Winthrop, near Clare's cottage, and West Aberdeen, where Bethany lived. The drive through the forest took twenty minutes, and shortly after it ended, a side road would lead Clare to Marnie's house.

I can do this. The path was clear, so she allowed the car some more speed. *As long as the storm lets up before the roads are too choked. As long as there are no accidents blocking the streets. I can do this.*

She reached for the phone to try Beth's number again, but before she could touch it, a strange noise made her look up.

ABOUT THE AUTHOR

Darcy Coates is the *USA Today* bestselling author of *Hunted*, *The Haunting of Ashburn House*, *Craven Manor*, and more than a dozen other horror and suspense titles. She lives on the Central Coast of Australia with her family, cats, and a garden full of herbs and vegetables. Darcy loves forests, especially old-growth forests where the trees dwarf anyone who steps between them. Wherever she lives, she tries to have a mountain range close by.